BUSINESS TRYST

Janna awoke slowly, her head swimming. She turned her head on the pillow. Not her own pillow, she groggily realized, too firm for eiderdown. But the scent lingering on the linen, an elusive aroma, jogged her memory. Nick Jensen.

She sat bolt upright, her head throbbing. She was in his bed. Oh, my God! No!

The image of Nick, the warmth of his body, the strength in his arms, whirled around her foggy brain. He'd kissed her—long, bittersweet kisses that promised much, much more. No. He'd never kissed her. She recalled now; she'd kissed him. The memory returned with belittling clarity. She'd thrown her arms around him, forcing herself on him.

Why? She didn't even like Nick Jensen. The shares. In her drunken state, her brain had short-circuited. She'd been trying to persuade him to give her the shares. How drunk had she been to use her body as a lure? Nick could have any beautiful woman he wanted . . .

Never Kiss a Stranger

Also by Meryl Sawyer

BLIND CHANCE

MIDNIGHT IN MARRAKESH

MERYL SAWYER

Never Kiss A Stranger

A DELL BOOK

Published by
Dell Publishing
a division of
Bantam Doubleday Dell Publishing Group, Inc.
New York, New York 10103

ISBN: 0-440-20682-0

Printed in the United States of America

Published simultaneously in Canada

June 1992

10 9 8 7 6 5 4 3 2 1

RAD

This book is dedicated to the memory of Jan Krall, who taught us the meaning of courage and gave us a love for all time.

and

With gratitude to these authors who've shown me the meaning of friendship. "Cochise has spoken."

Olga Bicos, Debbie Harmse, Nancy Wagner

A special thanks also to Jill Barnett, Kat Martin, and Gloria Dale Skinner for their support.

ACKNOWLEDGMENTS

R. G. Robinson, M.D.
Poison Control Center
Mifsud Tours, Valletta, Malta
Ministry of Tourism, Floriana, Malta
Farsons Brewery, Malta
Air Malta
Maltese Consulate, New York
Embassy of Malta, Washington, D.C.

A special thank you: To the wonderful people of Malta who took the time to discuss their history, their traditions, and their hopes for the future with me. Researching a book is always more than taking notes and visiting scenic places like Malta's fabulous beaches and historic sites. In the end, it's the people who give the story meaning.

contents

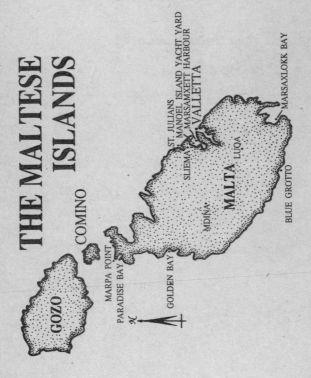

THE MALTESE
ISLANDS

GOZO

COMINO

MARPA POINT
PARADISE BAY

GOLDEN BAY

MDINA

MALTA

LUQA

ST. JULLIANS
MANOEL ISLAND YACHT YARD
MARSAMXETT HARBOUR
VALLETTA

SLIEMA

MARSAXLOKK BAY

BLUE GROTTO

prologue

From Here to Eternity

Malta 1941

"The way to love anything is to realize it might
be lost."

G. K. Chesterton

Malta: April 1941

"Who would stow away on a RAF flight into a war zone?"

"A reporter," answered Pithany Crandall's supervisor as they waited in total darkness to intercept any wireless communications the Axis forces might transmit. "He pretended to be one of the intelligence officers being flown here."

A spurt of static caused Pithany to adjust her earphones, but when nothing else came over the radio, she said, "He must be crazy."

"No crazier than a girl who spends her life in an underground cave spying," said an unfamiliar male voice from the back of the dark limestone cavern.

On the wall Pithany saw a huge shadow cast by the flickering glow of a candle that was immediately extinguished. Pithany knew the man was the reporter by his Scottish burr. She hadn't met him, but all Malta was talking about the reporter.

"I'm eighteen—hardly a girl."

"Really?"

His voice had a smile to it as well as a Scottish accent, making her wish she could see him, but the underground bunker didn't have any light. To conserve fuel, Pithany switched on the lamp only when recording radio messages.

"How did you get in here? This is a high security area."

"He has permission to interview you, Pithany," her supervisor said. "You talk to him. I'll let you know if anything comes over the wireless."

As the reporter fumbled in the darkness, sitting beside her on the bench that had once been a church pew, Pithany pulled off her headset, letting it dangle around her neck. His body touched hers and she realized that the shadow on the wall hadn't exaggerated his size.

"Ian MacShane," he introduced himself, "from the *Daily Mirror*."

"Pithany Crandall."

"How many languages do you speak?" His tone sounded conversational, not at all like a reporter.

"Italian and German. Some French." She assumed he knew everyone on Malta spoke Maltese, the Semitic language unique to the island, in addition to English, the official language. When he didn't respond, she added, "I guess I speak German better than almost anyone—from going to school in Switzerland. That's why I'm here."

"Do you spend all your time in the dark like this, waiting for something to come over the wireless?"

"Yes. The blockade means the island is short of fuel" —on cue, her stomach rumbled—"and food, but we can hold out as long as we have the petrol for the RAF to defend us."

"I see," he said, but she wondered if he really understood what it was like to live with Mussolini threatening invasion and the Luftwaffe based in Sicily at Malta's back door.

"Don't you get claustrophobia working so far underground?"

"No. I pass the time trying to decode what I hear. I'll

bet today's coded communiqué from General Rommel means another convoy is coming this way to resupply his Afrika Korps."

Ian MacShane leaned closer, and she tried to guess his age. His deep voice and the fact that he was reporting the war, not fighting it, made her think he was about forty.

"Don't try to fool me," he said. "I know we've stolen the German coding machine, Enigma. There's a new RAF Type X cipher machine in the next tunnel, unraveling messages using the Germans' supposedly unbreakable code. We have their information before the German High Command does."

"How did you find out?" Pithany bet ninety-nine percent of the people on Malta knew nothing of the top secret machine.

"Good sources. A nose for news."

A high-pitched wail echoed through the chamber, signaling yet another air raid. Although they were safe here well below ground level in the cavern, the Special Liaison Unit was located adjacent to Grand Harbor, the enemy target. Every time the Luftwaffe bombed the British ships using the port, the SLU suffered minor damage.

"Bloody hell," MacShane muttered.

"At least radar gives us advance notice," she said while they waited for the bombs to fall. At first, the islanders hadn't trusted the newfangled gadget—now they relied on it.

Muffled by the dense limestone walls, the noise from the advance wave of the attack, Junker 88s, penetrated the cavern. The second wave, the larger Stukas, zeroed in on the target next, dropping louder more deadly bombs. Antiaircraft guns, shore defenses, and the ships in Grand Harbor fired on the enemy, increasing the noise.

In the all-encompassing darkness, Ian edged closer to

Pithany, putting his arm across the back of the pew, resting it lightly, warmly against her shoulders. Her first reaction was to move away, but his nearness was comforting. The limestone bunker reverberated, dropping fragments of rock from the low ceiling and filling the dank air with dust.

Ian brought his arm down and held Pithany in a grip that was surprisingly muscular for a middle-aged reporter. Although she wasn't afraid, Pithany remained within the reassuring circle of his arm. The headquarters had taken fifty direct hits so far with no casualties, but she felt inexplicably drawn to this man whose face she could not see.

When the church bells signaling the all clear replaced the rumble of bombs, Ian didn't move his arm, and she didn't pull away. He discussed the siege with her until her shift was over. By holding on to the rail mounted in the wall, they found their way out of the tubular labyrinth of catacombs built centuries ago by the Knights of Malta to house slaves. Pithany stepped into the sunshine and searched her purse, her eyes squeezed shut. After ten hours at her post, she needed dark glasses to combat the light. Even wearing them, she'd have a headache that would last for hours.

Ian slipped his RAF aviator sunglasses onto her face. "So this is what you look like, Ace."

"Ace?" She cracked one eyelid. A pair of the most engaging blue eyes she'd ever seen squinted down at her from a face that could have sold thousands of war bonds. He smiled, an intimate smile that revealed a dimple. A single dimple. She opened both eyes wide and took a better look. Ian MacShane wasn't forty. He couldn't be a day over twenty-five.

She prayed that she'd remembered to comb her hair before coming to work, but then decided it didn't matter. The handsome reporter would never look twice at a short girl with hair the color of dust and eyes that couldn't decide if they were gray or green.

"Ace." The lone dimple moved slightly in a cheek that was overdue for a shave. "That's your nickname in London. Not only do you send the most accurate messages, but you relay the clearest ones to the British base in Alexandria."

Pithany looked at the ground, not sure if the tears stinging her eyes came from the light or from knowing that she was making a difference. *Ace.*

Ian took her arm, guiding her past the limestone rubble of friends' homes. In the distance the Mediterranean glittered azure bright in the late afternoon sunlight, its waves lapping peacefully on the shell-shocked shore.

"Look." She pointed to what had once been a fine medieval building. "This time the Nazis hit Palazza Ferreria."

"Damn shame," Ian said. "I like Valletta. It reminds me of a city in King Arthur's legend. I almost expect to see a knight—in full armor—riding a charger down one of these narrow streets."

Pithany smiled to herself. She hadn't expected the reporter to view Malta the way she did. Valletta, the capital, had been built on a peninsula. Sitting high and proud, protected by medieval ramparts, it overlooked a deep-water harbor on each side. Although the Royal Navy now used both harbors, giving the sea around Valletta a modern look, the city itself remained true to its heritage. Cobbled streets too narrow for cars were flanked by buildings the Knights of Malta had constructed during the Crusades. As a child Pithany had played on these streets, pretending a knight in shining armor—with the requisite white charger, of course— would ride up and carry her away.

As they walked inspecting the damage from this round

of bombs, she noticed Ian's limp and decided that was why he wasn't in the service.

"How about having dinner with me?"

She laughed. "Where would we eat? Everything's rationed right down to the last crumb of bread."

"An RAF pilot gave me a loaf of fresh bread and a sausage."

"Anthony Bradford?" she asked, unable to keep the animosity out of her voice. Anthony had asked her to join him for dinner several times. How was it he always managed to have surplus food?

"Is there a problem with—"

"No." Pithany had no intention of airing Malta's dirty laundry. War meant shortages that bred a thriving black market. She suspected Anthony Bradford—unlike the other RAF pilots—was making money on the side.

That night, Ian brought the food to what remained of her home, and she and her father gratefully accepted the reporter's generosity. The rationing system limited each person to a quarter of a loaf of bread a day. They hadn't seen a sausage in months.

Pithany assumed this dinner would be the last she'd see of Ian MacShane, but she was wrong. The next day, when her shift was over, he was waiting for her.

"I was wondering," he asked as she tried to conceal her surprise at seeing him by shielding her eyes against the late afternoon sun with a raised hand, "if you have time to help me?"

"With what?" she asked, immediately suspicious. No doubt he wanted to pry classified information from her.

"I need to know a bit about the Knights of Malta. Background for my story. Figured you'd know."

"First of all, the proper title is Knights of the Order of St. John of Jerusalem. When the Moslems drove them from the Holy Land, they came here." She kept her answer short, not saying the knights were driven from several other countries before settling in Malta. Why bother with an in-depth explanation when the reporter was really probing for confidential information?

He took her arm to guide her down the street, smiling and revealing the dimple. "What year was that?"

"At the end of the thirteenth century," she answered, not deceived by his winning smile. He could get this information from dozens of more attractive women; he had an ulterior motive for singling her out.

"Just what did they do during the Crusades?" he asked, sounding genuinely interested.

"Malta was a base for the knights coming from Europe, trying to retake the Holy Land from the Moslems. Each country had its own auberge or headquarters."

"You mean the French had one, the Italians another? That sort of thing?"

"Yes. The knights came from the most affluent families in Europe, so money poured into Malta. The beautiful buildings in Valletta were built during this period. The—" She cut herself off, deciding he wouldn't be interested in the details.

"Go on," he prompted, sounding genuinely interested.

"The grid pattern of Valletta's streets was the first of its kind—a revolutionary idea back then when cities were like Topsy—they just grew."

They picked their way through the rubble strewn across the streets by the bombs. Several times Ian slipped his arm around her to guide her through particularly hazardous areas. Each time his strong arm circled her waist she recalled her thoughts about him and she felt herself blush. She realized he was out of her league, but somehow he kept creeping into her daydreams. But knowing he was using her, taking advantage of his good looks to try to pry top secret information out of Pithany angered her. She reminded herself she'd been bred to be polite, unfailingly polite, and refrained from telling him what she thought of his tactics.

"When did your family come to Malta?" Ian asked.

"Just after the British recaptured the island from Napoleon and it became a colony. Like a lot of the Maltese we have relatives in England." She hesitated a moment, thinking of her younger sister and praying she was safe. "My sister, Audrey, is with friends in Kent." Pithany didn't add the friends were the Earl of Lyforth's family because she didn't want Ian to think she was bragging. The earl was one of the wealthiest and most powerful men in England.

"At least she's out of London," Ian said. "The Nazis are bombing it almost as heavily as they are Malta."

Pithany shuddered to think what would happen to Audrey should the Germans invade England. Although Pithany was ten years older than Audrey, they were very close. They'd written three times a week while Pithany had been away at school, but the war had cut off the mail service. It had been months since any mail had reached Malta.

"Don't worry about her," Ian said, slipping his arm around her again. He seemed to be using any excuse to touch her.

She pulled away. "I may be just eighteen, but I take my job seriously. I'll never reveal confidential information."

Ian's black brows furrowed. "I never thought you would."

There couldn't be any mistake about the sincerity in his voice or the puzzled look on his face. Either he was an accomplished liar, or he wasn't after top secret information.

"Let's get one thing straight. You don't ask me about my sources or what I'm going to report, and I won't ask you about anything confidential. Deal?"

Pithany nodded. "Then . . . then what do you want with me?"

A slow smile revealed the intriguing dimple as he took her into his arms. "You, Ace. I want you."

Before she could pull away, his lips met hers. There was tenderness in his kiss and the way his warm hands roved across her body pressing her to him. Even though Pithany had kissed a few boys—quick pecks—she knew this was an expert's kiss. She threw her arms around him, no longer questioning his motives.

By June, when Hitler invaded Russia, Pithany realized that she was in love with Ian MacShane's blue eyes and single-dimpled smile. Although he was so handsome he ought to be ashamed, Ian didn't seem to know every woman on the island gazed at him with undisguised longing. No doubt they wondered what in the world he was doing with that Plain Jane bookworm, Pithany Crandall.

Ian's "Report from Malta," broadcast weekly to London via Radio Malta, catapulted him from an unknown reporter to a ranking war correspondent. No other reporter had managed to get to the besieged island. His success gave him celebrity status, but Ian didn't seem to notice.

When she wasn't on duty, they spent their time together. It seemed completely natural and unplanned when their kisses became heated embraces that led to their making love. Ian acted as if he cared very much for her, but he never said the three words Pithany wanted to hear.

One night they were sitting on Valletta's stone ramparts. They often came to the high wall erected by the knights during the Crusades. Sometimes they sat on the Grand Harbor side and watched the ships being hastily repaired between air raids. But tonight they were on the north side of the Valletta peninsula, looking at Manole Island. Before the war the island had been an elite yacht club where her father had kept their boat. The facilities had been hastily converted into a submarine base. But in the light of a full moon—a bomber's moon—the water shimmered in moonstruck waves, its beauty undiminished by the war.

"Ian," she said, and he smiled the slow smile she adored. She leaned over and kissed his dimple. "I love you."

The dimple vanished. "Don't."

Pithany's throat tightened. How could she have been so silly? Of course, he didn't love her. She was merely a diversion. She hopped off the wall and ran down the cobblestone street, thinking that when the war was over Ian would return to England a celebrity. He would have his pick of beautiful women.

"Pithany," he called after her, his footsteps heavy on the cobbled stones. She kept going, but he caught her, grabbing her shoulders from behind. He spun her around. "I love you." He gazed into her eyes, then shook his head. "But it won't work."

The word "love" brought a dizzying jolt of relief. "Why won't it work? We love each other."

"Do you think Sir Nigel would want you to marry a boy from a slum in Edinburgh who doesn't even know his father's name?"

Pithany knew her father didn't approve of her seeing Ian. She'd stood up to her father, explaining they were in the middle of a war. Tomorrow might never come.

"How happy do you think you'd be living on a reporter's salary?"

"I'd be happy with you," she answered honestly.

Ian cupped her chin with his big hand. "You'd be bored with me in no time. I don't know a single line of Keats or the dates of the Crimean War."

It had never occurred to Pithany that Ian was ashamed of his lack of education. She stared directly into the blue eyes she would always love. "Sometimes the school of hard knocks is better than an Oxford education. You're the most interesting man I know—or ever hope to meet. I want to have your children, two girls and three boys."

His dimple appeared, highlighting his pleased grin. "You've got it all figured out, haven't you?"

"You bet."

Throughout the summer they made plans for the future, too in love to let the near starvation gripping the island affect their happiness. Malta, hemmed in by mines, surrounded by the Italian fleet, and hounded by the Luftwaffe, didn't have supplies to last through the winter. The stoic Maltese had reconciled themselves to the suffering. But now they were terrified their beloved island would fall to the Nazis because the most crucial shortage of all was fuel for the RAF planes. When they could no longer defend the island, the Nazis would invade.

Finally, word came of a Royal Navy convoy heading their way. As it neared Malta, the people held their breath. Would this one get through where others had failed? Ian met Pithany on the day the convoy was set to arrive, a smile on his face. He pointed to the sky.

"A *xlokk*!" Pithany cried, reverting to native Maltese in her joy. Opaque low-hanging clouds, more typical of May than fall obscured the sky. What began in the African desert as a dusty sirocco picked up moisture as it crossed the sea. By the time a *xlokk* hit Malta, it was a dusty fog driven by warm wind. The Luftwaffe wouldn't send planes aloft in this weather, and the Italian Navy, who lacked radar, couldn't attack.

"Come on." Ian hugged her. "Everyone's down at the docks."

If Pithany lived to be a hundred, she knew she'd never forget that moment. Standing beside Ian, his arm around her as usual, she waited along with the entire population of the island. Through the mists came the first escort ship disguised by camouflage paint. Bands played "Rule, Britannia" and the mob cheered, some people openly weeping. Pithany kissed Ian, amazed that despite the horrors of war she'd found love.

As she broke off the kiss, Pithany caught Anthony Bradford staring at her from the ranks of RAF fliers standing nearby. Deep within her something clicked. "Are you doing a story on Tony Bradford?"

"No, but I'm reporting him to the RAF command when I get to Egypt."

Pithany didn't ask what his report would say. She never asked Ian about his stories; he never inquired about the top secret information she had. But she knew Ian was too good a reporter not to be investigating the disappearance of valuable artifacts from Malta's numerous cathedrals during the daily air raids.

Cleopatra's Chalice, the island's treasured piece, had recently disappeared. St. Paul had been shipwrecked on Malta en route to Rome to be judged before Caesar. The islanders had rescued him and he'd converted them to Christianity. When he'd left, he'd presented his hosts with a chalice he'd commissioned from a local silversmith. They'd named it after Cleopatra because the Egyptian queen was considered the most beautiful woman in the world.

Ian drew her away from the celebration. "You know the magic carpet is on a quick turnaround."

Pithany nodded. The convoy—known on the island as the magic carpet—had to be unloaded as fast as possible. The minute the weather cleared the Luftwaffe would descend on Grand Harbor. The fleet needed to be in open water where they stood a chance.

He gazed at the ships, then at her, his eyes suddenly sad. "I'm going with them."

A silent sob rose in Pithany's throat. She'd known this day would come. Ian wanted to report from the African front.

"Will you wait for me?" he asked, as if there were some question about it.

"I'll wait forever, if necessary."

"Remember our code word, Falcon."

How could she forget? From now on, whenever the word falcon was included in an Allied radio transmission that meant Ian was on that ship or with those troops. She'd know where he was all the time.

"I have something for you." He slipped a silver ring onto the third finger of her left hand. Then he raised his hand to show her a larger, more masculine version of the same ring.

He really meant it; he was coming back for her. The tears that she'd kept at bay now trembled in her eyes. She ran her finger over the top of the wide silver band with the distinctive four-pronged Maltese cross, the symbol of courage and loyalty. He squeezed her hand, his ring covering hers. She didn't say anything. If she spoke she'd beg him to stay.

"This is for you too." He pressed a small derringer into her hand.

"Why?"

His eyes had an intent, serious look that she'd never seen. "To kill yourself."

"No! I could never—"

Ian put both hands on her small shoulders. "Let's be totally honest with each other. With the Enigma machine, the Allies have access to all the Axis messages.

We know what they're going to do before they do it. Has it done any good?"

"No," she admitted. She'd never told anyone, but she knew the British had warned Stalin well in advance of Hitler's invasion. Even so, the Nazi juggernaut had stormed across Russia.

"The Nazis can't afford to let the most strategic port in the Mediterranean remain in British hands. And don't think the Luftwaffe has missed the radio masts all over the island. They know this is the Allies' prime listening post."

"You're right. They'd invade, but Mother Nature has protected us," she said, thinking of the rocky beaches too treacherous for landing craft. The few sandy beaches were backed by steep cliffs. As the British had discovered at Dunkirk, an invasion from the sea might easily end in disaster. "I guess they could send in paratroops."

"Not likely," Ian said. "There isn't an open area close enough to the port. Those tiny fields are riddled with stone fences. They'd have more troops with broken legs than not."

"Then why worry?"

"They'll sail into Grand Harbor. How long do you think the shore defenses and the RAF can hold them off?

"We survived Süleyman," she said with pride. The islanders reminded themselves that Süleyman the Magnificent had sent his entire fleet to Malta. Against the awesome strength of the Ottoman Empire at its zenith, the Christians had prevailed.

"When was that?" he asked, his tone mocking.

"1565." Ancient history, she thought, glancing at the silver ring. "Why did you give me this if you think the Germans will come and I'll have to kill myself?"

He pulled her into his arms. "I'll be back and we'll have those five kids. But just in case, keep the gun with

you. If the Germans land, you'll be one of the first people they'll want. Don't let them take you. Remember
what they've done to the members of the French Resistance."

"I'll keep the gun with me."

They spent their last hours together, while the ships
were being unloaded, making love in a deserted bomb
shelter and planning their future. She wished she could
have his child now—just in case—but the cramps in her
abdomen and the condoms he always used forced her to
accept reality. Their children would have to be conceived after the war. If ever.

"Remember, Ace," Ian said when they parted. "I'll be
back."

She sat on the stone ramparts and watched the ship
take Ian out of the harbor, out of her life. A bittersweet
current swelled within her bringing cherished memories
of their times together. His laugh, his dimple, his smile.
His kiss. How could she face the endless days in a dark
catacomb knowing he wouldn't be waiting for her? She
knew if she'd begged him, Ian would have stayed. But
until he'd come into her life, she'd never known love.
She loved him too much not to let him follow his destiny.
Even if it didn't include her.

part one

THE GOOD DIE YOUNG

FIFTY YEARS LATER: 1991

1

*

There had never been a mule in Muleshoe, Texas, and no one in that tumbleweed junction had ever eaten gold. Nick Jensen decided the old-timers back home could have been wrong about the mule. Perhaps one dark night a mule—from God knows where—had wandered through Muleshoe bound for the badlands of New Mexico. But he'd stake his life that none of the folks in his hometown had ever eaten gold. They were too practical, too hardworking to eat what was meant to be worn or spent. So, what the hell was he doing?

Eating gold.

"Mr. Avery should be here any minute," Nick said, checking his Seiko. Where the hell was he? Scott Avery was never late.

"I am sure he will be here soon," said Hito Tanaka.

Tanaka's two companions nodded their agreement, but the three sets of brown eyes never left the chef's hands as he used a sable brush dipped in gold dust to coat the sushi. For contrast, the chef sprinkled *kuro goma*, black sesame seeds, on top and then arranged the sparkling sushi on a red lacquer tray.

Samisen musicians played in the background, stroking the guitarlike instruments with picks. Overhead spotlights illuminated the sushi chef's preparation area and the alabaster counter where the men sat on stools too short for Nick's long legs. Like silent shadows, geishas hovered in the darkness behind them. With a deep bow the chef presented his creation to the four men. Tanaka gestured, indicating Nick, the honored guest, should take the first piece.

"Let's wait just a few more minutes," Nick said, stalling and hoping Scott would show. With a few charming words, Avery would make the executives from Honsu forget about Nick and he wouldn't have to eat the sushi. Not that he didn't like sushi, but he drew the line at eating gold.

Ride with the tide and go with the flow, he reminded himself. What would Amanda Jane have said? She would have laughed at his predicament. Nick's mental image was of her cooking macaroni and cheese, laughing and happy with life. With him.

Nick smiled at the men, giving them the Texas grin that usually got him out of rough spots. Tanaka's inscrutable expression didn't change, but Nick knew what the man was thinking. The Japanese were punctual to a fault, arriving for meetings ahead of time.

When Hito Tanaka, executive vice president of Honsu, Japan's largest advertising firm, had asked Scott and Nick to lunch, he hadn't mentioned that they'd be having golden cuisine, the latest, and most expensive in Japanese dining chic. It was a supreme honor usually reserved for top Japanese executives, not middle management of American companies like Imperial Cola.

"Unfuckingbelievable," Scott had said when Tanaka had invited them. "Lucky for us old man Nolan's back in the States. We'll get to know the big cheese at Honsu personally."

Nick had realized immediately luck had nothing to do

with it. "Tanaka must know Mark is away because he never mentioned him."

"You're right," Scott had agreed. "Tanaka wants to see us alone. Why?"

Two days later, sitting at the exclusive sushi bar in the Ginza district, Nick still hadn't a clue as to why Tanaka had invited them to lunch.

"What kind of sushi is this?" Nick asked to fill the awkward silence. Scott's failure to be prompt was causing Tanaka to lose face. Senior executives were *never* kept waiting by middle management—especially in Japan.

"Tuna liver."

Christ! Raw liver dusted with gold. His stomach bucked—twice. With a wide grin to placate Tanaka, Nick reached for his *sake.* The iridescent haze floating on the top of the liquid stopped him.

Aw shit! More gold! Forget it, Nick thought, setting his cup down. He was leery of *sake,* anyway. His years in Japan had taught him to pronounce it correctly, *sah-kay,* but he avoided drinking it, remembering the name, *sake,* came from ancient Japan. It meant "chewing in the mouth" because it originated in the rice paddies where workers chewed rice and spit it into a communal barrel where the saliva fermented it. Again, Nick's stomach pitched.

The best *sake*—what they'd been served today—was *bijinshu,* "beautiful lady *sake*" after the virgins who'd traditionally chewed the rice for the *sake* the *samari* drank. These days, no one chewed the rice; it was chemically fermented. Good thing. Nick doubted there were enough virgins in Japan to produce the rice wine the Honsu executives alone put away at an average lunch. Still, he couldn't look into his *sakazuki,* cup, without thinking of rice swimming in spit.

"Sorry, I'm late." Scott Avery rushed up to them. "I just received word of a death . . . in my family."

Nick knew a bald-faced lie when he heard one, but the executives from Honsu didn't. They bowed and expressed their sympathy, instantly forgiving Scott's tardiness. Nick handed it to Scott. Only death could excuse him and let Tanaka save face.

Scott sat beside Nick and took the first piece of sushi. Relieved of the burden of waiting for a guest to begin, the three Japanese executives helped themselves and Nick took a piece. Scott talked nonstop as Nick had known he would, entertaining their hosts while Nick mixed a lethal amount of *wasabi* into his bowl of soy sauce and dipped the sushi in it, swishing it around until the gold washed off, leaving a residue of precious metal floating on the dark-brown surface. He dumped the sodden tuna liver rolled in rice and wrapped in seaweed onto his plate. He dissected it with his ivory chopsticks, pretending to be inexperienced at eating without a fork.

No one bothered to look at Nick. All eyes were on the chef as he prepared another round of sushi. This time, he rolled the rice and *anago,* sea eel, in a square of gold that had been hammered as thin as tissue paper.

"Would you like something else, Mr. Jensen?" Tanaka asked.

Taken by surprise because he had assumed Tanaka had forgotten him, Nick muttered, "Beer, please."

Geishas instantly delivered Sapporo to all the men. They reached for their wallets and Nick cursed under his breath. All he'd wanted was a Lone Star, but he'd triggered their favorite sushi bar game—The Nippon Derby. The men waited until Tanaka had placed five thousand yen under his glass and then they put their bets under theirs. Heads bowed and walking with dainty steps, the geishas went behind the bar. They took *udama,* fresh

Pharaoh quail eggs, from nests not much bigger than Nick's thumb.

"A-aa-y-aa-ah!" screamed the chef as he brandished his knife like a *samari* sword. At his signal, the geishas broke the eggs and dropped a yolk into each glass. The dime-sized yolks, bright yellow in the amber liquid, slithered to the bottom. The egg race was on. The first egg to rise to the top on the beer's effervescent bubbles would be the winner.

Nick doubted he'd win. During his five years in Japan, he'd been cursed with slow eggs. He whispered to Scott, "Where the hell were you?"

Scott kept his eyes on his beer glass although his egg had yet to lift off and Tanaka's was nearing the top. "I'll tell you later."

Nick handed his money over to Tanaka, again wondering why one of the most important men at Honsu had sought them out. Nick toyed with his sushi, taking only one other piece through a dozen gold-dusted specialities and twice that many rounds of *sake* while Scott talked, impressing them with his Wharton School bullshit.

No other nation revered labels the way the Japanese did, Nick decided. From designer handbags to Patek Philippe watches, they judged everything by its name. Scott Avery had attended all the big-name schools: Choate, Yale, and the Wharton School. No one in Tokyo had heard of Nick's alma mater, Hillcrest City College.

As the luncheon mercifully came to an end, Hito Tanaka raised his cup of *sake* to Nick. "Here's to a profitable relationship and another beverage like your Alabama Iced Coffee."

"*Bonzai,*" Nick replied with a Texas-sized grin. Sonofabitch! Now he knew why they'd been invited to lunch. On gold. He brought the *sake* to his lips but didn't drink it.

After the round of farewell toasts and compliments to

the chef, Nick and Scott thanked their host, then hailed a taxi.

"What was that all about?" Scott asked once they were slogging through heavy traffic back to their office.

"Mark Nolan's been promoted. You and I are going to be the new heads of the marketing division."

Scott drew his mouth into a taut line. For once, he was speechless. He finally asked, "Both of us?"

"Otherwise, Tanaka would just have invited the highest ranking man."

"You're right," Scott conceded. "But how did they know before we did?"

"Their investigators told them." Yessiree, there *were* things that they didn't teach at the Wharton School. It was common knowledge Japanese companies keep extensive dossiers on their employees. They hired squadrons of private investigators to ferret out the details of their private lives. Undoubtedly, they kept an even closer eye on their clients. Imperial Cola was Honsu's biggest account. It was in their interest to know what was happening, and if there was one thing Nick had learned during his stay in Japan, it was that the Japanese protected their interests. Tenaciously.

"What was that about Alabama Iced Coffee?" Scott asked absentmindedly and Nick assumed he was mulling over his new title, wondering how he was going to explain sharing it with a someone from Hillcrest City College.

"Alabama Iced Coffee was my idea."

"Impossible," Scott said, but his voice lacked its usual self-confident edge. "That was Mark Nolan's product."

"Right. I mentioned it to Mark, and he did all the hard work—nursing it through the corporate mumbo jumbo and overseeing the product development."

"Ah. You gave him the idea and he brought you over to Japan," Scott said as if that explained how Nick had made it through the corporate hierarchy to Imperial Cola's most profitable division.

Nick didn't answer. Sharing power with Scott Avery over the next few years until they were promoted to independent positions promised to be a royal pain in the ass.

"Why were you late?" Nick asked, deliberately changing the subject. "The death bit was great."

Scott literally went white under the deep tan he'd acquired while vacationing on Bali the previous month.

"Before I left the office . . . you got a call from Texas."

"My mother. Is she all right?"

"It wasn't about your mother. Someone called to say Travis Prescott had died."

Nick's stomach went into one long free-fall. Travis was thirty-four, three years younger than Nick. Dead? Impossible. "How?"

"Heart attack."

"No. He was a triathelete. In perfect health."

"It happens," Scott said and proceeded to rattle off the names of a few well-known athletes who'd died of heart attacks. "They're flying the body to Houston from Malta. The funeral's next Saturday. I guess you'll want to send flowers."

"I'm going back."

"Now? With this promotion about to be announced? You're crazy."

"If it hadn't been for Travis Prescott, I'd still be in the Houston warehouse hauling Imperial, not hawking it."

The late afternoon Texas sun blazed with only the faintest ribbons of clouds, scrims on the horizon, to mar the sky over Woodlawn Cemetery. Nick stood next to Travis's father, Austin Prescott, looking at the casket he'd helped select to bury his best friend. Only a smart aleck in the casket maker's ad firm would have named it "Tea Rose" when it was plain pine.

The mournful whistle of the westbound express from the train tracks beyond the sweet gum and mimosa trees took Nick's attention away from the minister's words. He felt the eyes of the other mourners on him and knew they were surprised by his presence. It had been five long, lonely years since they'd last seen him, standing near this very spot.

Nick stared at the pine box and tried to imagine Travis Prescott in it. He couldn't. Instead, Nick remembered the first time he'd seen his closest friend. Travis had been among the group of hotshot college boys assigned to the Imperial Cola warehouse in Houston as part of the management training program, "From the Bottom Up." Since his graduation from high school four years earlier, Nick had been working in the warehouse. Once a year the hot-shit kids appeared, letting the regulars know this was only a temporary stop on the hike up the corporate ladder.

Travis had been assigned to Nick's crew, and Nick had deliberately given him the grunt work, loading the trucks that serviced the vending machines. When he came to Nick at the end of the first week, Nick expected him to try to weasel his way into an easier job.

"How 'bout going for a brew?" Travis asked. "I'll buy."

"No." It pissed Nick off to know the college boy was trying to bribe him. He headed toward his pickup.

Travis caught up with him. "How 'bout coming to dinner one night this week?"

"Get this straight—" Nick jabbed Travis's shoulder with his index finger. "You want an easier job? Then get your butt into personnel."

"I'm not complaining about my job. I want to introduce you to my sister."

Nick almost laughed imagining Travis's sister. Must be stick-ugly or she wouldn't need her brother's help.

"She seems a little stuck-up, but she's not. She's just shy. She's seen you around the plant but you never—"

"Who the hell is your sister?"

"Mr. Robinson's secretary, Amanda Jane—"

Sonofabitch! "What's for dinner?"

The minister ended the grave-side service, and Nick guided Travis's father, obviously weakened by his prolonged bout with prostate cancer, to his car. They rode in silence back to the tract house where Austin, a widower, had raised Travis and Amanda Jane. Nick wondered how Austin would face the empty rooms and the overwhelming silence that would fall once the mourners left and Nick returned to Japan.

Austin's steps faltered as they came up the walk to his house where friends had prepared refreshments for the mourners. Nick put his hand on Austin's arm with the grim knowledge that within the year, they'd be putting Austin in the ground beside his wife and daughter. And son.

"Nick!" squealed one of Amanda Jane's friends. "Lemme fix you a plate."

The small dining room table at the far end of the living room had once been the setting of many laughter-filled meals. Today, people Nick hardly knew circled, filling their plates from Tupperware bowls of potato salad and ambrosia, selecting cold fried chicken from tinfoil platters, and heaping Ranch beans on top. In the corner a card table held a bottle of Southern Comfort and a bottle of Seagrams along with plastic cups and cocktail napkins left over from New Year's Eve.

Nick took a Lone Star from the styrofoam cooler under the card table. He polished off a few beers and three platters of food, thinking he really hadn't had a good meal since he left Texas. Darkness fell and the last

mourners finally left the Prescott house. He followed
Austin into the kitchen and watched in silence as the
older man took the Cuervo Gold Tequila and a huge
bottle of Tabasco sauce out of the cabinet. He mixed
equal parts tequila and Tabasco, tossed in a few ice
cubes and handed Nick one of the drinks. Nick wasn't
sure his stomach was up to a Bushwacker, but he took it
anyway, knowing that Austin was remembering the
nights he and Nick had sat on the back porch with
Travis, drinking Bushwackers and tending the barbecue.

Austin led him outside. "Let's set a spell." He
dropped into a webbed vinyl lawn chair. "How's your
ma?"

Nick started to say "the same" but changed it to,
"Fine. I'm driving up to Muleshoe to see her before I
leave."

For a few minutes Austin stared at the poplar trees
that formed a barrier between the small backyards.
"Life's too damn short."

"Yeah." Nick took a sip of his drink. It seared down
his throat, sending a burning vapor through his nostrils.

"Travis left you everything."

Hadn't Travis done enough? More than a friend, he'd
been like a brother. Better than a brother. Why hadn't
Nick patched things up? Because he never imagined
Travis would die. Nick had assumed his anger would
lessen, then he and Travis would settle their differences.
Now it was too late.

"He left you an Alfa Romeo and a speedboat. Some
shares in a hotel being built in Malta."

The heaviness weighing Nick down since he learned
Travis Prescott had died intensified, threatening to overwhelm him. The house, the memories, the emptiness.

"When I go"—Austin gestured to the house—"this is
yours, son."

Nick studied the stars. What the hell was he doing

living halfway across the world when the only people who'd ever loved him were here?

After a long silence, Nick changed the subject. "I don't like living in Japan."

"Why not?"

"It's small, crowded . . . unbelievably expensive." But it was more than that. "They're the opposite of Texans. We're an independent, ornery bunch."

"Got that right. And damn proud of it."

"In Japan, *kojinshugi*—individualism—is almost a crime. You're a company man. Your life's defined by your company and your position in it. There's some bullshit politics, for sure, at Imperial Cola. But we're not *afraid* to speak our minds." For a moment, he listened to the crickets' dirge, finally ready to voice the conclusion he'd reached at Travis's funeral. "I'm not going back."

"What about your promotion?"

"Life's too short. Why be unhappy?" Nick rose, went into the house and called Mark Nolan in Tokyo.

"You can't quit." The tinny echo from the satellite connection did nothing to hide Mark Nolan's anger. Nick listened patiently to the man who'd never forgotten his suggestion about marketing iced coffee in Japan. It had made Nolan's career and he'd arranged for Nick to be assigned to the marketing division. And when Nick had needed to get away from Texas five years ago, Mark Nolan had again helped him, bringing him to Japan.

"I appreciate everything you've ever done for me. But I'm not coming back."

Nick hung up, upset that he'd disappointed the man who'd championed him, but knowing he'd made the right decision. He sensed Austin needed time alone, so he headed toward the bedrooms. He paused outside the door to Amanda Jane's room, then opened it quickly as if he expected to find her waiting for him. He flicked on the light. Empty. Bare walls. The dresser had been stripped of her photographs. The only visible reminder of Amanda Jane was the lavender gingham bedspread. He mentally turned back the clock, remembering her anguishing over its purchase. At a garage sale.

He snapped off the light before the dark vortex of the past overwhelmed him. Nick went into Travis's old bedroom and sprawled across the bed, too tired to undress, hoping jet lag from the long trip would overtake him. It didn't. He took out the tape of *Clear and Present Danger,* the book he'd been listening to on the trip home.

He couldn't concentrate. His eyes were drawn up to where the wall met the ceiling. Years ago, Travis had taped a computer printout of his favorite saying: *"Ride with the tide and go with the flow."* Something about Travis's death didn't feel right. Nick went back out onto the porch and found Austin still nursing his Bushwacker.

"I 'spect you'll go over to Malta to sell the car and the boat." Austin took a swig of the Bushwacker. "There's some pictures yonder in the bill drawer."

Nick found the photographs in the kitchen and thumbed through them as he rejoined Austin. The boat Travis had left him wasn't just any boat. It was an expensive Donzi. He came to a snapshot of Travis with a brunet in a chain-mail bikini. They were anchored off some small beach on what looked like a tropical island, but must be Malta. Nick's marketing eye took over, seeing it as a perfect setting for a commercial.

He took a second look at the woman. She wore her dark brown hair shoulder length and it framed a face that featured almond-shaped eyes. She looked a little too sultry and wore more eye makeup than Nick liked, but he had to admit she was a looker.

He squinted hard and then held the next picture up to the porch light to be positive what he was seeing. No mistake. The snapshot showed Travis, buck-naked, with the same brunet—minus the bikini—straddling him, her head thrown back. She was either climaxing or damn close to it.

Jesus! Nick couldn't imagine Travis sending this to his father. Another, more damning thought hit him. Who'd taken the picture? Possibly, they'd had a camera mounted on the boat, but he doubted it. The grainy texture made him think the photograph had been taken using a telephoto lens. If so, how had Travis gotten the picture, and why had he sent it home?

" 'Peers that one got sent along by mistake." Austin shook his head, puzzled.

Nick studied the brunet's full breasts, evenly tanned so that the nipples were only slightly darker, and the curve of her bare hips. "What's her name?"

"Damned if I know. Never mentioned her. I got the pictures after he died." Austin came to his feet slowly. "She musta been pretty special. Travis never dated much after his divorce."

Nick hadn't spoken with Travis during the last several years, but he had no reason to doubt Austin. Since his wife had walked out on him, Travis had become withdrawn.

"Cain't believe he's dead. For crissakes, he was only thirty-four."

Nick nodded, his eyes drawn to the family photographs on the mantel. He asked the painful question he'd wanted to ask since he'd arrived. "Exactly how'd Travis die?"

"He'd been rentin' a guest house from a woman who owns a buncha hotels on Malta. He was havin' dinner with her when he had chest pains an' shortness of breath." Austin's voice rose a notch. "Mrs. Cranston— no Crandall—Pithany Crandall called the ambulance. My boy was dead by the time it arrived."

"They did an autopsy?" Nick asked.

"Yup. But I don't trust them foreign docs."

"Malta's not some backward nation. It was a British colony for over a century. I'm sure their doctors train in England and—"

"I don't care. I still ordered a complete autopsy done here. They sent tissue samples to the Mayo Clinic. I'll git the results in a week or so." Austin's belligerent tone softened. "Hell, cancer gets the Prescotts, not heart attacks. You know that."

Only too well, Nick thought, but he didn't comment. Bringing up the past was simply too painful. Still. Besides, Austin's mind was on Travis. Obviously, he didn't believe his son had died of natural causes.

"When you git to Malta, check on this Pithany Crandall and that gal in the picture. See what they know about Travis's death. If I don't make it, you find out what really killed my boy."

Nick wanted to tell Austin that he'd make it, but they'd never lied to each other. Not then. Not now.

Red-tailed hawks circled over the dusty prairie dog village, swooping low, looking for dinner, as Nick came to the outskirts of Muleshoe. The sun balanced on the horizon, casting a coral glow over the flat, endless expanse of parched land. The only sign of color was the pigweed bushes, a lush green against the dark soil. In another two months they'd be brown tumbleweeds blowing across the one-lane road.

In the distant sky he saw a formation of sandhill cranes heading for their winter nesting area on the far side of Muleshoe. The open terrain with the wind whistling across the prairie—so different from Tokyo— reinforced Nick's decision. The crowded Japanese subways and one-room apartment shoehorned into a concrete bunker were no place for a Texan. Nick wasn't sure what he'd do now, but with the money he'd saved and

Travis's legacy, he'd be able to support himself and take care of his mother.

Nick turned down the dirt road that crossed Running Water Draw. As usual, the creek was bone-dry—only flash floods filled it—with lizards and horned toads sunning themselves on the rocks. Two young boys were in the creek bed shooting at beer cans with BB guns. Nick smiled to himself, remembering the hours spent with his older brother, Cody, shooting at bottles.

He pulled up in front of the old farmhouse, finding it hard to believe he'd ever lived here. He hoisted his bag over his shoulder and went up the path to the clapboard house where he'd lived from the day he was born until his eighteenth birthday when he'd walked out.

He stepped inside. "Hello, Ma."

His mother jumped up from the faded floral sofa where she'd been sitting watching the evening weather report. She gave him a quick hug, standing on tiptoe. "Well, I'll be jiggered," she said, stepping back and looking him over. "You're all growed up. Look at you."

He'd been grown up for years, but it always came as a surprise to his mother. "You look good, Ma."

Nick meant it. Her hair was still black without a trace of gray, and her eyes were lavender-blue, a combination that, in her youth, had often prompted comparisons to Elizabeth Taylor.

She gave him a rare smile and pushed him toward the bathroom. "Wash your hands now. I reckon you're hungry. I've got supper ready."

As Nick walked into the bathroom, he looked around to see if his mother had used the money he'd sent to buy anything new. She hadn't. *What did you expect?*

She had a hot dog and Mojo fries on a plate alongside a tall glass of milk when he walked into the kitchen. At least the milk wasn't in his old Mickey Mouse mug, but he knew it still was up in the cabinet behind Cody's

Roadrunner mug. Nick smothered the hot dog in French's mustard, wondering when he'd begun preferring Grey Poupon. It was a long way from Muleshoe to Houston. Even longer from Tokyo.

She cut her hot dog, no bun, into dime-sized pieces. "This was always Cody's favorite meal."

He died when he was twelve, for crissake. If he'd lived, he might have loved sushi. Nick checked his watch. On the way up the path, he'd placed a mental wager that he wouldn't be in the house five minutes before his mother mentioned Cody. He'd won. He'd bet anything Ma still read Cody's report cards every day.

He ate in silence until the wall telephone rang and his mother motioned for him to answer it.

"Must be for you. I never git any calls."

You would if you stopped living in the past. "Hullo." The echo warned him that this call was coming from overseas.

"Nick, that you?" Mark Nolan asked.

"Uh-huh." Nick braced himself for an argument. But nothing could convince him to return to Japan. Too crowded, too expensive, too lonely.

"I have an idea," Nolan said. "What if I could arrange a transfer for you?"

"Where?"

"Malta. You could take over Travis Prescott's operation on a temp—" A whooshing sound drowned out his words.

"Where the hell are you?"

"In the subway at a public phone."

Nick realized something was up. Full transcripts of conversations in the office had a way of getting into Japanese hands. Whatever Nolan wanted to say needed to be kept secret.

"Can you hear me now?" Nolan asked.

"How can I run an operations division?" Nick wondered what strings Nolan had pulled. Marketing and operations were worlds apart. He'd never had any operating experience unless you counted the From the Bottom Up program, which he didn't.

"Don't worry about it. Malta's a small-potatoes division. Besides, it won't be for long."

"Oh?" Nick looked over and saw his mother waiting. He covered the mouthpiece. "I'm finished," he said, and she cleared the dinette.

"I've been promoted," Nolan said, confirming what Nick already knew. Scott's and Nick's promotions wouldn't be possible unless Mark Nolan had been moved up the corporate ladder, leaving a vacant rung. "I'll be at headquarters in Atlanta working on a top secret project."

"Iced coffee for the home market," Nick guessed.

"How the hell did you know?"

"Lucky guess. It's a hit in Japan and is being marketed successfully in Europe. Why not the U.S.?"

"I need you on my team, but my transfer doesn't go into effect for a while. Once I'm in Atlanta, I'll find a spot for you." Another noisy whoosh announced a passing train. "I've got the Malta deal all set up for you. Just hang in there until I send for you—six, eight months max."

The thought of all the reading operations generated—orders, shipping reports, sales figures—made Nick's head ache. But he'd be a fool to throw away an opportunity like this. Amanda Jane had always told him that he belonged at corporate headquarters. True, Atlanta wasn't Texas, but Nick figured he'd like it there. Anywhere but Japan.

"Great." Nick tried to sound enthusiastic, but the funeral and his return home depressed him. "Thanks."

Nick got the details and hung up. He wandered into the living room where his mother was crocheting and watching Vanna White turning letters on *Wheel of Fortune*. Vanna wore the latest in shopping mall chic and had his mother's rapt attention. Nick sat in the Naugahyde easy chair. A commercial came on and his mother turned to him.

"I've been transferred to Malta."

"That's mighty fine." She watched the Alpo commercial for a moment. "Malta's in Mexico?"

"No, Ma. It's an island south of Sicily—near Italy."

"You speak Italian?"

"No. They speak English there. It used to be a British colony."

"That so?" The commercial ended and his mother's eyes swung back to the television. "Isn't that where the Prescott boy was?"

He had a name. Travis. You met him a dozen times. "Yes."

She turned to him. "Too bad he passed on like that. Young. So young." Her loving gaze went to the sideboard where Cody's report cards were on display. A picture of Cody in his Little League uniform stood on top of a freshly starched doily. Beside it, the card from Hensley's Funeral Parlor read: YOU'VE GOT A FRIEND IN JESUS.

"Ain't it the truth?" His mother sighed, her martyred sigh. "The good die young."

2

✳

"Are you sure Shadoe hasn't told your sister who the father of her baby is?"

"I'm positive. Janna doesn't know." Warren Atherton kept his eyes on the platter of hors d'oeuvres, not on Shadoe Hunnicutt. He selected a wedge of pâté of pigs' feet and snails topped with *bottarga,* dried caviar.

"Who's Shadoe with?" Warren's friend asked, nudging him.

Warren shrugged and leaned casually against the towering Gog in ancient Guildhall where the Save the Rain Forest reception was being held. The light from the historic stained glass window behind the golden statue of the mythical creature, Gog, backlit Warren's ash blond hair and cast prisms of color across the shoulders of his dinner jacket. His eyes, which he'd inherited along with more titles than he could remember, had been dubbed "Atherton blue" by Queen Elizabeth I when she'd bestowed a title on the first Earl of Lyforth.

Warren kept those genetic blessings trained on his friend to avoid looking at Shadoe Hunnicutt. The low-cut black sheath that sculpted her body revealed an impressive cleavage and left little to the imagination, not that Warren's imagination needed any prompting. He'd seen the controversial redhead in a lot less.

"Lord Lyforth," said a passing guest. "Give my best to the earl."

"I'll do that." Warren kept his tone level. Four hundred years of arranged marriages had bred more than crystal blue eyes. He hadn't seen his father in months.

Suddenly someone shouted, "Ladies and gentlemen." A phalanx of policemen in riot gear had appeared out of nowhere. "Sorry to interrupt the festivities, but you must evacuate the premises immediately. *Walk* to the nearest exit."

Warren hurried toward the door. "The IRA," a woman nearby speculated. "They wouldn't."

"Do you think Guildhall is sacred to them?" It was a rhetorical question. They'd destroyed the Carlton Club, the bastion of conservatives. Not content, they'd planted the car bomb that had killed Ian Gow, a conservative MP, then fired on number 10 Downing Street. Headquarters for the City of London, the financial heart of England, Guildhall had a rich history dating back to the medieval Lord Mayors who wielded as much power as the reigning monarchs. Down through the centuries, the king always sought permission before entering the City. Even today the Queen was required to make a formal request before visiting the City.

The crowd rushed through the cobbled yard, barely aware of the wet mist, following the bobbies waving them across the street. Warren came to a stop behind a police barricade with his silk clad shoulder wedged against Shadoe Hunnicutt's bare one.

"Hello, Warren." Her red curls fluttered in the slight breeze as she looked at him with warm-brown eyes.

He watched the mist dampening her shoulders, threatening to trickle down into the valley between her perfect breasts where a rune-stone pendant hung from a silver chain. The odd shaped stone with its ancient carvings seemed out of place with the silk gown. But then, almost everything about Shadoe was intriguingly different.

"You must be freezing." He took off his dinner jacket and draped it over her, mumbling a few choice words about the IRA. Warren feigned intense interest in the police preparations to avoid talking to Shadoe. He reminded himself of his father's words, which at thirty-five Warren should be able to ignore, but couldn't quite: "She isn't our kind."

Indeed, she wasn't. Shadoe's father was a minor English noble who'd married an Italian actress. Shortly after Shadoe's birth, her mother decided the country life didn't suit her. She left her baby in Derbyshire and returned to Italy to star in numerous movies, taking off her clothes the minute the director yelled "action." Despite a proper English upbringing and the best schools, Shadoe had gained a reputation for being wild before she was sixteen.

At twenty Shadoe had married an Italian count, after floating down a Venetian canal in an armada of gondolas with Warren's sister, Janna, as a bridesmaid. During the candlelit ceremony in the Basilica di San Pietro, Warren sat in the last pew. The marriage lasted three years. Shadoe next married an American in a civil ceremony with Janna as her sole attendant. She divorced the Yank six months later, and she'd remained single until five years ago when she turned thirty. On her birthday, she'd sent Janna a telegram saying she'd married a Frenchman no one had ever heard of, in the surf on a small atoll somewhere in the South Pacific. She filed for divorce two days later.

After the failure of her last marriage, Shadoe had opened The Freudian Slip in Knightsbridge, a boutique that featured the finest in seductive lingerie. For the next few years, her amorous escapades took a backseat to her career. She'd become phenomenally successful, expanding her trendy shop into a thriving mail-order business. Warren wasn't surprised by her achievements. Shadoe Hunnicutt had talent—and more brains than most who gossiped about her.

She was far too intelligent, too independent to care what others thought. Until the baby. Shadoe protected her infant daughter, refusing to name the father, not even telling Janna, her closest friend.

"Did Janna go to Paris?" Shadoe asked, her voice a low, well-remembered whisper.

"Of course." His sister always accompanied his mother to the exhibitions of the couture collections. "Why wouldn't she?"

"She and Collis had a terrible row. Since he's leaving for America in a few days, I thought Janna might have stayed home. Her horoscope said not to travel."

Shadoe's penchant for astrology didn't bother Warren. He knew all about it. He hesitated; his inbred reluctance to discuss private matters made him pause, but he knew Shadoe was too smart not to guess Janna's marriage was in trouble. "They have rows all the time. They work it out."

"He's ruining her," Shadoe said so softly that Warren had to bend uncomfortably close to catch what she was saying. "Janna's not happy."

"It's Janna's life," he said, although he wholeheartedly agreed with Shadoe's assessment. His sister's husband was making her miserable. "There's nothing we can do about it."

"Lord Lyforth," shouted a male voice. Warren turned and saw a bobbie edging through the crowd. "Call this number at once. It's about the earl."

Warren left Shadoe and followed the bobbie, puzzled over who'd call him about his father. The telephone number on the slip of paper he'd been given was unfamiliar. It wasn't any of the Atherton residences, nor was it a West End exchange. The policeman led him up a back alley and into a bank being used as a command center.

"The call came into the Grand Hall," the officer explained. "We're monitoring all the lines into Guildhall."

They directed him to a telephone and he dialed the strange number. A young man answered, and Warren said, "This is Warren Atherton."

"Come quickly"—the voice had a hysterical pitch—"Reggie needs you."

Reggie? No one called Reginald Atherton, eighth earl of Lyforth, Reggie, not even his wife. Clearly, this was a hoax. "I don't know what you want, but I—"

"Pl-please"—the young man was sobbing now—"I think he's dead."

Paris: Midnight

Janna Atherton-Pembroke smiled at the baron who was her dinner partner as she put down her fork, its sterling tines reflecting the candlelight. Taking one more bite was out of the question. The *bratilles de canard aux lentilles* had followed a hearty portion of roasted rabbit in black-olive sauce topped by pickled pumpkin.

"The countess gets lovelier every year," the baron commented, his eyes sweeping down the long table to Janna's mother, Audrey Crandall Atherton, as the harpsichord player began a new song.

Janna nodded, thinking that as a child she'd assumed she'd inherit her mother's patrician profile framed by ash-blond hair and highlighted by deep green eyes. It hadn't happened. Janna's eyes remained a cloudy green that bordered on gray in certain lights and her hair was the color of wet sand. At thirty-four, she no longer coveted her mother's beauty. She accepted her resemblance to the other less beauteous Crandall women like her

Aunt Pith. At least she'd inherited her aunt's brains and emotional stability.

From down the table Pithany Crandall winked at Janna and mouthed, "Are we *still* eating?"

Janna nodded, stifling a giggle. God bless Aunt Pith. She always made Janna laugh, no matter how miserable she felt. Janna had always felt closer to her mother's older sister than she did her own mother. Aunt Pith seemed to know what Janna was thinking, while Audrey Atherton had never understood her.

"She's a remarkable woman," the baron commented, his attention focused now on Aunt Pith. "I understand you're helping with her new hotel."

Janna merely nodded, unwilling to discuss the business venture that had caused her latest quarrel with her husband. Because Collis was content to remain a professor at the London School of Economics, he expected Janna to be satisfied with her teaching position. She wasn't. It had always been understood that one day Janna would take over Aunt Pith's group of hotels on Malta. Collis had known this when he'd married Janna. But he'd chosen to ignore it, trying to mold her into a college professor. It hadn't worked, and until she and Collis reached an understanding they would just go on making each other miserable.

Janna excused herself and walked down the marble corridor, her footsteps echoing on the parquet floor and throwing a hollow sound toward the vaulted ceiling. The Andignes in the Rue de Varenne had been built in the late sixteenth century. This *hôtel particulier,* private mansion, on the Left Bank reminded Janna of her parents' town home on Belgrave Square in London. Like the Belgravia district, the Faubourg Saint-Germain was as exclusive now as when it had been built centuries ago. Today, the Faubourg and Belgravia both housed government ministries and foreign embassies. And a few elite families who had cleverly kept up with changing times, approaching the twenty-first century with titles and fortunes intact.

It would be easier to steal the Crown Jewels than to gain entrée to the private hotels in this *haute noblesse* area with its narrow streets and high walls that concealed extensive gardens. While many admired the Sixteenth Arrondissement's wide boulevards and majestic trees, Janna preferred the Faubourg. To her it was the reincarnation of eighteenth-century grandeur—a step back in time. She and her best friend, Shadoe, both loved the area, often pretending that they'd once lived here in the days of Marie Antoinette. When the twosome roamed the narrow streets, the friendly ghosts of the past welcomed them.

The Faubourg was as much home to Janna as her parents' Belgravia mansion or Lyforth Hall in Kent. Or Aunt Pith's home in Malta, Falcon's Lair. When Janna had attended the Sorbonne and then spent several years researching her paper, she'd lived in the suite Aunt Pith kept at the Hôtel de Suède. Janna had spent hours writing at a Louis Quinze desk that overlooked the private park behind Hôtel de Matignon, the prime minister's residence.

At the end of the hall, Janna stopped and slid back a boiserie panel, too preoccupied to admire the intricate wainscoting's fine detail. Deliberately hidden behind the paneling was a World War I style telephone. She hesitated before she dialed, wondering why she was wasting her time calling her husband. Undoubtedly, Collis would let the answering machine pick up her call as he had all day. She dialed anyway and waited until the machine delivered its message.

"Collis, it's me. Pick up the telephone, darling. Please. I need to talk to you. . . . Please."

No answer. She dropped the receiver into the cradle,

certain Collis was home. Soon he would leave for a lecture tour of the United States. He'd spend these last days as he always did before giving any lecture, rehearsing in their mirrored bathroom, checking his handsome profile from every angle.

She slid the panel shut, seeing Collis in her mind's eye soaking in the tub and rehearsing his speech on the state of the world economy. Damn him! She went back to the dinner party, wishing she could fly home tonight and settle their differences. But she couldn't. Tomorrow was the Lanvin exhibition featuring Claude Montana's designs. British Midlands Bank, owned by the Athertons, had acquired Lanvin several years ago. It was Janna's duty to accompany her mother to the showing.

She returned to her seat and found *mille-feuille au chocolat* had been served. She poked at the dessert with her fork and made polite conversation.

Pithany noticed the dejected look on Janna's face and silently cursed Collis Pembroke. Sometimes Janna was too much like her, Pithany decided. Neither knew when to give up on a man.

Pithany looked down the table and saw her younger sister chatting with her dinner partner. Audrey has Papa's eyes, Pithany thought, remembering her father with fondness and a deep sense of loss. Although over fifty years had passed since Pithany had stood on the dock and waved good-bye to her father as the boat took him to Gozo, she vividly remembered the concerned expression on his face. *Take care of Audrey,* he'd said, and Pithany had done her best. When the war had finally ended, Pithany immediately flew to England.

Audrey was no longer the tagalong little sister she'd been before the war. At thirteen she was already filling out, and anyone could see she would soon become a great beauty. In comparison Pithany had felt incredibly plain, worn down, and worn out by the war she'd thought would never end. Pithany told Audrey their father had died in the war, glossing over the truth. Audrey had dissolved into hysterical tears that were followed by a deep depression. Finally, Reginald Atherton, the earl's son who Audrey idolized, brought her out of it. Pithany never had the heart to tell Audrey their father had committed suicide, shortly after he'd arrived on Gozo.

From down the table, Pithany heard Janna laugh and recognized the false ring to it. Janna was still upset, so Pithany excused herself by saying she had a migraine and asked Janna to walk her home. Audrey remained behind visiting with her old friend, the baron, who would see her home later.

"Do you want to talk about it?" Pithany asked although she knew Janna was upset about Collis.

Janna shook her head. Pithany decided it was just as well. As much as she loved Janna, there was nothing she could do. Good thing Janna was standing up to Collis Pembroke now. If she didn't, Janna would have a life of misery doing what he wanted instead of what she wanted. The man was a consummate snob. Like Reginald Atherton. They both coveted money, but neither wanted to be caught making it. That was outmoded thinking as far as Pithany was concerned.

That attitude kept Warren Atherton, Janna's older brother, a prisoner of leisure, waiting to inherit the title. But the Earl of Lyforth intimidated everyone around him. Because Warren would one day be the earl, he received most of Reginald Atherton's attention. Naturally, Reginald ignored Janna.

They walked the short distance to the Hôtel de Suède. At the door, the hall porter greeted them with the news that Warren was waiting for them.

"Why would Warren fly in from London?" Janna

asked. "I thought he was attending the rain forest fund-raiser."

The suite was in total darkness. Janna switched on the light and Pithany saw her nephew sitting on the divan, his head thrown back against the cushions. His blond hair, normally neat, hung in hanks across his forehead. Although dressed formally, his dinner jacket was missing.

Janna dashed over to her brother. "Warren, what's the matter?"

"Father," he said, his voice choked with emotion. "He's dead."

"No," Pithany and Janna said in unison. "How?"

"Heart attack."

Pithany dropped to the divan beside Warren. Reginald Atherton was fifty-eight, ten years her junior. Too young to die.

"It can't be," Janna muttered, on the verge of tears.

Pithany's heart contracted, not for Reginald Atherton, but for Janna. Her entire life she'd loved that man and tried in vain to please him. Only to be shunted aside in favor of his son. Warren put an arm around Janna. At least, they loved each other, Pithany consoled herself.

But who would comfort Audrey? During the war she'd lived with the Athertons, worshiping Reginald and eventually marrying him. The handsome earl and one of the most beautiful women in the country: a match made in heaven, everyone agreed. Except Pithany. She found Reginald cold and self-centered, but her sister loved him with unquestioning devotion. Pithany prayed Audrey was strong enough emotionally to survive his death, but she had her doubts.

"I took Father's jet to get here," Warren said, obviously not realizing it was now his jet. "The pilot is standing by, ready to take us back. I have to tell Mother myself."

"She's still at the party," Janna said. "Shall we all go—"

"No!" Warren vaulted to his feet. "First, I want to talk to you two alone." He shoved his hand in his pockets and took a deep breath before saying, "I received a call from a hysterical young man saying Father was with him, and he was dead. I thought it was a hoax, but he sounded so bloody sincere I drove over to the Hammersmith address he gave me."

"Hammersmith?" Pithany had never known Reginald to venture beyond the West End. He regarded the working class area as a DMZ. "What on earth was your father doing there?"

"He a-ah"—his characteristic blush rose from beneath Warren's collar and swept up to his hairline—"was having an affair."

"No!" Janna exclaimed, frowning.

Pithany, on the other hand, wasn't surprised. From the first time she'd met Reginald, she'd sensed his aloofness stemmed from something more than typical British reserve. In Pithany's opinion Audrey's emotional troubles had been intensified by her loveless marriage. One thing was certain: The scandal of her husband dying at his lover's home would destroy Audrey.

"We'll have to hush this up," Pithany said. "Audrey can't find out about this woman."

For a moment, Warren studied his hand-lasted shoes. His troubled eyes finally met hers. "His lover wasn't a woman. It was a man in his late twenties."

"You're lying." Janna jumped to her feet and grabbed her brother's arm. "Why are you saying these things about Father?"

Pithany realized Warren was telling the truth. Reginald had been an insular man with no close friends and no love to spare for his family. He'd channeled all his energies into maintaining the facade of the perfect gentleman while living a secret life. Pithany came to her feet, put a restraining arm around Janna, and said to Warren, "Go on."

"I couldn't leave Father there like that. The press would have a field day. Mother would be humiliated. I took Father home and put him in his own bed. Then I sent for Dr. Osgood who confirmed Father had been having trouble with his heart. He'd suffered a mild heart attack last year. He was taking—"

"Heart trouble? Did you know?" Janna interrupted.

"Dr. Osgood said Father refused to tell anyone."

"There'll be an autopsy to confirm the cause of death." Pithany said, her mind scrambling for a way to protect Audrey.

"Yes. It may reveal Father died earlier. I suppose if they do an in-depth autopsy, it will show he was moved."

Janna embraced her brother. "Bless you for moving Father, for trying to spare Mother."

"There's never been a breath of scandal in this family. If this gets out Mother will be subjected to a double dose."

"Perhaps we can persuade Dr. Osgood to order a routine autopsy in Pildowne Crossing's small morgue rather than sending the body to London," Pithany suggested. She doubted Audrey's eggshell-thin composure could survive a protracted investigation. "Dr. Osgood has a special fondness for your mother. If you remember, he came every day when she was hospitalized." Pithany didn't add that Reginald spent most of his infrequent visits making certain word didn't leak out that his perfect wife had suffered a nervous breakdown. "I could persuade him to rush the autopsy, using Audrey's health as the reason."

"If they're just trying to confirm a heart attack," Janna added, "they won't look further. They won't discover you moved him."

"We'll have the funeral immediately," Pithany said. "That way, not only will they have added reason to rush the autopsy and inquest, but Audrey will be spared a long ordeal."

"Maybe," Warren said. "But we might have a worse problem. Blackmail."

Pithany suddenly felt old, older even than her sixty-eight years. "The man he was . . . with . . . what was he like?"

"Good-looking. Italian. Gian Paolo is his name. I gathered he was"—Warren took a deep breath—"just a one-night stand. Even so, he seemed genuinely concerned. He suggested I take Father home. He was so sincere and I was in shock. I didn't give his motives a thought until I was halfway to Lyforth Hall, then I began to wonder. Did he have an ulterior motive? He may be planning to blackmail me. Moving a body has to violate some law."

Janna turned to Warren. "You're positive none of the servants saw you bring Father upstairs?"

"Absolutely."

"Don't worry," Janna assured him. "If this Italian talks, it'll be your word against his."

By the time they broke the news to Audrey, telling her their father had died at home, and took the Atherton jet back to London it was almost 4:00 A.M. Janna let Warren and Aunt Pith take the nearly catatonic Audrey in the limousine to Lyforth Hall while Janna took a taxi home. From the moment she'd heard of her father's death, Janna had wished Collis was with her.

Minera Mews was deserted when the taxi let her out, but Janna moved quietly, careful not to awaken her neighbors. The alleys behind the Belgravia town houses had originally been stables and servants' quarters. Over the years the mews had been converted to elegant maisonettes whose prices rivaled those of the original town houses even though they were narrow and packed together closer than cigars in a box. Janna let herself in and silently dropped her things in the keeping room.

As she started up the stairs to their bedroom, she heard Collis's voice. Was he still in the bathroom rehearsing at this hour? She decided he must be more nervous about speaking to the Institute of Economics than he'd admitted. No wonder. Questions from members of the Washington think tank had left prominent men sputtering.

Janna smiled to herself, remembering the night she'd met Collis Pembroke. She'd delivered her paper on "The Actual Cost of the French Revolution" at a seminar given by the London School of Economics. The paper had taken her several years in Paris to research, and she was absolutely euphoric that it had received enthusiastic acclaim. Cambridge Press was publishing it as well as several university presses in the United States and Europe.

After presenting her paper, she had taken her seat, relieved the ordeal of public speaking was over. The keynote speaker, Collis Pembroke, walked up to the podium. Handsome men didn't usually impress her because they seldom had the intelligence to match their looks. Collis lounged against the podium, without a single note, and delivered an in-depth analysis of the future of the Common Market that mesmerized everyone, including Janna. At the reception afterward she was introduced to him.

"Excellent paper," he said. "First-rate research."

"Thank you." Her words came out smoothly, not reflecting the surprise and encouragement she felt. Collis Pembroke not only spoke with the polish of a thespian, he knew more about finance than she could ever hope to learn.

"You know"—he paused and smoothed back his flawlessly combed brown hair—"you have an intellectual gift, a rare talent for analyzing the financial nuances of—" He looked beyond her, his intelligent blue eyes surveying the crowded hall. "Let's go somewhere private and evaluate your findings."

At dawn they were still discussing eighteenth-century French economics. Unlike the other men she'd dated, Collis wasn't intimidated by her intelligence. Nor was he awed by her family name because the Pembrokes of Northumberland were a titled family, too, although their land had been sold until they now owned nothing more than a small manor house. Collis supported himself by teaching and consulting on economic trends.

Tonight, as Janna climbed the stairs to the bathroom, she thought of how upset Collis would be to hear of her father's death. From the moment she'd brought Collis home five years ago, the two men had forged a close bond. She rounded the corner, coming toward the mirrored bathroom and wondered how to explain the sordid circumstances of her father's death.

Ahead, reflected by the mirrored walls was the profile that never failed to make women take a second look. She paused, deciding that no matter how many times Collis upset her, she loved him. The shock of her father's death had shown her how very much she needed her husband. She belonged here with him, not spending time in Malta helping Aunt Pith. Stepping forward to tell him how wrong she'd been, Janna saw the other figure sitting in the Roman tub with Collis.

"What were you saying?" the girl asked, taking her blond hair in one hand and lifting it over her head, exposing full breasts above the foaming bubbles.

Collis had no idea what he'd been saying. But with Annabelle Swarthmore words didn't matter. Under the water, he slid his hand up the length of her thigh. In-

stantly, her legs parted. Even underwater, he could tell
she was ready. She was insatiable, completely insatiable.

She dropped her long hair and the already wet ends
fell to her breasts as they bobbed in the water. She wiggled forward, pressing herself flush against his cupped
hand and she drew his head down to her lips. He opened
his mouth and her tongue shot in, questing, probing.
Demanding. Easing two fingers inside her, he matched
the rhythm of her tongue.

"What were you saying?" she asked between heated
kisses.

"You have a rare talent"—he replied as her hand ca-
ressed his penis—"for . . . finance." She stroked back
and forth, short staccato jerks. "An intellectual gift for
understanding the nuances of international marketing."

"The goods. That's what you are plain and simple,"
Janna told her reflection in the baroque mirror. She'd
run all the way from Minera Mews to her parents' town
house and rushed upstairs to her old bedroom. Breathing hard, holding back tears of shock and betrayal by
sheer willpower, she eyed herself in the mirror that had
watched her grow from a precocious child to an inquisi-
tive adolescent to a woman. She touched the cold glass,
creating a halo of vapor around her finger where it met
her nose in the mirror. "You're nothing to look at, are
you?"

"Just average," she answered for the mirror. "But
you're 'the goods' to Collis."

"The goods": Janna had never paid any attention to
the Sloanies' definition of a great catch. She'd never had
much in common with the West End debutantes who
haunted the shops around Sloan Square. To please her
mother, she'd taken her bows with them, but that was
all. After her debut, Janna had traveled for several

years, studying archeology and art before attending the Sorbonne.

So when Sloanies referred to "the goods" as marriage material of the highest water—money and a title—Janna never thought in those terms. She would have married the man she loved regardless.

"You should have seen through Collis," she whispered to her reflection.

There had been a thousand little clues that should have told her money was paramount to Collis, not that she had much now—just a small inheritance from a distant relative. But Aunt Pith had made it clear Janna would inherit her fortune. One incident stood out in Janna's mind, crystallizing the truth for her at last. Over her objections, Collis had insisted on selling the stocks Aunt Pith had given them for a wedding present and buying the house in Minera Mews. "For you," he'd said, then he'd renovated the house to suit himself. The *pièce de résistance* was the mirrored bathroom where he could practice his lectures. The only corner of the house Janna could call her own was her closet.

"He manipulated you," she admitted. "And you let him."

She turned away from the mirror, the tight band of irrevocable loss cinched in another notch. Tonight she'd lost two men that she'd loved deeply, totally—a father and a husband.

Neither of them had loved her.

Reginald Atherton, eighth Earl of Lyforth, was laid to rest on a sunny April morning three days after his untimely death. If anyone questioned the rush to send him on to chapter eternal, the great club in heaven, they attributed the haste to her ladyship's fragile emotions. For the funeral, the women in the family wore charcoal-gray suits and large brimmed hats with honeycomb veils while Warren Atherton wore a dark navy suit. Stiff upper lips were *de rigueur.* Any show of emotion, of course, would be in exceedingly poor taste.

Janna stared, unseeing, at the closed casket, oblivious to the deep shadows inside the family's chapel or the hundreds of wreaths and floral tributes lining the stone walls. She couldn't imagine her father inside the coffin. Since she'd learned of his death, Janna had kept telling herself: There must be some mistake. He isn't dead. This thought niggled at the back of her mind until she drove to the morgue and demanded to see the body.

The attendant at the small funeral parlor in Pildowne Crossing had taken her to the back room where they were hastily preparing her father's body. Aunt Pith had persuaded Dr. Osgood to order an autopsy performed locally and a brief hearing rubber-stamped the coroner's findings: heart attack. The funeral was set for the next morning.

Inside the funeral parlor's back room, her father had already been dressed in his morning coat. She gazed lovingly at his face, expecting the handsome man she remembered from childhood. Instead a face with shriveled skin clinging to the skull greeted her. The mortician whispered that the taut skin came from the rigors of the autopsy. His comment barely registered.

She touched her father's hand. "Oh, Father, we never knew you. Did we? You never let us. But we loved you anyway."

Now, sitting in the family pew, she didn't see the inlaid walnut coffin. She saw a shrunken form robbed of the patrician air she always associated with him. Warren touched her gloved hand, signaling it was time to leave the church. The Athertons led the somber procession to the adjacent cemetery where the previous seven earls were buried. The coffin was borne the short distance in a

carriage drawn by matched bays draped in black crepe
that brushed the ground.

Janna tried to concentrate on the grave-side service,
but couldn't. Her mind kept drifting to her father's secret life. Collis's secret life.

The casket was lowered into the ground. Audrey
stepped forward supported by her sister, Pithany, and
Warren. Janna reached into a long velvet box lined with
scarlet satin and handed her mother a single white rose.
For a moment Audrey's hand trembled and her eyes met
Janna's. Despite the veil, Janna saw her mother's pupils
were dilated and her eyelids red-rimmed. Janna smiled
reassuringly and squeezed her mother's hand. Her
mother pressed her lips to the rose, slowly turned, and
tossed it on top of the coffin.

Janna took her brother's place, holding her mother's
arm, while Warren Atherton, now the ninth Earl of
Lyforth accepted the hand-sized sterling silver spade. He
dug into the mossy earth held in a silver bucket. The
moist dirt slid from the spade in a slow stream and
landed on top of the rose with a dull thud.

Afterward the cortege followed the Atherton Daimler
through the village of Pildowne Crossing where all the
curtains were drawn out of respect for the deceased, and
hand-picked flowers or homemade wreaths sat on
porches. The procession wound down the country lane
toward Lyforth Hall, taking almost two hours for everyone to assemble at the estate.

Janna went through the motions, greeting the distinguished guests, but one thought kept haunting her: We
all loved him, but none of us really knew him.

Collis Pembroke raced the car he'd hastily hired at
Heathrow down the narrow lane toward the Atherton
estate. Like a preening swan, Lyforth Hall floated on a
sea of immaculately tended grass shaded by stately oaks.

Every time he saw the weathered stone mansion, its chimneys wreathed in ivy and the scores of leaded glass windows sparkling in the sunlight, Collis thought of Ramsford Park, his family's dilapidated home in Northumberland. England's financial might, now, as in the past was centered in the south. Collis was positive that geography, not genetics, had led to the decline of the Pembroke fortunes. But for him, that was over.

With Reginald Atherton's death, Janna's trust would be augmented by an inheritance that even death duties couldn't diminish. Collis envisioned purchasing a country home, a villa in Marbella, and a Jaguar. But the material rewards couldn't compete with the power Collis would gain. Reginald had respected him, putting Collis's opinion ahead of those of other family members, especially his son. Collis had written the speeches the earl had delivered in the House of Lords and had given him financial advice.

Now Collis was prepared to take control of the Atherton fortune. Warren certainly didn't have the brains for it. Janna and her brother were extremely close. Warren would listen to his sister. And Janna would do whatever Collis told her. He was positive he'd taken the right stance with her when she'd wanted to go into business with that old bat, Pithany. He'd heard the pleading messages Janna had left on the recorder. She was ready to cave in.

Collis double-parked the car and raced up the stone steps and into Lyforth Hall, cursing himself for missing the funeral. *Look concerned,* he told himself as he went over his alibi. He'd been so busy going over his notes for his tour of the U.S. that he hadn't read the papers or turned on the telly. Busy! He smiled at his favorite reflection in the entry mirror. He *had* been busy. He'd crawled out of Annabelle's arms just in time to catch his plane to Washington. He would be on it now if he hadn't picked up a *Times* on his way into the terminal.

When he read the article, Collis had been surprised they were burying Reginald so quickly. He'd died Friday evening and they were burying him Monday. It was strange, just as it was strange that none of the Atherton servants had come to Collis's home to tell him the news when he hadn't answered the telephone. He assumed the family thought he was in Washington because he'd never told Janna exactly which day he was leaving.

He stepped into the Great Hall and found hordes of mourners, sending the deceased to the hereafter as they always did with a feast worthy of Fortnum and Mason's and quaffing the dear departed's private stock.

Collis didn't see Janna, but spotted Shadoe Hunnicutt, Janna's closest friend, standing alone and walked over to her. "Where's Janna?"

"In the garden with the family."

Collis turned his back on Shadoe. He'd discouraged Janna's friendship with the flamboyant redhead. She never made a move without consulting Tarot cards or wondering if she was being motivated by past life experiences.

Secretly he admired her intelligence and her business acumen. He used her business insight whenever he taught a seminar on small businesses that showed the cunning way a clever entrepreneur could discover a niche in the market no one else had seen.

Collis walked through the French doors that led to the vast gardens maintained by a staff of gardeners supervised by a horticulturist. Collis cursed his family's poverty, but consoled himself with the thought that at least his family had legitimately earned their title. The Earl of Lyforth had received his title from Queen Elizabeth—for valor between the sheets, or so the centuries-old rumor went. Of course, *his* ancestors had been rewarded for battlefield achievements.

Collis rushed out to greet Janna, who was talking with Aunt Pith. "Darling, I—"

Janna turned away from him, her eyes hostile. A patch of guilt-driven sweat broke out on his forehead. *She can't know,* he assured himself, *she's just upset over her father's death.* Pithany swept past Collis without even a nod. He'd always hated the old biddy, resenting her closeness to Janna, but he'd tolerated her, knowing she'd leave Janna her fortune. Janna walked toward the Elizabethan knot garden, and he followed.

"Darling, I'm so sorry. I didn't realize your father had died. I was going over my speeches. I didn't listen to the news or read the papers." She removed her hat and regarded him with a detached coolness that he'd never seen. His apprehension increased. "You know how wrapped up I get in my work."

"You were ah . . . rehearsing your speech?"

"Yes." His tension eased slightly.

"You didn't get any of my messages?"

"You know how I am." He tried for a contrite tone. "I was wrapped up in my work."

"You were . . . wrapped up? Too wrapped up to answer the telephone?" He nodded. "Too wrapped up to read the papers?" He shrugged apologetically. "Too wrapped up to turn on the telly?"

"You know how wrapped up I—"

"You were wrapped up, all right. With a busty bimbo who has 'a rare talent for finance.' "

Collis gasped for air as if he'd been buried six feet under with the earl. Janna must have returned and seen Annabelle. How could he have been so stupid to bring another woman into his home? "She doesn't mean anything," he assured Janna. "I'm devoted to you. You know that."

"I've known something was going on for months. But you lied and lied. You kept saying: *'You're crazy, Janna. Don't be so suspicious, Janna. You're imagining things, Janna.'* You made me question my own sanity."

Collis knew he'd made a severe tactical error. Her father's death would leave Janna vulnerable, needing him more than ever. He could have persuaded her to do anything had she not caught him. He fumbled for a way to recoup. "I'm sorry. I've been such a fool. You know how it is. Women throw themselves at me." He gestured to his handsome face. "When you look like this—I resisted . . . but she kept after me until—"

"I'm filing a divorce petition in the morning."

He put his arm around her. "Darling, don't do that—"

She pivoted away from him. "Don't 'darling' me. I've been a fool long enough."

Collis watched her go, temporarily beaten. He knew better than to argue with Janna when she was this angry. But he'd get her back. She'd come around—she always did. He wasn't giving up the Atherton fortune so easily.

3

✠

On the evening following his father's funeral, Warren sat in Lyforth Hall's library. The walnut shelves, running from floor to ceiling, contained the best of English literature, from gold stamped first editions to bound volumes of *Punch*. On the wall opposite the mullioned windows overlooking a side garden was a stone fireplace with the Atherton coat of arms chiseled into it. A slow burning oak log cast tendrils of light across the Aubusson rug, its floral garlands faded by countless soles tracking across it to the burled walnut desk the eight—now nine—earls had used, preferring this room to the smaller study.

Warren rocked back in the leather chair. God, he hated this. He'd thought the pressure was over when Aunt Pith had convinced Dr. Osgood to arrange a simple autopsy to spare Audrey a long ordeal, and they'd gotten through the funeral without any mishaps. Even better, nothing had been heard from Gian Paolo. Now this.

The telephone on the desk buzzed, indicating a message from within Lyforth Hall. He picked up the receiver, hoping this wasn't more trouble.

"Sir"—the butler's voice came over the line—"Miss Hunnicutt is here. She has something for the countess."

He doubted his mother was up to visitors. She'd made it through yesterday's ceremony thanks to Dr. Osgood's medication. "Have Miss Hunnicutt come in here."

Warren straightened his tie and smoothed back his hair over his ears, thinking he needed a haircut. The door opened and Shadoe walked in, wearing stone-washed jeans that looked as if she'd been spooned into them and a man's hacking jacket over a rust-colored turtleneck sweater that matched her hair.

He welcomed her with a smile, then said, "Mother's not up to seeing anyone."

"I brought her a present." From under the jacket, Shadoe produced something white that looked like a small feather duster except for the gloss-black nose and matching eyes. Its long bangs had been tied on top of its head into a topknot that looked like a silk powder puff.

"A Maltese dog?"

"Yes. Your mother has always wanted one."

A pang of guilt shot through Warren for not thinking of this himself. For years, his mother had wanted a Maltese like one of Aunt Pith's, but his father despised any animal you couldn't hunt a fox on. "Let's take it upstairs."

They walked to his mother's suite in silence. Warren knocked on the door and the maid answered. His mother lay propped up against a flotilla of silk pillows piped in French ribbon. Her chin-length blond hair was carefully combed into the classic pageboy she'd worn for as long as Warren could remember. She wore a silk bed jacket edged in Alençon lace that matched her green eyes.

With a wan expression, she asked, "Is Dr. Osgood here?"

Warren checked his watch. The doctor visited three times a day. "He'll be here any minute. Shadoe's come" —he reached for Shadoe's hand—"to give you something very special."

Shadoe's soft fingers curled around his and gave him a

slight squeeze. "This is Von Rommel," she said, handing the small dog to his mother.

The handful of fur snuggled against his mother's chest and yawned sleepily, unfurling a pink tongue not much bigger than a matchstick.

Audrey smiled, the first smile he'd seen since she'd learned his father had died. "Adorable, simply adorable. Thanks, awfully." She cuddled the dog to her bosom. "Just this morning I told Pithany I wanted one of her puppies. Her Maltese has a litter, you know. Since it would be coming from out of the country, the poor little thing would have to spend six months in quarantine before the authorities would let me have it."

"I'm glad you like him. Now, you've got to take care of him. Von Rommel needs you."

"Don't worry," Audrey assured her. "I'll brush him myself and take him for walks. When I'm shopping in Harrods, I'll leave Rommie in their kennel with his own pillow and bowl."

He heard the maid admit Dr. Osgood. Out of the corner of his eye, Warren looked at Shadoe, who was smiling fondly at his mother. Shadoe was the most sensitive woman he knew—in tune with people's feelings.

"Ellis, look." His mother beamed at Dr. Osgood and held up the now sleeping dog.

"I see you're feeling better."

"Yes. Much better." His mother cradled "Rommie" to her chest and kissed the top of his head, her eyes on Dr. Osgood.

Shadoe tugged on Warren's arm, and they slipped out and went down the stairs to the porte cochere where her beat-up Austin Mini was parked.

"It was very thoughtful of you to bring Mother the dog. Thanks."

She glanced up at him, her eyes luminescent in the near darkness. Her look was so galvanizing it sent a tremor through him. He put his hands in his pockets to keep himself from taking her into his arms.

"Janna needs you now—more than ever," she said, getting into her car.

Warren watched the tail lights until they disappeared. Leave it to Shadoe to guess the problem. She was amazingly intuitive. Except when it came to him; she never seemed aware of his true feelings for her.

From the recesses of his mind, where he'd suppressed it, came the news he'd learned just before Shadoe's visit. Part of him still refused to believe it. But Peyton Gifford had shown him irrefutable evidence. Even if he hadn't, Warren would have taken his word for it. Since before Napoleon, one Gifford after another had been the Athertons' solicitor. Unlike most attorneys who salivated at the mere thought of lucrative litigation, Gifford, Gifford, and Cavendish did not. They were unfailingly honest, loyal, and above all, discreet.

Warren went upstairs to the music room where Janna had been all day. He paused, his hand on the polished newel post, and wondered if he should let Aunt Pith handle this. From what Gifford had told him, Aunt Pith had been instrumental in convincing his father. Through the years, Aunt Pith had been the backbone of the family. She'd divided her time between England and Malta, always being on hand when needed. But she wouldn't be around forever.

You have to tell Janna yourself. You're the head of this family now.

Warren opened the door and found Janna sitting in an overstuffed chair and listening to Yo Yo Ma's latest CD. Strains of the premier cellist's music filled the room where previous generations had gathered to hear harpsichord or pianoforte recitals. Those instruments were in the attic now replaced by state-of-the-art McIntosh equipment. He picked up the remote control from the

table next to his sister and pointed it at the infrared
sensor.

The music stopped and Janna studied her brother as
he seated himself in the armchair beside hers. His handsome face looked pinched, drawn. She sensed something
was wrong. "You've heard from that—that man."

"No." A telltale flush crept up Warren's neck, as it
always did when he was acutely uncomfortable—the
only chink in his otherwise patrician armor. "Peyton Gifford left about an hour ago."

"He has divorce papers ready for me already? I only
called his office this morning."

"He came about the will." Warren's tone had a
strange edge to it. "He wanted to talk to me before the
official reading."

"Oh." Her father's death and Collis's betrayal had left
a yawning emptiness, almost as if this were some horrible nightmare, and she was trapped, suspended in an
alien world. Who cared about the will? Money couldn't
bring back the dead. Or buy love.

A silence more worrisome than anything he'd said
filled the room. Janna thought the estate might be in
some financial difficulty, but discarded the idea immediately. After all, Collis had been advising her father.

Warren finally spoke. "You know I love you. I've never
been as close to anyone as I have you."

Apprehension replaced her thoughts of Collis. Her
brother never used the word love. They loved each other
deeply, of course. But saying it aloud signaled some impending crisis. "What's wrong? Please tell me."

His brows drew together in an agonized expression.
"Father left you out of his will."

It took two full seconds for her head to clear. "Out?
You mean nothing? Absolutely nothing?"

"Yes, but don't worry. I'll take care of it. He should

have left you"—his words came out in an angry rush— "the shares in Aunt Pith's new hotel."

"No," she said, unable to keep the hurt from her voice. "I won't take anything Father didn't intend me to have." Her brain reeled trying to make sense of this. Her father's holdings were vast and unlike many other noble families' fortunes, the Athertons' hadn't been diminished by time. Her father had undoubtedly left numerous bequests to servants, family retainers like his solicitors, and God-only-knew how many charities. She'd always assumed he'd leave her an inheritance to supplement her small trust. A token to demonstrate his concern for her future welfare.

But no. Not one pence for her. Then she realized why he hadn't. "Father thought being Aunt Pith's sole heir was enough." Aunt Pith had told the family years ago that because Warren would inherit the Atherton estate, Janna would inherit her sizable estate, which she'd built out of the ruins of the war. It made sense, but still, Janna's insides trembled at the slight.

"No. That's not why," Warren said, his voice unsteady, his face becoming alarmingly red. After an uncomfortable silence he added, "You're not his daughter."

Not his daughter, not his daughter, not his daughter. Like a curse, the words echoed through her brain as she struggled to make sense of this. "You mean . . . Mother and some other man? I don't believe it."

Warren took her hand in both his. There might have been tears in his eyes, but in the semidark room, she couldn't be certain. "You're not Mother's daughter, either. You're adopted."

"Adopted? That's ridiculous. Look at me." She pointed to her face. "Everyone says I resemble Aunt P—" Her voice faltered. "But I don't. Do I?"

"Yes." He squeezed her hand. "A little, I guess. We all

see what we want to see. The family always said you took
after Aunt Pith. We believed them."

Shock caused the words to wedge in her throat. Finally, she managed to ask, "Do you know who my real
parents were?"

"A woman from Malta and an American naval officer
stationed there when it was a NATO base."

"I'm an *American*?"

"It's not a four-letter word, you know."

"Really?" She couldn't keep the sarcasm out of her
voice. Reginald Atherton regarded Americans as a sub-
species.

"Are my parents still alive?"

"Gifford didn't know," he responded, his nervousness
echoing noticeably in the large room. "Maybe Aunt Pith
can tell you. She arranged the adoption."

"Why would Father adopt me when he already had
you? He did legally adopt me, didn't he?"

"Yes. I saw the documents."

"Then people must know. Everyone must have realized Moth—Audrey hadn't been pregnant."

"No. No one outside the family—and the solicitors—
know. Mother wasn't well for several years after I was
born. She had a prolonged case of postpartum depression. No one saw her for months. Gifford told me when
you arrived, no one questioned it."

The nagging in the back of her mind refused to be
stilled. "I can't imagine Father adopting me. Obviously,
he never wanted me." She closed her eyes in despair,
admitting the truth: He'd never loved her—despite her
continuous attempts to win his affection—because she
wasn't his daughter.

"Gifford says Aunt Pith convinced him."

She gazed into the Atherton blue eyes she'd looked up
to and loved her entire life. Even worse than knowing
her parents had never wanted her, even worse than los-

ing Collis, was the loss gnawing at her now. "I'm not your sister."

Warren stood, pulled her to her feet, and held her, stroking the back of her neck the way he had when she was six and had fallen from her pony, the way he had when she'd almost broken her neck chasing Bentley Horgath down the slopes at St. Moritz. The way he had when she'd come to Lyforth Hall for the funeral. Without Collis.

"I mean it," he said, his voice low, choked. "I love you. You're my sister. This won't change anything between us."

It was a lot of money, Pithany thought, hanging up the telephone. The quote she'd received for a security system for Falcon's Lair, her home in Malta, was high, but a necessary expense. Two days before she'd joined Janna and Audrey in Paris to preview the couture collection, Travis Prescott had suffered a fatal heart attack in her home. When she'd returned from the futile trip to the hospital, she discovered someone had broken into her villa. She'd worked for several days with her housekeeper, Clara, but found nothing missing. They'd straightened Travis's belongings as well, but they had no idea what the thieves might have stolen from him although several valuable items like his money clip hadn't been taken. The whole incident upset Pithany.

Face it, Malta isn't the same sleepy island of your youth. There were numerous Libyans and Algerians attending the university. Irrefutable evidence linked Malta with the bomb that brought down the Pan Am jet over Lockerbie, Scotland. British oil field workers—a scruffy, transient lot—shuttled in and out of Malta on their way to Libya. And most damning of all in Pithany's estimation: Thousands of German tourists jammed the beaches they'd so zealously bombed fifty years earlier.

The native Maltese still knew each other—too well. The island's small size and the numerous intermarriages kept the community close-knit. But times had changed. The robbery rate, once nonexistent, was rising. It saddened Pithany, but she braced herself for it. She'd lived through worse.

The loud rap on the door of her room startled her. She hurried from the desk to answer it. "Janna, what's wrong?"

The soft plum-colored cashmere dress Janna wore deepened the color of her eyes, which were now a hostile green. "Reginald has left me out of the will because I'm not his child. Why didn't you tell me I was adopted?"

"He didn't even leave you the shares in the Blue Grotto?" Pithany hedged. "He promised me—"

"Why didn't you tell me I'd been adopted?"

The moment Pithany had dreaded since she'd first held Janna, just minutes old, had come. "I wanted to tell you—dozens of times—but I was sworn to secrecy."

"Do you know who my parents are?" Janna asked, every syllable clipped with anger.

Pithany was tempted to tell the whole truth, but Janna might not believe her. Worse, Janna might blame Pithany. She couldn't risk losing Janna's love. What Janna needed now was Pithany's strength, her love. With Collis's betrayal and Reginald's will coming at the same time, Janna was vulnerable. Later when, Janna had grown more accustomed to the situation, Pithany would tell her everything. For now though, Pithany would merely prepare Janna with a few carefully chosen facts. "Yes. I knew your parents."

"Knew?" Janna slumped onto the sofa. "Then they're dead."

"Yes. Your father was a United States naval officer stationed in Malta with the NATO forces. He was killed in a freak accident during naval maneuvers. That's why he didn't marry your mother. She died of a liver infection several years ago."

"I never had a chance to know either of them," Janna said, her voice filled with heart-wrenching despair. For the first time since they'd learned of Reginald Atherton's death, and Janna had told her about Collis, tears welled up in Janna's eyes. "My parents must have had relatives. Surely, I have cousins or—"

Pithany sat beside her and put her arm around the one person on earth she'd kill for. "Your mother, Gloria Attard, lost her entire family during the war. She grew up in the Carmelite orphanage in Valletta. Your father was an only child. His parents are probably dead by now. We could check." Pithany chose her next words carefully. "There aren't any relatives except a few distant cousins in America. We verified all this when Audrey adopted you. Reginald needed to be assured no one would appear to claim you." And embarrass him.

"Why did my mother give me up?"

The plaintive note in Janna's voice brought tears to Pithany's eyes. "Gloria couldn't offer you the kind of life the Athertons could."

"I wouldn't have cared." Tears crested in Janna's eyes. "Did she ever ask about me?"

"She left Malta right after you were born," Pithany answered with deliberate evasion. "I only learned of her death from the Carmelite nuns who heard from her occasionally. I understand she never married."

Janna's mind spun with bewilderment. Alone. She was alone in the world. She always had been, but hadn't realized it. She stared off into the distance for a moment, and then asked, "How did you convince the Athertons to adopt me?"

"Audrey was no problem. She'd had a difficult time conceiving Warren. She had to go to a Swiss clinic to do

so. I knew there wouldn't be a second child and Audrey
wanted a daughter."

"And Reginald?"

"I convinced him to do it for Audrey. You see, Audrey
is very much like my father. He suffered from chronic
depression. In those days, we didn't know what it was, or
how to treat it." Pithany held Janna's hand in both of
hers. "I never told Audrey, but Father killed himself.
When I realized she had the same condition—it's very
often inherited—I made certain Audrey had competent
medical care. I also tried to make certain Audrey was
happy. She was desperate to have a daughter."

"We've all spent our lives making Mo—Audrey
happy," Janna said with an edge of resentment in her
voice.

"Don't be too hard on her. Now that we know about
Reginald's secret life, it's easy to understand that her
marriage couldn't have been a happy one. She tried very
hard to be a good mother to you, didn't she?"

"Yes. She did her best, but I always felt closer to you."
Janna hesitated a moment. "If . . . if Audrey hadn't
adopted me, would you have?"

"Of course." Pithany forced herself to ask the next
question. "Would you have wanted that?"

"Yes," Janna said, her voice unsteady. "Whenever I
visited, I used to pretend I lived with you, and I was
never going home. I didn't fit in with the Athertons—no
matter how much Warren tried to help."

Pithany closed her eyes. It hurt too much to cry.
"Come home with me now. I'd love to have you. There's
plenty of room at Falcon's Lair. It's time I trained you to
take over for me."

"I don't have any right. I'm not your niece."

Pithany's heart stalled, but she managed to keep her
voice level. "Once I'd hope to marry, but the war ruined

my plans. Fifteen years later you were born. You've always had a special place in my heart. I built the hotels for you. I've always known that one day you'd take over for me. You're like a daughter to me."

4

What a pain in the butt. In Muleshoe, there'd have been a flash flood that would have sent Running Water Draw over its banks and the whole storm would have been over in ten minutes. But here in Malta, the thirsty limestone forming the island soaked up the deluge that continued hour after hour. To make matters worse, the power had been out for the last two hours.

Nick yanked off the Walkman's earphones, having listened to the conclusion of *Clear and Present Danger,* and wondered if it was time to check on Millicent and her three Maltese pups. The luminescent dial on his watch read ten thirty. Pithany had asked him to let Millicent out at ten since she wouldn't be home until after midnight.

He felt his way across the living room—three days wasn't long enough to know the guest house where Travis had lived well enough to move faster in the dark —to the French doors that faced the main house. House? Hell. Falcon's Lair was bigger than the largest building in Muleshoe, Hensley's Mortuary. He looked out into a moonless night and a torrent of wind-driven rain. He knew the swimming pool lay between his guest quarters and the main house, but he couldn't see it. He silently cursed not having a flashlight. With his luck, he'd fall into the pool on the way to let the damn dog out.

Too bad he hadn't asked Miss Crandall where she

kept a flashlight. When she'd left that afternoon for the bridge tournament, Nick had been sunning himself after swimming. There hadn't been a cloud in the sky. In the two weeks Nick had been on Malta, sunny days and warm nights—typical weather, he was told—had been the rule. Somehow he'd known the storm was coming. He should have searched for a flashlight.

Malta reminded Nick of someplace, but he couldn't quite remember where. It might have been a picture book he'd read as a child about King Arthur and his knights, but he couldn't be certain. He'd immediately felt at home on the island, admiring the inviting beaches that contrasted sharply with the villages that seemed to be throwbacks in time with their narrow, cobbled streets and storybook homes that appeared to have been built during the Middle Ages.

Nick decided that he couldn't wait any longer for the rain to stop. The dog hadn't been out for hours. Holding his raincoat over his head, Nick streaked across the pool area, cutting a wide swath to avoid the pool. In the blinding rain and total darkness, he tripped over some damn plant and stumbled into the side of the house. One hand on the limestone wall, one hand holding the raincoat above his head, he groped in the darkness, deciding he'd overshot the door leading into the servants' quarters and kitchen. He stepped into a puddle and water filled one shoe. "Aw, shit!"

He found the door and fiddled with the key until it opened. Millicent shot out, nearly tripping him, and disappeared into the darkness. Closing the door to keep the rain from coming in, he hoped the dog had enough sense to return when she finished her business. After dropping his raincoat on the tile floor, Nick took off his shoes and socks. No sense in tracking mud all over the place.

In the distance he could hear the pups yipping. Hands

in front of him, he felt his way across the small service area that he'd only seen once when Pithany had shown him how to take care of the puppies. His nose told him he was close. Three puppies. Over five hours. The whelping area in the adjacent room had to be a minefield of turds.

He opened the door into the kitchen and checked a few drawers, looking for a flashlight, but didn't find one. Scratching at the backdoor told him Millicent had returned. He stumbled to the rear door and eased it open a crack. The dog charged in. The pure white of her coat made her more visible than anything else in the darkness. He reached down to pick her up, thinking he'd have to use his raincoat to dry her off. She shook, showering his face with water, then hightailed it toward the kitchen.

"Dammit!" Why hadn't he shut that door? He'd been warned Millicent would hide from her puppies if given half a chance. She'd reached the end of her rope—the sixth week. Now that her pups had been weaned, she'd had it with motherhood. She would try to sneak away from her pups whenever she could and hide. What was he supposed to do now? Search the entire house when he couldn't see a damn thing?

Cursing under his breath with every halting step, he groped in the darkness, finding his way through the kitchen into the dining room. He had his mouth open, ready to yell, "Cookie. Cookie"—the only sure way to get the dog to come—when he heard the strident sound of breaking glass. Just his luck. Millicent must have knocked over a pricey crystal piece on one of the coffee tables in the living room.

Trusting his memory that the Mediterranean style villa had a large open foyer with no furniture to trip him, he hurried in the direction of the living room. He halted about where he remembered two—or was it three?—steps down into the mammoth room.

He opened his mouth to call, "Cookie." The word stalled in his throat. Ahead, he detected movement—little more than a black shadow in an even darker room. Not a dog. A man.

A trace of light—so faint as to be nonexistent—came through a parted curtain. He guessed the intruder had broken one of the panes on the French door and had entered the villa, opening black-out drapes that were usually drawn against the unrelenting Mediterranean sun.

Nick flattened himself against the wall, certain the man hadn't seen him in the all concealing darkness. It was impossible to tell much about the intruder. Shapes were discernable only by varying degrees of darkness.

He waited to see what the person would do, remembering Pithany telling him about the robbery that had taken place the night Travis had died. The main house had been searched, but Travis's guest house had been thoroughly ransacked. When Nick packed his friend's things to send to Austin, he hadn't been able to find the Filofax that Travis always used or his camera. Malta was a small island. Nick figured this was the same thief, or he knew the thief. The man wasn't getting away from him.

He squinted hard at the raincoated man, his hat drawn low. There was something long in his hand. A knife or a long-barreled gun, but not a flashlight. He must have one in his other hand. Soon he'd switch it on and discover Nick unarmed. It took a split second for Nick to decide what to do.

He charged across the room. With a flying tackle he hit the man full force, knocking him down. They landed on the tile floor, a jumble of limbs, with Nick on top. The weapon bounced across the floor with a metallic clank.

Nick groped for the intruder's arm, intending to pin it behind his damn back before hauling the guy to his feet. His hands encountered something surprisingly soft. He double-checked.

A woman?

No!

Yes!

Aw, shit!

She moaned and gasped for breath. Nick jerked his hands from her breasts almost muttering an apology, remembering in time she had broken into Falcon's Lair. Women were every bit as dangerous as men. This one had come armed.

She thrashed, trying to get away, but he had her trapped beneath his body. His ear inches from her mouth, she cut loose with a yell that could have been heard two hundred miles away in Libya.

"Knock it off, lady!"

She flailed at him. One hand went for his face but he ducked. Her nails caught him just below the ear, raking down his neck.

"Cut it out!" His nose was just inches from hers. He had the shadowy impression of a pale face as she tossed her head from side to side. She yanked at a fistful of his hair, pulling it with surprising strength. He grabbed her throat, intending to frighten her. "Don't make me hurt you."

She bit his wrist, sinking her teeth in. Pain shot up his arm, but he ignored the impulse to let go of her neck. Suddenly, she went limp. He jerked his hand off her neck. Had he killed her? He wasn't choking her that hard, was he? The bile rose up in his throat. The only thing he'd ever killed was a rattlesnake in Running Water Draw. He jumped to his feet, praying she was still alive. Stumbling sideways, he banged into a table, stubbing his toe.

The "dead" woman vaulted to her feet and streaked in what he judged to be the direction of the front door. She wasn't getting away from him. He rushed after her, catching her by her shoulders and pulling her backward. Stumbling and bumping into a sofa, he lost his balance and fell onto it, landing with her on top of him.

"P-please don't hurt me." The tortured whisper had an unmistakable British accent. "I'll give you whatever you want, just don't kill me."

"Kill you?" He hauled her to her feet, but didn't let her go. "I won't hurt you if you hold still while I call the police."

"You're calling the police?"

"Hey, lady. You broke into this house." He dragged her with him, intending to use the telephone in the kitchen.

"I belong here. I'm—"

He stopped. "Belong here? What are you talking about? You broke in."

"I rang and rang, but no one answered the bell," she said, her voice trembling. "I thought Aunt Pith would be here, or Clara."

Aunt Pith. Clara, the housekeeper who was in Gozo with her daughter for the weekend. Obviously, he'd roughed up one of Pithany's relatives. He released her. "What about the weapon in your hand?"

"Weapon?" She sounded genuinely puzzled not to mention scared spitless. "You mean the tire iron? I used it to break a window pane to get in. It was raining so hard that I was afraid to drive down the hill with the streetlights out. Aunt Pith wouldn't want me to spend the night in the car."

"Who are you?"

"Lady Janna Atherton-Pembroke. Pithany Crandall is my aunt." Some of the fear had left her voice, replaced by a more self-confident tone. "Who are you? What have you done with Aunt Pith?"

"Nick Jensen. I rent the guest house. Your aunt's playing in the bridge tournament. She asked me to take care of Millicent and her puppies."

"Do you normally attack innocent women?"

"I thought you were a thief. Didn't your aunt tell you about the robbery?"

"Well, yes. But—"

"How the hell was I supposed to know you weren't a burglar?"

"I suppose you're right. Aunt Pith wasn't expecting me until the weekend. I see she didn't mention me," she admitted, but there was an uppity edge to her voice. "Now, if you're satisfied, I'm going to my rooms."

Even in the darkness, Janna had no trouble finding her way up the stairs. She'd spent so many holidays at Falcon's Lair that she knew it as well as her own home. But she clung to the bannister, her stomach fluttering, her heart knocking against her chest. Without question, she'd thought he was going to kill her. He'd frightened her so much that she'd used her title, Lady Janna, something she never did.

She stopped halfway up the stairs and waited for her pulse to return to normal. It didn't. She could still feel the weight of Nick Jensen's tall body trapping her and see his ugly face, a dark shadow, looming above hers as he choked her.

She slowly felt her way into the suite of rooms that had been hers for as long as she could remember, a flicker of apprehension coursing through her, heightening with each footstep. Nick Jensen was lurking around downstairs. She found her way through the sitting room to her bedroom and told herself he wasn't a dangerous man. The whole incident had been a mistake. Still, she locked the door behind her.

She tossed her raincoat aside and collapsed, fully clothed, onto her bed, feeling shaky and weak. The back of her head throbbed and she touched it gently, finding a lump where her head had struck the tile floor.

She lay there, her thoughts swinging pendulum-fashion from anger to reason to anger again. She'd given him an excuse to attack her. No one had ever manhandled her. She could still feel his hands on her breasts and the unbearable pressure of his body. And the voice that conjured up images of six-guns and branding irons.

Dimly aware that the rain had stopped, leaving a somnolent dripping from the eaves, she closed her eyes, trying to relax after the white-knuckle plane landing and the terrifying incident downstairs. She didn't know she'd fallen asleep until she awoke to a sodden mass on her chest licking the tip of her nose. A scream died on her lips. "Millie?"

The poor thing was drenched; she'd catch her death. Janna rose clutching the wet dog and went into the bathroom to dry her, wondering what Nick Jensen had really been doing in the house. Certainly not taking care of Millie. Had he been snooping around, looking for something to steal? Goodness knows, Falcon's Lair contained countless valuable art objects and paintings.

She toweled Millie off and wrapped her in a dry bath sheet. As she went back into the bedroom, she heard a voice in the hall.

"Cookie. Cookie. Cookie."

Janna unlocked her door. "Aunt Pith. I'm in here. I've got Millie."

"I wasn't expecting you," Aunt Pith said, but even in the darkness, Janna heard the welcome in her voice.

"I finished what I had to do. I want to start to work

with you right away." There wasn't anything in London for her anymore.

Flashlight in hand, Aunt Pith entered the suite. "Oh, my," she said, reaching for Millie and handing Janna the flashlight. "How did you get so wet?"

Janna sank onto the sofa and let out an exasperated sigh. "That Jensen man must have let her out and forgotten her."

Aunt Pith sat beside her, cuddling the dog. "Millie probably got away from him."

Janna described the incident downstairs finishing, "I don't trust that man."

"It was a mistake, that's all. Nick thought he was protecting my property."

"But he tried to strangle me. Don't you think that's going too far?" She couldn't understand Aunt Pith's attitude. Janna had always been able to come to her with the tiniest bruise, the smallest scratch, the silliest complaint and get sympathy. "I'm not comfortable with him living in the guest house. He frightens me."

It was more than that. From the moment he'd spoken, she'd had the strangest sensation that went beyond fear. Had she met him somewhere? Impossible. She'd remember that accent. Still, she couldn't shake the feeling that she knew him.

"He's . . . so big. So—so . . . ugly."

"Ugly?" Aunt Pith smiled indulgently. "He can't help what he looks like. It takes an inner spirit to be a truly good person."

Janna took this comment as a direct criticism of Collis Pembroke. Aunt Pith had never cared for him. Janna had sensed that from the start. But she hadn't fallen for Collis because he was handsome. She'd thought he loved her as much as she loved him.

"I advise you not to alienate Nick Jensen. We need him."

"Whatever for?"

"Have you spoken to Warren in the last few days?"

"No." She didn't like the look on Aunt Pith's face in the shadowy backwash of the flashlight. "Gian Paolo," Janna guessed, although she couldn't imagine what he had to do with the Texan.

"He's disappeared."

"An answer to our prayers."

Aunt Pith smoothed the now sleeping Millie's fur, looked at Janna, then at the exhausted dog. "When they had the official reading of the will, Warren discovered Reginald had left Gian something very valuable."

The too familiar knot formed in the pit of Janna's stomach. "Why didn't the attorneys tell Warren sooner? They certainly wasted no time in telling him about me."

"They didn't notice. Reginald left a great many bequests."

Janna fought the surge of resentment welling up inside her. She reminded herself to keep her mind focused on the future. Not the past. "What did he leave him?"

"Thirty-five percent of Crandall Hotels. I sold Reginald a substantial interest in order to raise money to build the Blue Grotto." A tight frown corrugated her brow. "I expected to buy back his shares soon. I never thought he'd die. Even if I had, I would have assumed he would leave you those shares."

"I'll buy them back," Janna said. "Warren will lend me the money."

"We'll have to find Gian first. Meanwhile, be nice to Nick Jensen. He owns twenty percent of the company."

"Why would you sell anything to him?"

Aunt Pith sat stiffly erect. "Raising money to build the Blue Grotto wasn't easy. The Bradfords convinced banks here it was too risky. I asked Reginald for part of the money. The remaining twenty percent Travis Prescott bought. Nick Jensen is his heir."

Janna had never met Anthony "Big Tony" Bradford but for as long as she could remember, he'd been her aunt's rival. He owned numerous businesses on Malta including hotels that competed with Pithany's. "And you're afraid Anthony Bradford might acquire both men's shares and take control of your hotels."

Aunt Pith nodded solemnly. "He has brought his son, Curt, into the business. They've made it clear that they'll never be satisfied until they control all the hotels on Malta. I can't let that happen. I've worked a lifetime building my business."

"Don't worry. Warren will locate the Italian and convince him to sell. I'll get those shares from Nick Jensen."

Nick knew the power had been restored when the lights in Falcon's Lair went on, shining through his bedroom window. He went into the bathroom and inspected the scratch on his neck and the bite on his hand. Great. Tomorrow everyone in the office would stare and speculate about his wild weekend. His left leg was numb from slamming his knee against the floor when he'd tackled Her Royal Highness—Lady Janna. How was he supposed to know she wasn't a thief?

He recalled Miss Crandall mentioning her niece, who was going into business with her. Called her Janna, not *Lady* Janna with some double-barreled last name. Pretentious as hell. He'd heard that voice too often in his nightmares. The raised final consonants and clipped diction. *"I'm going to my rhewms."*

The entire time he'd been in Japan, he'd avoided the women from the British Embassy. They looked like the women back home but their accents reminded him of his sixth grade teacher, Mrs. Mooth. She'd been sharp; he'd give her that. She'd zeroed in on Nick's problem on the first day. And no matter how much he smiled, she'd tormented him through the longest year of his life. Then she'd finished him with his mother. Finished even to this day.

Better get used to the accents, Buddy. You're here for at least six months. Just his luck, everyone on the island spoke English with a British accent.

The telephone rang and he went into the sitting room to answer it, assuming that, at well after midnight, it was a wrong number. "Hullo."

"Nick?"

"Austin. How ya' feeling?"

"Cain't complain." His voice sounded far away despite an excellent connection.

"Listen. I haven't been able to find Travis's girlfriend yet. No one in the office knows anything about her. His landlady, Pithany Crandall doesn't know either. I—"

"Got the autopsy report back."

Nick's sixth sense kicked in. "Not a heart attack?"

"No. Poison."

The dull ache that he hadn't been able to escape since learning of his friend's death intensified. "What?"

"They claim he ate oleander blossoms or leaves or branches or—hell, I don't know."

"Travis wouldn't eat an oleander." Nick's mind scrambled to make sense of this. Death by oleander? Sounded like something from a third-rate mystery novel. "Why the hell did the coroner here say heart attack?"

" 'Peers the symptoms are the same. Chest pains. Shortness of breath."

"There must be some—" He started to say "explanation," but he and Austin never lied to each other. Not then, not now.

"What about the Crandall woman? Suppose she . . ."

Not a chance, Nick thought, relying on his instincts. Then he remembered Pithany Crandall's strange behavior when she'd met him. Almost had a heart attack herself. But the minute she learned that he was taking over the local bottling facility, she'd insisted—adamantly insisted—he move into the guest house Travis had been renting. "Why would Pithany Crandall murder Travis?"

5

✴

Nick frowned, his eyes intense under drawn brows. "What did you serve Travis the night he died?"

"Just what I told you the day you arrived," Pithany answered, seemingly at ease with the question. "Nothing has changed."

"Go over it for me again. Maybe you left something out."

"Travis had been invited for high tea, not dinner, and he arrived late, which was unusual. He brought me a hostess gift—something he always did. He had wonderful manners, you know. It was a small jar of honey."

Nick wasn't surprised. Travis craved honey. Slathered it on toast every morning. No matter how much Amanda Jane teased him that he would get fat, Travis never gave it up.

"He had a cup of tea and a Bath bun with honey—"

"What kind of tea?" Nick wanted to see if she would give him the same answer she did the first time.

"Orchid tea. He'd tried all my teas but it was his favorite."

Same answer she'd given when Nick had first come to her home and inquired about his friend's death.

"We were waiting for Clara to bring out the trolley with the sandwiches and desserts when Travis had his first pain. He—"

"That's all he ate?" Nick cut her off. He couldn't

stand to relive his friend's final, agonizing moments. Had he known he had been poisoned? Had he known he was going to die?

"Yes, that's all Travis ate," Pithany answered, regarding him with a speculative gaze. "What makes you ask? Is something wrong, Nick?"

"He didn't die of a heart attack." Nick paused a moment, hoping to elicit some telltale response. Nothing. "He was poisoned. Oleander poisoning."

Pithany's body stiffened in shock, her astonishment obviously genuine. "I—I can't believe it. How?"

"I was hoping you could tell me. Did he say where he'd been?"

"No, but I assumed he'd been on his boat. He usually spent Sundays down at the yacht club."

"Did he mention anyone, anything?" Thinking of the final minutes of his friend's life, Nick forced himself not to close his eyes in a vain attempt to block any image her words might bring.

"No," Pithany said quietly. "He kept insisting he'd be all right. I'm certain he didn't know he was dying. Suddenly, he blacked out and his heart stopped beating. Clara and I tried to revive him but . . ."

Where were you when Travis needed you? Nick asked himself, not for the first time.

Pithany twisted her silver ring with the Maltese Cross and it caught the morning light. "Travis was a special person. Did he tell you how we met?

"It was at a reception at the Auberge de Castile, the Prime Minister's office. He took pity on an old lady and asked me to dance. We began talking and I found out he was looking for a new apartment. I suggested he rent the guest house."

Nick wasn't surprised Travis had asked Pithany Crandall to dance. He'd always befriended people. The more someone needed him, the better a friend Travis became. No one knew this better than Nick.

A full half hour early for his lunch meeting, Nick strolled down the gangway of the Royal Manole Yacht Club, looking for slip 666 where Travis's boat was moored. He'd gone directly from speaking with Pithany to the Prefecture of Police, Albert Attard. He'd already received a FAX from the Houston authorities and had reopened the investigation into Travis Prescott's death. From there, Nick had come to the yacht club and asked if anyone remembered seeing Travis the day he died. A waiter thought he might have seen Travis in the Corsair Bar, but whether it was that afternoon or some other, he wasn't sure. The members Nick asked barely knew his friend's name.

Nick wasn't surprised. Unlike his sister, Travis hadn't possessed remarkable good looks. He'd been quiet, unassuming, the kind who made few friends. But when he did, he was the best . . . Nick stopped himself, wondering if the four years Travis had spent here had been as agonizingly lonely as the time Nick had spent in Japan. They should have written, made arrangements to meet, called. Something.

Nick forced himself to admire the string of yachts—nobody called these mothers boats—Med-moored, tied stern first to the dock. Slip 664 housed *Humble Aboat*. Nothing humble about it. Bigger than his mom's house in Muleshoe. The next one was over fifty feet. *Classea* had a score of deckhands polishing the brass. Obviously, there was money in Malta—lots of it.

He didn't have to double check the slip number on the next dock box. The name on the transom in bold navy script stopped him dead in his tracks. *Amanda Jane*.

Perfect name. What else would you call a boat this sleek, this beautiful except to name it after someone equally so? He ran his hand over the smooth finish, remembering the used boat he and Travis had bought to water-ski on Lake Howland. They'd painted *Dip Ship* on its transom themselves. Amanda Jane had screamed, of course, but they teased her, the way they always did, telling her their first choice had been *Wet Dream*. He laughed, oblivious to the staring deckhands, remembering the good times. The love.

Keeping the unhappy memories temporarily at bay, he stepped onto the boat. The *Amanda Jane* wasn't as impressive as her neighbors, but she was an expensive race boat designed with the Italian flair for style. He resisted the impulse to check the instrument panel—no doubt it was loaded with gadgets he and Travis once dreamed of —and went to the navigation station and searched for the Captain's Log. Nothing.

The log would have told who'd been on this boat and when. Nick could have learned the name of the mysterious woman in the photograph. Had the same person removed both the Filofax and the log, making it impossible to track Travis's movements? Nick collapsed into the captain's chair and stared out over the indigo water to the limestone peninsula ringed by a bastion of stonewalls protecting buildings that had been built during the Crusades. But he was too preoccupied to appreciate the beauty of the ancient city, Valletta.

He kept wondering who could have poisoned Travis. The local police hadn't gotten very far with their investigation, but they had contacted a medical expert who'd told them oleander poisoning acted quickly. It stood to reason that Travis had eaten something either at the yacht club or at Falcon's Lair that had killed him.

Nick's gut feeling about Pithany Crandall said it wasn't her, but all signs pointed to—

"Naw," Nick muttered, half under his breath. The old gal was really fond of Travis. There was always the possibility it had been an accident. He might have stopped for a bite on the way to Falcon's Lair and accidently been poisoned. Hell. That didn't seem likely either. Why would he stop to eat when he was already late for high—highfalutin as far as Nick was concerned—tea, which substituted for an evening meal? Besides, Travis was never late. Except on the night he died.

Nick didn't realize how long he'd been sitting there, brooding over his friend's mysterious death until the wake of a passing *dghajsa* rocked his boat. Like all the fishermen's boats, the water taxi was painted vibrant shades of green, yellow, and red with touches of blue. They reminded Nick of the pictures of gondolas he'd seen, but Pithany had told him these wooden boats were Phoenician designs brought to the island by early settlers. On each side of the bow a fierce-looking human eye had been painted—Osiris's eyes to ward off evil spirits. Nick came to his feet with an overwhelming sense of loss. Where had Osiris been when Travis Prescott had needed him?

A glance at his watch told him he was late for his lunch with Curt Bradford. Nick hurried down the gangway to the dock where the tenders from the larger yachts were moored. The tender for *Siren's Song*—the same size as *Dip Ship*—was waiting. The white-uniformed sailor helped him aboard and then cast off.

Nick looked back at the *Amanda Jane,* her bow bobbing in the gentle swells of Marsamxett Harbor, wondering why Curt Bradford had invited him to lunch. The information dossier provided by the company for managers indicated the Bradford family was one of the wealthiest on the island. In addition to a string of hotels, they owned several industrial operations, most notably the bottling facility that was a joint venture with Imperial Cola. It was currently operating under a long-term contract with no problems in sight. It seemed odd that

Curt Bradford would insist on meeting Nick so quickly. He dismissed his suspicions as holdovers from his days in Japan, where every move was calculated to correspond with business interests.

Even though he'd been on the island less than two weeks, Nick had noticed the easygoing manner of the Maltese. They operated on what Texans would have called Mexican Standard Time, meaning if it should have been done yesterday, you'd be lucky to get it *mañana*. He struggled to adjust his mind-set, still attuned to Japan.

Nick whistled under his breath as the tender pulled up to *Siren's Song*. On her deck groupings of chairs and tables surrounded a crystal-blue swimming pool with a mermaid painted on the bottom. Two more uniformed sailors led Nick down the companionway to the dining room overlooking the pool and left him to wait.

A glass-top dining table that could easily seat two dozen people was supported by a gold-leafed mermaid. Two places had been set with bone china featuring a daisy chain of mermaids around the rims. In the center of each plate was SIREN'S SONG in raised gold script. A smoke-glass mirror with the same mermaid etched into the glass formed the far wall.

Nick watched the deckhands cleaning the pool for a good ten minutes, wondering if he was deliberately being kept waiting. *You've been in Japan too long.* He went over to the bar and made himself a Bushwacker in a crystal glass with SIREN'S SONG on it, using all of the Tabasco in the small bottle.

"Sorry I kept you waiting," said the man coming through the door. "I was on a conference call with my people in Paris, Vienna, New York, London, and Hong Kong."

Nick turned to the dark-haired man, who was thirty-five or so, several years younger than Nick, and decided he was in for a lunch of name-dropping. "I made myself at home."

"I'm Curt Bradford." He extended his hand, his dark brown eyes studying Nick intently.

"Nick Jensen," he said, deciding most women would find Curt handsome, but there was something too perfect about his overfinished good looks that made Nick uneasy. He'd never been comfortable around men who dressed like mannequins. Too prissy to help out in a fight. Curt confirmed Nick's suspicions by pouring himself a white wine, then checking his reflection in the mirror.

"Is this your first operations assignment?" Curt asked as they sat down to lunch.

"Yes," Nick answered, instantly alerted by the seemingly innocent question. Curt had to have dealt with enough Imperial-Cola managers to know it was standard practice for the company to have their managers run at least one operation stateside before sending them abroad. So why the dumb question? Or was it a savvy question? Was Bradford wondering why Nick had been sent to Malta without stateside experience?

Curt nodded to the servant to go ahead and pour the wine. "Marsovin Special Reserve, produced in the Bradford vineyards west of here."

Nick sipped the wine. "Excellent."

"Do you sail?" Curt asked. When Nick shook his head, Curt continued, "You'll have to come out with me. I'll teach you. I have a fifty-foot race boat, *Lethal Weapon*. I'll be practicing for the Downwind Regatta that'll be held next month."

"Sure." Nick chafed at Curt's patronizing tone. "That'd be mighty fine."

While servants wheeled in a trolley with a covered silver dish on it, Nick decided Curt Bradford was definitely after something. He didn't need to give sailing lessons to a man who couldn't possibly compete in his league. Yacht racing consumed more money than Nick would ever make in his lifetime. Judging from the swank Royal Manole Yacht Club, whose members included the crowned heads of Europe, Greek tycoons, and German industrialists, Nick thought that Curt Bradford had plenty of companions to sail with him. True sailors, not Texas tinhorns more at home on powerboats.

"A cassoulet of *fenek* and *fagioli*," Curt said as the servants ladled a serving onto Nick's plate. "Our national dish."

"So why call it a cassoulet like it's French?"

Curt looked at him blankly for a moment. "You'll see it on most menus as stew."

He took a bite—great stuff—hoping he hadn't insulted Curt. Nick would have to learn to keep his mouth shut. The company insisted its executives maintain low profiles, blending in with the local culture, participating in the daily life as if they were natives, not Americans. "Stew, casserole, cassoulet. What's in a name?" He took another bite, nodding appreciatively. "Better than a T-bone. So, what's fenek and fag . . . fag—"

"*Fagioli*, a Maltese bean. *Fenek* is rabbit."

Nick stopped chewing. Aw, shit. Not Thumper.

"Next Saturday night we're throwing a party at our home in Mdina to celebrate the *festa* for St. Christopher. I'd like you to come and meet my father."

"Great. I'd like that." Nick ate, carefully selecting the beans and other vegetables, leaving the meat aside.

"I guess you were close friends with Travis Prescott." Curt shook his head. "What a tragedy. So young."

As usual, Nick's instinct had been correct. If Curt knew Travis and Nick had been close, he knew a lot more about Nick than he let on. "Did you know Travis well?"

"Not as well as I would have liked. But I did sponsor

him for membership in the Royal Manole Yacht Club. The waiting list is years long, you know. But I got him admitted in six months."

Nick couldn't imagine why Bradford would do this for a man he hardly knew. "Do you know his girlfriend?"

Curt paused and checked his handsome reflection in the smoke-glass mirror. "No. Why?"

"Just wondering. I heard he had a girlfriend, but I haven't been able to locate her."

"Why do you want to find her?"

"Travis didn't die of a heart attack. He was poisoned." Nick studied Curt. "Oleander poisoning. I think he was murdered. If I found the woman, perhaps she could answer a few questions."

"Murder?" Curt's gaze shifted from Nick's to the mirror then back to Nick again. "I doubt it. It was probably an accident."

"No one eats oleander by accident."

"I suppose you're right, but I can't imagine why anyone would kill him." Curt gestured to the servants and the table was immediately cleared.

And he could care less, Nick decided, watching Curt take a bite of the chocolate ice cream that had been served. Nick stuck his spoon in the artfully molded ice cream, but didn't eat. Something told him Curt Bradford knew more than he was saying.

Curt finished his dessert, and then patted his lips with the linen napkin, leaving a chocolate smudge on the mermaid's tail. "You know, Travis and I had agreed to a personal business deal shortly before he died."

Nick steadied himself, realizing this was the reason he'd been invited to lunch. None of the scenarios he'd imagined had included Travis. "Oh?"

"He'd agreed to sell me his stock in the Blue Grotto Corporation."

Nick's sixth sense went on alert, telling him Bradford was lying. "You have signed documents?"

"No," Curt hedged. "A gentleman's agreement."

Liar. "I hadn't planned on selling."

Bradford shrugged, indicating the sale was of little importance to him. "Over three million Maltese lire— roughly a million U.S. dollars."

Once so much money might have impressed Nick. No longer.

"I'm prepared to up the offer," Curt added smoothly. "Say, ten percent more."

"Let me think about it."

"I'll top any offer you get. Just give me the last look."

Nick had been swimming in corporate waters long enough to recognize a dorsal fin when he saw one, and he could tell the difference between a dolphin and a shark.

Curt stood on the deck and watched the wake left by the boat taking Nick Jensen ashore. The damn Texan was angling for more money. That old bitch, Pithany Crandall, would top Curt's offer and the bidding war would be on. He went into the salon, saying, "I told Big Tony it wouldn't work. Jensen would be a fool not to see what Pithany Crandall would give him."

"Don't worry about it," Rhonda said, tossing her head confidently so that her dark hair shifted across her shoulders. "It was just the opening round." She locked the door.

Curt dropped onto the sofa. An idiot would know the Texan wouldn't accept the offer, but still Curt dreaded facing Big Tony. His father would crucify him with a single look and proceed to harangue him for hours that he was nothing but a no-good playboy not fit to run the Bradford empire.

"What did you think of Nick Jensen?" he asked as

Rhonda sat beside him, sliding her arm around his neck and caressing his earlobe.

"Wraparounds," she whispered in his ear, although they were alone. "Just looking at his long, long legs made me wonder what they'd be like locked around mine."

"You're horny." Years ago, they'd discovered that watching each other while hidden behind one of the two-way mirrors Big Tony used to spy on people was a sure turn-on.

"Definitely," she said, running the tip of her tongue over the coiled ridge of his ear. Quicker than a snake, she grabbed his hand and eased it up under her dress to her thighs.

He deliberately teased her, playing his fingertips across her soft skin. If he moved his hand higher, he knew he would find she wasn't wearing panties—did she even own a pair?—but he didn't, instead skimming her smooth thighs with his fingers. She sighed, throwing her head back, sending long brown curls down her bare back. Curt kissed the nape of her neck, where it met her shoulders, one of her most sensitive spots, sucking slightly, tasting her spicy perfume.

He was uncomfortably hard now, aching to mount her, but she was too demanding a mistress to take for granted. To her, foreplay was an art form, and he was the master. His mouth barely off her tanned skin, he asked again, "What did you think of Jensen?"

She laughed, her special laugh that was really a sustained giggle. "Don't worry. We'll get those shares."

He inched his hand upward, and she sucked in her breath while his fingers moved deftly, expertly stroking her. She exhaled, a prolonged sigh.

"Don't worry," she whispered, gazing lovingly at him from beneath half-lowered lids, "I'll take care of him for you."

* * *

Janna paused at the landing, gathering her thoughts before going downstairs for dinner. In the distance, she heard the Texan's distinctive drawl. The sound of his voice made her listen more closely. His voice was familiar, oddly familiar. She didn't know anyone from Texas.

Then she remembered his body crushing hers, his hand locked around her throat, his brutish face looming above her, concealed by the dark but terrifying nonetheless. She took a deep breath and reminded herself the incident had been a mistake. She'd broken into the house; he'd overreacted. What mattered now was getting those shares.

She proceeded down the stairs, prepared to be sweet to Nick Jensen. With that Italian holding so much stock, Aunt Pithany needed Jensen's shares to consolidate her position. With her hostess smile in place, she walked into the room.

Nick Jensen politely stood up, a full head taller than Janna. "Hullo."

"Hello." She looked up into the most arresting blue eyes she'd ever seen. Deep, intense blue that could easily be mistaken for brown at a distance. Straight black hair, a few weeks overdue for a trim framed a face that could have sold an ocean of men's cologne.

"Hey, I'm mighty sorry about last night. Did I hurt you?"

She shook her head, noting the scratch on the side of his neck. Had she done that? He smiled at her, a ten-gallon grin to match his ten-gallon voice. A single dimple—didn't they come in pairs?—appeared in his cheek. She watched closely. Just one. A Lone Star dimple.

"I'm sorry I scratched you. I was frightened."

She turned away and walked to the bar. How had she ever gotten the impression he was ugly? True, it had been too dark to see him, but something should have tipped her. She returned with her gin and tonic, and sat on the sofa beside Aunt Pith.

Nick studied Janna while Pithany gave them an update on the alarm system to be installed next week that would prevent mistakes like last night's. Short, Nick thought, but cute with that wholesome girl-next-door appeal: Her green eyes dominated her face. She vaguely reminded him of someone he'd met. Of course, Pithany. Janna was a younger version of Pithany Crandall, which meant Janna would age well. Her figure would remain trim and her sandy blond hair would mellow into a becoming silvery gray.

Despite her smile, Janna didn't fool Nick. Not for one damn minute. She didn't like him. Looked at him like she'd been expecting Frankenstein. His knockout smile, which he rarely used because he didn't like to encourage women, hadn't thawed the lady. He tried not to compare her to the only other woman who'd taken an instant dislike to him, Mrs. Mooth, his sixth grade teacher. Letting something that had happened so many years ago color his judgment was childish.

Clara called them to dinner and Janna watched Nick, recalling her immediate attraction to another handsome man—Collis Pembroke. He'd brought her nothing but heartache. At least she didn't have to worry about falling for Nick Jensen. All she wanted from him were those shares.

"Cold ox tongue," Janna told Nick who was staring dubiously at the first course. "Sliced paper thin and topped with green peppercorn sauce. It's an island specialty. Try it. You'll like it."

Nick ate a piece the size of a split pea, then said, "I understand you'll be running Pithany's company. Is your husband going to help you?"

"I don't need his help. I—" Janna stopped, realizing how shrewish she sounded. She had no intention of telling anyone in Malta about her impending divorce. When Audrey was over her husband's death, Janna would tell people. Besides, just saying Collis's name brought a wellspring of hurt and anger she couldn't disguise. "What I mean is that Collis will be busy teaching in London. Aunt Pith needs me here."

Nick rearranged the ox tongue on his plate, thinking Janna's marriage wasn't a happy one.

"Actually, I need both you and Nick," Pithany said. "I've decided to retire immediately. For years now, I've wanted to show my dogs, but I've been too busy. Audrey"—she smiled at Nick—"that's Janna's mother, will be coming with me. She wants to show her Maltie too. I'm leaving in a few days."

"Now? Before the hotel even opens?" Janna couldn't believe it. The Blue Grotto had been years in the planning. Aunt Pith had gambled everything to build this hotel. How could she casually make this announcement without telling Janna beforehand?

"It's almost completed. You"—again Pithany lavished a smile on the Texan—"and Nick can handle it. The key management is already in place. All that's left to be done is supervise the decorating and oversee an advertising campaign. We're very lucky Nick inherited that stock. He's an advertising expert, you know."

Janna didn't know and could care less. Aunt Pith's announcement astounded her. Bringing Nick Jensen on board was utterly ridiculous. Aunt Pith should have offered to buy him out. As Clara served the main entrée, it occurred to Janna that she might be selling Aunt Pith short. This gambit could be some complicated plan to persuade Nick to sell.

Nick feigned intense interest in the veal he'd been served, surprised that Pithany hadn't asked to buy his shares. Since his meeting with Curt Bradford, Nick had checked into the situation and discovered the families were arch rivals. Pithany was up to something, but what exactly remained a mystery to him.

"What's an expert in advertising doing managing a distribution center?" Janna asked.

Nick heard the edge in Janna's voice. Evidently, Pithany hadn't discussed asking Nick to help with Janna. Interesting. "I'm in Malta getting field experience."

"Just what was your job in Japan?"

"Marketing." Nick didn't elaborate, understanding she didn't want his help. Her tone irritated him. Letting her emotions show wouldn't get her far in the business world. A shark like Curt Bradford would swallow her whole. "I guess you've had a lot of business experience."

"Not really," she admitted. "I taught a class in networking for female executives. But my brother and I have been investing for years. Before the war in the Middle East, we made a good deal of money with a company that sold Velcro to the sheiks. They use sheets of it to keep jockeys on their mounts during camel races."

Nick thought she might be putting him on but her earnest expression and her aunt's pleased smile told him she wasn't.

"Right now," Janna continued, "we also own part of a small company that manufactures plastic corks. You know, the Portuguese have a monopoly on the cork market. They've driven the price so high that small vineyards, especially in France, can't afford them. The plastic corks are doing quite well."

Nick kept his smile to himself. Two flakey investments qualified her to run three hotels and open a new one? Maybe the old gal was becoming senile after all.

"Janna wrote a paper on finance that was quite well received," Pithany told him. "She researched it for three years using primary sources. I have a copy. Would you like to read it?"

"Aunt Pith, I'm sure Nick isn't interested in the true cost of the French Revolution."

Got that one right. Nick smiled at them, the good ole boy grin he relied on to get him out of tough spots. He didn't read anything he didn't absolutely have to and certainly not long-winded intellectual bullshit on the French Revolution. The two women weren't playing with full decks. If he didn't like Pithany so much, Nick would have sold out to Curt Bradford. Janna didn't know diddly-squat about business and would probably run the company into the ground.

They were served their coffee and dessert, British style, in the living room rather than at the table. Nick decided to mention the Bradfords to test their reaction.

"Curt Bradford invited me to a party his family is giving this weekend."

"Don't miss it," Pithany said enthusiastically. "It's one of the best *festa* parties of the year. They hold it at their palace in Mdina." She warmed up his coffee, saying, "Janna's going, but I won't be in town."

Nick glanced at Janna. If she had any negative feelings about the Bradfords, they didn't show.

"You two should go together," Pithany added. "Mdina will be jammed—"

"Aunt Pith, I'm sure Nick has a date he'll be bringing." Janna turned to Nick. "Mdina is an old city dating back to Roman times, so the streets are narrow and parking is impossible. I—"

"I'm not taking anyone," Nick said. "Let's ride together. You can show me the way. I'm lost around here without a map. For some reason, I keep thinking places are in the opposite direction of where they actually are."

"Really?" Pithany asked. "Like what?"

Nick shrugged, sorry he'd mentioned this. "I had a meeting in Mosta. I started driving north from my office in Valletta."

"It's south," Janna said. "Didn't you see the signs?"

"Yeah, and I turned around." He didn't mention how confusing he found reading the vowel-short Maltese words. Luckily, the island was only four miles long. How lost could he get?

"Nick," Pithany said. "Where do you think Mdina is?"

"South near the airport."

Pithany smiled, an odd, satisfied smile.

"No," Janna said, "It's way north of there."

"You two had better ride to the *festa* party together," Pithany said. "Finish your coffee. I'm exhausted. Could you check on Millie and the pups for me?"

"Sure thing. I'll close the kitchen door this time," Nick said, then added, "Thanks for dinner."

Pithany smiled at him, not her polite smile, but the intimate smile she usually reserved for her immediate family. Janna couldn't understand it. Aunt Pith wasn't impressed by remarkable looks. She'd never warmed to Collis.

Janna finished her coffee, feeling awkward being alone with Nick. He made Collis appear ordinary looking. But, she reminded herself, she hadn't fallen for Collis Pembroke's handsome face. He was a genius, gifted with an intelligence rarely seen. Nick Jensen possessed average intelligence, nothing more.

She looked up and found him studying her with those disturbing blue eyes. He smiled, the slow smile again, and his lone dimple appeared. He was awfully sure of himself, she decided, and the effect he had on women. She forced a smile, letting him think he'd charmed her, determined to get those shares. She was tempted to ask him right now, but decided against it. Aunt Pith must have something up her sleeve to have asked a total stranger to help Janna run the company.

"I'll check on Millie," Janna said, putting her cup down. "You don't have to come."

Nick jumped up. "No bother."

He followed her through the kitchen, carefully closing the door behind them, into the butler's pantry where Millie and the pups were. Millie had been separated from her three pups by a mesh fence. They could see their mother and have the comfort of her presence without being able to nurse. They'd been weaned, but would revert if given the opportunity. Millie yipped with delight when she spotted them, jumping around like a kangaroo. Janna lifted her out of the pen.

But it wasn't Janna that Millie wanted. Instead of licking Janna's face as she usually did, Millie pawed the air, wiggling in Janna's arms, trying to get to Nick.

"Give her to me, Shorty." Nick took Millie from her.

"Shorty?"

He grinned at her, flashing his silly dimple. "From up here"—he examined the top of her head—"I have a great view of your part . . . Short-stuff."

Janna had never minded not being a great beauty like Audrey, but she despised being short. What she wouldn't give for Shadoe's long, long legs. But she refused to let Nick know about her adolescent insecurities. She reached down to the three mewling pups and picked up her puppy.

"Taxila," she told Nick, who was getting a face wash from Millie.

"Yo Taxi," he said, and her puppy lapped the air in the small space separating her from Nick. "Great name."

"Taxila," she said, ignoring his teasing, "is an ancient Buddhist ruin in Pakistan." Obviously, the Texan had no appreciation for archeology.

He nuzzled her puppy. "You don't look ruined to me."

"Taxila is just pet quality. That means he can't be shown because he doesn't meet kennel club standards."

Nick raised Taxila's hind leg and peeped at his privates. "Looks mighty fine to me."

Janna stifled a cutting retort at the Texan's crude sense of humor, remembering Aunt Pith needed his shares. She managed a smile.

Nick lay on his back, staring at the ceiling in the guest house, thinking about Janna. Shorty. Fit her to a T. And she didn't like it, not one bit. Could have called her Sourpuss. The woman had absolutely no sense of humor.

Janna Atherton-Pembroke was probably an intellectual snob. Three years researching a paper on the cost of the French Revolution? Jeezus! And she'd named that cute puppy after a Buddhist ruin in Pakistan of all places? What kind of a mind came up with something like that? He had to admit he was intrigued. He couldn't decide what it was about Janna that interested him. Maybe it was because she didn't like him, pretending she did to get his shares.

The situation with the stock provided a challenge. For the first time in five years, he was enjoying himself. Japan had been a grind. The closed society, open to foreigners only on a business level, fostered loneliness, he realized. Malta was different. Here, Nick felt comfortable with the language, the people. More than comfortable. Actually, he felt as at home here as he did in Texas.

A knock on the guest house door brought Nick to his feet. He hurried into the sitting room. He swung the door open and found Pithany Crandall.

"I brought you Janna's paper." She handed him a bound volume that if shredded would be enough for several ticker-tape parades.

"Thanks," Nick muttered.

Pithany glanced over her shoulder to the lighted window on the second floor. Janna's room, Nick realized.

Had to be. The best suite in the house, overlooking the pool.

"May I come in?"

Nick could hardly say no. She owned the place. He stood aside and she walked in quickly. She seated herself in one of the chairs opposite the wicker sofa. Nick plopped down, facing her.

"About the shares Travis Prescott left you."

Nick made a mental wager that she'd top Curt Bradford's offer by ten percent.

"I'm willing to pay you to hold on to your shares until your company transfers you to the Atlanta office."

Atlanta? No one was supposed to know about his arrangement with Nolan. Jeeezus. The Japanese employed a slew of sleuths; Bradford must have used a private dick. Now Pithany Crandall. He was in the wrong business. Should have been a private eye. He'd have made a fortune. "Why?"

"I sold those shares to Travis Prescott because he planned on making Malta his home. Did you know that?" He must have looked shocked because she continued, "You hadn't spoken with him very often lately, had you?"

Beyond words, Nick shook his head, her condemning statement all too true. He wondered if Pithany knew what had caused their separation. "We weren't as close as we once had been."

"Travis lived right here for over four years. We had dinner together two—sometimes three—times a week."

It suddenly struck Nick that Pithany Crandall had been lonely. Her business kept her busy all day, but the nights at the big house must have been lonesome.

"I liked Travis very much. He'd made a lot of money in the stock market, so when he offered to buy shares in my company, I let him. I never imagined he'd die." Her eyes clouded with genuine sadness. "I miss him."

Most people would have found the age difference between Pithany and Travis a barrier, but Nick understood. There was something about Pithany Crandall that had drawn him to her immediately. Knowing she'd befriended Travis made him like her all the more.

"I need your help with the Blue Grotto. It's been my pet project."

"Then why retire? Wait until it's built."

"Janna would turn to me every time there was a problem. She has to learn to stand on her own." She paused and smiled at Nick. "As part owner, you could help her and she'd have to listen."

"If she didn't, I could threaten to sell to the Bradfords, right?"

"Precisely. Will you help me?" When Nick nodded, she added, "I don't want you to mention a word of this to Janna."

6

✳

The House of Lords was proof positive there was life after death. Liberal leader, Jeremy Thorpe had pointed this out some twenty years earlier; Warren Atherton couldn't have agreed more. He'd been formally presented the previous week, but this was the first session he'd attended. He eyed the rows of white-haired men, many with hearing aids, others nodding off although the peers had not yet been called to order. What are you doing here, he asked himself, examining the ornate room dominated by the raised dais and empty throne used only used by the Queen on ceremonial occasions.

In the weeks since his father's death, Warren hadn't been able to reconcile himself to the circumstances surrounding the heart attack. The scene with Gian Paolo replayed over and over in his mind even more frequently now that he'd discovered their relationship had been a long-term affair. The father he'd looked up to his entire life—and foolishly tried to emulate—had been a coldhearted stranger who'd cut Janna out of his will, leaving her legacy to his homosexual lover.

Taking his father's seat in the House of Lords would be a new beginning. It had been cold in his father's shadow. Now he was the Earl of Lyforth.

Only a quarter of the seats in the chamber were filled —a typical day. Warren walked forward with a purposeful stride, smiling at the white-wigged Lord Chancellor, who presided over the area reserved for the clergy. Several Anglican bishops were present as well as the chief rabbi, Immanuel Jakobovits. Warren didn't check for any Catholics; it had been almost five hundred years since a Catholic leader had ventured into the chamber. And he'd lost his head.

On one side of the gold-canopied room were benches for Conservative Party members while the other side was reserved for the Labor Party. Cabinet officers, front benchers, traditionally filled the front rows while back-benchers took seats behind them. Warren was tempted to establish himself as an independent peer, cross-bencher, by sitting on the Labor side. Everyone expected the Earl of Lyforth to become a ranking Tory. He'd spent his entire life in conservative circles. He belonged with the Tories; he'd never agreed with Labor policies. Warren accepted the welcoming smiles of his father's friends, but slipped into a back bench beside Baron Colwyn. The former leader of a rock band and one of the youngest men present had been granted a life peerage. His title, unlike Warren's, wouldn't pass to his son. Still, Warren felt more comfortable with Colwyn, who had a reputation for independent thinking.

The debate began and Warren's thoughts wandered. He missed Janna and wondered if she were any happier. He owed it to his sister to find Gian Paolo and buy back the stock, but so far the private investigator hadn't found a trace of him.

The debate concerned whether the government should joint-venture a factory with the Japanese in the economically distressed area of Manchester. Warren had been following the controversy in the papers. He'd spoken to friends in the business community and had formed an opinion on the subject. As he listened, it occurred to him that the peers were missing the point.

Warren told himself to keep his thoughts to himself. After all, this was his first day.

But he astonished himself by asking for the floor. Ignoring the peers and the television camera routinely recording the proceedings, Warren said, "Why should Her Majesty's government finance Japan's economic imperialism? Do they want to help the unemployed in the Midlands? Of course not. They want bases in every European country in order to win the global manufacturing war. They're afraid when England unites with the European Community that the group will limit imports from Japan. But"—he paused for dramatic impact—"if they've already established manufacturing facilities here, how can they be shut out? They can't. Then the Sumo financiers will be free to take English industries to the mat—just as they targeted America's television and copier industries—until they eliminate the competition."

The peers were gaping, several turning up their hearing aids, and the sprinkling of onlookers in the gallery had moved into the front row.

"Ladies and gentlemen," Warren continued, smiling at Baroness Elliot and author, P. D. James, the only women present on the house floor, "I believe we have a moral obligation to vote no on this issue. To do otherwise would sacrifice our industry for a short-term gain."

It wouldn't be an intellectually popular speech, Warren realized. Some would even accuse him of Japan-bashing, but he had spoken his mind. The great thing about the House of Lords was that you could say what you wished without concern for the political consequences. No one could take Warren's title from him.

When the vote was taken, the house refused to back the government's plan by a wide margin. Warren knew it was a token objection. The House of Commons could override their decision. Since unemployment was a key issue, it most likely would.

Warren left the chamber and found his Jaguar in the members' car park. The red monitor light on the telephone was blinking. His service instructed him to call Sherlocks Plc. He did and was put through to the investigator he'd hired to locate Gian Paolo.

"He's living in Sheriff's Lench, working as a *sous*-chef at the Sheriff's Lench Manor."

"Great," Warren said, "I'll handle it from here."

All the questions he'd already mulled over concerning his father and his secret life returned. Along with his anger. Killing the little Italian was his first thought, but that wouldn't do Janna any good. Now that Pithany had put her in charge of the hotels, Warren was more committed than ever to helping. He didn't want Paolo to sell his shares to someone else. If the Bradfords knew he had the stock no telling, absolutely no telling, what might happen.

Warren admitted he needed help. This had to be handled delicately by someone who could be trusted with the family secret. His solicitor, Peyton Gifford, was his first thought, but he discarded the idea. Too pompous. Gian Paolo was hardly more than a kid; the Italian needed someone he could relate to like—Warren thought a moment—like Shadoe Hunnicutt.

Annabelle was sucking Collis's big toe, sending shivery tremors of anticipation up his bare leg to his groin. She gazed up at him, her brown eyes accented by sweeping lashes, her blond hair tumbling free across her breasts, barely hiding her nipples. Collis motioned for her to come to him. She did—an inch at a time—running the liquid tip of her tongue up his calf where she paused to rub her breasts against his shin. With moist kisses, she edged up his thigh.

He was ready, more than ready, for her. "Hurry up, angel."

That was all the encouragement Annabelle needed. Her avaricious mouth circled his distended shaft, sucking with surprising strength. He groaned, telling himself to take deep breaths—not to lose it just yet. Mercifully, she pulled back in the nick of time and hovered over him, smiling. She wasn't really beautiful. In a few years her tits would tickle her waistline and her milkmaid prettiness would fade into matronly plumpness. But he didn't care. When he was with her, he lived for the moment. For what she could do to him.

She moved aside and ran her fingertips across his chest, until his breathing slowed a bit. Then she leapt on him, gloving him in wet heat. Sitting upright, she rode him, her breasts swaying, her hips moving rhythmically with each thrust almost as if she were posting on a Thoroughbred.

I am a thoroughbred, Collis thought, cursing the Athertons. He gritted his teeth, trying valiantly not to come too soon, not to disappoint Annabelle. He concentrated on his ancestors, condemning them for not having had the foresight to climb in the sack with a crowned head as the first Earl of Lyforth and countless other nobles had. After all, at least four of the noble dukes alive today were descendants of Charles II's bastards. Collis could easily have been one of them instead of an impoverished Pembroke.

He had no intention of dying on the dole. Positive he could get Janna back—soon, he recalled his visit to Lyforth Hall earlier that afternoon. The present and Annabelle were momentarily eclipsed.

Collis had appeared uninvited to have tea with Audrey. This would have been an unforgivable *faux pas* except, of course, for a member of the family. Warren had cornered Collis after the funeral and had warned him that Audrey's health was too fragile for her to know about the divorce. That dovetailed perfectly with Collis's scheme. Since Audrey had always seconded Reginald's opinion on any subject, Collis decided he'd use Audrey to get Janna back.

"Do you think Janna should be bothered running a hotel?" Collis asked as they had tea in the sun room. "It's not a suitable occupation."

"No?" Audrey said, her eyes on a rat-sized dog with a frieze of white fur. The little beast had dragged in the priceless antique prayer rug Reginald had kept in front of the fireplace in his private study and was chewing on the silk fringe.

Collis leaned across the Georgian tea service separating him from Audrey and touched her arm to get her attention. "It's time Janna had a baby. Don't you agree?"

"A baby? I'd love to be a grandmother."

Collis smiled into his teacup. A baby? He despised ankle biters with their snotty noses and wet nappies. Every time Janna had mentioned having a baby, he'd refused. But now he was willing to do anything. He took Audrey's hand and said, "I know I can trust you not to mention this to anyone. Janna and I have had a bit of a tiff. Nothing serious, mind you. She seems to think having a career is more important than motherhood. You know better, don't you? Reginald would never have wanted his daughter working like a commoner."

Audrey regarded him with that vacant look he often thought she used to hide her true feelings. "Reginald?"

"Believe me, Reginald and I were close. I wrote all his speeches, you know. He never wanted his children involved in the trades." He leaned closer, his tone intimate. "Why don't you discuss it with Janna and convince her to come home and have a baby?"

"Oh, my," she gasped. A wet spot had appeared on the prayer rug. She picked up the tiny dog. "No, no, no!"

She kissed him on the nose and cooed. "No can do, Rommie."

"Will you talk to Janna for me, Audrey?" He used the smooth voice guaranteed to hypnotize audiences.

"Yes. I'll be in Malta on Saturday." She stood, clutching the wiggling dog. "I've got to run along now. Ellis will be by any minute with my medication."

"Have mercy! Have meeerr—cy!" Annabelle moaned in Collis's ear jerking him back to the present.

It took Collis a full second to realize he wasn't at Lyforth Hall but in bed with Annabelle. And still as erect as Cleopatra's Needle. That Egyptian obelisk, nothing more than a rough-hewn pillar of stone on the Victoria Embankment, had always seemed phallic to him. He was still as rock-hard as that old relic, giving Annabelle what she needed.

The buxom blonde dangled her tits in his face. "Suck me."

Collis obliged her, but wondered how much longer he could delay his climax. Concentrate, he commanded his aching arms, his cramped legs. He concentrated, loving Annabelle, loving what she did to him. He focused on what he'd learned after Audrey had left him at Lyforth Hall.

Satisfied that he'd been successful with Audrey, Collis had wandered into Lyforth Hall's east wing where he and Janna had a suite of rooms. Around a corner, he met Reginald's man. The valet seemed lost in the manor where he'd spent the last thirty odd years.

Collis paused, thinking one day soon he would be needing a good man. "I'm sorry for your loss."

The old man nodded, his receding hairline emphasizing wise but sad eyes. "So young."

"Were you with him . . . at the end?"

"No. He was alone with his son."

Strange. Reginald and Warren hadn't spoken in

months, since Collis had told him that his son and
daughter had invested in plastic corks—of all things. On
the afternoon that Reginald had died, Collis had discussed an upcoming speech with the earl. He had mentioned going to dinner with a friend—not driving to
Lyforth Hall.

"I didn't know his lordship was here until Dr. Osgood
arrived." He shrugged his stooped shoulders, shaking his
head. "I didn't know Lord Warren had come home either. Someone called for him several hours earlier, but
he wasn't here, so I told him to call Guildhall. I was
certain he would be there."

Strange, Collis thought. The unexpected reconciliation between father and son. Very strange.

"You're killing me! Absolutely killing me!" Annabelle
screamed, bringing him back to the present with a jolt.

The moment he realized where he was, he climaxed in
a flash that sapped his muscles of their strength. How on
earth had he held out so long? Annabelle flopped forward across his chest, her nose against his.

"You were wonderful," she moaned, eyes full of ado-
ration. "Didn't I tell you it would be more fun if I tied
you up?"

"If we knew the hour Paolo was born, not just the
date, wouldn't we get a more accurate horoscope reading?" Warren asked, indulging Shadoe's penchant for astrology. He wasn't certain why she relied on an assort-
ment of metaphysical crutches from astrology to Tarot
cards to the more offbeat rune stones. But she relied on
them, and often her predictions were startlingly accurate.

"Yes." She leaned toward the driver's seat, making it
hard for him to keep his mind on the road. "But it
wouldn't change the results."

"I hope you're wrong." So far, Shadoe had read the

Tarot cards, checked Gian's astrological profile, and cast
rune sticks. She claimed all the signs were negative. Still,
Warren was counting on greed to persuade the Italian.

"You have no now idea how much I want to be wrong.
I'd hate for Janna to be hurt." Her brown eyes, varie-
gated with amber like fine tortoiseshell, were more serious than he'd ever seen them. "I don't have any close
friends. I never have had. When I was a young girl and
first came to Huntington everyone snubbed me. The first
night no one would eat with me. I sat alone while several
of the girls talked in deliberately loud voices . . . about
my mother. Janna left her friends, joined me, and chatted nonstop so I wouldn't hear the other girls."

Warren knew Janna had defied Reginald Atherton
when he told her not to see Shadoe. She'd refused and
had asked why he thought Shadoe wasn't "their kind"
since he hadn't even met her. His father had replied the
nobility used names with classical or biblical origins: Diana, Elizabeth, Sarah, Mary, Caroline. Janna had been
named after Janus, a Roman god. Anyone with a crazy
name like Shadoe had *déclassé* parents—not our kind.

Warren cursed himself for not having had Janna's integrity. He should have told his father to go to hell. And
kept on dating Shadoe. God only knew Warren hadn't
come close to loving anyone else in the last fifteen years.

"Janna's the best kind of friend. She's never criticized
my marriages. She's never pried about Chloe's father.
She loves me, not because of who I am, but in spite of
it."

Shadoe turned away, facing out the window. After a
long silence, she said, "Gloaming, that's what the Irish
call this time of day. A cross between gloom and glow. I
wonder if Janna misses it. We used to go for a walk
about on Huntington's trails—roaming in the gloaming
—each day after the sun set."

Until her comment, Warren had hardly noticed the

sun had slipped below the horizon. The mauve-hued twilight peculiar to England at this time of year would linger, suspended between the light of day and the dark of night, for hours. Because Malta was so much further south, day and night were sharply defined. Janna would enjoy brilliant sunsets but miss the gloaming.

Warren recognized the echo of loneliness in Shadoe's voice. He wanted to pull off the road and take her in his arms to comfort her, but decided that was too big a step. Over the years, they'd eased into a comfortable friendship—nothing more.

In silence they drove through the gently undulating hills north of Stratford. Nestled amid fields of wheat and hillside pastures, the five hamlets known as the Lenches retained the picturesqueness of the better known Cotswolds villages with their half-timbered cottages and thatched roofs. The Lenches hadn't encouraged the tourism that congested the Cotswolds. Warren decided the residents, who valued their peace and pastoral lifestyle, had been wise not to offer lodging in the area. Tourists wishing to visit had to stay in Stratford or Evesham, limiting their numbers. Until now. Apparently Gian Paolo was working in a recently opened inn.

Thinking of the Italian, Warren's temper flared. He reminded himself to remain calm. Shadoe, who knew the whole story, had advised him to tell Paolo the truth. The shares were rightfully Janna's, and Warren was prepared to compensate him handsomely for them.

The distances between the Lenches were short, so Warren slowed, observing the PLEASE WATCH OUT FOR OUR CATS sign posted alongside a hedgerow. The serpentine lane wound through Church Lench and Atch Lench with their Norman churches and adjoining cemeteries filled with Celtic crosses. He braked, coming into Sheriff's Lench. "Keep your eye out for Sheriff's Lench Manor."

"That's it." Shadoe pointed to a redbrick manor

house that appeared to have been recently refurbished. On the walk, a stone horse's head stood guard atop a brick pedestal. SHERIFF'S LENCH MANOR was written in Gothic letters on a sign attached to the post.

Warren parked his Jaguar in the nearly full lot adjacent to the manor. "It seems as if tourists have found the Lenches."

Shadoe wasn't listening. Her eyes squeezed shut, her hands clutching the rune stone she always wore, she said a magic rune, then looked at Warren, her expression concerned. "For luck. For Janna."

His anxiety heightening with every footstep, Warren guided Shadoe into the inn. Although it had been remodeled, the manor house retained a musty odor of old stone and time-worn tapestries. They walked into the oak-paneled public room where a dozen people were gathered at tables sipping evening drinks or playing darts.

"It's 'im! It's 'im!" screeched the barmaid, pointing in their direction. "It's 'im wots on the telly."

Warren looked over his shoulder to see who'd come in behind them. No one.

An overweight man with a bald pate sprouting wisps of black hair dashed up to them. "My Lord," he said as if experiencing the second coming. "You do me the honor of visiting my humble—"

"Yer Grace," interrupted the barmaid, who'd rushed up. She dipped one knee, obviously not knowing he wasn't a duke and that his title didn't merit a curtsey.

The proprietor elbowed the girl aside. "We watched you on the evening news. We agree England doesn't need Japanese money."

"Hear, hear," said several of the patrons who'd gathered around them.

Shadoe looked up at him, her brown eyes puzzled. He hadn't mentioned the speech because he'd forgotten it.

His mind had been focused on explaining the situation with the Italian to her.

"Thank you," he responded, dismayed that his speech had been replayed on the news. The activities in the House of Lords were routinely televised during the session, but were rarely replayed during prime time. "I merely stated my opinion. Many will disagree, but that's the way I feel."

"Keep it up."

"We need more like you."

"Give 'em hell," said one elderly lady.

After a round of handshakes, slaps on the backs, and offers to buy him a drink, Warren led the proprietor to a quiet corner.

"We'd like to speak with Gian Paolo," Shadoe said.

He eyed them with curiosity saying, "Right this way. He's in the kitchen helping the chef."

They walked through the buttery, the fragrant scent of jugged hare mingling with black pudding filling the passageway. Warren's stomach rumbled a counterpoint to the rapid-fire thudding of his pulse. They entered the kitchen, its walls hung with polished copper pots and pans.

"Gian," called the proprietor. "You have visitors."

The dark-haired man looked up from the cauldron he was tending, his eyes wide. He looked into the pot as if he hoped by ignoring them, they would disappear.

"Gian," said the proprietor, "don't you know who this is?"

A prolonged moment of silence, then the glum reply, "Yes."

"Is there someplace where we could speak in private?" Warren asked.

The owner of Sheriff's Lench Manor was delighted to be of service and showed them down a long stone corridor. Judging from the black soot on the walls, it had once been lit by rush lights. Warren took Shadoe's arm while the owner prattled on about his recently opened inn. Gian Paolo followed in silence like a hound brought to heel with a choke chain.

The owner left them in his private parlor. Shadoe sat on the sofa and patted the space next to her for Gian to sit. Warren took the chair opposite them, somehow managing to smile at Gian.

"What do you want?" Gian asked. Fear accented every syllable, overwhelming the trace of an Italian accent.

Caught off guard, Warren scrambled for an answer that would allow him to ease into a discussion of the stocks. He'd incorrectly assumed Paolo might be planning to do his family harm. What was *he* afraid of? Paolo had nothing to lose—the Athertons everything.

Shadoe touched Gian's arm, and he turned to her, the fear in his eyes dimming slightly. "Why are you afraid?" she asked.

Gian shrugged, watching Warren out of the corner of his eye.

"It must have been difficult since the earl passed on." Shadoe said, her voice filled with genuine compassion.

"Yes. We saw each other almost every day for the last twelve years—since I was seventeen."

Warren almost gagged, imagining his father picking up Gian when he'd been in his late teens. Warren was no stranger to homosexuality. From his days at Eton when many younger boys fagged for senior students, he'd accepted it as a part of life. His close friend, Dexter Thorpe-White, preferred men and it never interfered with their friendship. But his father? God, no. What would his mother do if she found out?

"I can't believe he died so suddenly." Tears crept into Gian's eyes. "I wasn't prepared to live the rest of my life without him."

"Is that why you came here, to make a new life?" Shadoe asked.

"I was hiding from him," Gian said, his eyes on Warren. "I knew, no matter what I said, you'd think I'd tell someone about Reggie. But I never would. I loved him too much. I knew he'd never want people to know our secret." He slumped back, his expression one of defeat. "I guess you're going to have me deported."

Warren almost broke into a smile; Gian was here illegally. Joy died as quickly as it had surfaced. Deporting the Italian wouldn't keep him from inheriting. It would only alienate him and might make it impossible to purchase the shares.

"We wouldn't do that," Shadoe assured him. "Warren's here with wonderful news."

"I gather my father was quite fond of you. You'd been"—Warren paused, seeking a polite term—"friends for a number of years."

"We loved each other."

Gian's simple statement uttered with such honesty threatened to snap Warren's composure. He wondered if his father could possibly have loved, really loved, this man. Or had it merely been a form of lust Warren didn't understand? He admitted he hadn't a clue. Warren hadn't known his father; he'd accepted the illusion Reginald Atherton had carefully created. His father had cared enough about this Italian to leave him what rightfully belonged to the daughter who'd worshiped him her entire life.

What about me? Warren asked himself. He'd allowed his father to bully him. Only these past few years had Warren rebelled. His father had been adamant about no Atherton dirtying his hands making money. But Warren had become interested in several businesses and had invested his money. He'd hidden his activities until his father had somehow discovered what Warren and Janna had been doing. His confrontation with his father—their last conversation—had been bitter. His father's untimely death had riddled Warren with guilt. He shouldn't have gone to his grave not speaking to his only child. Favoring his lover.

"My father wanted to be certain you'd be comfortable should anything happen to him." Warren took his cue from Shadoe, disguising his deep-seated resentment. "He left you a sizable bequest."

Blinking back tears, Gian said, "He'd promised to give me money to open my own restaurant."

Warren immediately saw the approach he should take. "He left you shares in a corporation. If you sold them, you'd be a wealthy man—about half a million pounds."

"A million pounds."

Warren's temper ignited, but he kept his face a mask of congeniality. "That's way above market value for the number of shares—"

"No. It's not. That's how much Anthony Bradford paid me—"

Warren vaulted to his feet. "You sold those shares already?"

For the first time, Gian smiled at Warren not Shadoe. "Yes. I signed the final papers this morning."

The gloaming had deepened into a plum-colored hue, brightening Sheriff's Lench Manor with a candle's glow of light while high above them a lover's moon nudged aside a cloud. Shadoe and Warren hurried down the flagstone footpath toward his Jaguar.

"It's not your fault," Shadoe tried to reassure him.

"I'm not certain Janna or Aunt Pith will agree. I should have found Paolo first. What I want to know is how Bradford even found out Paolo inherited the shares."

"That man is obsessed with getting Aunt Pith's hotels.

I guess he had a detective checking on the stock. Bradford's like a vulture, circling, ready to pounce. He knows Aunt Pith had to sell stock to raise money to build the Blue Grotto. He'd like nothing more than to see it fail. Then Bradford would have control of all the hotels on Malta."

Warren opened the car door for Shadoe. He glimpsed her shapely legs as she climbed in. He struggled to keep his mind on the Italian. He got in the car and inserted his key in the ignition, but didn't start the motor. Unable to dispel the powerful surge of emotion gripping him, he turned to Shadoe. "Thanks for coming with me. I don't know what I would have done without you."

"I knew he wouldn't sell. The cards—"

"What do the Tarot cards say about us?" The words were out of Warren's mouth before he could stop them. "Us?"

Fifteen years vanished in a second, leaving him a twenty-year-old boy again, breathless with anticipation. He touched her shoulder where her russet hair fell in a floss of curls and slipped his hand around her neck. Her eyes, luminous in the gloaming, never left his. Parting her lips, she lifted her chin to meet his kiss. He traced the fullness of her lips with the tip of his tongue, wondering how he'd resisted her all these years. The brush of her tongue against his caused a jolt of desire more intense than any he'd ever experienced. Both arms around her, his hands tangled in her long hair, Warren released his pent-up desire in a series of intimate kisses.

Shadoe pulled back. "No. Warren. I don't have anything to do with men anymore. I'm celibate."

Both hands on the steering wheel now, Warren frowned, the shock of her statement hitting him full force. Shadoe Hunnicutt—celibate? Impossible. But he'd known her too long to think she'd lie.

"I'm serious, Warren. I haven't made love to a man since I divorced—"

What about the way you just kissed me? he wanted to ask, but didn't. "What about your baby?" Her baby had arrived long after she'd been divorced. She couldn't have been celibate then.

"My relationships with men never worked out," Shadoe said, obviously sidestepping his question. "I want what I've never had—a family. I love Chloe. She's all I need. I'm all she'll need."

Warren knew neither of Shadoe's parents had wanted her around. He gave his own mother credit. A bit fey at times, she'd tried hard to be a good mother. He'd also had Janna and Aunt Pith. They unquestioningly loved him. What would it have been like to have grown up alone? Unloved.

"Surely, Chloe's father cares—"

"No," Shadoe replied, a note of finality in her voice. "My mother left me with my father, and he never cared a whit about me."

"That doesn't mean all men . . . Chloe needs a father."

"I'm going to have to be both parents." Her unyielding tone took his spirits even lower.

For a long moment silence filled the car as the light of the moon overtook the gloaming. Shadoe touched his hand, saying, "Chloe will never know her father."

Warren opened his mouth to protest, believing Shadoe wasn't being fair to cut the child off from the father. Men cared—as deeply as women.

"I used a sperm bank."

For a minute he thought he'd misunderstood her, but she added, "Artificial insemination."

"Why?" he asked. She was easily the most beautiful, desirable woman in London—the last woman to need a sperm bank.

"I always wanted a family, but I couldn't find the right man."

When Warren looked back on the wasted years, the time he should have been with Shadoe, an unbearable depression settled over him. "Shadoe, I'm sorry I let my father come between us. I—"

"It's all right," she said with the understanding tone he always associated with her. "It wasn't in the cards."

"You're wrong. I'm the man for you—"

"No," she said emphatically. "It wasn't meant to be. I have a baby now. I have to support her, build for the future. I intend to remain celibate."

Warren sensed that now wasn't the time to change her mind. Her course was set—no man included.

"If there's ever anything I can do for you . . . or Chloe, please let me know."

"We're fine," she said, but he detected the slightest hesitation.

"We're friends. You know that. I'm not just any man. I'm Janna's brother. There must be something I can do to help you."

"Well, I have been thinking about buying a place in the country, so I can take Chloe out of the city on weekends. But I have to save money to send her to school. She's not going to Huntington. I was miserable there. I'm going to send her to the European School in Culham."

"Really?" Her idea surprised Warren. The schools, several in Belgium with locations in Italy, Germany, Holland, as well as England, specialized in educating students as Europeans not as students from a specific country. Early on, Warren recalled, they were taught a second language and then a third. Maybe a fourth. He wasn't certain. The classes were mixed, reflecting the twelve nations of the European Community. With the uniting of the community, Europe had undergone an enormous change. These students would be equipped to face the future in a way even the students of Britain's most elite schools wouldn't be.

"I'll give you whatever money—"

"I won't let you *give* me anything. I'm expanding my lingerie shop into locations in Hampstead Heath, St. John's Wood, and Regent Park. They won't be as expensive as the Freudian Slip, so I'm calling them Pantasy. I'm having trouble at Barclay's. They don't want to loan me money even though my credit is good because they think lingerie shops are risky businesses. I need someone to help me convince—"

"I'll take care of it," he promised.

He turned on the engine and the Jag purred to life. The wheels churning in the loose gravel, Warren drove toward the road. What a fool he'd been. Never again. He'd change Shadoe's mind. She still loved him; she just wouldn't admit it. Yet.

part two

✳

DEAD RINGER

7

✳

Janna held the Mizrahi cocktail dress up to herself
and examined her reflection in the mirror, unable to decide if the soft coral made her look too washed out. She
tossed it onto the bed, then picked up the black Lacroix.
Too simple? Usually, she had no difficulty deciding what
to wear, But the *festa* tonight at the Bradfords' was special.

She wanted to impress the Bradfords and let them
know she was here to stay. For years, she'd heard about
them. Once someone had pointed their yacht out to her
as it sailed past Cap Ferrat. But she'd never met Anthony Bradford or his son, Curt. Their high-rise hotels
were famous, of course, not only for their size but for
the scores of tourists they brought to an island whose
main industry was tourism. In contrast, Aunt Pith's hotels were small, fashioned in the European tradition of
elite hotels that catered to visitors who signed the register giving their home addresses as manor houses or
schlosses. Janna wondered how the Bradfords would re-
act when they learned she would be taking over for Aunt
Pith. She welcomed the challenge, certain from what her
aunt had told her, the Bradfords would try to buy her
out. Or force her out.

Unable to decide what to wear, she tossed the dress
aside and walked through the French doors onto the
balcony. She took a deep breath, enjoying the promise of

summer in spring's fragrant flowers and the warmth of the air. Behind her the late afternoon sun was sinking ever lower, deepening the shadows around Falcon's Lair, claiming more and more of the pool area in its dusky veil. In the distance she saw the deep blue water of St. Julian's Bay with dozens of vibrantly painted *luzzijiet* bobbing in the surf as the fishermen unloaded their catches. Even at this distance, Janna could see the white Osiris eyes flashing from the bows.

Below in the garden, Aunt Pith sat on the swing facing the water, seemingly unconcerned that her plane was leaving in two hours. Not for the first time, Janna noticed the bent-willow swing built for two was set at an odd angle. As much as she loved Aunt Pith, Janna admitted she was strange at times. No one could talk her into moving the swing a quarter turn to the south so that it faced the picturesque bay rather than the open sea.

Janna had been stunned to learn Aunt Pith had never planned to ask Nick Jensen for his shares. Her total lack of concern after devoting her lifetime to building her hotels astounded Janna. Odder still, Aunt Pith was now leaving to show her Maltie on the international kennel club circuit when the crown jewel of her hotels, the Blue Grotto, was just two months from opening.

She saw Nick come out of the guest house. He slung his towel over a chair and dove into the pool with a grace Janna found surprising considering his size. Edging back into the shadow of her doorway, she watched as she had for the last several days when he returned from work and swam a few laps, fascinated by the precision of his butterfly stroke. His formidable shoulders broke the water, then sliced downward with a powerful thrust while his long legs kicked in perfect time with his arms, propelling him forward at a rapid clip but without the wild splashing she associated with the stroke. Until she'd seen Nick execute the stroke, she couldn't imagine why it was called the butterfly.

Nick finished and Aunt Pith left the swing and went over to talk to him. Janna was too far away to hear what she said, but the smile on her face painted too clear a picture. She was taken with him. Why? It wasn't like Aunt Pith to be charmed by a handsome man. Collis had given it his best with no response.

A soft knock brought Janna to her door, reminding herself tonight was the night. Never mind about Aunt Pith, Janna intended to ask Nick for those shares.

"Iva?" Janna called "yes?" in Malti, expecting Clara, the housekeeper.

"May I come in?"

Recognizing Audrey's voice, Janna swung open the heavy plank door. Her mother and Dr. Osgood had flown in that morning to join Aunt Pith on the canine show circuit.

"Am I bothering you?" Audrey asked.

"No. I'm just trying to decide which dress to wear tonight." She gestured to the bed beyond the sitting area,

"You're meeting the Bradfords. Wear the Lacroix. Black becomes you." Audrey sighed and Janna wondered if she could possibly have guessed that Janna now knew the truth about being adopted. "Be careful of Anthony Bradford."

"I didn't realize you knew him."

"I—I met him once . . . a long time ago. He frightened me."

Janna wasn't surprised. Many people frightened Audrey. Those who didn't know her well thought her a consummate snob. Janna knew better. Despite her beauty, or perhaps because of it, Audrey was acutely shy.

"Do you have a moment to talk to me?"

"Of course." Janna motioned to the sofa in the sitting area.

Audrey sat, then arranged the folds of her knit dress over and over. She finally asked, "Do you enjoy running a business?"

"Yes," Janna answered honestly. "It's a lot of work. It keeps me busy all day and into the night." *I don't have time to think about Collis.*

"What do you do exactly?"

"I'm just learning so far, but I'll be overseeing the three hotels. The fourth, the Blue Grotto, is almost finished. It'll be taking up most of my time."

"You don't find it demeaning . . . or common?"

"Heavens, no. If it's good enough for Aunt Pith—"

"Business is awfully fascinating," Audrey said, her blue eyes fired with more enthusiasm than Janna could remember. She wondered if Dr. Osgood had changed her medication. "I have an idea. I want your opinion."

Janna smiled encouragingly. She couldn't remember Audrey having an idea that hadn't first been Reginald's.

"I want to open a shop on Beauchamp Place."

"Lovely, lovely." No one knew designer clothing like Audrey Atherton. A shop on Beauchamp Place among a bevy of designer shops would be perfect. In Reginald's absence this would give Audrey badly needed direction. "I'm certain Lanvin will arrange for you to open a store—"

"I want to open a designer shop for dogs. I even have a name for it—Haute Dog."

Too stunned to speak, Janna did manage to smile. Audrey nattered on and on, babbling with delight about all the ideas her Rommie had given her. One simply could not find the proper products for a pampered pooch.

Audrey explained her plans to sell Burberry slickers, Pierre's Perrier, and a line of canine cologne to be called Eau de Rommel. Janna disguised her shock behind an encouraging smile. Obviously, this project had been well thought out—a first for Audrey—and meant a lot to her. Janna listened patiently, uttering appropriately enthusiastic comments until Audrey finished. As Audrey left, Janna promised to give Haute Dog her full support.

Janna decided Audrey was right and put on the black dress. She carefully applied more makeup than usual, shadowing her eyes to bring out the green and adding extra blush. She took out the falcon pendant Aunt Pith had given her for her eighteenth birthday. The golden falcon head custom-crafted by Bulgari had a feathery ruff of jonquil diamonds alternated with ice-white stones and riveting eyes of matched emeralds. Earrings, smaller versions of the falcon heads, completed the set. She took a step back from the mirror.

The only time she'd looked better had been on her wedding day. She'd worn Aunt Pith's gift then, too, Janna recalled with a stab of bitterness. She'd been so happy that day. Totally in love. *Never mind, don't look back. Concentrate on the Bradfords. On the future.*

Her telephone rang and she went to answer it, thankful Collis didn't have her newly installed number. He'd sent ten pounds of chocolates from Charbonnel et Walker with "I love you. Forgive me" written in gold on them. When the Atherton jet had arrived, there'd been a custom arrangement in a willow basket—a miniature Kew Gardens—from the Sherwood Florist. She'd given the candy and flowers to Clara, realizing that not once in their marriage had Collis thought to stop at one of the flower stands that could be found on every other corner and buy her a simple bouquet.

She answered the telephone, and Warren asked, "How are things?"

"Fine." His voice reminded her of how much she missed him. "I'm meeting the Bradfords tonight."

"Call me later and tell me how it went."

"Tonight I'm also going to convince Nick Jensen to sell me his shares."

"Pay whatever you have to. I'll back you."

Almost thirty-five years of togetherness had taught Janna to gauge Warren's moods as well as he could judge hers. Something was wrong; she heard it in his voice. "What's the matter?"

"We found Gian Paolo."

"He wants a bloody fortune for his shares."

"I wish it were that simple." Warren paused, and a cold, sinking feeling surged through her. She gripped the receiver more tightly as he continued, "He's already sold them to the Bradfords."

"Oh, no," she said, unable to hide her disappointment. "Aunt Pith has legally assigned me her shares—forty-five percent of the stock. I'm certain I can convince Nick Jensen to sell me his shares. That will consolidate my position, but the Bradfords could still give me trouble."

An unexpected image of Nick flashed across her mind: When he finished swimming, he would sweep his hair back with both hands and then vault out of the pool. With Gian Paolo's stock in the Bradfords' hands, Nick shares became crucial. She had to buy them immediately. Before the Bradfords did.

Driving Janna to the party, Nick drove west into the setting sun that had almost melted into the sea, coating the stone-terraced fields with a bronze sheen like a candle's glow. His first glimpse of Malta had been from the air as the sun set on the tiny island. A goldfish swimming south had been his instant impression of the shape and color of the island. He'd assumed the amber hue came from the spectacular sunset, but the next day he'd discovered all of Malta was the color of an apricot because the buildings were constructed from the same golden limestone that formed the island.

He slowed on the narrow road to overtake a horse-drawn *karrozzin*.

"Lovers," Janna said as Nick swung wide around the carriage, its curtains drawn. "Has anyone told you about *passeggiata*?"

He knew all about the sunset social hour when the Maltese walked around the streets, stopping in sidewalk cafes or at neighbors' houses to chat, but he let Janna give him a scholarly history of the custom. She was trying so damn hard to be sweet. He intended to play it for all it was worth. It would be interesting to see what she'd do when he refused to sell.

"I like Malta," he said, "much better than Japan. You won't find the Japanese strolling the streets enjoying life. They work twelve-hour days minimum."

"Don't they have labor laws?" she asked, motioning for him to watch out for the donkey cart overloaded with pumpkins coming from a side road.

Nick slowed, automatically looking to his right for the rearview mirror. Then he remembered it was on the left. Drive on the left side; mirror on the left side. "Yes, but the companies coerce employees into volunteering to work overtime. Anyone who refuses, finds himself out of a job."

"One life—one company. They don't change employers the way we do."

Nodding, Nick let the cart pass and pressed on the accelerator. Janna surprised him. He would have bet she didn't know the company was everything in Japan. Slave labor, he decided, not unlike the blacks who had been brought from Africa, warehoused in the catacombs under Valletta, and shipped to the New World.

"That dedication has given them the edge," Janna said. "Not to mention the restrictive trade barriers.

Their government supports their businesses in ways ours can't."

"It isn't that simple," Nick said, though he was encouraged to see she had some idea of life beyond the silver spoon set. "They're intelligent, dedicated to hard work. I admire them."

She pointed for him to follow the sign for Naxxar. Nick stole a glance at her. He had enough of an eye for style to recognize an expensive designer gown when he saw one. Black silk, clean lines that sculpted the body but not too tightly. The low neckline suggested an interesting cleavage without being too revealing. The subtle dress was a perfect backdrop for the pendant. Nick had never seen such a striking piece of jewelry. There was something almost haunting about it. Probably the emerald eyes. No matter which way he looked, they followed him.

Confirmed what good ole Fitzgerald had said. The rich were different. Hell. Janna's mama traveled with her personal doctor. And they had their own jet to zip them off to Rome, Geneva, and London for a pack of dog shows.

For the first time, it occurred to Nick he was rich. A million dollars wouldn't buy the Atherton jet or the Bradford yacht, but it would go a long way in Muleshoe. He toyed with the idea for a moment, barely hearing Janna telling him to circle the roundabout and follow the signs for Rabat. What would he do if he had the cash in hand? He couldn't think of anything except buying Austin time. And money couldn't even do that.

"I read your paper." Nick was tempted to say it had taken him hours to plow through the sucker. She'd backed up every statement with reams of statistics. When he'd finished it, he'd revised his opinion of Lady Janna. Only a single-minded dedication could have produced that work. He'd checked on her investments. Chic

Sheiks Sheets and Pop Your Cork were both returning handsome profits. With dedication, she could learn to run the hotels. As long as she didn't try to write a paper about it.

"You did? What did you think?"

"You could have said it in a page: The revolution cost France its supremacy in the arts, music, finance—you name it. And handed it to England," Nick replied, unable to resist the urge to tease her. She looked so damn serious, staring at him with those dusky green eyes.

"I had to support my thesis with facts."

Nick grinned at her. Yessirree. No sense of humor. She got pissy in a hell of a hurry. That was the trouble with the rich. Too many people kiss-assed them just because they were rich. They weren't used to hearing the truth.

They drove in silence until Nick spotted Mdina on the bluff. Thrust outward like the bow of a ship, the walled city was located on a promontory facing west, overlooking ribbons of stone-terraced fields that stair-stepped down to the sea. Nick slowed, getting into a line of cars inching up the hill. They entered the ancient citadel through a medieval-style gate and found a parking place.

"How old is this place?"

"Mdina dates back to Roman times," Janna said as they walked along the street cobbled with amber limestone toward the Bradfords. "The Knights of St. John first lived here, then moved to Valletta because it was on the water. With so many Crusaders passing through, it was a better location."

"The knights got the island dirt cheap," Nick said, recalling what Pithany had told him. "One falcon—a real bird complete with a leather hood—a yearly tribute to the good ole Holy Roman Emperor."

"I'm surprised you know about it. Most Americans

think the Maltese falcon is a jewel-encrusted statue like the one in the movie."

Nick stopped and Janna stood beside him, looking up at him. He was momentarily distracted by the way she tilted her head, the curious look in her eyes. He stared at the golden falcon's head, resting provocatively at the rise of her breasts. "Like this falcon?"

He decided Janna thought he wasn't very smart. He wasn't surprised. Like dumb blondes, good-looking men weren't expected to be intelligent. At times he liked to foster that notion. He used the down-home routine on people and let them believe he was a dumb cowpoke. More than once, allowing someone to underestimate him had given Nick the edge. With Janna, though, he was constantly tempted to show her. And tease her.

"Speaking of falcons," he said when she didn't respond to his comment, "Why does Pithany call her place, Falcon's Lair?" In the short time he'd been in Malta, Nick had noticed the Maltese used names rather than numbers for their homes. Some were pretty weird: Casa Iguana, Bull's Nose, Pinky Banana.

"I don't know exactly. Aunt Pith says falcons are the most intelligent birds around. That's why Maltese falcons, peregrines, have always been prized. When the sheiks hunt, they use falcons."

Nick had no idea anyone still hunted with falcons. But what did he know about people who Velcroed their jockeys to camels? "Why lair? Bears have lairs. Falcons use nests."

"It's Scottish for lore. You know, knowledge or learning."

Nick was still puzzled. "What do falcons know?"

Janna shrugged, the falcon pendant shifted its emerald eyes catching the light. "Everything . . . I guess."

They arrived at a walled compound, its fortresslike wooden doors held open by servants in red uniforms with gold buttons and epaulets. Inside, a courtyard with a fountain in the center had clusters of scarlet bougainvillea covering the high walls. Strings of pearllike lights wreathed the trees and hung from the half-dozen balconies of what Nick could only describe as a palace. Old though, must date back to the Crusades. Nick scanned the crowd grazing at the long buffet tables and talking in clusters as they sipped drinks. Janna touched his arm, and he bent down to hear her above the band playing in the far corner.

"Will you introduce me to Curt Bradford?"

Tony Bradford stood alone on the balcony, surveying the crowd below. His *festa* party, the first of the season of celebrations honoring various saints, would be followed the next day by a religious service. Afterward a priest would carry the church's relics through the village, leading a parade of the faithful, which meant everyone not in prison. A converted Catholic, Tony attended because it was expected of a man in his position, but he'd never shared the religious fervor of the Maltese. Still, his traditional *festa* party, the most lavish on the island, gave him an immense sense of satisfaction. He invited only the most important people and they came because he was a rich, powerful man. He thought of himself as the Duke of Malta.

Tonight, his usual pleasure was heightened by anticipation. Janna Atherton-Pembroke had accepted his invitation, ending years of snubbing by the clannish Crandalls. Pithany wasn't coming—she'd never give him the satisfaction—but she'd sent Janna. Why? Pithany Crandall was up to something. After pitting her hotels against his for decades and gambling on an expensive new resort, she'd suddenly given Janna her stock. Now she was going to trot around the world showing her dog. On the surface, it appeared to be a mistake in judgment.

But years of experience with Pithany warned him to be wary.

Tony thought he'd at last cornered Pithany when she sold almost half of the stock in her company to raise money to build the Blue Grotto. He'd miscalculated. Travis Prescott had died before selling the Bradfords his stock. And now, this Nick Jensen refused to sell. Anthony was too savvy to assume Jensen could be easily persuaded. With the Texan living in Pithany's guest house, she would have the upper hand.

Pithany had made a tactical error in selling the Earl of Lyforth those shares. He chuckled to himself. He'd outwitted her—for once—by snapping up those shares. Too bad Pithany didn't realize Tony held their game's trump card. He knew exactly who Janna was.

He'd kept track of Janna from the moment she was born. As long as she'd stayed tucked away in England she wasn't a threat. He'd always assumed Pithany would die and Janna would sell the Bradfords the hotels. But with her flitting around Malta making noises about living here permanently and running the hotels, he had to take action.

The couple coming through the gate below caught Tony's eye. Instinctively he knew the petite blonde was Janna. He'd read the investigator's quarterly reports on her, but hadn't asked for pictures. He couldn't bear it. She turned, saying something to a tall man who was bending down to hear her. Tony gripped the wrought-iron balustrade. A grim sense of déjà vu made his heart race.

How vividly he remembered Pithany wearing black the last night they'd been together. Back then, she'd been a year older than Janna, thirty-six. But the eyes, the body, the hair somehow reminded him of Pithany even though Janna didn't really look like Pithany Crandall. A lifetime of bitterness surged through Tony as he remembered begging Pithany—for the final time—to marry him.

The light refracted from the pendant around Janna's neck. Even at this distance Tony could feel the falcon's accusing green eyes. He'd known about the pendant, of course. He even had a photocopy of the sales receipt. But he hadn't been prepared to see Janna wearing it. The falcon. Tony's nemesis.

Just when Tony had grown accustomed to Janna reminding him of Pithany so much that it made his throat tighten, the tall man with Janna looked up. It couldn't be! Shock, raw and primitive, seared through Tony. He closed his eyes for a second, telling himself he was seeing things. But his vision was as sharp as it had been when he'd flown for the RAF during the war. He took another look. No mistake.

Where the hell did Pithany find that man?

"Get Curt up here," Tony yelled to a passing servant.

"A command performance," Curt said to Rhonda. He followed the servant upstairs to see what Big Tony wanted. A summons from his father was rarely good news. He wished the old man would hurry up and die so he could do as he pleased. Big Tony was bent on establishing a dynasty and Curt, the sole male heir, was the one to do it. Never a day went by without Big Tony reminding him that he was neglecting his duty.

"Who's that with Janna Atherton-Pembroke?" Big Tony asked the moment Curt joined him.

It took Curt a minute to find the only woman he didn't know among the guests. "Nick Jensen."

Big Tony's eyes never left Nick Jensen. "What did the investigator's report say about Jensen's family? Does he have relatives in Scotland?"

"No. His mother's side goes back to some place called

the Alamo and his father's people came over on the *Mayflower*."

Big Tony grunted, the way he always did when he didn't believe something. He turned, hate etching every feature, especially his black eyes. He ran his hand over his forehead, smoothing back hair the color of pewter, a gesture Curt found himself often using, a habit he was determined to break.

"Get our investigators to do another report on Jensen, an in-depth report this time. Pithany Crandall is trying to pull a fast one."

"Why? Their initial report was thorough. I read it several times. His first job was with Imperial Cola. He's been with them ever since. The only interesting thing—"

"I read the goddamned report, and I'm telling you that there's more to Jensen than what's in it."

Curt didn't bother arguing; he never won.

"Take a good look at Janna. That's breeding . . . class."

To Curt she was a cut above plain, saved from it by big green eyes and a nice figure, but not his type at all. He couldn't imagine her doing anything kinky in bed.

"I don't see what's so special—"

"You wouldn't." Big Tony jabbed Curt with his finger, "But you are going to marry her."

"She's married."

Big Tony kept his eyes on Curt. "She's filed for divorce. Women fall all over you. It shouldn't be too hard to get her interested in you."

He knew how to handle his father's demands to marry and produce an heir before Big Tony died. At thirty-four, Curtis Whiting Bradford was an expert at evading matrimony. Although Big Tony didn't know it, Curt loved, deeply and totally, and had for years.

He trooped downstairs and rejoined Rhonda, not as shaken by Big Tony's demands as he had been when he was younger. Time was on his side. The old bastard couldn't live forever.

"What are you going to do?" Rhonda asked after he'd recounted his conversation with his father.

"The same thing I always do when Big Tony locates the perfect wife for me."

Nick didn't see Curt Bradford, so he escorted Janna around the courtyard, proud to be with her. She talked easily with people without a hint of the snobbishness he'd expected. They were a good team. She introduced him to her business acquaintances, and he made certain she met the few people he knew. They wound up at the buffet table near a life-size ice sculpture of a mermaid.

Janna helped herself to what appeared to be meatballs. *"Bragoli*—beef olives." She smiled knowingly at him. "You're a bit of a picky eater, aren't you? You hardly touched the ox tongue last night."

He stabbed a meatball with a sterling silver toothpick shaped like a sword—the rich were different—and took a bite. "Excellent." He took another. "I did eat the veal. It was the best I've had."

Giggling, Janna dropped her used toothpick into a silver cup. "That wasn't veal. That was sweetbreads."

Sweetbreads—the pancreas. Yuck! In Texas they fed the innards to the hogs. He ignored Janna's smirk and had another meatball. She spread some pâté on a cracker and ate it.

"Good," she said. "But not as good as Aunt Pith's." She made another and handed it to him. "Try this. You'll like it."

"You know there's more cholesterol per ounce in *pâté de foie gras* than anything else in the world?" he teased. "Wanna send my cholesterol count into the stratosphere?"

"It's not *foie gras,*" she said as he was about to take a bite. "It's *fenek pâté.*"

Aw, shit! "Not Thumper on a cracker." He gave her back the pâté.

"You're going to starve around here."

"Naw. I survived in Japan. Even learned to eat that mush they serve for breakfast."

Nick looked up. Coming toward them were Curt Bradford and a knockout brunet—the naked woman in the picture with Travis.

8

✤

Janna looked up, following Nick's gaze to the couple approaching them. She heard him whisper "Curt Bradford." The sense of anticipation she'd experienced all evening heightened. She watched Curt, her competition, the man determined to acquire Aunt Pith's hotels. He was handsome and obviously very sophisticated with an air about him that reminded Janna of Italian men.

"Glad you could make it," Curt said to Nick, then turned to her. "You must be Janna. I'm Curt Bradford."

"Hello," Janna said, delighted her voice sounded natural. "Lovely party."

"Thanks." Curt smiled at the woman beside him. "This is Rhonda Sibbet."

With one dismissive flutter of her wispy lashes, the striking brunet's gaze swept over Janna, and finding nothing worthy of note she gave an almost imperceptible nod, then turned a devastating smile on Nick. Janna stood up taller, finding it impossible not to stare at Rhonda. The feathery dress she wore skimmed every line of her well-endowed body, accenting her long legs and revealing more of her bosom than any nightgown Janna owned.

"I'm a friend of Travis Prescott's," Nick said.

Janna couldn't imagine why he'd say that. He was scouring Rhonda with an intense gaze that left no question that he'd been mesmerized. Nick treated Janna like his kid sister, teasing her at every opportunity. What did she expect? A handsome man would never be interested in her. She reminded herself that she didn't care what Nick Jensen thought as long as he sold her those shares.

Rhonda inclined her head, a coquettish movement that set cascades of dark brown hair in motion across her bare shoulders. Obviously, she was as taken with Nick as he was with her.

"Do I know Mr. Prescott?" Rhonda asked Curt but her brown eyes were still on Nick.

"No," Curt said so quickly he almost cut Rhonda off. "He managed the Imperial Cola operation before Nick." He turned to Janna. "Rhonda spent the past year at her villa in Monaco. Does your brother still keep his yacht there?"

Something about the conversation seemed odd to Janna. "The *Audrey Rose* is moored in Puerto Banus."

"Aaah, Marbella," Rhonda said to Nick. "Don't you love it?"

"Never been there." Nick's tone was so terse that Janna turned to look at him. He was smiling. No dimple.

"Janna, why don't you and I go into the library and discuss the hotels?"

As if on cue, Rhonda grabbed Nick's arm. "Let's dance."

Nick followed Rhonda to the area where a parquet dance floor had been put over the uneven cobblestones. Lying bitch, he wanted to shout, but he reminded himself not to lose control. Rhonda Sibbet was the woman in the photograph. No mistake. When he'd joined Curt for lunch on the yacht, Nick had suspected Curt knew more about Travis than he'd admitted. They were both lying. Why?

The hotel stock. Had to be. Why else would the Bradfords seek out Travis? Why would they lie about it now? Could it be that they knew something that could help find his friend's murderer? His sixth sense kicked in, telling Nick to be cautious. Go slowly. Better play this close to the chest.

"A carioca," Rhonda said, sliding into his arms, positioning herself closer than necessary.

Nick had no idea what kind of dance a carioca was but judging from the music it was Latin American. The only dances he knew were the Cotton-Eyed Joe and, of course, the two-step waltz.

"Samba," Rhonda directed, "then move your hips a little like this." She demonstrated a gliding, undulating movement Nick could never hope to imitate.

He tried to follow her, thankful that the dance floor was so crowded that no one could see him making a fool of himself. He avoided looking at Rhonda's breasts, twin soccer balls thrust upward like cocked Colts. Her dress was in just as bad taste. Someone had scalped a posse of peacocks to come up with this number. The dress fit so tightly that the overlapping feathers seemed to be growing from her skin. Nothing like the becoming black dress Janna wore. Sexy as hell without being cheap.

"You're sure you never met Travis Prescott?"

"Positive. I never forget a man," Rhonda said with a breathy whisper Nick assumed she intended to be seductive.

"I thought I saw a picture of you two on a boat. Musta been a mistake."

Her false eyelashes shadowing her cheeks flew up. For a moment she looked stunned, then her eyes boldly met his. "Where did you see this—this picture?"

"Texas. At Travis Prescott's funeral."

"Couldn't be me. I just returned home last week. I've been living in Monaco."

Nick was tempted to press further, but figured she'd only lie. He would have Austin send him the photo, then he would take it to the police. Let them get the truth out of her.

"How about taking me water-skiing tomorrow?" She deliberately brushed her breasts against his chest.

"I'm busy," he lied.

Her lower lip turned outward in what some men might have thought was a sexy pout. The music ended and Nick guided her off the dance floor. He looked around for Janna but didn't see her. The band struck up a beat that sounded like rock 'n' roll.

"Lambada," Rhonda said, dancing in place. "Let's go."

Nick followed her out onto the floor again, figuring a rock tune meant he'd be dancing without touching his partner. They walked into the crowd. Rhonda stopped, slammed her body flush against his, and locked her arms around his neck. Before he could push her away, she began moving to the beat of the music, bumping and grinding against his pelvis. A quick look to his right, then to his left told him Rhonda wasn't doing anything unusual. All around dancers were gyrating against each other. As close to screwing as you could get and still have your clothes on.

Nick pried Rhonda off him. "Lambada—lumbago," he fibbed, his hand on the small of his back. "Let's get a drink. My back's killing me."

"If we combined the hotels, we'd have the lock on the tourist industry in Malta," Curt said to Janna, his voice as smooth as the Marosivin private reserve he'd served her.

She put the glass down; the little bit she'd drunk seemed to have gone to her head. "Aunt Pith's concept is to have smaller hotels that cater to Europe's elite, not high rises that attract hordes of tourists on Thompson tours, who tote back Maltese crosses by the dozen. Plastic crosses."

Her answer startled Janna. She'd been bred to prize tact. What was she doing? Trying to alienate Curt? She'd better not; she planned to live on Malta. She intended to heal the riff with the Bradfords, not make it worse.

"I understand," Curt said, his polished tone not quite masking a challenge. "That's how Pithany Crandall saw the company. But what about you? Times have changed. Tours are the lifeblood of hotels."

"Not my—" She stifled another surprisingly blunt response. "There's room for different types of hotels."

He rose and poured himself another drink from a bar cleverly hidden in an Egyptian sarcophagus. What kind of man was Tony Bradford? she wondered, planning on meeting him later. Curt's father had painstakingly renovated this old palace dating back to medieval times, but this particular room was out of context with the rest of the architecture. Why would he decorate it like a mummy's tomb?

From the bar Curt smiled at her and she forced a smile. She'd pried a few details from Aunt Pith and knew Curt had a reputation as a playboy with a lust for gambling and women, lots of them. During the past hour she'd learned Curt was quite shallow. He seemed to have few real interests outside of racing his boat and his race cars. His interest in the hotels seemed halfhearted at best. She decided his father, Tony, must be the power behind the business. The man determined to control Aunt Pith's hotels.

"Your aunt has gained a reputation for being anti-German."

"She's never gotten over the war, not completely." Janna disagreed with Aunt Pith on few things. Her continued dislike of Germans was one of them. Fifty years. Wasn't it time to forgive and forget?

"Germany is Malta's largest trading partner," Curt pointed out. "They're insulted when our best hotels snub them."

Janna banked a smile. Imagine! A Bradford admitting the Crandall hotels were superior. Aunt Pith would laugh.

"I can see you don't care for our private reserve," Curt said. "Let me get you some chardonnay."

Janna wanted to tell him a few sips had already made her woosy—she wasn't much of a drinker—but had the feeling she'd insulted him by not drinking the first glass. She studied him, recognizing that Curt's interest in her, like his concern about the hotels, was feigned. She'd learned at least one thing from her experience with Collis Pembroke. A handsome face and a charming smile didn't deceive her. Not anymore.

Curt brought her the chardonnay and sat beside her, taking a seat so close that there was less than a hand's span between them. "To our hotels." He clinked his glass against hers.

Janna took a polite sip. The wine was too sweet with a hint of spice she'd not tasted in other chardonnays. She started to put it down, but he tipped the rim of his glass to hers.

"To us."

Janna gulped down a swallow, telling herself what she saw in Curt Bradford's eyes couldn't be there. He edged closer; Janna felt shaky all over. He touched the falcon pendant and she let out a sigh of relief. Everyone was fascinated by the pendant. For a moment there . . . He gazed into her eyes again. This time there wasn't any mistaking his intention.

"I've been wondering about this mirror." Janna scooted sideways until she was in the corner of the sofa and pointed at the mirror on the wall behind them. On the pediment a pharaoh had been chiseled into the rose limestone. Egyptian hieroglyphics formed the border of the unusual mirror.

Curt closed the space between them, took her glass, and set it aside. "It's the false door to King Tut's tomb. Uncle Tony bought it at a Sotheby's auction. The mirror replaced the rotted wood."

"Not Tut's tomb," she said, her mind scrambling for a polite exit. His blatant look of sexual interest made her nervous. "Unis-ankh. He lived several centuries before Tut."

He laughed. "You'll get along great with Big Tony. He's crazy about ancient Egypt."

Janna was about to inquire why he called his father "Big Tony," when he slipped his arm around her shoulders. "I was wondering," Janna said, trying to talk her way out of the uncomfortable situation, "why your father used a smoke mirror. Wouldn't a regular mirror have reflected the room and made it seem larger?"

Curt's mouth swooped down and his parted lips met hers in a hard kiss. Had she not known better, she would have thought he was being deliberately cruel. She gagged, pushing him away, her arms curiously weak.

He kept kissing her, murmuring, "Let's go out to my yacht just the two of us."

She shoved at him with all her might. "Stop it!"

He pressed her deeper into the glove-soft leather, his hand on her breast. Just as she was about to hit him, someone knocked at the library door and Curt loosened his grip. Janna stumbled to her feet. Her head spinning, she tripped over the Persian rug, landed against the door, fumbled with the antique latch, and finally yanked it open. Nick stood in the hall with Rhonda beside him.

"Take me home," Janna said. The words sounded as if they'd come from a stranger's lips. Her tongue felt heavy, thick.

Janna let Nick pull her to him. His strong arm around

her waist, he ushered her down the hall and out into the courtyard. By the time they'd passed through the gate into the street, her breathing had almost returned to normal. Despite the warmth of the spring night, she felt chilled and leaned closer to Nick.

"What happened back there?"

"He—he made a pass at me." She felt silly saying it, but she couldn't put into words exactly what had happened. It was almost as if he'd deliberately set out to frighten her. Or worse.

Nick stopped, his arm still around her, bringing her to a jarring halt. "Don't bullshit me, Shorty. I'm the one who had you on the floor in the dark. You damn near scratched my eyes out. You wouldn't panic just because Bradford came on to you."

"That was different. I thought you were going to kill me. I was fighting for my life."

He accepted her explanation and they started to walk again, faster this time. Janna had to hurry to keep up with Nick's long stride. Her knees felt wobbly, so she stopped. "Let me take off these heels."

They started down the street again, but this time Nick didn't touch her. She wished he'd put his arm around her again. Even with her shoes off, her steps were unsteady. Suddenly, the whole thing—her father's death, the move to Malta, the Bradfords—seemed like a dream to her. She'd wake up any minute and find Collis sleeping beside her. She giggled and it grew into a full-throated laugh. An unbecoming, totally unladylike laugh.

"Shhhh. Hush," Nick said, halting. "You'll wake up the whole town."

His comment only made her laugh harder, unable to get control of herself. "Nick," she said between giggles. "No one lives here."

"C'mon. There's got to be two or three thousand people in Mdina."

"No. The Bradfords live here—"

"Rhonda told me Curt has a place in Sliema."

Janna took a head-clearing breath; she didn't seem to be thinking too coherently. "All right, Tony Bradford lives alone in the palace with his servants. The point is only two other families live in Mdina. That's why they call it the 'Silent City.' "

"Are you drunk?"

"Honest. During the day, people are here, tourists and bureaucrats working in government offices. Basically, no one actually lives in Mdina. It's been a ghost town for centuries."

He looked around, noting the dark buildings, lit only by the full moon. "Don't that beat all." He took her high heels from her and stuck them in his suit pocket and put his arm around her again. "We're outta here."

She snuggled against Nick and walked along until they came to a semicircular opening in the buttressed wall that formed the perimeter of Mdina. "This"—she nudged him to the right—"is my favorite spot. Do you know what these holes are for?"

"They fired a cannon from here."

"Good guess, but wrong. The knights kept cauldrons of boiling oil at these turnouts. If the enemy tried to scale the wall—"

"Whammo, french fries."

He moved to the edge and looked down the several hundred feet to the ground. She leaned against the wall and tried to guess what he was thinking. A cat's-paw of wind lifted the hair across his brow; he didn't bother to smooth it back into place. Slowly, he turned to her with a look so galvanizing that she automatically moved closer to him. In the opalescent light of the hunter's moon, his eyes appeared black. Though she'd been chilled a few minutes ago, heat now suffused her body, making her light-headed and increasing the tingling in her legs.

For one wild, wanton moment she longed to run her fingers through his hair. To kiss him. *Don't you dare.* But her body seemed to have a will of its own. Nothing could have made her back away. She looped her arms around his neck and smiled up at him, touching the thick hair at the nape of his neck.

"Janna, how much wine did you drink?"

She should have been insulted; she never overdrank. But her mind didn't seem to be able to hold a thought long enough to voice it. She managed to hold up one finger.

"That's all, Shorty?" He rumpled her hair. "You sure?"

She gazed at the magnificent man in her arms with a sense of wonder, moving closer. A quiver built deep in her stomach and fluttered upward. From the remotest part of her brain a warning bell sounded. She almost pulled away. Then he smiled, a slow, slow smile. The dimple appeared. She stood on tiptoe and kissed it.

His breath warm against her cheek, he turned slightly. Their lips met, soft and barely parted. She touched her lips to his, caressing his mouth more than kissing it. Tracing her tongue across his lips, a dreamy intimacy gripped her. She hardly noticed his arms circling her. His tongue expertly slid between her lips, seeking hers with a masterful thrust. The tip of her tongue met his and she eased it slowly over his, taking her time, letting the swelling sensation between her thighs build and build.

Crushing her to him, he kissed her with a savage intensity Janna had never experienced. She instinctively tilted her hips upward against his; for a moment he paused, his lips deserting hers. The smoldering heat, building inside her, demanded more. She pressed herself against him, thrilled at the insistent pressure of his arousal. Lowering his head, he met her lips again.

Some distant voice in her head kept telling her to stop, but she allowed passion she hadn't known existed to guide her. When he angled his hips to one side, she let his leg edge between hers.

"You fooled me . . . Lady Janna."

With one swift motion, he positioned her in front of him, drawing her up on tiptoe. Palms clutching her bottom, he eased her up against his taut shaft. Hesitantly at first, then with the flame of desire driving her, she moved against him.

"This your idea of the lambada?"

"I need . . . I need . . ." She forgot what she was going to say. Looking up at the crystal-white stars, she tried to focus, but they kept dancing around in dizzying circles to the beat of the party music playing in the distance.

A group of late arrivals came up the street.

"Aw, shit!"

Janna felt Nick tugging on her to leave. She slumped against him, her legs suddenly useless. She staggered sideways, grabbing for Nick, but she lurched into the wall. The stars cycloned around her, spinning in a whorling vortex until the ground came up to greet her.

Nick drove up to Falcon's Lair and heaved a sigh of relief. What should have been a twenty minute drive had taken him over an hour. Since coming to Malta, his usually infallible sense of direction seemed to have failed him. He kept thinking he was heading in the wrong direction. All those damn signs he couldn't read slowed him down—Gzira, Ta'Xbeix, Qormi, Zurrieq—sending him around the roundabouts two or three times. For a country whose official language was English there were countless signs in Malti. 'Course he hadn't counted on his guide passing out. He shook Janna. "Wake up. You're home."

She didn't move, still sitting slumped against the passenger door where he'd put her after carrying her to the car. The house was dark; Nick realized everyone had already left for Rome. Clara had gone by now too. She'd caught the last ferry to Malta's sister island, Gozo, where her daughter had just had a baby. Nick had no choice but to carry Janna to her room. He got out of the car, went around and eased her door open. Dead weight, she fell into his arms.

Halfway up the path to the front door, Nick remembered he didn't know the code for the newly installed alarm system in the main house. He shook Janna again, harder this time. Her head lolled across his shoulder, but she didn't wake up. Nick went to the guest house and somehow managed to hold Janna while he unlocked the door and punched his code into the alarm system.

He stood, cradling Janna in his arms, and tried to decide where to put her. His bed seemed to be the best place. There she could sleep until morning. He settled her under the covers, tucking the sheet under her chin. After changing his clothes, Nick headed to the sitting room, a pillow tucked under his arm, to spend the night on the sofa.

Passing through his bedroom, Nick saw Janna had tossed the covers aside. A shaft of moonlight sparkled across the falcon pendant, refracting spears of light in the dark room. He moved closer, drawn by the softness of her face. Sleep had erased the carefully controlled expression she usually wore. She looked almost pretty with her upturned nose and the gentle slope to her cheek. Her lips, barely parted, were extremely sensual. Alluring.

Jeez-us! What the hell are you doing? He hightailed it into the sitting room and flopped down on the sofa. He couldn't be attracted to Lady Janna. She was highfalutin as hell with all her intellectual bullshit—naming her puppy after some damn ruin—and married to boot. He told himself he was just plain horny and needed to find some professional action. But he still couldn't erase the scene at the wall from his mind.

He'd gone for Janna. Almost took her—standing up—right where the knights had boiled their damn oil. What could have gotten into him? An adorable smile and eyes as big as Texas, staring up at him as if she'd seen him—truly seen him—for the first time. For a minute there an echo of his past had triggered emotions he'd thought were gone forever. He thought she cared about him. But no, she was drunk and itching to get laid like all the other women in his life.

Lots of women had wanted to roll in the sack with Nick. Only one had loved him.

"You can't keep your pecker in your pocket." Big Tony's voice boomed, threatening to awaken the ghosts in the "Silent City."

Curt didn't answer. Years ago, he'd learned to let his father's tirades run their course. This time, though, a smoldering hatred he'd never seen fired Big Tony's eyes.

"What did you think you were doing pawing Janna? You don't handle a lady like that. Now she won't come near you."

That was exactly what Curt had planned. He'd known enough prim English women to realize Lady Janna Atherton-Pembroke would reject any man—no matter how irresistible—when he got rough with her. If Jensen hadn't appeared, Curt would have made certain Janna never came near him again. What he hadn't counted on was Big Tony watching him from behind that damn Egyptian mirror. Curt had assumed he'd be out hobnobbing with the President of Malta, not spying on Janna.

"I think we have a better chance of getting the shares from Jensen, anyway."

"What makes you the expert?"

"Rhonda says Jensen's really taken with her."

Big Tony snorted his disbelief, then said, "I won't rest until I have control of Pithany Crandall's hotels. For once in your life, you could have helped me, but you blew it.

Curt bristled and for the first time let it show. "I can get those shares from Jensen, you'll see."

"Get out of my sight," Tony said, and Curt headed for the door, anticipating spending the rest of the night in Rhonda's arms. "Just a minute. Don't forget to get the goods on Jensen. I want to know everything about him from the moment he was born."

Janna awoke slowly, her head swimming, a metallic taste in her mouth. The moon cast spangles of light across her face, but left everything else in darkness. She turned her head on the pillow. Not her own, she groggily realized, too firm for eiderdown. But the scent lingering on the linen, an elusive aroma, jogged her memory. Nick Jensen.

The night he'd mistaken her for a burglar, she'd noticed the woodsy aroma. Noticed it in the car. Noticed it as he hustled her away from the Bradfords. Noticed it when she'd kissed him. Kissed him? She sat bolt upright, her head throbbing. She was in his bed. Oh, my God. No!

She looked around, her eyes now accustomed to the dark. Thank heaven, he wasn't with her. She ran her hands down her body and realized her clothes were still on. Nothing could have happened. Could it? She slumped back against the pillow and tried to remember.

The image of Nick, the warmth of his body, the strength in his arms whirled through her foggy brain.

He'd kissed her, long, bittersweet kisses that promised much, much more. No. He'd never kissed her. She recalled now; she'd kissed him. The memory returned with belittling clarity. She'd thrown her arms around him, forcing herself on him.

Like any whore in the *Gut*. Once she and Warren had ventured down Strait Street, Malta's red-light district where prostitutes had plied their trade since before the Crusaders. Whores had aggressively grabbed Warren, thrusting their nearly bare breasts against his chest. Rubbing their hips against his. Exactly the way she'd thrown herself at Nick.

Why? She didn't even like Nick Jensen. The shares. In her drunken state, her brain had short-circuited. She'd been trying to persuade him to give her the shares. How drunk had she been to try to use her body as a lure? Nick could have any beautiful woman he wanted—like Rhonda. The only way Janna could wrest the shares from him was with money.

She struggled to remember just how much wine she'd consumed. Less than a glass. That couldn't make her drunk. The acrid taste in her mouth reminded her of the strange aftertaste of the wine Curt Bradford had served her. Had he put something in it? A sleeping pill? An aphrodisiac? Why would he? Rich, handsome men like Curt had their pick of women.

A sickening sensation gripped her. As much as she'd embarrassed herself with Nick, it could have been worse. Had Nick not happened along, the drug might have taken effect. She might have succumbed to Curt's advances. Never! Janna stared up at the ceiling, her shame deepening. The way she'd been acting anything was possible, she conceded. Before tonight she would have bet anything she would never have kissed Nick Jensen.

Where was Nick? She didn't want to know. She

wanted to be gone before he returned. He'd never believe a handsome man like Curt would stoop to drugging women. He'd think she was making an excuse.

She jumped up and found her high heels next to the bed. She grabbed them, then saw her purse on the dresser beside a large photograph in a silver frame that caught the moonlight. She took a quick look: a strikingly beautiful woman with long dark hair. She tiptoed across the limestone tile through the adjacent sitting room to the door.

"Where are you going?"

Hand on the brass knob, she halted, thankful the darkness hid her face. "Home." Ready to bolt, she opened the door, realizing she needed Nick's shares. If she ran now, she'd only have more difficulty facing him later. She closed the door. Behind her, the lamp snapped on.

She turned slowly and saw Nick sitting on the sofa with Taxila on his lap. Dressed in cutoff jeans, his thick hair hopelessly rumpled, he watched her with an expression she couldn't read. For the first time, she realized Nick usually smiled, not the lone dimple smile, but a casual smile meant to put a person at ease. She'd give anything to have him smile now.

She forced herself to look into his blue eyes. "I apologize. I—I hope I didn't embarrass you by behaving like . . . like . . ."

Nick heard the hesitation in her voice and gave her credit for facing him. "You thought by sleeping with me you could get my shares."

"No. Really, I didn't," she said, and some part of him wished he could believe her, but he was no fool. "I want the shares, of course, but I don't know what happened. I —I guess I had too much to drink."

He wanted to say something sarcastic, but the pleading expression in her eyes stopped him. "It's happened to everyone." He motioned for her to sit.

Janna took the chair opposite Nick, pretending not to notice he was half dressed. His bare torso, which she'd seen each time he swam, seemed even more formidable at close range and more densely covered with dark hair. She kept her gaze on her puppy sitting on his lap, her sense of mortification increasing. Even drugged, where had she found the nerve to kiss him?

"Now's a good time to discuss the shares. I'm not selling."

"But I can offer you—"

"Not interested." He stretched his long legs and leaned back, letting Taxi lick his hand.

Janna didn't believe him. He was angling for more money.

"Pithany sold those shares to Travis because she believed he'd help her. I intend to take his place."

"Name your price."

"No amount of money can make me change my mind."

She didn't know what kind of game he was playing, but common sense told her not to alienate him. She managed a tight smile.

Janna rose to leave, not fooling Nick for a minute. She hated him. "Wait a minute. What do you know about the Bradfords?"

"I've never met Anthony Bradford. As you know, tonight was the first time I met Curt."

"I'm curious. If they're so rich—shipyards, vineyards, a software company as well as hotels—why the hell do they want Pithany's hotels so badly?"

Curt watched the burly sailor, Greek by the look of him, through the one-way mirror in the stateroom on *Siren's Song*. The stocky man gawked at the lavish furnishings, then turned to Rhonda who was sitting on the king-size bed. The black lace on the scarlet negligee she wore matched the trim on the black satin sheets.

"Come here, sugar," Rhonda said.

The sailor walked toward her, tugging at the crotch of his trousers, the fullness of his erection obvious. Curt hoped this wasn't going to be a wham-bam job. Those were a bore. He liked a hot, sexy show. Rhonda craved it.

Rhonda pulled the Greek onto the bed. Immediately, he unhitched his trousers, but she stopped him, clamping her hand over the navy twill covering his bulging penis. "What's your hurry?"

He muttered something in unintelligible Greek as Rhonda unbuttoned his well-worn shirt. He shucked it with an impatient jerk of his muscular shoulders. Aggressive, Curt decided, even more aggressive than the last man Rhonda had picked up in the *Gut*. The sleazy bars and flop joints housed the transient sailors—a tough lot at best—who came through Malta on a regular basis. Rhonda seemed to be selecting more and more assertive types to bring to the yacht for their little games.

Rhonda eased the man back against the satin sheets, then ran her long nails through the dense hair on his chest. He grabbed at her gown and tore it off her shoulders, exposing evenly tanned breasts. Her nipples, slightly elongated, were spiraled tight. She arched her back, offering him a perfect breast. He took it and sucked so noisily while kneading the other with a huge hand that Curt could hear him on the other side of the mirror.

A white-hot flash of jealousy arced through Curt. He wanted to kill the damn sailor. Instead, he unbuckled his trousers and freed his erect penis, his eyes on the couple on the bed.

Rhonda evaded the sailor's questing hands and eager mouth long enough to remove his pants. The thicket of hair on the man's chest covered his torso all the way to his groin. Short and surprisingly thick, his cock stood at attention.

"Meaty, really meaty," Curt said to himself, knowing what Rhonda was thinking. None of the others had been built quite like this man. Achingly hard now, Curt fought the urge to kill.

Rhonda palmed the man a few times. He pushed her aside and reached for his pants. He took out a foil wrapped condom. This one was smart, Curt decided, zipping up his trousers and confining a painful erection. The sailor flipped Rhonda onto her back, spread her thighs with his knee, then entered her with a noisy grunt.

Rhonda gasped, her usual cry of pleasure. Curt burst through the door into their stateroom, uncontrollable anger flooding his brain. He stood over the couple, not missing the rapt pleasure on Rhonda's face.

"You sonofabitch!" Curt yanked the man backward, yelling "Mifti, Aasd, get in here."

The sailor began to say something, but Curt caught him with a brutal—and totally unexpected—punch to the gut. Mifti and Aasd, Curt's crewmen, burst into the cabin. They dragged the stunned man toward the door while Curt landed a few more merciless blows.

Behind Curt, Rhonda giggled. He left the crew to beat up the hapless sailor and dump him back on Strait Street. If the man told his incredible tale, who would believe him?

Curt unhitched his trousers, his eyes on Rhonda. When the crew had burst in, she'd covered herself, but the outline of her slim legs beneath the satin sheet revealed her still-spread thighs. He yanked back the sheet, then paused a moment to admire the body he adored.

"You bitch," he said, still playing their little game.

"You cheating bitch." He whacked her bare bottom. "Don't ever let me catch you with another man."

He couldn't control himself. Their lovemaking, which usually lasted quite a while after one of their little shows, was over quickly, but Rhonda didn't care. She curled up against his chest. A long, lingering kiss she usually reserved for foreplay followed.

"Curt," she whispered with the breathy voice he loved. "We might have a problem. Nick Jensen thinks he's seen a picture of me . . . and Travis Prescott."

"Impossible," Curt replied, but a frisson of alarm pricked at him. The big Texan spelled trouble; he'd known it from their first meeting. "Why would he think that?"

Rhonda examined the lacy edge of the sheet. He knew her too well not to realize she was upset. "When he was in Texas, he claims to have seen a picture . . . of Travis and me on a boat."

"I took those shots from *Siren's Song* with a telephoto lens. Prescott didn't even know they existed. One couldn't be in Texas." He rose, positive he was correct, but his sense of unease grew with each breath. "They're over there in the drawer."

Rhonda pulled him back. "I already checked. One is missing. Travis must have sent it to his father."

"Unfuckingbelievable! How did he get it?"

She shrugged apologetically. "Remember, he asked me to put the pictures you took of the *Amanda Jane* in the packet he was mailing to his father. On the same roll were the telephoto shots. One must have gotten mixed up or stuck to another. I watched him put them in the envelope." She took a deep breath. "I was even with him when he mailed them."

"How stupid—"

"I'm sorry. Don't be angry. You know how much I love you. It was a mistake."

He would have punched any crewman for less, but not Rhonda. She was the only person who had ever loved him. The only woman he'd ever loved. "Don't worry, angel. I'll take care of Jensen."

9

The next morning Janna took the first Air Malta flight to Rome. She reached the Countessa d'Bianci's villa where Aunt Pith was staying with Audrey and Dr. Osgood. They were out, so Janna waited in Aunt Pith's suite looking out at a fountain spraying arcs of water into the air. The streams thinned on the downward plunge to become iridescent droplets in the sunlight as they fell to the koi pond ringing the fountain. Except for the few hours she'd slept in Nick's bed, she hadn't been able to rest. Her mind should have been dulled from lack of sleep, but it wasn't.

No matter how long she mulled over why Curt had drugged her, it remained a mystery. But Nick's question was right on target: Why *did* the Bradfords covet Aunt Pith's three—about to be four—hotels? Even if they combined Aunt Pith's hotels with theirs, it would be a small slice of their financial pie. Their wealth centered on the Bradford shipyards and was augmented by several other lucrative businesses. The hotels ranked close to last on a list of their assets.

Aunt Pith had to know more than she was telling. Her behavior since Janna had moved to Malta had become increasingly peculiar. It was impossible to understand why she would leave—to show her dog, of all things—just when the Blue Grotto was nearing completion.

Equally perplexing was Aunt Pith's refusal to pressure Nick Jensen into selling his shares.

The door to the suite opened and Aunt Pith walked in. "Janna, what are you doing here? Has something happened to N— to the Blue Grotto?"

"The hotel is fine. I came because I wanted to talk to you . . . about the Bradfords."

Aunt Pith crossed the room and sat near Janna saying, "What did you think of Anthony Bradford?"

"I spent time with Curt, but I didn't meet his father." She hesitated a second. She disliked not telling Aunt Pith the whole story but Janna had already decided not to worry her. "I gather Curt isn't particularly interested in the hotel business." When Aunt Pith didn't comment, Janna continued, "I flew here to ask you why the Bradfords are so determined to acquire your hotels."

"Your hotels now," Aunt Pith said quietly.

Janna nodded, again experiencing the awesome burden of taking over the business Aunt Pith had so painstakingly built. "The hotels would never be more than a decimal point in their empire. Why the interest? Nick tells me they've offered him twice the market value for his shares." She studied her aunt for a moment. "There's more to this—this rivalry than you're telling me, isn't there?"

"Rivalry?" A note of cynicism colored Aunt Pith's voice. "I suppose you could call it that. I think it's an obsession. Anthony Bradford is obsessed with money and power."

"You clashed with him after the war," Janna said, "when you both built hotels."

"No. The trouble started during the war. To impress Hitler, Mussolini declared war on England and France. He didn't have the nerve to cross his border into France, so he bombed Malta, a tiny island with a half-dozen rusty RAF Hurricanes to protect it. You can imagine how thrilled we were when more RAF fliers arrived to defend us. Most of them were wonderful men."

Janna knew Aunt Pithany's hotels were always available—free of charge—to any British soldier who had helped defend Malta. Many were regulars, returning year after year in January and February when the bleak English winter was at its peak and Malta's sunny beaches beckoned.

"Whenever there's a war shortages occur. On an island that depends on ships to bring fuel and food, it's worse. I believe Anthony Bradford came prepared to corner the black market. He ruthlessly sold supplies at astronomical prices to the highest bidder, ignoring thousands of needy people who couldn't pay his price. I can't prove it, but I think he was responsible for the disappearance of church relics during air raids. One piece, Cleopatra's Chalice, was a national treasure. It was almost pure silver embellished with precious emeralds, but it wasn't the monetary value that made it so important. It had been a gift of St. Paul, thanking the islanders for rescuing him when he'd been shipwrecked off Malta."

Aunt Pith fidgeted with the silver ring on her finger, examining it as if seeing it for the first time even though she'd worn it for as long as Janna could remember. "There was one r-reporter who was investigating him. Ian MacShane."

The way Aunt Pith tripped over "reporter" and the softening of her expression at his name alerted Janna. Although Janna had always been close to Aunt Pith, she'd never mentioned him. "Was he a friend of yours?"

"More than a friend. Much more." Aunt Pith's earnest eyes clouded with visions of the past. After an awkward silence, she said, "I loved him with all my heart. Fifty years hasn't changed how I feel."

Janna had never heard Aunt Pith speak with such emotion. Such love. "Where is he?"

Fascinated, Janna listened while Aunt Pith took her back in time to December, 1941.

Midnight was rapidly approaching as Pithany sat in the underground bunker monitoring radio messages, but Rommel's forces pounding the British in North Africa had gone to bed for the night. Her earphones on, Pithany put her head down on the table beside the wireless receiver. With luck, she could get a little sleep before the shift changed. She preferred the day shift because the heavy air traffic kept her busy, and she didn't have time to worry about Ian.

As the North African campaign intensified, the volume of shortwave radio messages that Pithany translated increased. The Maltese listened and tracked troop and ship movements, knowing an invasion could come at any moment and vowing not to be taken by surprise. Pithany translated Morse code from shortwave messages in German or Italian, and rushed them to her superiors seconds after they'd been broadcast. Because of her ear for detail, she had been selected to record the longer range radio transmissions intended for the high command in Berlin which were dispatches in ultramodern codes.

The reward for her long hours in the darkness were messages from Ian. Never mind how he did it, he always managed to persuade a radio operator to tag the word "falcon" on to a transmission, letting her know where he was. The last she'd heard "the falcon" had moved from the British headquarters in Alexandria, Egypt, to join the frontline troops in Libya. His reports relayed by Radio Malta to the BBC in London indicated he was in the trenches with the men. Where he wanted to be, she reminded herself.

When she wasn't worrying about Ian, Pithany worried about her father. Like many of the islanders, he suffered "bomb happiness." Doctors claimed the severe bouts of depression were caused by nerve endings being deadened by the deafening noise of the prolonged bombing. The victims walked the streets during air raids, oblivious to the noise or the danger. Her father, like so many others, had lost his ability to concentrate. Although only in his early forties, he seemed to be growing senile. She was thankful her mother wasn't alive to see it.

A burst of static snapped Pithany to attention. The strength of the Italian transmission told her this was a shortwave message she could translate herself. For longer range dispatches the Germans used a series of complicated codes that were impossible to decipher—although Pithany always tried. Those messages had to be relayed to Bletchley Park, England where the Enigma machine operated. Once they'd been decoded by the machine, the information was sent back through Malta where Pithany and her coworkers directed them to the appropriate commanders.

She hesitated for a fraction of a second, wondering if she should turn on the light. Since she and Ian had met the convoy months ago, few supplies had reached Malta. Fuel was critically low—again. She flicked on the lamp, certain any message sent at this hour was important.

She rapidly recorded the dispatch. Halfway through, she realized it wasn't in any code. This was butchered German obviously translated on the spot by some Italian whose grasp of the language was limited to "Heil Hitler." But the news of the aerial attack that was taking place as she listened stunned Pithany. Forgetting to turn out the light, she rushed into the adjacent tunnel to awaken her superior whose job it was to alert Lieutenant General William Dobbie, the British governor-general in charge of Malta.

"You sure you got this right?" her superior barked. "I've never heard of Pearl Harbor."

Neither had Pithany, but by that evening the entire

population could locate the cluster of Pacific Islands. The Maltese sympathized with the Hawaiians who were poised for an invasion by Japan. The Maltese were isolated on an island, too, threatened with invasion. The following day, America declared war and Malta celebrated. With the Americans on their side, the outlook for the future seemed less grim.

Several days later, the news came that the British had reinforced the besieged North African garrison at Tobruk. "The Falcon" was among the first troops there. Things were improving, the Maltese reassured each other. Even the unusual weather couldn't dampen their spirits. The icy winds—*gregal*—blew in from Mt. Etna, bringing snow for the first time in a decade.

On Christmas Eve, 1941, Pithany went to church with her father. Bundled in blankets, she listened to the sermon reminding the Maltese that the citizens of Leningrad, under siege since September, had it worse than they did. Thousands had starved to death; no one on Malta had starved—yet.

She prayed for everyone whose life was in jeopardy because of the war, especially for those in the Nazi "work" camps. President Roosevelt's wife, Eleanor, had convinced the Nazis to release noted child psychologist, Bruno Bettelheim, from a "work" camp called Dachau. Pithany had monitored enough messages from resistance fighters to already know what wasn't common knowledge yet. "Work" camps were really death camps. Few would be as fortunate as Bettelheim.

"I know, God, you're too busy with this unholy war to pay attention to one lonely woman's problems. But if you get a chance, make Papa well. Keep Ian safe, please. Even if you can't bring him home to me."

Guiding her father out of the church lit only by smoky homemade tallow candles, Pithany saw Tony Bradford motioning to her. She left her father with friends and joined Tony.

He smiled, his usual brash smile that never failed to remind Pithany of childhood tales she'd heard about the pirate, Dragut. Four hundred years ago when Malta had withstood a harrowing siege from Süleyman's Turkish navy, the murderous pirate had joined forces with the knights. Because he'd died defending Malta, he'd been forgiven for his sins and Dragut Point on Marsamxett Harbor had been named for him. In Pithany's opinion, Tony—like Dragut—was a necessary evil.

"Fix Christmas dinner for me tomorrow," he said, his voice low. "I'll bring a rooster."

"Where did you get one?" She couldn't conceal her anger. Once the roosters crowed, heralding sunrise along with the bells of Malta's three hundred churches ringing for the first mass of the day. Now the bells rang only to signal the all clear after an air raid. No one had seen a rooster since summer.

He merely smiled.

"I'm not interested. We're having *soppa ta L'Armia* like everyone else." The widow's soup of potato peels wasn't very appetizing, but Pithany refused to eat well while her friends starved.

She turned to leave; Tony caught her arm. "Mac-Shane's not coming back. But I'm planning to stay on Malta and make a life here." He cupped her chin, forcing her to look directly into his dark eyes. Through the worn fingertips of his RAF gloves, she felt the heat of his hand. "Give me a chance."

She walked away, her heart refusing to believe what her mind knew was true: Chances were Ian wouldn't return. Already, he vied with the American, Edward R. Morrow, as the best war correspondent. After the war, Ian could have any job. Any woman. Pithany's insecurities returned, a heavier weight than the war, the severe rationing, or her father's illness.

In early January of 1942 Pithany was again on the late night shift. There had been no message with the code word "falcon," but she knew Ian was still with the British forces in Tobruk because he hadn't missed a weekly broadcast. A hiss of static came over the wireless followed by guttural German. A tremor of apprehension clutched at her gut. She'd come to realize some messages weren't in code. The Nazis deliberately broadcast certain messages uncoded, knowing the Maltese were listening.

She flicked on the light and recorded Hitler's directive number thirty-eight to Field Marshal Kesselring. Regarding the enemy occupying the island of Malta: "They shall be destroyed."

Pithany doused the light and felt in her pocket for the derringer Ian had given her. With Malta being used as a base for air and sea forces supporting Tobruk, the Nazis couldn't afford to let the island remain British. The Germans would invade them or bomb Malta into oblivion.

Her shift over, she ambled down the serpentine tunnel, its walls covered with the spongy fungus that grew during the wet season. She walked into the blinding January sunlight, her hand shielding her sunglasses. Toward her strode a tall man, little more than a black shadow to her watering eyes. Her heart slammed to a stop, then beat in double-time. "Ian?"

"Miss Crandall?" the shadow asked.

She halted, disappointment welling up inside her. "Yes?"

"I have a letter for you"—he shoved a folded piece of paper into her hand"—from Ian MacShane."

She clutched the paper, knowing it would be some time before her eyes adjusted to the sunlight enough to read. "Have you seen him? How is he?"

"Skinny. He has a beard." The soldier chuckled. "Like everyone else, he has Rommel's Revenge. But he's alive. I'm ferrying spare parts in a RAF plane. MacShane asked me to bring you his letter." He looked over his shoulder. "I've got to go."

"If you see him, please give him a message for me. Tell him . . . tell him I love him. I'm here waiting. Waiting for him."

The soldier left and Pithany sank to the ground. Her vision slowly returned, pitted by black spots that would last for hours. She unfolded the letter, barely noticing its soiled edges. The handwriting appeared childlike; one *s* was backward.

Dear Ace,
   The worst is yet to come. Keep the gun with you. Always remember I love you. Nothing in this crazy world makes sense except love. Not for one minute would I trade fame or money for loving you.

Through tear-blurred eyes she turned the page and read the final three lines. Then she pressed her lips to his signature, asking God to watch over him.

Evidently Ian had inside information. The following day instructions came for the Maltese to remain in bomb shelters and set up communal "victory" kitchens rather than returning home after each air raid. Pithany and the other workers were given instructions for the speediest way to destroy the radio equipment used by Y Services. All across the island, men prepared to disable the hundreds of radio masts used to receive and transmit Allied messages as well as listen to German dispatches. The clergy supported their efforts: the church bells would remain silent and would ring only to signal an invasion.

The Luftwaffe pounded Malta, upping two raids a day to four or more. Even if the islanders had been allowed to go home, they couldn't. Gypsy encampments sprang up around the entrances to shelters. Each day after her shift, Pithany joined her father at one such encampment. She would find him sitting instead of being out with the men who were foraging in the ruined buildings for anything they could burn. It was now crucial to conserve what little fuel they did have for the RAF.

Pithany tried her best to give her father courage even though the exhausting hours in the tunnel sapped her energy. But all that interested him was reading *The Times of Malta*. Despite the heavy bombing, the paper had never missed an edition.

Each day, he'd rattle the newspaper under her nose saying, "You see, Pithany Anne, the Nazis are bombing Malta more than they are London. Why?" She would explain to him how Malta's role as a fleet base and intelligence center was causing havoc with Rommel's supply line. Her father would grunt his understanding, then he'd fall silent for another day.

By March, the food supplies had been consumed. Bread, the staple of the Maltese diet, was baked under government supervision to deter theft. Its crisp crust was usually tastier than its cousin, French bread, but it became heavy when potatoes—some said sawdust—were used to extend the minuscule reserve of flour. The islanders knew better than to complain. They had nothing else to eat except carob beans and prickly pears—animal fodder. Some of the men did manage to bring in a few fish with lines strung from shore, but the island was too heavily mined for them to sail to the fishing banks where they could catch enough fish to make a difference.

On April 15th, Lieutenant General Dobbie summoned the islanders to St. John Square. Before the war, the square had been the site of the outdoor market where people brought carts of goods and bartered until noon. But today, Pithany stood beside her father and looked up at the weary Dobbie standing on the steps of St. John's Co-Cathedral, the knights' own church. She marveled that a bomb hadn't destroyed the baroque masterpiece.

An even more impressive miracle was the number of people still alive despite the bombing and the blockade. Hundreds had been wounded in the air raids. No one had starved yet, but many were weakened by malnutrition. They were a brave lot, she thought, proud to be Maltese.

"I have a message from King George VI," Dobbie called out over a megaphone. " 'To honor her brave people I award the George Cross to the Island Fortress of Malta to bear witness to a Heroism and Devotion that will long be famous in history.' " Dobbie beamed his approval to the astonished crowd. "Let me remind you of Queen Elizabeth I's words when this island faced Süleyman and the overwhelming might of the Islamic empire: 'If the Turks shall prevail against the Isle of Malta it is uncertain what further peril might follow to the rest of Christendom.' "

Dobbie raised a weary hand to forestall the group's cheers. "I could say many things, but I think Nelson, the greatest naval commander that ever lived, said it best. At the battle of Trafalgar, facing the combined forces of the French and Spanish navies, Nelson told his men: 'England expects every man shall do his duty.' Here on Malta, we know our duty. The world is counting on us. We won't let them down."

A cheer went up; but her father merely stared ahead.

Pithany whispered to her father, "The king gave us the cross for withstanding a hundred days of continuous air raids. Even London hasn't been subjected to as many bombs. Never have so many tons of explosives fallen on one place."

"Don't be fooled," her father said. "The cross is just a morale booster. The end isn't near."

Pithany didn't answer. At times her father's sharp insight returned, and he became as lucid as he'd once been. But if the war didn't end soon, he might slip over the edge forever.

She left him in the square playing *brilli* with his friends and walked to her job. Tony Bradford caught up with her in front of the *Auberge de Castile et Leon.* Once the most impressive of the inns that housed the knights, the *auberge* had been severely damaged by bombs.

"I hear your father's getting worse," Tony said, almost sounding concerned.

Pithany kept walking.

"He'd be better off on Gozo."

"Wouldn't we all?" She couldn't keep the bitterness out of her voice. The Maltese republic consisted of three islands, Malta, Gozo, and Comino. Comino was too small to be much more than a sandy cay once used by boaters for Sunday outings. But Gozo with its rolling hills and placid beaches—but no military installations—was a safe haven. The Germans didn't waste bombs on it. When the war began, some Maltese were farsighted enough to ship their loved ones to Gozo.

"I can get him there," Tony said, emphasizing "I."

She banked a scathing retort, realizing this might be the only chance she had of saving her father. But she doubted she had anything valuable enough to trade for passage on a boat. "How much?"

He studied her, his dark eyes intense. "Nothing."

She didn't believe him—Tony was notorious for making money whenever he could. What was he after? It didn't matter. This might be her only opportunity to get her father to the safety of a village where life had some semblance of normality. Away from the thunderous noise of the continual bombing, her father might recover.

"How soon could you arrange it?"

Tony smiled, a knowing smile that said: Everyone has a price. "Tomorrow night."

Pithany discovered that tomorrow night meant they had to begin their journey at dawn the next morning. With fuel so precious, they were forced to ride in a donkey cart to Marfa Point through *nebbia,* the cold wet fog that blew in from Italy. Without success Pithany tried to chat with her father as they rode, realizing this might be the last time she saw him. She'd long since stopped worrying about herself, but she couldn't help being concerned about him. Maneuvering through the mine-ridden channel between Malta and Gozo would be a challenge for the captain of the boat. Surviving on Gozo would be her father's challenge. He had friends there. But no one to love him.

Her thoughts, as they usually did, turned to Ian, and she wondered how he was. The *nebbia* had lifted, and a typical sunny day revealed the lush rolling countryside Ian had never seen. In the short time he'd been on Malta, they'd never gone beyond Valletta. When he returned, they'd picnic at *Ghajn Tuffieha,* Pithany promised herself. The spring surrounded by a copse of trees and wild fennel had been her mother's favorite spot. Ian would love it.

"No!" Her father pointed to a sign that read: MAR-SAXLOKK BAY, indicating it was ahead of them three miles.

"Remember, Daddy," she explained patiently. "I told you all Malta's signs now face in the opposite direction. We know where we're going, but strangers won't. It worked in France. The Resistance turned the signs around and delayed the Nazis. In the confusion, many Resistance leaders escaped. If the Nazis land here—" She stopped; his eyes had that vacant look again.

It took them the entire day to travel from Valletta to Marfa Point. In a car it would have taken them less than an hour, but Pithany didn't mind. This was her first chance to enjoy the countryside resplendent in its spring cloak of wildflowers. By midsummer the heat would turn the green hills to amber until fall came and Malta experienced its "second spring" with another crop of wildflowers.

Marfa Point came into view with the deserted pier the Malta-Gozo ferry once used for its daily run.

"Look! Black crows!" Tony pointed to the sky, using RAF slang for the Luftwaffe.

Pithany and the driver followed Tony's lead and jumped from the cart. Tony hauled her father—oblivious to any danger—from the cart. They hid among the huge boulders surrounding Marfa Point. The "crows" flew in low. Evidently, they'd spotted the cart because they strafed the road.

"Sonofabitch! Look at all the bullets they have to waste," said Tony.

Pithany watched the donkey, its spindly legs trembling, praying he wouldn't be hit. Before the war, Joey had belonged to Abdul, the baker. One of the most welcome sights on Malta had been lop-eared Joey with his harness of jingling bells, coming up the street delivering fresh baked bread. Like all the other work animals gentle Joey, accustomed to children's pats and the cheerful greetings of adults, had been commandeered by the military.

The next plane came in even lower than the first. A burst of shots kicked up dust on the road. The following plane flew in—lower still—taking a direct bead on the terrified donkey. Joey bolted, charging down the slope out of sight, the cart rattling behind. Pithany cursed the Nazis. They were notorious for firing on farmers caught in the open during an air raid. But to torment helpless

Joey was senselessly cruel. But what did she expect? She'd heard enough reports to know mercy wasn't in the Nazi vocabulary.

The last of the planes passed and the group crawled out from among the rocks. They raced across the road and peered down the embankment. At the bottom lay Joey, the cart on top of him. He whimpered, a piteous, almost human sound.

It took Tony, the driver, and Pithany to push the cart off the donkey. Joey valiantly tried to stand up, pawing the grass with his front hooves, but his hips were crushed, several broken bones piercing the skin, starkly white against his bloodied coat.

"Sonofabitch," Tony cursed the animal.

"It's not Joey's fault," Pithany said. "Put him out of his misery."

"With what?" Tony asked. "I'm off duty. I'd have to go back to the base to get my gun."

Pithany drew the derringer out of her pocket and handed it to Tony. He looked puzzled, but didn't question her. With one hand on the donkey's snout to steady him, he aimed between Joey's soulful eyes and fired a single shot. The donkey's head flopped to the ground, ears sagging backward. From the small hole between Joey's still-open eyes trickled a stream of blood.

"Get to Biskra fast," Tony ordered the driver, naming the nearest village. "Tell Josef to bring his cart and men just as soon as the Krauts head back to Sicily."

Pithany didn't have to ask why Tony needed the men. She stared at Joey; his tortured eyes pleaded with her. The men would butcher him and sell every ounce— bones included—on the black market. She bent down and eased the donkey's eyes shut, then paused to run her hand over his long ears. "You can't butcher Joey. He's like a pet."

"Would you rather people starve?" Tony handed her back the gun.

Pithany shook her head. People were forced to eat anything now. Just last night one of the men living in their shelter had bought a skinned rabbit on the black market. It looked suspiciously like a cat to Janna. Rabbits, once assumed to be impossible to eliminate, had vanished. People had turned their house cats loose months ago. A few wily ones could still be found foraging for rats around the shipyards.

Her father came over and put his arm around Pithany. "I'll never forgive the Germans," she said. "They've reduced us to this." Her father pulled her away. "Goodbye, Joey," she said over her shoulder.

Pithany let her father lead her to the old ferry landing where they sat down on pilings shattered by Nazi bombs. In the distance they heard the Nazis pummeling Valletta. Soon the Luftwaffe turned north swooping low over the hills on the horizon where lookout points were. They weren't coming their way this time; they were targeting the antiaircraft guns on the west facing beach.

For the first time in months her father talked, reminiscing about the days when the family would trek on Malta's trails. At lunch, her mother would open the wicker basket her father carried and they'd have a picnic.

"Life was simpler then," her father said.

How well she remembered those days. She could still see her younger sister, Audrey toddling along, trying to keep up with her. And Pithany could vividly recall her mother stopping to talk to the widows dressed in black and sitting in doorways making lace. Her mother would pause to chat with them, bringing the inland villagers news of "the city," Valletta.

"Do you miss Mama . . . still?" Pithany asked. Her

father had been extremely depressed when his wife had died, but she'd been gone for years now.

He studied her for a moment. "I'll always miss her. When you love someone that much, you don't forget them. Not ever." He smiled, his old familiar smile. "But your mother isn't gone. She lives on in you. We all live on in our children. That's eternal life. You have no idea what a comfort you've been to me since Emily passed on. I couldn't have raised Audrey without you."

She put her arm around him, resting her head on his shoulder. Was she making a mistake, sending him away when he might need her?

"You're just like Emily," he continued. "You have the Crandall hair and eyes, but you inherited your mother's inner strength. She would have handled this war far better than I have."

"You'll be fine, Papa. I promise. On Gozo there's food. You'll be safe there."

Her father looked over his shoulder. Behind them Tony was supervising a group of men hurrying to butcher Joey before the sun set. She couldn't look. Her father drew her close. "I know what you've done. You've given me a chance at life. I just hope it's not too big a sacrifice."

She shoved all thoughts of Tony Bradford aside. She could deal with them tomorrow in the lonely darkness of the tunnel. Or in her even lonelier hours off duty. She wouldn't let Tony spoil her last hours with her father.

Her father pointed to the horizon where a dark shadow moved, threading through the whitecaps. The boat from Gozo approached. The little girl in Pithany cried out: *Don't leave me, Papa.*

In silence they clung to each other, neither verbalizing the bitter truth. These could very well be their last moments together. When the boat pulled up to a piling, using it for a pier, having skillfully avoided the mines,

Pithany couldn't hold back the tears. In a silent parade, they dribbled down her cheeks.

"The tears of history. Men and women saying good-bye, separated by a war not of their making. In the end, many will die, more will suffer but the world won't change." He handed her his handkerchief. "Promise me you'll take care of Audrey." He stepped onto the boat.

"I will, Papa," she promised, thankful Audrey was in the relative safety of England with family friends, the Athertons.

"If something should happen . . . to either of us . . . remember, you never lose those you truly love. Not even death can take them from you. They live on. Forever in your heart."

10

✳

The sun was rising, casting misty bars of light through the *nebbia* when Pithany and Tony returned to Valletta. They stopped at a broken-down hut on the outskirts of the city. A trio of men rushed out to unload the donkey meat and the few burlap sacks of vegetables and fruit brought over from Gozo by the boat that had picked up her father.

"Why don't you give the food to Father Cippi?" Pithany asked, trying once again to convince Tony to do the right thing. Although she couldn't imagine eating any donkey meat herself, many on the island were desperate enough not to ask what they were eating. "He keeps lists of what each shelter has received. He would distribute the food fairly."

Tony smiled, the same cocksure grin she'd instinctively mistrusted from the moment she'd met him and trusted even less since witnessing his cavalier attitude in carving up Joey for profit. "You're nuts. I'm not giving up the bundle I'll make on this."

Pithany turned away from the cart. Blood dripped from the wooden slats. In her mind she could still see Joey's soft brown eyes pleading with her. That image faded, replaced by the memory of her father standing on the ship's stern waving good-bye. She'd watched as they navigated the channel, fingers crossed, praying they didn't hit a mine. Unlike Joey, fate smiled on the ship. It skillfully avoided the mines.

Tony came out of the shed. "Let's go. I'm on duty in two hours."

He walked her to the crossroads where trucks shuttled goods from the docks to Luqa Field, the RAF base. Here Tony could catch a ride while she walked to her shelter. He waved to an approaching truck.

"Tony, I can't thank you—I don't know how to thank you enough." She tried to force more gratitude into her voice. It wasn't that she was ungrateful, but the incident with Joey had solidified her negative feelings about Tony Bradford. If there's ever anything—"

"I'm off Friday. I'll pick you up at five."

"I'm scheduled—"

"Trade shifts." Tony jumped on the truck's running-board.

Before she could answer, Pithany was left standing in the road, the truck lumbering away, sending rooster tails of dust from beneath the tires. She walked to her shelter thankful she didn't have to report to Y Services for a few hours. As she went, she realized just what the price was for letting Tony help her father. Romance? No, more likely he was interested in sex.

Why? There were many prettier, wealthier girls he could have chosen. Why would Tony seek Pithany out? Unquestionably he had from the very first. Even before Ian had arrived, Tony had been friendly to her. Overly so. Why?

She still didn't have a clue when Friday night came. Pithany hadn't bothered to trade shifts. She hoped she could discourage Tony, show him she wasn't interested. When she emerged from the skein of tunnels after work, a sliver of a moon lit the rubble that had once been the knights' majestic buildings. She was thankful for the dim light; it would allow her eyes to adjust without the pain-

ful headaches sunlight caused. Out of the darkness
emerged an ominous shadow blocking the moonlight.

"I told you to trade shifts." Tony's voice cut through
the silent night as deadly as any Luftwaffe bomb.

Remembering what he'd done for her father, Pithany
steeled herself to be pleasant. "You didn't give me a
chance to explain why I can't go out with you."

"What in hell are you talking about?"

"I'm engaged," she said, holding up her hand with the
silver ring. "I'm going to marry Ian MacShane."

Tony hauled her into his arms until his nose was
inches from hers. "No. You're not. You're going to
marry me."

She gasped.

"We're perfect for each other."

"I love Ian. I'll never love anyone else. I can't marry
you."

"You don't have any choice." He turned on his heel
and walked away, his words echoing through the deserted streets.

A premonition of danger gripped her. She caught up
with him. "Why me? Any girl on this island—"

"None of them are Crandalls from Devonshire, are
they?"

She stopped dead in her tracks, the truth all too clear.
Her father was the youngest son of Baron Chilton, Oli-
ver Crandall. They could trace their ancestors back to
the Norman Conquest. Even now, while Pithany was en-
during the hardships of war, her younger sister, Audrey,
was being sheltered by the Athertons. Cedric Atherton,
the Earl of Lyforth was one of the wealthiest, most powerful men in England. And an old family friend. The
Crandalls had entrée to British society; a door even a
regiment of RAF medals could never open.

Ever since the British had wrested Malta from Napoleon, a Crandall son—never the heir, of course—had

been sent to the island to look after family business interests. Under the Union Jack, the island and the Crandalls prospered. But the Maltese branch of the family suffered "the knight's curse"—some claimed it was caused by the water collected in rooftop cisterns—never producing sons. Pithany's father had come to Malta to take over from his childless uncle.

"The curse" plagued her father's generation in a way it never had previous Crandalls. Nigel Crandall was one of three sons. Surely, one of them would have been expected to produce a male heir. But no—curse of curses —their wives bore only girls. Pithany's two uncles had died before the war. She knew beyond a doubt her own father would never remarry. That left Pithany Anne Crandall the heir to the Crandall properties in Malta with impeccable social connections in England.

"I can handle your father's businesses," Tony said, his voice suddenly as soft as the moonlight falling on the bay. He touched her cheek; a gesture that was surprisingly gentle. "You provide the class. Our children will be educated in England. Marry anyone they want."

"No. Never—"

"You don't think I'm the only one who's interested in the Crandall connections? Why in hell do you think MacShane wants to marry you? When this war's over, he can land any job. But his sons won't waltz into Eton or Harrow unless they have what you people like to call breeding."

Pithany turned and charged up the narrow street, tripping over debris scattered by the night's bombing. Ian couldn't be so cold, so calculating. He loved her. She might have had her doubts earlier, but the letter had erased them. He'd asked her to marry him—not to gain a position in British society—but because he loved her.

Ian MacShane possessed one of the rarest of personality traits—integrity. During his weekly radio broadcast, he emphasized the troops' courage. Unlike some reporters, he never practiced yellow journalism, harping on war's seamier side—donkeys served up on the black market as aged veal or high command mix-ups that cost lives. If he'd been the scheming, conniving man Tony would have her believe, Ian would have tried to make her divulge confidential information that she'd learned. But he never had. If Tony had been in the same position, he would have tried to wring every last bit of top secret information from her.

Pithany didn't see Tony Bradford again for weeks, and she wouldn't have missed him except that she wanted to ask him to return the gun Ian had given her. She thought about the gun more when Rommel's spring successes in the desert put the British forces valiantly holding Tobruk at risk. If Tobruk fell most people assumed Malta would be next.

In late June, Pithany was washing her clothes in a bucket of rainwater she'd collected and cursing the Luftwaffe's bombs for destroying the water pipes, when she heard shouts from the vendor delivering *The Times of Malta.*

"Extra! Extra! Read all about it! Rommel breaks through lines at Tobruk!"

Pithany dropped the wet dress and raced, barefoot, down the street. Her foot cut on a shard of glass, she barreled through the pitch-black tunnel, going by instinct, to her post with the Y Services. She rounded the bend then slammed to a stop. All the lights were on; operators huddled over tablets of paper, recording messages.

The watch supervisor waved her over and shoved a headset at her. "If Tobruk falls, we're next," he said.

Pithany clamped her headset to her ears, then removed it and gave it a good shake, hoping to clear the lines. When she put the headset on again, she realized it was functioning properly. With so many radio messages competing for airspace, frequencies were jamming. She concentrated, desperately trying to record messages before other dispatches "stepped on" them. She prayed for the British soldiers. For Ian. Where had he been when Rommel breached the British lines?

Surely, he'd taken cover, opting to use his skills as a reporter to bring the battle alive for his listeners. But she wasn't positive. Ian regretted the childhood injury that had prevented him from serving his country. He'd been left with a permanent limp from a rugby accident, but Ian ignored his bad knee. When the Germans stormed the British lines, she knew he wouldn't grab his pencil while the others did the fighting. Uniform or no uniform, he would fight alongside them.

Through the longest day of her life, Pithany listened, diligently transcribing messages. Memories of flawless blue eyes and a single-dimpled smile threatened to interfere. She forced her mind to focus on the scrambled transmissions, knowing lives were at stake. She worked around the clock, her heart aching at Rommel's *blitzkrieg* advance. By dawn the following morning she knew the score: a complete rout. Still, the British refused to admit defeat.

Four hours later, they were forced to formally surrender.

The silence of despair hung over the Y Services. No one bothered to turn out the lights. Pithany barely heard her supervisor instructing the operators to listen even more carefully to German transmissions: Malta had to anticipate the exact moment of invasion in order to destroy valuable equipment. She longed to know about Ian. Was he among the thousands taken prisoner?

"I know you've worked three back-to-back shifts, but I need you even more now. Are you up to it?" When Pithany nodded, her supervisor added, "Listen to ship movements. Let me know which of our ships are coming here."

She listened eagerly, hoping Ian had made it to a ship, but knowing the chances weren't good. Tobruk was a small port; not many ships had been anchored there. The British had defended the city to the last moment—choosing surrender over retreat. Not many men could have made it to a ship before the Germans captured them.

Those ships that did escape sent a short radio message and then maintained radio silence so they couldn't be tracked by the U boats hounding Allied ships. Most ships were bound for Gibraltar, she discovered after listening to numerous transmissions. She assumed that meant the British were abandoning Malta. After all, the island was much closer to Tobruk than Gibraltar. She slipped her hand into her pocket automatically reaching for the gun. Gone. She'd forgotten Tony still had it. It didn't matter. Some months ago, Pithany had admitted to herself she wouldn't honor her promise to Ian. She couldn't take her own life.

Late that night when Rommel's men were undoubtedly celebrating their leader's new title, Field Marshal, conferred upon him by the Fuehrer as a reward for his successful North African campaign, Pithany picked up a message from a British supply ship hastily leaving Gazala for Malta. A single word followed the brief message: falcon.

"Thank you, God," Pithany whispered. She closed her eyes and a mental map of the African coast appeared. Ian must have been with the forces at the Gazala Line due west of Tobruk. He would reach Malta at dawn.

Despite being so weary she could hardly hold her pencil to record messages, she smiled, the first heartfelt smile in months. Ian was coming back to her. At last.

As the night passed transmissions from land bases

slacked off. Though she could have left, she stayed at her post. Other operators were picking up increased radio traffic from German boats sailing toward Tobruk. Vultures homing in after a kill. To reach Malta, Ian's ship HRM *Nelson* would have to pass through a Nazi dragnet. *Don't let them spot the* Nelson. *Please.*

"What's the weather like?" Pithany called out to the other operators during a lull in radio transmissions.

"Crystal clear. Full moon."

"God," she whispered to herself, "send a *xlokk,* or a *nebbia* or something. Anything but a 'bomber's moon.'"

A squawk over the wireless became a short message: The Germans had spotted the *Nelson.* Pithany dropped her pencil, clamped both hands over her headset, slamming it flush with her ears and mentally translated incoming transmissions. Head bent, eyes closed—for once she cursed the light—she listened. Praying. She estimated the *Nelson's* position at about an hour off Malta's coast. Maybe, just maybe, they could make port before the wolf pack closed in.

Seconds later the *Heidelberg* fired the first torpedo. A second. A third.

"SOS," signaled the *Nelson.* "SOS."

"Somebody help them," Pithany screamed.

Her supervisor touched her shoulder. "Only the bloody Nazis are in their zone."

Pithany groaned. Despite the Geneva Conventions, Nazis never picked up survivors.

"Abandon ship. Abandon ship." The radio operator on the *Nelson* relayed the captain's message.

The *Heidelberg* instructed her sister ship the *Pruller* to fire on the disabled *Nelson.*

"No," Pithany moaned. "Give them a chance. Let them launch the lifeboats."

"Direct hit," responded the *Pruller.*

Pithany imagined Ian treading water in the choppy

seas, still brutally cold at this time of year. Perhaps he'd been sucked under and even now was fighting, courageously struggling, his lungs bursting, desperately trying to reach the surface.

"Dear Lord, take him quickly. I beg you. Don't let him suffer."

Did it hurt to die? she wondered. It must. Cold. Alone. A watery unmarked grave. The last three lines of the single love letter Ian had written replayed, its words long since memorized.

If anything happens to me, Ace, look for me in the shadows, in the darkness. We met without a light to guide us. And out of the dark came the greatest gift of all—love. A love for all time.

"A love for all time," she whispered to herself. "A love for all time."

In that instant, she knew he was gone.

Images swirled blurred by the tears in her eyes: Her father waving good-bye—maybe forever; Joey lying in the green grass, his soft ears covered with blood; Ian smiling the single-dimple smile she loved.

A desperate dialogue ran through her thoughts. Things she'd wanted to share with him. Loving words she had longed to whisper. Now she would never have the chance.

"You said you'd be back," she screamed. "You promised. You promised. You . . . promised."

Janna put her arms around Aunt Pith, wanting desperately to say something—anything—but not knowing what. She'd never seen Aunt Pith, not once in all the years they'd been together. "I'm sorry, Aunt Pith. So sorry."

Sorry, such a hollow word, Janna thought. Overused.

It didn't bring an iota of comfort. The agony of losing
Ian MacShane etched her aunt's face. Janna felt it, too,
realizing for the first time why Aunt Pith had never married. Instead she'd given the love meant for Ian to Janna
and the rest of the family.

Aunt Pith wiped her tears with a lace handkerchief.
"Goodness. I didn't mean to cry." She gazed into
Janna's teary eyes and continued, talking more to herself
than to Janna. "I got over the loss. Really, I did. After a
time days would go by and I wouldn't think of Ian. As
years passed, images blurred. I couldn't remember his
face exactly. I never had a picture, you know, just my
memory.

Janna understood that his memory alone had sustained her. One great love had touched Aunt Pith's
heart, firing her soul and lingering forever. A love for all
time.

"I would try to recall our talks but they refused to
come. That's when I discovered you can't call memories
up at will and relive the moment," Aunt Pith said. "Our
minds don't work that way. Something has to trigger a
memory for it to reappear as real as if it were happening
again. That's why when people die they don't truly leave
us. They're in the scent of spring flowers, in the sunset,
in a song. One day just last year— Never mind, I sound
like a silly old lady."

"No. You don't. Tell me, please."

"Last year there was a fire at the shipyards. It was
midday and naturally, I was working in my office in Valletta. The wind blew the smoke in my window. Suddenly,
an image as sharp as you are to me now sprang from the
recesses of my mind. I could feel—I swear I could feel—
Ian's arms around me, his lips against my ear whispering
it would be all right. We were in a bomb shelter and a
fuel storage tank had been struck. It smelled exactly like
the smoke coming from the shipyard fire. I'd almost for-

gotten that particular air raid until then. I wouldn't let the staff close my windows. I'm certain they thought I was crazy."

A surge of guilt swept through Janna, overwhelming the pain Aunt Pith's story evoked. All these years, Janna had taken the love Aunt Pith had offered for granted, never asking herself if Aunt Pith was happy. When Janna had told Aunt Pith about Collis's betrayal, she'd comforted Janna.

There'd been no one to comfort Aunt Pith.

Alone. Absolutely alone. Janna couldn't imagine it. Aunt Pith and Warren—even Audrey—had been there to guide Janna and love her. She put her arms around her aunt and hugged her. "Aunt Pith, I never told you how much I love you." She squeezed harder, the words stalling in her throat. "I don't know what I would have done without you."

Aunt Pith smiled, a wise but melancholy smile. "I didn't mean to make you sad. Don't think I haven't had a happy life. You've been a joy to me. From the moment you could talk, you had the sharp eye for detail, the memory, the ability to pick up languages quickly. You reminded me of myself."

"Too smart for my own good." Janna studied Aunt Pithany a moment, realizing they were alike in many ways. "I'll bet you were too. Did you frighten the boys away?"

"Most of them."

"Me too. I didn't have very many girlfriends, either— except Shadoe. Even Audrey found me strange."

"Don't blame Audrey. She's like my father. I believed his problems were caused by 'bomb happiness.' But I came to realize he'd been depressed his whole life. Back then, we didn't know how to treat it. That's why I've insisted Audrey have medical attention even though Reginald would have preferred to ignore her problems."

"Chronic depression." Janna smiled. "It's hereditary. I've often wondered if I'd get it. Now, that's one thing I don't have to worry about. It appears as if Tony Bradford will be my biggest problem." Janna hesitated a moment, reluctant to bring up the past, unwilling to cause her aunt more pain.

"You're wondering what happened after Ian died," Aunt Pith said, looking directly at Janna, totally in control once more. "Actually, Tony was quite kind. He'd been flying back and forth from Malta to Bardia where the British were regrouping. After one mission, he brought me flowers from Bardia. He also returned the gun Ian had given me. I still have Ian's gun," she said wistfully. "It's in the bottom drawer of my nightstand. I hate guns, but I kept his for sentimental reasons. Of course, it's never been used."

"You didn't need Ian's gun. The Germans never invaded Malta."

"No. Montgomery took command of the British forces and drove Rommel from El Alamein and Tobruk. The Soviets had launched a counteroffensive at Stalingrad. Late 1942. The tide of the war had turned, but we didn't know it. Tony kept asking me to marry him, but I refused."

"He was certainly persistent."

"Yes. Understand one thing. Anthony Bradford isn't called 'Big Tony' for no reason. He's physically large with an even bigger ego. He was obsessed with creating a Bradford dynasty—and still is. Tony came out of the war a rich man from his black market profits. He acquired the shipyards and purchased a palace in Mdina."

"Did he try to buy your father's businesses?"

"Yes. He insisted I could never rebuild my father's three hotels without marrying him."

"But he did marry, otherwise Curt wouldn't be here."

"Tony Bradford married a month after you were born.

Fifteen years after we'd first met. Curt was born the following year. It wasn't a happy marriage. Tony's wife moved home to Zurrieq a number of years ago. She died recently."

"Even after all this time, Tony wants your hotels?" Janna found such an obsession difficult to imagine. It suggested a man who was mentally unbalanced.

"Yes. Remember, it took me years to get approval to build the Blue Grotto."

Janna vividly recalled the nasty fight. Tony had blocked her permit to build on the undeveloped coastline, championing the Maltese hunters who used the bluffs around the Blue Grotto Lagoon. The hunters would sit by the hour with small bird cages a short distance away. When flocks of birds migrating from Europe to Africa flew over Malta, they were attracted by the caged birds' songs and swooped low to investigate, only to be killed.

Janna had spearheaded the tactic that finally secured the permit. Although the sport dated back to the knights themselves and was an integral part of the island tradition, Janna arranged a media campaign that shamed the hunters. The birds they shot weren't killed for food, just for sport. And many being killed belonged to the saintly ranks of the endangered. The tourist industry tipped the scales when it received complaints from tour groups insisting the slaughter stop. Pithany was awarded her building permit and hunting in the area was stopped.

Pithany managed a wan smile. "I think he hoped to wait me out and then buy out my heirs. Since he discovered you were planning to help me, Tony has aggressively tried to acquire my stock."

"You should have told me all this years ago." Janna realized that in many ways Aunt Pith played it close to the vest. She'd had to rely on herself—alone—for so long that she rarely confided in anyone. Even Janna.

11

*

"High tea. Jeee-zus!" Nick said under his breath, cursing himself for accepting the invitation. He knotted his tie, then checked his reflection in the mirror of his London hotel room. "Admit it, Tinhorn, you're curious." He wanted to see what the Athertons would do next to get his shares, so he'd agreed to join Warren Atherton for tea.

Besides satisfying his curiosity, meeting the Earl of Lyforth had provided Nick with an excuse to duck out on Mark Nolan and his new wife, Glennis. The group of Imperial Cola executives in London for meetings on the joint venture with Tewkes Beverages was having an early dinner before going to the theater. Warren's invitation had given Nick a good reason not to join them.

"Tea?" he muttered, shaking his head at his reflection. In Muleshoe, if two men had something to discuss, they said, "Meet'chu at Wiseacres." And they would settle their differences over a brew in the dark bar with country music blaring from the jukebox. Didn't work that way in Japan. It wasn't going to be that way in England either.

Nick assumed Pithany had called Warren and let him know Nick was coming to London on business. Three days ago when he'd checked in at The Dukes in St. James, there had been a message from Warren. He'd invited Nick for dinner at his club but Nick had been too busy with meetings to join him. Then Warren had pressed him into coming for tea.

The earl was in a hell of a hurry to meet you. Nick adjusted the lapels of his suit, realizing the Athertons weren't simply interested in buying his shares. They were desperate. Nick ventured a guess that the Bradfords had gotten their hands on more stock—even though no one had mentioned it.

For a moment Nick wondered what Janna had learned when she'd gone to Rome to discuss the Bradfords with Pithany. He doubted Janna's aunt would tell her the whole truth. Nick had been willing to return his shares for exactly what Travis had paid for them. He didn't have the heart to make a profit off the woman who'd befriended Travis. But Pithany had refused his offer, and she had asked Nick not to sell anyone his shares until he was transferred from Malta. Her insistence that he not reveal their arrangement to Janna puzzled Nick. Had to be some kind of weird test that would force Janna to hound Nick, believing she could wrangle the stock from him.

He checked his watch and saw it was too early to get a taxi to the Belgravia address Warren had given him. Nick turned on the television and flipped the channels, searching for CNN. He clicked past one channel and the name "Lyforth" caught his ear. He turned back.

A starchy-looking man in a trench coat was speaking into the microphone. The words "recorded earlier" were printed across the bottom of the screen. "The Earl of Lyforth has just addressed the House of Lords recommending restricting licenses of television networks operating via satellites."

The man beside the reporter appeared to be about Nick's age, perhaps a year or so younger. If central casting had been contacted, they couldn't have found anyone who fit the part better. Tall and lean with wheat-colored hair and pale blue eyes, Warren Atherton fit Nick's image of a modern-day earl: distinguished—just short of being stuffy.

The reporter thrust the microphone at Warren. "What prompted your speech today?"

"I'm outraged at the British Satellite Broadcasting program, *Heil Honey, I'm Home*. It's offensive, in bad taste, and what's more it demeans the struggle we British underwent to defeat Hitler."

Warren gazed directly into the camera, his look so sincere that he seemed to be saying: I have your best interests at heart. Charisma. Nick knew it when he saw it. So few men possessed it. Couldn't buy it. You were either born with charisma or would never have it.

"For those viewers not familiar with this television program," the reporter continued, "let's run a few clips."

Nick watched as short segments from a sitcom about the domestic life of Adolf Hitler and Eva Braun flashed across the screen. The actors spoke with New York accents but were shown living in a run-down Berlin apartment building. Their trials centered around their nosy Jewish neighbors, the Goldensteins. This episode made fun of Neville Chamberlain coming to dinner to discuss "peace in our time," only to have the pushy Goldensteins arrive and get drunk.

"I believe," Warren said when the clips finished, "the commission needs to review the types of programming these channels are planning *before* granting them licenses."

"Stay tuned," the reporter said. "I'll be interviewing Hayim Pinner, Secretary General of the Board of Deputies of British Jews after this word from our sponsor. I'll be back straight away."

Nick didn't have time to listen to Pinner, but he could well imagine what he thought about this program.

Pithany Crandall wouldn't appreciate the program either, Nick decided as he rushed downstairs. He sympathized with her. She'd literally spent years underground fighting the Nazis. To her it would never be a laughing matter.

The doorman hailed a taxi for Nick. The driver immediately noticed Nick's accent and launched into a tour guide's explanation of how the nearby St. James Palace had been built by Henry VIII and had been home to the ruling monarch for much longer than Buckingham Palace. If Nick wanted to watch the changing of the guard without getting into the mob at Buckingham Palace, he could see them at the courtyard opposite Marlborough House. Nick said, "Interesting," now and again, but he wasn't really listening.

It took longer than Nick had expected to slog through rush hour traffic—it hadn't looked very far on the map—to reach Belgravia, a neighborhood where a couple of million bucks wouldn't get you noticed. Rows of Georgian town houses, stately trees, pricey cars decorating the curbs. Flags hung from various embassies along Eaton Square, drooping in the damp fog rolling in off the Thames. The area reminded Nick of what London must have been like a hundred years earlier before security cameras, bodyguards, and attack dogs became necessities.

They turned onto Loundes Place and stopped in front of a house that was even larger than the others. Nick paid the driver and rushed up the steps, noting the Grecian urns—probably the real thing, not phony repos like those in Hensley's Funeral Parlor—filled with dozens of daffodils and a small white flower Nick didn't recognize. He thumped the fox head knocker and straightened his tie.

A uniformed butler escorted Nick through the marble entry lined with what had to be Impressionist paintings.

Old moolah. Didn't exist in Texas. Nick hadn't encountered it in high-tech Japan either, but here it surrounded him. He followed the servant into a large room where several people were gathered, preparing himself for a full court press by the Athertons. Trimmed in gold, the barrel ceiling featured some artist's vision of heaven with bare-assed angels romping through clouds playing harps and blowing kisses at each other. He hardly noticed the dynamite redhead sitting alone, because his eyes were drawn to the far side of the room where Warren and Janna were standing by the fireplace. Janna was smiling at her brother, a trusting, loving smile. Then she laughed at something he'd said.

Instinctively, Nick stepped back. The sight of Janna and Warren—their affection for each other so obvious—brought back a riptide of memories. Nick recalled arriving at the Prescotts' for the first time years ago. Austin had sent Nick out to the backyard where Travis and Amanda Jane were tending the barbecue. Nick had come to the sliding door and stopped, watching Amanda Jane and Travis across the yard. He'd been struck by their obvious closeness. Their love.

Until that evening in Houston, Nick hadn't been able to name what he'd been missing. Missing his entire life. As the aroma of sizzling steaks hit him, the truth hit him harder. His mother had always walked a mental tightrope, never quite falling off, but always on the verge. She was incapable of love. She hadn't even loved Cody. His brother's death had merely given her something besides her ex-husband to cry over.

What Nick wanted, what he needed, was his own family to love. He wouldn't desert them the way his father had. He'd be there at every Little League game. Hell, he might have daughters. What did they do? He wasn't sure. But he was positive carousing till dawn in honky-tonk bars with shitkickers and their broads was as much a dead-end as life in Muleshoe.

He remembered that Amanda Jane had looked over at him, her smile making her pretty face even prettier, her brown hair and eyes even sexier. He had watched her countless times at the plant, listening to the other guys' crude remarks, but he'd never spoken to her. He had believed Amanda Jane was too good for him. She gave him another encouraging smile. The smile that changed his life.

Nothing like the frosty stare Janna was giving him now. She'd looked up, obviously not expecting him. So serious, so uptight. He didn't know why he always had the urge to tease her, but undeniably he did. To throw her off balance even more, Nick forced himself to come up with his killer grin. By the time Janna had responded with a hesitant smile, her brother was halfway across the room.

"Come in," Warren Atherton said, his hand extended. He introduced himself, shaking Nick's hand with a firm grip.

As Warren introduced him to several men, Nick waited with a heightened sense of curiosity, expecting one of them to be Janna's husband. None of them was. Warren escorted him over to the sofa where the dazzling redhead was sitting and introduced them. The timbre of Warren's voice altered subtly, and Nick realized Shadoe Hunnicutt was more to Warren than "an old friend of Janna's."

Nick sat down beside Shadoe while Warren went to greet a new arrival. "So you've known Janna a long time," Nick said, trying to ease into some discussion of Janna's husband, curious about the man.

"Since France," Shadoe responded, looking him square in the eye, "when we met you."

Nick was seldom at a loss for words; this was one of

those rare moments. He wasn't the type of man women forgot—or confused with someone else. That fact hadn't made him conceited. More often it embarrassed him. "Wasn't me. I only recently met Janna in Malta."

"In the dark." A statement, not a question.

Nick quickly looked across the room at Janna. Her back was to him, but his gaze lingered on her hair. She'd had it cut since he'd seen her in Malta last week. Clipped in varying lengths, it gave her a more casual look. He wondered exactly what she'd told her friend about him. Had she mentioned Mdina? "Janna told you."

Shadoe shook her head. "She'll always meet you first in the dark. It's fate."

Was she teasing him, making fun of him mistaking Janna for a burglar?

"You were with us during the flight to Varenne," Shadoe said, her voice as soft as the pale yellow dress she wore.

"Nope," Nick said, deciding because Shadoe was Janna's friend didn't mean she had a brain in her head. She obviously had him confused with someone else. "The only time I visited France, I flew in and out of Orly. I've never been in Varain."

She smiled a strange smile and touched the unusual stone pendant she was wearing. Weird. Definitely weird.

"But weren't you drawn to a certain part of Paris? Didn't one area interest you more than others?"

"Not really. I did the usual tourist bit: the Louvre, the Eiffel Tower, Arc de Triomphe."

"That's it?"

He hesitated, then confessed, "There was one thing that really intrigued me."

"Varenne?" she asked expectantly.

"No. The sewers. They're fascinating. All that going

on beneath the streets. I really liked the tour of the sewers."

"You don't remember, do you?" she asked, clearly disappointed. "Most people don't. They just have a vague feeling of familiarity about a certain time or place. When you studied the French Revolution didn't you feel . . . sense you'd lived back then?"

Jeee-zus! The rich were different. They could afford loony-tune friends. He looked around for someone to rescue him. Janna was watching him, but when he caught her eye, she quickly looked away. "Couldn't even tell you the exact date of the French Revolution. Peasants were starving and that ditsy queen said to let them eat cake."

"I don't know how that rumor got started, but she never said that. Ask Janna."

Nick waved at Janna and she crossed the room. He didn't give a damn about what the queen of the guillotined dilettantes had said; he wanted to get away from Shadoe Hunnicutt. She was a knockout, but a few bricks shy of a full load. Reminded him of his mother.

Janna walked up saying, "We'll be serving tea in just a few minutes." She sat in the chair opposite them.

"I was explaining to Nick that Marie Antoinette never said: 'Let them eat cake.' Correct?"

"That's right. Years afterward, someone reported she'd said that, but no one who lived when she did ever mentioned it. Most scholars assume it was one of those stories that gains credibility with time."

Nick grinned at her, one of his dimpled smiles, taking perverse pleasure at how uncomfortable Janna looked when he did. "But the peasants were starving and good ole Marie was living high on the hog, so—"

"Actually, there isn't any evidence that the peasants were any worse off than they had been in previous years. But there had been unusual weather conditions that caused a mold to form on the grain. It was harvested anyway and made into bread. The theory many scholars accept is the bread baked from this contaminated grain caused a mild brain fever that made people irrational. A form of mass hysteria."

Just then, Warren came up. "Janna, if you like, we're ready for you to serve tea."

Nick jumped up. "I'll help."

"Thanks, but—"

"I'm dying to hear more about that mold." He took her arm and guided her across the room to where a servant had wheeled in a silver trolley of sandwiches and pastries.

"What's with your friend? She seems to think we met in some past life. In some town called Varain."

"Shadoe believes in magic runes, reincarnation, Tarot cards, astrology," Janna said as they reached the cart.

"You don't go for that b.s., do you?"

She looked up at him, but didn't quite meet his eyes. "Not all of it."

"Do you call an astrologer before you make a move, like Nancy Reagan?"

"No," she said, her tone defensive. "But I do check the paper every morning. Millions do, you know. Why else would every paper and many magazines publish horoscopes?"

"They're printed because people want an easy answer, an excuse."

She poured the tea through a silver strainer, then added hot water from another pot.

"I suppose you believe in reincarnation and past lives too."

Janna shrugged. "I'm not certain. It's possible—"

"C'mon. You're educated. How can you go for that?"

She leveled her big green eyes on him, her expression serious. "Many people have been hypnotized and regressed back in time. They speak languages they don't know in this life, and accurately describe places that they've never visited. I think it's entirely possible that some people have lived before and will live again."

"And you think you lived during the French Revolution?" When she nodded, he asked, "Did someone hypnotize you?"

"No. I've always experienced a certain—I don't know how to describe it—affinity for the time period."

Nick couldn't believe she was serious. "Do you think we met back then during the French Revolution?"

"It's possible. Shadoe believes—"

"Who was I supposed to be?" He decided to play along with her, sensing she was embarrassed.

"One of Count Fersen's men."

"Who the hell was he?"

"A Swedish nobleman who tried to help Marie Antoinette escape."

"Who were you?" he asked, not believing there was any truth to this, but curious.

"A friend of Marie's," she said, her eyes downcast. "You and I tried to help her escape."

"And?" He waited, but she didn't say anything. He was tempted to tell her this was a screwball idea, then it hit him. "And what about us?"

Instead of answering, she picked up a cube of sugar with a pair of silver tongs and dropped it into the tea.

"We were lovers," he guessed.

Head down, she nodded, adding another cube of sugar to the tea. "Shadoe thinks you are de Polignac, one of Fersen's men. We were very good friends."

No wonder she'd invested in Velcro for camels. If Janna bought this past life bit, you could sell her anything. He leaned close and whispered, "I want you to know you were terrific in bed, but I had a hell of a time unlacing your corset."

She almost smiled as she plopped a third cube of sugar into the tea.

"What happened in the end?"

"The guillotine."

"Jeezus! What a way to go."

"Jersey, Hereford, or Shorthorn?" she asked, still not looking him in the eye.

"Longhorn. In West Texas they raise Longhorn cattle."

"Actually, I wanted to know what kind of milk you prefer in your tea."

Milk in tea? Yuck. "Just sugar." He watched her put yet another cube of sugar into the tea. Her fingers were tapered with buffed nails. He could almost feel them furrowing through his hair. Forget the past lives bit, he wanted to tell her, remember Mdina. This life. She handed him the cup and saucer. He put his fingers over hers, being deliberately clumsy so he could touch her. Soft. Every bit as soft as he remembered.

She appeared flustered, but her voice didn't show it. "We have cucumber, tomato, or watercress sandwiches—"

"C'mon, Shorty. You call those itty-bitty things sandwiches? Shoot, they don't even have crusts."

She shook her head in mock disgust, and he asked himself what it would take to make her laugh, really laugh.

"Try this." She put a pastry on a plate and added a scoop of lumpy looking whipped cream. "A Bath bun with clotted cream from Devon. I guarantee you'll like it."

The guests had gathered around the trolley, selecting sandwiches, fruit, and pastries while Janna served the tea. Nick stood nearby awkwardly holding his cup and saucer in one hand and the dessert plate, fork, and napkin in the other. Warren appeared with Shadoe.

"Come sit with us," Warren said. "I haven't had a chance to talk with you."

Nick followed them, and let Shadoe sit beside Warren before sitting opposite them. He set his tea down on the table and concentrated on eating the Bath bun while he waited for Warren to bring up the stocks.

"I've been studying how your company established itself during the Second World War."

"One soldier to carry the ammo and two to carry the Imperial Cola—or so I'm told." Nick assumed Warren was patronizing him by discussing his job.

"But after the war, Imperial Cola consolidated its successes by joint venturing facilities with important local businesses."

"Yes," Nick agreed. "We've made similar arrangements in most countries. Here we're allied with Tewkes. In Malta our bottling partner is Bradford Beverages."

Nick intentionally gave Warren an opening to discuss the Bradfords and the shares, but he didn't take it. Instead, he said, "Once you've become part of the local economy, it's impossible to oust you."

"We've had our problems. India, for example. We wouldn't reveal our secret formula, and they kicked us out. Frenchmen drink wine and bottled water. Soft drinks, even cola, finish a poor third."

"Generally speaking, don't joint ventures protect foreign businesses? What I'm concerned about, Nick, is several joint ventures Japan is proposing for the UK."

Nick polished off the Bath bun and the last of the clotted cream—great stuff but what the hell happened to the tea?—pure sugar. "What companies are involved?"

"I put a stop to an automobile plant, but now Turabo Industries wants to joint venture a textile plant in the Midlands."

"Our textile industry has been losing market share for

a number of years," Shadoe said, her eyes not on Nick but on Warren.

"This could very well solve some of our unemployment problems. But what's the down side? Am I worrying needlessly that our country will be taken over by foreigners?" Warren gave Nick that earnest look he had used during the television interview. "What do you think?"

Nick factored in what he knew about Warren Atherton—nothing—and the possible consequences of what he would tell him. "Anything I say is off the record, understand? I don't have any confidential information. What I'm going to tell you is a matter of public record, but I don't want my views to cause problems for Imperial Cola. Japan's their biggest market."

Warren nodded solemnly. "I understand. I take it you're not too keen on Turabo Industries."

"It's one of Japan's oldest and most respected textile companies. Founded sometime in the late 1800s. Recently, Hensho Enterprises bought all the outstanding shares. A *yukuzu*—a gangster—Yoshio Yosuma heads Hensho. He's boss of an underworld syndicate known in Japan as the Yamaguchi-gumi gang."

"I didn't realize Japan had a serious criminal element," Shadoe said. "I always think of their society as prizing honor and their good names."

"Appearances can deceive," Nick said.

"Tell me more about Henshu," Warren said.

Nick spent the next hour giving Warren a rundown of the *yakuza* as well as an overview of what to expect when doing business with the Japanese. Looking over Warren's shoulder, Nick could observe Janna without appearing to be rude. Now and then she would use her fingers to comb through her hair, not quite accustomed to the new style. Nick liked it. Her ruler-straight hairdo had detracted from her best feature, her large expressive eyes.

He smiled inwardly, recalling their earlier discussion. So she believed in past lives and thought they'd been lovers. Interesting idea. Not the past lives, but the lovers. It might account for why she'd been so passionate in Mdina. But it didn't explain why he'd been so ready to make love to her.

When the last guest had gone, Janna finally joined them. "What's going on over here?" she asked. "You three haven't been very social."

Nick moved over, giving Janna no choice but to sit on the loveseat beside him. "We were talking about Japan."

"I know how concerned you've been about some of their joint ventures," Janna said to her brother.

"Nick has been very helpful." Warren turned to Nick. "Shadoe and I will be in Malta in a few weeks. Let's spend more time talking about this."

Nick rose to leave, still expecting Warren to mention the stocks, but he didn't. "Thanks for inviting me." He shook Warren's extended hand. "See you in Malta."

"I'm driving out to Hampstead Heath. Let me drop you at your hotel," Janna politely volunteered. "It's on the way."

He followed Janna through a massive kitchen and out a back door that led to what once must have been the carriage house. Parked inside were a Range Rover and an Aston Martin Lagonda. Janna opened the door to the Aston Martin.

"My brother's," she said apologetically.

Nick climbed in, puzzled that Warren hadn't discussed the stock. Undoubtedly Janna would. He glanced at her. Dusk and the deep shadows in the carriage house masked her profile. She hesitated, her hand on the keys in the ignition. Slowly, she turned and faced him. The coach lamp behind the car cast a mellow light across her face embellishing the gentle curve of her cheek, the fullness of her lower lip.

"Nick . . . about the other night . . . I . . ."

Nick smothered a groan. "You're not going to apologize again, are you, Shorty?"

"Yes. I—"

He leaned across the small space separating them and came nose to nose with her. He expected her to pull back, but she didn't. Her controlled expression in place, she gazed at him. The only evidence of her uneasiness was the death grip her fingers had on the leather-wrapped steering wheel. Not for the first time, he asked himself what she really thought of him. Before the incident in Mdina, he'd been positive she disliked him. The smile that he'd once relied on to convince women to hike their skirts hadn't fazed her. Until that night.

If he hadn't been stone-cold sober, he would have thought he had imagined it. The scene had replayed in his mind more times than he cared to admit. He kept telling himself that she was married, that he'd known love too well to settle for a night in the sack. Still, she'd affected him in a way he'd never experienced before— and didn't know how to handle except to tease her.

He forgot he intended to tease her about Marie Antoinette. The urge to kiss her overwhelmed him. His hand spanned her chin and tilted her head back. He touched his lips to hers—just to see if they were as soft as he remembered. Even softer. Slightly parted. Pulling her into his arms, he edged his tongue forward. She responded to his kiss with a moment of hesitation. Then she shyly brushed the tip of her tongue against his and curled her arms around his neck. Her fingers traced through the thick hair at the back of his head, urging him on. Sexy, damn sexy.

What the hell are you doing, cowboy? His conscience kicked in, reminding him that he had a married woman in his arms. He released her, saying, "Okay, Short-stuff. We're even. You can loosen up now. I've come on to you. Now I can be embarrassed, not you. No more apologies. Agreed?"

A moment of silence, then a suffocated whisper: "Agreed." She quickly turned away, cranking on the ignition. Gunning the engine, she shot out into an alley barely wider than the sleek sports car.

Although it was almost seven, the prolonged twilight illuminated the car enough for Nick to see the vivid scarlet coloring Janna's face. He swore under his breath. Why the hell had he kissed her? He'd only made a bad situation worse.

"Is Hampstead Heath very far?" he asked, using his most casual tone, striving to smooth things over.

"No," came the tight-lipped response. "It's in north London."

"Meeting your husband there?"

She kept looking straight ahead; there was a long pause. "Collis is in America . . . lecturing."

Collis? Some name. Lecturing? He imagined her husband: short, tweed jacket, a pipe, Coke-bottle glasses.

"I'm going to see Professor Kaye. He's an expert on World War II. He's written twelve books on the war. I met him while researching my paper on the cost of the French Revolution. I'm hoping he has a photograph of someone my aunt met during the war. I would like to surprise her with his picture."

Nick was touched by the affection he heard in her voice. Obviously, she cared very deeply for her aunt. He had the distinct impression Janna was closer to Pithany than she was to her own mother. Someone else might have found that odd, not Nick. For a moment, he thought of the Prescotts. He'd been closer to them than his own family.

It occurred to him that Janna's family life might not

have been any happier than his. There could be no mistaking the fondness she felt for her brother, but Nick wondered about Audrey Atherton. He'd only met her briefly when she'd come to Malta with her doctor and that spoiled mutt. Audrey was a real beauty, like his mother, but again like his mother she seemed emotionally unstable. And what about Janna's father? No one had mentioned him to Nick. Not once. He must be dead or Warren wouldn't have the title.

Something inside Nick thawed a little. And a feeling infinitely more dangerous than sexual attraction surfaced. He didn't want her upset with him. He was beginning to genuinely like her. A lot.

"Did you ask your aunt about the Bradfords?"

She slowed the car for the snarl at Hyde Park Corner and ventured a glance in his direction. "Yes. During the war Tony wanted to marry Aunt Pith, but she didn't love him, so she refused." Janna nudged the car forward, refusing to let a taxi bully her aside. "He's had a grudge against her ever since. For years, he successfully blocked her building the Blue Grotto."

Nick doubted "a grudge" adequately explained a vendetta that had dragged on for over fifty years. "Sounds like more than a sore loser to me. Tony Bradford must have a few loose screws."

Janna nodded her agreement. "Have you ever met him?"

"Nope. I've had lunch with Curt, though."

The light changed and the car edged forward. Nick had planned to go home after tea, change his clothes, and explore London on foot, but suddenly a surge of loneliness swept through him, a feeling that he'd fought more and more since moving to Malta. Must be all the friendly people speaking English, he decided. In Japan, he'd been content to spend as much time alone as possible. When he wanted company, he listened to a book on tape. Now that wasn't enough.

"Want some company on the ride to Hampstead Heath?"

Janna's head swiveled toward him. She risked a quick glance, then concentrated on bringing the car to a stop. "You would probably be bored."

"Would your friend mind if I came?"

"He'd like it. Professor Kaye can ramble on for hours about the war." She faced him, her expression puzzled. "You're really interested in coming with me?"

He stifled the urge to make some smart-ass remark. Teasing her only got him into trouble. "Sure."

They drove north until they came to Regent's Park with Janna giving him a guide book explanation of local landmarks. He sensed Janna was relaxing so he didn't interrupt, but nodded encouragingly and said, "Uh-huh" now and then.

They drove past Primrose Hill, a spacious mound covered with the lush grass of late spring that Janna told him was called cow parsley. A group of boys were running in the twilight unfurling multicolored kites. One bright yellow kite had the face of a Mutant Ninja Turtle on it and the message RIDE THE WIND, DUDES written across the bottom.

"Kites are dangerous," Nick said without thinking.

"Kites? Dangerous?"

"What if one gets caught in an electric line?"

"I'm sure most boys know better than to go up after it."

"Just takes one cocky kid—" Nick cut himself off.

Janna kept her eyes on the trail of exhaust sputtering out of the Austin Mini ahead of them. "Did someone you know get hurt trying to get his kite?"

Nick was forced to answer. "Yeah. He was killed."

"How awful." She turned toward him. "Were you with him?"

"Yes." Jee-zus. Why hadn't he kept his mouth shut? He didn't want to discuss this with her.

"I'm sorry, that must have been terrible. How old were you?"

"I was ten. Cody was twelve."

"Twelve? Then your friend was old enough to know better. Don't blame yourself."

"You wouldn't feel that way if it had been your brother." Nick couldn't believe he'd brought up Cody's death. He'd rarely talked about it. Even now, almost thirty years later, his brother's memory triggered a dull ache. And the question: What would he have been like had he lived?

"I should have stopped him." He could still hear himself yelling to Cody to be careful, but his brother, as usual, thought he knew more than Nick and hadn't listened.

"I'm sorry. How tragic for you, for your parents." She paused a moment, then asked, "They didn't blame you, did they?"

"My parents were divorced just after I was born, so my mother raised us alone." Nick let it go at that. His mother hadn't blamed him for not stopping Cody. After all, his brother was older, bigger. Smarter. But she never forgave Nick for not being the one who went up the pole.

Janna must have realized she'd opened an old wound because she immediately launched into a rapid-fire explanation of how all London's parks had once been linked from Hampstead Heath in the north to the Thames in the south.

"Look back," she said.

In the distance the London skyline sparkled against the deepening dusk and through a slow-moving fog wending its way northward. The view was so impressive that Nick had a difficult time thinking of anything to say that didn't sound trite. "Postcard view."

"Most tourists never get as far north as Parliament Hill," Janna said as she drove along the perimeter of the Heath.

Hampstead Heath was much more natural looking, less cultivated than the carefully planned royal parks, Nick decided. Trees with hollow spaces in their trunks and low-spreading branches flanked numerous ponds filled with ducks settling in for the night. She turned the Aston Martin down a narrow street and came to a stop in front of a redbrick house whose backyard bordered the park.

They walked up to the door in silence and rang the bell. The door immediately swung open and an older man Nick judged to be at least eighty greeted them. Tall, gaunt, arctic-white hair and beard. He looked like a character from the Old Testament. He bear-hugged Janna with a familiarity rare among the British.

"I brought a friend along," Janna said when he released her. "This is Nick Jensen."

"Gerald Kaye," he said, squashing Nick's hand with a powerful shake. "My friends call me Gerry."

Gerry ushered them down a long hall. "I'm sorry about your father, Janna. Give your mother my condolences. How is she bearing up?"

"Better than we expected."

Nick kept his eyes on Janna. A slight frown marred her forehead. Apparently, she'd recently lost her father. No wonder she seemed so unhappy, so serious. Why the hell did her husband leave her when she obviously needed him? She was sensitive, perceptive. Hell, she'd dragged details of Cody's death out of him. And guessed his mother blamed him. Losing her father must have been a blow. No wonder she didn't often smile.

Gerry ushered them into the library. Leather bound books lined the shelves of two walls from floor to ceiling. A map of Europe as it had been during the Second World War hung on the wall, surrounded by fascinating photographs of planes and ships used during the war.

"Sit, sit." Gerry motioned for Nick and Janna to take seats on the sofa while he settled into a faded chintz armchair.

"Gerry, were you able to locate any photographs of Ian MacShane?" Janna asked.

"No, but I know all about him. MacShane was an orphan who grew up in Glasgow's back alleys. He came to London and initially worked as a runner in Fleet Street. He convinced someone at a radio station to give him a chance to do some reporting. He was excellent at it. Natural talent. He bluffed his way onto an RAF plane and flew to Malta at a time when no other reporter had been able to reach the island. He sent word back to the radio station that he'd do exclusives with them if they would reprint his broadcasts in the *Daily Mail*, the paper he'd once worked for. They did. Overnight, he became famous."

"Wasn't there a file photograph taken for the paper or the radio station?"

Nick observed not only the distress on her face, but the rising disappointment in her voice.

"There might have been, but the Nazis bombed the building."

"Surely, someone there took a picture of him when he was in North Africa. By then he was quite a celebrity."

"I checked all my files. Nothing. I rang up several other authorities on the war. No one has a picture of Ian MacShane."

"Thanks for trying. I was hoping . . ."

"I have complete transcripts of all his reports. I'll give you those. Do you really need a picture?"

"It's for my aunt. A picture would make her very happy. She was going to marry Ian. But when he went down with the *Nelson*—"

"Wait," Gerry interrupted. "You've got the story wrong. Ian MacShane wasn't aboard the *Nelson.*"

12

✳

Caught off guard, Janna didn't know what to think. Aunt Pith had been convinced Ian had gone down with the *Nelson,* but Gerald Kaye was a leading authority on the war. "Are you positive? If Ian had lived, I'm certain he would have contacted my aunt."

"MacShane was in Bardia two days after Tobruk fell. Then he disappeared; he never filed another report."

"If he'd been killed, wouldn't his body have been found?" Janna asked. "He was famous. The BBC must have searched for him."

Gerry shrugged. "In the chaos of war anything can happen. It was assumed he died."

"Maybe he was injured, suffered amnesia, and is still alive somewhere," Nick suggested.

"No. MacShane was too well-known for someone not to have recognized him if he'd been wandering around. I interviewed the last person to see MacShane alive for *Back From Hell,* my book about the North African campaign after Montgomery assumed command of the British forces." Gerry rose, adding, "Let me find those notes. They're in the basement."

Janna gazed out the window hardly seeing the moonlit garden's hedge where honeysuckle and tea roses rambled, naturally tumbling onto the flagstone path that led into the heath, or the stone dovecote where Gerry kept his homing pigeons. She couldn't imagine what she was going to tell Aunt Pithany. All these years her aunt had been certain Ian had been aboard the *Nelson.*

"Be prepared to never really know what happened to Ian MacShane," Nick said quietly.

"You don't understand. My aunt has lived the last fifty years loving a man she believed went down with the *Nelson.* How can I tell her that she's wrong? She'll need to know what happened just the way you want to know what really happened to Travis Prescott." Janna met Nick's eyes. He was nodding thoughtfully. She assumed her words had triggered memories of his friend. "Have the police learned anything new about his death?"

"The morning you flew to Rome, they came to Falcon's Lair and questioned Clara. They confiscated the baking supplies to run tests on them for oleander contamination. But they're not going to find anything."

"Why not?" she asked, noting the solemn expression on his face had intensified, a sharp contrast to his usual easygoing manner and ready smile. She understood that he felt as deeply about Travis as she did Aunt Pith.

"Your aunt and Clara ate more than Travis did that day, and they've been using the same supplies since— except for the honey. Clara used it once or twice, then the ants got to it. She threw it out."

"Travis must have eaten something just before he arrived for tea."

"It's the only explanation—"

Gerry walked in, carrying a manila file folder. "Here's what we want." He sat down and thumbed through it. "March 11, 1979. I interviewed Ralph Evans, who told me that he and MacShane had traveled from Gazala to Bardia together. Evidently, MacShane had missed boarding the *Nelson.* The last time Evans saw him was in a waterfront bar in Bardia. MacShane left to meet a RAF pilot he knew."

"Did he mention the pilot's name?" Janna asked, immediately thinking of Tony Bradford.

"No. My notes indicate I asked, but he didn't know. Evans had expected to see MacShane the next day, but he never showed. Evans's unit regrouped and he left Bardia."

"No one else saw MacShane after that night?" Nick asked.

"He vanished." Gerry leaned forward, elbows on his knees, fingers interlaced, and thought for a moment. "Perhaps he was killed and the body improperly identified. It's also possible his body is buried in an unmarked grave in Bardia."

"I wanted to give Aunt Pith a picture of Ian. Something to make her happy." Even to her own ears Janna's voice sounded anguished. "Instead I'm going to give her news that will make her miserable."

Nick put his hand on her arm. "Why don't we do a little more investigating before telling her anything?"

We? Since when had he become a part of this? She looked down at his large, square hand now patting her arm reassuringly. His exceptional looks threw her off balance because they rekindled painful memories of Collis Pembroke. But unlike her husband, Nick Jensen wasn't self-centered. He obviously cared deeply for his friend. And he seemed genuinely concerned about Aunt Pith.

"You're right. I don't want to upset Aunt Pith. She's been wonderful to me—better than a mother." She met Gerald's observant eyes and felt guilty remembering she'd left Rome so absorbed with Aunt Pith's story that she hadn't taken time to say hello to Audrey. "Don't misunderstand. My mother is wonderful. If either of us even sneezed she took us to Dr. Osgood."

"But you felt closer to your aunt," Nick said, his hand still on Janna's arm.

She nodded, unable to ignore the warmth of his hand, his supportiveness. Would Collis have been as sympathetic? No, he didn't like Aunt Pith. But what was Nick's game? She couldn't decide why he'd asked to come with her. He obviously enjoyed baiting her. For a foolish moment back in the garage, she'd allowed herself to respond to his kiss only to find out he'd been teasing her. She tensed, renewed embarrassment engulfing her and sending a flush up through the tan she'd acquired in Malta.

"Is Evans still alive?" Nick asked Gerry. "Could we talk to him? Maybe he'll remember something else."

Gerry lifted his eyebrows, expressing his doubts. "Let me ring a few associates and see."

"I'll contact the authorities in Bardia," Nick told Janna. "Let's find out if they buried any unidentified bodies around the time Ian disappeared."

Gerry stood. "I don't know about you two, but I'm hungry. How about joining me for a bite? Bachelors make damn lousy cooks, but I whip up a mean Welsh rarebit and a passable black pudding."

"Sounds great," Nick said.

"Nick adores Welsh rabbit," Janna said, unable to resist the opportunity to tease Nick even though her heart wasn't in it. Her thoughts were on Aunt Pith. "He can't eat enough rabbit."

Puzzled, Gerry looked first at Nick and then at Janna, but he didn't comment.

Nick walked beside Janna down the hall toward the kitchen. "I know the difference between rarebit and rabbit," he told her with one of his mischievous smiles. "Melted cheese on toast. Better than a bunch of itty-bitty sandwiches."

Janna smiled, determined to put her relationship with Nick on an even keel. There wasn't any reason they couldn't be friends. Pithany had advised Janna to give

Nick a chance to help her. She understood the wisdom
of her aunt's advice. She needed Nick in her camp. She
couldn't afford to let her enemies lure him away.

Collis Pembroke lay with his head on Annabelle's am-
ple bosom, the telephone receiver against his ear as he
waited for the butler in Countessa d'Bianci's villa in
Rome to call Audrey to the telephone. "Hello, Audrey,"
he said when she finally answered. "How is the dog show
going?"

"Who is this?"

"Collis." It irked him that Audrey didn't recognize his
voice. "I called to find out if you were enjoying the
show."

"You're awfully sweet."

Collis gave the receiver a gratified smile; Audrey was
easy to manipulate.

"I spent the day listening to lectures on characteristics
of various breeds," Audrey continued. "Did you know
that about ten percent of the Dalmatians born are deaf?
They have to be 'bucketed.' Drowned. Imagine such a
barbaric practice in this day and age. Of course, Maltese
don't have that problem. They've been carefully bred.
They don't have trouble learning to widdle in the right
place the way Dalmatians do."

"Interesting," Collis said, although he believed Rommie "widdled" wherever he pleased. He listened to another slur on Dalmatians, a claim that they "widdled"
one hundred proof uric acid—more potent than other
dogs'—guaranteed to wipe out an English garden with
one lift of the leg.

Audrey sounded different, rattling off facts and trivia.
Like Janna. Funny, he'd never noticed they had much in
common. Audrey paused for a breath and Collis asked,
"Did you have a chance to talk with Janna?"

"Oh, my. Oh, my. What can I do with a daughter like her?"

Collis sat bolt upright. "What did Janna say?"

"I tried to convince her that this idea of going into business was awfully common—something an Atherton should never do. But Janna wouldn't listen."

"What about having a baby?"

"Out of the question. I spent hours, believe me, hours, but she's determined to divorce you."

Divorce? Warren had stressed how important it was to keep the impending divorce from Audrey. But Janna had told her. The finality of the situation hit Collis for the first time.

Audrey sniffled.

What did *she* have to cry about for God's sake?

"Nothing can change Janna's mind. I tried, honestly, I tried. She was in Rome several days ago and I spent hours begging her but . . . it's hopeless."

Collis rang off, hardly letting Audrey say good-bye. Why was he surprised his ploy hadn't worked? Janna had a stubborn streak. Her love for him had always been a card he played, persuading her to do what he wanted. She couldn't have become immune to the old Pembroke charm.

"What is the matter, Collie?" Annabelle asked.

Collis grunted and pressed the television's remote control. Warren Atherton's face filled the screen. A stab of envy, as sharp as real pain, knifed through Collis. Atherton knew nothing—absolutely nothing—yet here he was the golden boy of the chat show circuit. Everyone was convinced the earl was destined for the political stratosphere. Rumors were already circulating about a possible cabinet post.

The hell with everyone, Collis thought. If they couldn't see that he, not Warren, had the credentials to give advice, then they could rot in hell. What did he care? But he did care. He loved lecturing under the guise of teaching because it gave him center stage and an adoring audience. He envisioned himself on the telly night after night, lecturing to an entire nation.

Then Janna would be sorry she'd divorced him. He wouldn't need her anymore. Janna had been an asset: her family name, her ability to talk to strangers, her intelligence. Marrying her had elevated him from the fish and chips lecture circuit to monied circles. He'd parlayed her connections, but it had been his speaking ability that had earned him his current status as Britain's financial guru.

He'd never loved Janna, of course, but he'd been fond of her. He preferred women who weren't so intellectual, women who didn't give him the feeling they were competing with him. The marriage might have worked had she remained the adoring woman that she'd been on their first dates. But she'd changed. It was her own fault he'd taken up with Annabelle.

He clicked off the television, cursing the Athertons. He savored the thought of humiliating Janna and Warren. There had to be a way to disgrace the Athertons while increasing his own net worth. He pondered the situation, dozens of highly implausible scenarios running through his head.

"Collie," Annabelle whispered, and he turned to see her smiling up at him, her golden hair splayed across the pillow. She handed him a bottle of Kama Sutra oil. "Your turn."

His gaze skimmed her naked body, taking in the fullness of her breasts as they sloped to her gently rounded abdomen. Her legs were parted, as usual, revealing baby soft inner thighs. He drizzled the oil, zigzagging it across her chest, down past the swatch of curly blond hair to the tops of her thighs. He set the bottle aside, trying to push thoughts of the Athertons aside as well.

He smoothed the oil across her breasts, circling the jutting nipples. He cradled one between his finger and his thumb rolling it in the scented oil. She arched upward, moaning slightly, her legs even more widespread. Insatiable. Completely insatiable.

If only the Athertons could see him now. Janna would be devastated, Warren shocked, dumb Audrey dumbfounded. They could all go to bloody hell. If he didn't need Janna's money—

Collis kept rubbing Annabelle, palming the inviting mound between her thighs, his thoughts preoccupied. How much money was he losing with this divorce? The teacher in Collis took over. Access the problem first and then find the solution, not the other way around. How much had Reginald left Janna? The old boy was a queer duck. He might not have left her as much as Collis expected. Worse, he could have left her property like the house in Toquay. In this market, selling might take years —if he could convince her to sell.

Collis needed to know the contents of the will. He considered asking Audrey, but he doubted anyone had given her the details. Annabelle's moans became louder. He looked down into her blue eyes, heavy-lidded with passion. An idea sprang into his mind, a flash of brilliance that came to him, as usual, full-blown and startlingly clear.

"I'm a genius. A fucking genius!"

In one swift movement she looped her leg over his and mounted him. He expelled a long breath, asking himself how she managed to excite him in a way no other woman ever had. She rocked from side to side as she rode him.

"Collie, you are going to marry me, aren't you?"

* * *

"Was I too . . . hard-line?" Warren asked Shadoe as they drove home from the BBC Studios in Ealing after he'd appeared on television.

"No. You convinced me," she said, her eyes on Warren. "Just because Italy has agreed to a variety of joint ventures with the Japanese doesn't make it right for us."

With difficulty, he kept his eyes on the swarm of tail-lights ahead of him. Ever since tea late that afternoon, he'd been with Shadoe. He didn't know any other way of getting her to change her mind about him except to spend time with her and give her the opportunity to really know him.

Warren found her comfortable, enjoyable. Ever since he could remember, women had pursued him, not for himself, but because of his social position. These women talked relentlessly, trying too hard to entertain him. Frequently, they boldly chased him. Like his friend, Gerald Grosvenor, Duke of Westminister and Britain's wealthiest man, Warren had received numerous marriage proposals. Since he'd inherited his title the situation had become worse.

"What did you think of Nick Jensen?" Warren asked, curious to know Shadoe's impression of the handsome Texan. On the drive over, she hadn't mentioned him.

"I like him very much. I'll never forget how he helped us during the French Revolution. I hope he and Janna have a chance this time to let their love grow."

"Nick and Janna were together in a previous life?" Warren knew Shadoe was convinced she and Janna had been friends of Marie Antoinette. It had started as an adolescent fantasy, but they continued to talk about it particularly when they visited France.

"They've been together several times, I think. I can't be certain because I was only with them once. But Nick is always killed before they spend very much time together."

"I see," Warren said, sensitive to Shadoe's belief in karma. "Nick was with you and Janna when you tried to help Marie Antoinette escape with that Swedish diplomat . . ."

"Axel Fersen," Shadoe said. The brake lights of the car in front of them turned her red hair crimson and illuminated the seriousness of her expression. "Axel loved Marie very much, but he'd been afraid to tell her. When it became clear she was going to lose her life, he tried to help her escape. Nick was one of his men. He met Janna for the first time in a dark alley. She was delivering one of Marie's messages. It was *un coup de foudre*—love at first sight. They had three wonderful days together then—" She shook her head sadly. "Nick and Janna are old souls searching for each other. They'll keep meeting somewhere in time until fate brings them together."

She couldn't be serious, but she was. Warren maneuvered the Range Rover along Old Brompton Road, analyzing Shadoe. Years ago Janna had told him her theory about Shadoe's obsession with the supernatural. Since Shadoe had grown up alone, deserted by her mother, shunted aside by her father to be raised by the cook and a series of maids, she hadn't received proper guidance. She'd developed her own system of values and had been exposed to a variety of cult beliefs the servants had taught her.

Warren recalled his own youth and blessed Aunt Pith for keeping the Atherton family together, insisting Audrey take them to church. His father ducked out— spending most weekends in the city—but every Sunday Dr. Osgood would come for Audrey and the children and drive them to services. Although Warren wouldn't describe himself as a religious man, his moral code had been shaped by sectarian beliefs, not a hodgepodge of ideas derived from cults and Eastern religions.

Things might have been different—Shadoe might not have become a prisoner of her astrological chart—had Warren not allowed his father to convince him to stop dating Shadoe. During the fifteen miserable years afterward, he'd concentrated on being the model heir while she'd rocketed through numerous men. He'd thought her disastrous marriages proved his father was right—Shadoe wasn't their kind. Until she told him about the baby. Now he realized she had merely been searching for love and the security of the family she'd never had. Warren intended to give her what she needed—now, not in some damn future life.

"Is your mother still planning to show Rommie?" Shadoe asked, her voice low.

"Definitely. She's hired a full-time trainer and she's devoting herself to following the show circuit until he's ready." He glanced at Shadoe but she looked away. "I want to thank you for giving her the dog. He's her reason for living."

"Warren, I . . . that is, my friend. He . . . aaah the man who gave me the dog. Well, he wasn't entirely certain about Von Rommel's parents."

"What do you mean? He sent Mother the kennel club papers."

"You see, my friend, John, wasn't positive who Von Rommel's father was." She stopped, measuring him for a moment. "John was in Hyde Park one day with his Maltese. He was inspecting the posts along Rotten Row, looking for the one he'd sponsored. Remember, the posts had been melted down during the war to make bullets and they've only recently replaced those along the bridle trail."

"Yes. My father paid to have several posts installed," Warren said, not quite concealing the edge in his voice. "Go on."

"John didn't realize his Maltie was in heat. They're so

small it's hard to tell sometimes. Anyway, he lost track of her for a moment. The next thing John knew she was rogging with one of those— What do you call those small dogs from Mexico, the kind without much hair?"

"Chihuahuas?" His voice rose in dismay. "You mean Rommie's father is a Chihuahua? How did John get papers?"

"He took his bitch to a friend who had a male. When the dog became pregnant, they conveniently assumed the male Maltese was the father and registered the puppies, but John always had his doubts. The father preferred males. John kept Von Rommel rather than give him away and chance his being bred or shown. I convinced him to sell me the dog because I thought a full-grown Maltese would be perfect for your mother. She wouldn't have to worry about chewing or housebreaking. I never expected her to show him."

"I don't know what my mother will say," Warren said, attempting to disguise his irritation.

"It won't be the first time it's happened. Didn't Queen Elizabeth's corgi mate with Princess Margaret's dachshund and they had a litter of corgshunds?"

"Yes. But they never tried to show them."

As he turned the car down Cranley Mews, the ridiculousness of the situation hit him. Shadoe had obviously been working up the courage to tell him. She was as honest as she was sensitive. Compared to everything else going on in the world—in his life—one Maltese with bogus papers wasn't worth worrying about. Or upsetting Shadoe. He had best be prepared: Life with Shadoe would be a series of magic runes and mutts masquerading as Malties.

"My mother has never bought anything except goods produced by royal appointment. She'll assume Rommie is show quality. Let her believe it. What can it hurt?"

* * *

"Janna," Gerry said, "you're not listening."

"I'm sorry," Janna said. Her thoughts had been drifting away—back to Aunt Pith and Ian—all evening. She doubted Gerry had noticed. He'd been busy entertaining Nick with stories of the war and pictures of planes and ships. From what she could tell Nick had been fascinated.

"It's late," Nick said. "Almost midnight. We'd better be getting back."

Gerry escorted them to the front door saying, "I'll give you a ring as soon as I know if Evans is still alive."

"I would appreciate it," Janna said.

Gerry paused, his hand on the doorknob. "You know, there might be a way of getting a picture for your aunt."

"I thought you checked everywhere," Nick said.

"I did," Gerry answered, his eyes on Janna. "This would be a very special picture. Janna would have to help."

"I would do anything to get her a picture."

"For several of my books, I've used a woman named Laurel Hogel who lives in Surrey. If you go to her and tell her about the person, not just general facts anyone could know but intimate details, she'll do a sketch for you."

"You mean describe him?" Janna asked, upset that she knew nothing beyond the fact that Ian had been Scottish. Nothing. She'd asked several times, but Aunt Pith had been reluctant to describe him. Evidently it was too painful.

"No. You wouldn't physically describe the person, but tell about him. Laurel is a psychic artist. She receives a mental image of the person from what you tell her."

"How does she do it?" Nick's tone was openly skeptical.

"I don't know," Gerry admitted, "but it works. I've told her about several men who had died in the war. I wanted pictures for my books but wasn't able to locate any. Laurel produced sketches for me. When I showed them to their relatives, they were amazed that a woman who had never met them could do their portraits."

Janna ignored Nick's incredulous expression. "Do you think it'll work?"

Gerry nodded. "What have you got to lose? Would you like me to ring her and set up an appointment for you?"

"Yes. Please do."

Janna barely heard Nick and Gerry say good night; her mind was on Laurel Hogel. She'd never heard of psychic artists, but if Gerry, the scholar's scholar, had used her, Janna was willing to try.

Nick opened the car door for her. "You're not going to visit that woman, are you? You don't believe in that bull pucky, do you?"

She settled herself behind the wheel and waited for Nick to get in. "Yes. I want a portrait for Aunt Pith."

"Jeez-us. There's a sucker born every minute—all of them are women."

"That's not fair," she snapped. "Psychics have helped find lost children, kidnap victims. Many police departments consult them. In the Soviet Union, scientists don't question psychic power. When they discover someone with the talent, they put them in training programs to maximize their potential. What do we do in the West? We make people prove over and over that they're not faking by having them read decks of cards and things like that."

"I'm familiar with psychics. Some are the real thing, but a lot of people claim to do psychic readings as an excuse to fleece people. A psychic artist just sounds too screwy."

"What about Gerry? He's a scholar. He's used her."

"Maybe she's for real, but you'll never convince me. I think it's all a crock like past lives and astrology."

Janna turned the key in the ignition. Nick thought she was a nut. Out of the corner of her eye, she saw he was smiling. "I never said *I* believed in past lives or astrology."

"Could have fooled me. Over tea you seemed pretty convinced."

Janna felt her face getting red and was thankful for the dark interior of the car. She could strangle Shadoe. Janna had told her about meeting Nick. Immediately Shadoe had insisted they'd known Nick in a previous life. "What I'm convinced about is that if—and that's a big if—if I've lived before it must have been during the French Revolution. I love that period in history."

"I guess so. You spent years researching it."

"To be honest, Nick, I find it very embarrassing that Shadoe brought it up. Even if I did live then, I'm positive you weren't around."

"How can you be so sure?" He sounded as if he were about to laugh.

"I'd know it. I'd feel it."

"Damn! I always wanted to unlace one of those corsets they wore back then. Didn't they wear a lot of petticoats too?"

"A dozen at least, sometimes more."

"Forget it! I would have been too exhausted undressing you to make love to you."

The teasing tone of his voice made her smile, but the thought of him making love to her kept her cheeks warm. She had to admit that she found him very attractive. Sexy.

"Are we going to sit here all night idling the engine until we run out of gas?"

"Sorry," she said, then put the car into gear and sped

off. "I don't think anyone knows the possibilities of the human mind. I'm going to give Laurel Hogel a try."

"I guess it can't hurt," Nick conceded, but he didn't sound convinced.

They drove through the nearly deserted streets. Janna wasn't aware that she'd been silent to the point of rudeness until they reached Green Park, and she realized they hadn't spoken. "Did you enjoy Gerry?"

"If I'd had one history teacher like Gerry, I might have liked the subject."

"You seemed to like his cooking, too. You had three helpings of Welsh rarebit and two servings of black pudding."

"Great stuff. Especially the pudding. What's in it?"

Janna swallowed a smile and looked right at Nick, glad the oncoming tide of headlights along Piccadilly made the interior of the car bright. "Pigs' blood."

"Oooo-kay. Very funny. Now tell me the truth."

She turned right on St. James, then looked at him again. She didn't want to miss a thing. "It's the truth. Honest."

The expression on his face was worth the wait through dinner, resisting the urge to tell him what was in the black pudding he was wolfing down.

"You're dead meat, Shorty. Know that? You'll be sorry."

She turned down the narrow lane off St. James that lead to The Dukes. "I live in fear."

She stopped in the cobbled motor court and waited for him to get out. He didn't move, but sat looking at her. His sexual magnetism went beyond the magazine slick handsomeness Collis possessed. Her pulse surged with excitement. She cursed her fatal flaw: attraction to handsome men.

"Do you have plans for tomorrow night?" he asked.

She regarded him warily, expecting retribution for the black pudding. "Why?"

"I could use a little help."

She chalked up the earnest tone in his voice to softening her up to play some trick on her, the way he had earlier when he had kissed her. "Help with what?"

He looked down almost as if he were talking to someone hiding under the dashboard. "There's a big company dinner. One of those fancy affairs over at the Savoy. I don't know anyone here. Hell, at times like this a man needs to be married."

He paused and she was tempted to say he had gotten what he deserved by remaining a bachelor. The world was full of wonderful single women. Undoubtedly that was the problem. Like Collis, Nick Jensen had all the women he wanted. Why settle down?

"It's hard to be alone at a rubber chicken dinner," Nick continued, "with an old fogy's band playing all night."

He couldn't be asking her out. He knew she was married; he'd asked her about Collis. She waited, still anticipating a joke.

"It would be a big help if you came with me." His words came out in a rush. "As a business associate. After all, we own those hotels."

He cocked his head to one side and looked at her for the first time since bringing up the party. It dawned on Janna that it had been difficult for him to ask her. It was even more difficult for her to answer.

13

✳

It wasn't really a date, Janna assured herself as she walked into the Savoy with Nick. She wasn't certain why she'd agreed to come. She could have spent the evening with Warren, or she could have visited Shadoe and played with Chloe. But here she was.

"There's Mark," Nick said, waving to a stocky man across the lobby.

Janna stole a quick peek at Nick, somewhat surprised he owned his own dinner jacket, but not that he looked so handsome in it. The admiring glances women were casting in their direction, the same looks she remembered only too well from her years with Collis, didn't surprise her either. Those legions of women salivating over her husband had made her feel insecure. Deep down she must have known Collis encouraged female attention. Thrived on it. He never walked into a room; he made an entrance, smiling at his adoring fans.

She ventured another look at Nick. His eyes were focused on his friend and the blowsy blonde at his side, not at the crowd. Janna studied the woman, estimating her to be about her age. This must be Glennis, his friend's wife. On the way here Nick had talked about Mark. From the tone of Nick's voice when he'd discussed his recently married friend, Janna knew Mark was very important to him.

Nick introduced her as Janna Atherton-Pembroke, omitting her marital status.

"You look great," Nick told Janna as he handed the cloakroom attendant the sable she'd borrowed from Audrey's closet.

He'd said it simply, without his teasing smile, and she felt herself tense. "Thanks."

She touched the pearl choker that she'd taken from Audrey's jewelry box, a double strand of nine millimeter pearls each perfectly matched. The gown might as well have belonged to Audrey, too. She'd bought the moss-green dress for Janna from Marc Bohan, formerly head designer for Christian Dior. He'd been enticed to London to revive the staid image of Hartnell, famous as the salon where the Queen Mother shopped. From the backwaters of fashion, Bohan had elevated Hartnell to the forefront of British design. Janna knew the dress became her—Audrey's clothes sense was infallible.

But to double-check, she'd tried on every dress in her closet—some of them several times—before selecting the green sheath.

Nick put his hand on the back of her waist and guided her down the hall into the Lancaster Room. Janna started to give Glennis a brief history of the hotel, but stopped. Glennis was watching Nick. Janna had seen that look before—when women eyed Collis. Nick was saying something to Mark and didn't notice his friend's wife.

"Oh, Lordy," Glennis said, entering the ballroom. "We don't have anything like this in Atlanta."

"It's modeled after a ballroom in a French chateau," Janna said as they crossed the large room.

What made the Lancaster Room so impressive in a city filled with distinctive architecture was the light, Janna thought. The mellow glow of chandeliers and wall sconces was reflected off the polished parquet floors and the panels of beveled mirrors imported from France in the previous century. The unusual lighting and the musicians playing classical music enhanced the feeling of stepping back in time.

"This is our table," Mark said, pulling out a chair for Glennis.

"Sit here, Nick." Glennis patted the chair next to her. "Tell me all about that earl."

Nick must not have heard her because he turned and introduced Janna to several passing executives. Then he maneuvered Janna into the seat beside Glennis, who didn't have the good manners not to look disappointed.

"Glennis has been pestering me all day, wondering how your tea with the earl went," Mark said.

Glennis looked past Janna to Nick. "What was his house like?"

"I didn't notice," Nick said, nudging Janna with his knee. "I was too busy eating."

"Imagine, an earl," Glennis said, her southern accent elevating Nick to immortal status.

"How'd you meet Lyfield?" Mark asked Nick, making it obvious he didn't know she was "that earl's" sister.

"Lyforth. The Earl of Lyforth—Warren," Nick said, and Glennis's mascara-embalmed lashes widened. "I'm renting his aunt's guest house."

"I've been dyin', simply dyin' to visit Malta," Glennis said to Mark, her eyes on Nick. "Haven't you, honey?"

It was all Janna could do not to gaze at the fifteen-foot ceiling and pray for deliverance.

Nick took her hand. "Let's dance."

Walking out to the floor, Janna glanced around. There were more than a dozen single men sprinkled through the large group.

Nick gathered her into his arms, saying, "I'm not much of a dancer."

"And you're not much of a liar, either." Thankful for

her stiletto heels, she looked directly into his blue eyes. "You didn't invite me because everyone had their wives. You invited me to protect you from Glennis."

For a moment he looked stunned, then he chuckled, a deep rich sound that seemed to vibrate through her. "You know, Short-stuff, you're too smart for your own good. Mark's first wife couldn't stand living in Japan. She divorced him. He came back to the states and married the first woman he met."

"A double-edged sword—you want her to like you, but not too much. If I protect you, will this make up for the black pudding?"

He smiled, a slow smile. The single dimple appeared. "Maybe. If you're real good at it."

All evening she ran interference for him, keeping Glennis at bay by querying Nick about the cola wars and dancing with him between every course. Somehow she even managed to listen attentively to the speeches during the trifle. According to the speaker, her fellow countrymen were prepared to give up their tea for Imperial Cola.

Dinner over, they headed for the dance floor again as the strains of a Strauss waltz filled the room. This time Glennis wouldn't take no for an answer. Janna had been monopolizing Nick all night. She watched Nick whirl away, Glennis pressed flush against him.

"I've got two left feet," Mark told Janna.

"I don't mind," Janna said, and she meant it. She felt sorry for a man who loved a woman determined to throw herself at another man. She couldn't help wondering if her situation with Collis had been as obvious. Had everyone pitied her?

"It's about time Nick started dating again." Mark's eyes were filled with genuine concern. "I never thought he'd get over Amanda Jane's death."

Death? Who was Amanda Jane? Janna struggled to

conceal her shock. Obviously, Mark thought Nick had told her about himself. "I'm sure he'll never really be 'over' her."

"I didn't mean he'd forget his wife. How could he? She helped him every way she could. Even put him through school. Such a tragedy."

His wife? Somehow she'd had the impression Nick had never been married. Her gaze skipped over the dancing couples until she found Nick. He mouthed "Save me" over Glennis's shoulder.

"I imagine Austin Prescott is a wreck. Losing his daughter to cancer was hard enough, but having his son murdered has got to have destroyed him."

"Of course," Janna said, her voice strained. Travis Prescott had been his brother-in-law. No wonder Nick was determined to investigate his death. Why hadn't he told her what their relationship was?

She glanced across the room and met Nick's eyes. Over the chattering Glennis's shoulder, he smiled and winked. She realized Nick hid behind his ready smile. An insular man, he avoided revealing details of his private life. She'd prodded the story of his brother's death out of Nick, but she sensed she wouldn't be able to manipulate him into discussing his wife. "Did you know the Prescotts?" she asked, deciding Mark might be her only way of finding out more.

"Sure. I started in the Texas marketing division. Austin Prescott was in sports promotions. We worked together on a project. He introduced me to Nick at a company barbecue just after Nick'd become engaged to Amanda Jane. Was she ever gorgeous." He looked at Nick, shaking his head sadly. "Anyway, Nick and I hit it off. He mentioned an idea he had for marketing iced coffee."

Gorgeous? Naturally. A statuesque blonde, no doubt. No. A stunning brunet. She vaguely remembered the picture in Nick's room. She struggled to keep her mind on the conversation. "Iced coffee? Like what Imperial Cola is doing with Bessel?" She recalled reading an article about the Swiss company joining Imperial Cola in producing iced coffee and tea drinks.

"Yes, but we were *years* ahead of them," Mark said with pride. "When I proposed Nick's idea to the honchos in Atlanta, they said: No way. But I convinced them. I nursed that puppy through God-only-knows how many test markets. Then we brought it out in Japan."

"How did it do?" she asked, her mind still on Amanda Jane.

"Great. I moved to Japan to supervise the project. That's why Nick called me five years ago when Amanda Jane died. Poor guy was miserable. He needed to get away. I brought him to Japan, and I wasn't sorry. He's a marketing genius. I plan to bring him to corporate headquarters in Atlanta as soon as I can."

Mark continued to talk, but she hardly listened. She couldn't stop looking at Nick. And wondering. For five years Nick had mourned his wife's death. Remarkable devotion, like Aunt Pith's. Fifty years. She'd loved Ian, cutting off all possibility of marrying anyone else and having the children she wanted. A painful knot formed in Janna's throat, choking her with the realization that she would never experience such a special love.

Moments later the full impact of Mark's words kicked in: Nick would be leaving. Stop wondering about his private life. Obviously he didn't want her to know—concentrate on the stock. How could she convince Nick to sell *before* he left?

The dance ended and Nick rushed over, Glennis clinging to his arm.

"What were you two talking about?" Nick asked Janna as they began another waltz.

"You," she said. "Mark was telling me about how you

came up with the idea for iced coffee, and how successful it was in Japan." She hesitated, wondering if it was
her imagination or was Nick holding her closer now than
he had all evening? "Nick, do you have any ideas for
making the Blue Grotto a premier hotel—quickly?"

The flicker of surprise in his eyes told her he hadn't
expected to be asked for advice. She must have given
him the impression that she didn't value his opinion. In
truth, she hadn't. He'd appeared to be a transplanted
Texas doomed to the lowest echelons in the corporate
hierarchy. Wrong. Dead wrong. There was a power and
depth to Nick Jensen that fascinated her.

"Aunt Pith has the key management in place. All I
have to do is supervise the advertising campaign, but I
don't have the experience to promote the Blue Grotto
without help," she said, being completely honest. "I'm
concerned the type of hotel Aunt Pith has always run—
catering to Europe's elite—is an endangered species."

He regarded her silently for a moment, his penetrat-
ing blue eyes not giving away his thoughts. "I think
you're right. The Blue Grotto is bigger than her other
three hotels. It'll need to be at capacity constantly to
make a profit—not to mention recouping the building
costs." Nick whirled her in a slow circle, bringing her
even closer. Evidently, he'd gotten used to dancing with
Glennis the limpet. "Divers."

"Divers?" she asked, while asking herself why she
hadn't noticed the slight cleft—the merest indentation—
on his chin. "You mean scuba divers?"

"Fastest growing market in the travel business. I'm a
diver myself. I know."

"So is Warren. I've wanted to learn to dive but the
thought of toting all that equipment." She rolled her
eyes.

"Lousy schlepp-to-thrill ratio, I agree."

"What ratio?"

"A marketing term for the amount of gear required for a sport versus the fun. Like diving, skiing has a lousy schlepp to thrill ratio, but again it's a sport that lures travelers with money, the market you want."

"Malta does have spectacular diving. The fluorescent rocks that make the Blue Grotto beautiful attract a variety of fish."

"Make videotapes and send them to dive shops, sports stores, and travel agencies. Then watch what happens."

"You're right. If people saw how beautiful Malta is, they would come. A travel brochure makes it look like another sun-drenched island. A video would show that it has grottos even more spectacular than the Isle of Capri and diving better than the Barrier Reef."

"Get your brother to narrate it."

"Warren? He's not a professional—"

"You've seen him on TV. He could sell bikinis to Eskimos."

The music stopped. Janna started to step away, but Nick didn't move his arm. He was too engrossed in relating the importance of charisma in advertising. Not until the band began a fox-trot did Nick release her.

"Let's say good night to Mark and Miss Magnolia. Isn't there a bar around here somewhere? Let's have a drink and talk about this more."

They left the Nolans with a group of Tewkes Beverage executives and went into the American Bar and found seats in the corner, taking a table not far from the piano.

"Nice place." Nick nodded approvingly at the small bar. "Food was a lot better than I expected."

"Escoffier was the chef here at the turn of the century. He's regarded as the most creative chef of all time, so the hotel still uses most of his recipes. Richard D'Oyly Carte built the Savoy. He'd made his money as the impresario who promoted Gilbert and Sullivan operas. Nothing but the best suited him. The Savoy still makes its own mattresses and has Irish linen specially woven for sheets—"

"Jeez-us. Do you know you sound like Ms. Facts-on-File half the time?"

"Do you know you smile *all* the time?" she retorted, stung by his comment.

"Don't you like happy people?"

"Are you happy, Nick, or do you smile to distract people?"

His expression darkened with an unreadable emotion.

The waiter came up and they ordered. Janna chided herself for baiting Nick. Why had she let his comment draw a sarcastic remark? The answer came with startling swiftness: Collis. Too often he'd taunt her for sounding like "a pseudo-intellectual." He wanted to be the only intelligent one in the family. As usual, the thought of her husband made her heart skip painfully.

"It's cute," Nick said as the waiter left.

"What's cute?"

"The way you spout all those facts."

She had no idea if he was teasing her; he didn't smile. "The point I was about to make was that D'Oyly was a premier promoter, and here we are a hundred years later in his bar discussing ways to promote a hotel."

He weighed what she'd said for a moment, his expression still serious. "Don't compete with the Bradfords for the same market. They're relying on older travelers to come to their hotels and spend money in the casinos. Go for a younger group who's more interested in sports like diving, wind surfing, and sailing. Remember they're educated. Let them know about architectural sites and ruins like that place that looks like Stonehenge."

"Tarxien?"

"Yeah. And when you shoot those videos be certain the seas are flat. The image younger travelers have of

Malta probably comes from the Bush-Gorbachev Summit."

Janna groaned. "A *xlokk* hit Malta. Spume shot into the air with each breaking wave. People joked, calling it the Salt Water Summit. They didn't understand that the Mediterranean is more saline than most other bodies of water. It looked worse than it was."

Nick's mouth puckered, suppressing a smile. She realized she'd sounded like a textbook again. Mercifully, the waiter arrived with their drinks.

The next afternoon Janna drove south to Surrey for her appointment with Laurel Hogel. The sun had nudged through the tightly packed clouds to brighten the late spring countryside as she turned down the lane and came to a stop in front of the address she'd been given. She picked up the transcripts of Ian MacShane's broadcasts that Gerry had given her and wished that Nick were with her. She'd invited him, but he'd refused saying he was spending the day in Lyme Regis, leaving her with the unpleasant feeling he didn't want to be with her.

Why Lyme Regis? she wondered. It was really off the beaten track for someone on his first trip to England. Never mind. Nick Jensen was a complex man; she wasn't going to understand him any better by thinking about him so much. She needed to concentrate on the psychic artist.

The half-timbered house, one in a row of several, sported an English garden full of well-tended flowers. Janna had expected a sign—an outline of a palm with the words Psychic Artist underneath. But no, this appeared to be a cozy cottage typical of the English countryside. She walked up the steps and tiptoed around a marmalade-colored cat sunning himself.

Janna's knock was answered immediately by a woman

in her mid-sixties. Her hair had once been a sandy blond but now was mostly gray. Kind green eyes a shade or so darker than Aunt Pith's welcomed her.

"You must be Gerry's friend, Janna," the woman said, wiping her hands on a yellow gingham apron.

"Yes." Janna tried not to look as if she'd been expecting a woman in a turban and flowing robes. "Mrs. Hogel?"

"Call me Laurel." She ushered Janna across the parlor to a large conservatory facing the backyard. "Sit. Sit. Let me fetch the tea."

Janna settled into a wing chair upholstered in faded chintz and inspected the room. The walls were covered with chalk portraits that left no question that Laurel Hogel was an extremely gifted artist. Despite her talent, Janna couldn't help being skeptical. How could anyone do a portrait of someone they'd never met?

Laurel returned carrying a tray with a teapot and a platter of teacakes. "How do you take your tea?"

Janna told her, then added, "Gerry didn't mention your fee—"

"My dear, I never charge. I help when I can. A happy face is payment enough." She took her tea over to the easel and set it down. She sat on the high stool behind the easel. "Tell me about your friend."

"He wasn't my friend. He was my aunt's friend." Janna went on to relate Ian and Pithany's story, leaving out some of the more intimate details. Laurel listened attentively, nodding now and again and drinking her tea. Half an hour had passed but Laurel had yet to pick up her colored chalk. "Are you getting a feeling for him? Or is this useless? Since I didn't know him, maybe I'm not conveying his image . . . or essence or whatever."

"No. I see him, quite clearly actually. He had a miserable childhood. He had difficulty writing or . . ." She paused and looked out the window into the garden where the marmalade cat was stalking a wily blue jay who flew into a tree and scolded the hunter. ". . . or reading. Maybe both."

"He had a very poor education—Glasgow just before the war."

"It wasn't his education. Something else was wrong. For some reason he had trouble reading although he was extremely intelligent." She waved her teacup. "But his real problem was his mother. She deserted him."

A too familiar ache welled up inside Janna. Deserted. The way she'd been. No. Not the same, not at all. She'd had Aunt Pith, Audrey, and Warren. And Shadoe. Reginald Atherton had never loved her, but she couldn't equate that with what Ian must have suffered. She should stop feeling sorry for herself.

"Ian was happy in London, away from memories of his mother. But he was even happier in Malta—despite the bombs. He found what he'd been searching for, love." Laurel picked up a piece of chalk and began to draw. "Ace"—she smiled at the canvas—"he loved her with all his heart. A love for all time."

Ace! A love for all time. The words hit Janna like a blast of icy wind off the North Sea. She had deliberately not mentioned Ian's pet name for Aunt Pith or the final line of his note, believing it was too personal, too private. The last vestiges of her skepticism vanished.

Janna waited while Laurel sketched furiously, entranced by the image on the canvas. Curious to see, Janna started to rise but Laurel frowned and motioned for her to stay put. She was afraid of breaking Laurel's concentration, so she remained seated, staring at the back of the easel. Now and then, Laurel stopped and inspected her work, squinting myopically at the sketch.

"He promised he'd come back," Janna said helplessly.

Laurel looked up, her hand poised midair. "He would

have, my dear. He would have if that man hadn't killed him."

"What man?" Janna gasped. Never once had she suggested to Laurel that Ian had died. She'd been reluctant to tempt fate. Some part of her believed he was still alive. Somewhere.

Laurel dropped the chalk. "Oh my. I should have sensed you didn't know."

"Are you positive Ian MacShane is dead?"

"Yes. A man—I can't make out his face because it's in the shadows—fires a gun point-blank here." Laurel pointed to her temple.

Just above her left ear.

14

�֍

South Street? What stupid sonofabitch would take a classy name like Strada del Palazzo and change it to South Street? That didn't sound nearly as prestigious as it should, Tony thought as he stood on the balcony of his office and looked down at the cobbled lane flanked by majestic buildings. The pinnacle of Tony's career had been the construction of the Bradford Enterprises building on the street where the most important businesses in Malta had their headquarters. While many islanders, including Pithany Crandall, bemoaned the loss of the Auberge de France, which had once housed the French knights, Tony believed the Nazis had done the world a favor by leveling it with a bomb. His building, more Bauhaus than medieval, was superior to that old relic.

Across the street, Louis Hyzler, president of the Bank of Valletta, waved to Tony from his desk next to the *gallariji*. Louis had removed most of the brightly painted wooden slats enclosing the balcony. Centuries ago *gallariji* had been used to conceal the strictly cloistered women who had been allowed outside alone only behind enclosed balconies.

"Those were the days," Tony muttered to himself, thinking of Pithany Crandall. Women belonged at home, not out in the business world, challenging men. "What the hell is she up to with Nick Jensen?"

Tony walked back into his office, sat down, and flipped

through the private investigator's report on Nick Jensen. His father had been the only son of a wealthy Bostonian family who could trace their ancestors back to the *Mayflower*. The father had come west to Cannon Air Force Base as a pilot and married a beautiful local girl, who'd given him two sons, but the marriage hadn't survived the couple's return to Boston. Not surprising. A hick and a blue blood. Nothing in the report seemed unusual except the time gap between Nick leaving school and entering college.

The Texan had barely graduated from high school, then worked for several years in a Imperial Cola warehouse. Why he'd suddenly quit and entered college was a mystery. No doubt, having a wife to support him—a clever ploy—had fueled his interest. He'd attached himself to Mark Nolan, another shrewd move. Nolan was now in corporate headquarters, maneuvering to have Nick transferred to Atlanta.

Tony knew exactly how to handle Nick Jensen. He pressed the monitor, signaling his secretary to show in the Texan. Tony had purposely sent for Nick and then kept him waiting. The door opened and Nick Jensen ambled in, a smile on his face, not appearing the least bit ruffled over waiting an hour. With a quick glance, Tony examined Nick, from his dark hair to linebacker shoulders to his three-piece suit. Deep inside Tony a shudder of premonition hit him like a revolver being cocked. The same feeling he'd had when he'd spotted Jensen at the party.

Tony rose and extended his hand. "Anthony Bradford," he said, deliberately not apologizing for the delay. "Call me Tony."

Nick Jensen introduced himself, shaking Tony's hand with a knuckle-crushing grip. And smiling. He was too stupid to know he'd been humiliated. Tony looked into

Nick's blue eyes, his apprehension increasing. That
face . . .

Tony motioned to the chair opposite his desk, then sat
in his own leather chair. His sense of uneasiness grew as
he studied Nick. At the *festa* party it had been dark; Tony
could have been mistaken. But now, at close range he
saw that his initial impression had been correct. For the
first time in years, Tony questioned his judgment. He
must have missed something in the report on Jensen.

Tony shifted in his chair; uncomfortable prickles of
sweat rose across the back of his neck. Behind Jensen's
smile lurked something that turned Tony's blood to ice.
Reminding himself that he earned the title "Big Tony"
because he was ruthless, Tony shook off the disturbing
memories. Nick Jensen was nothing but a dumb-ass
Texan, no match for Tony.

"My son made you a generous offer for your stock in
the Blue Grotto Corporation. What's it going to take to
close the deal?"

"I'm not interested in selling."

What a cocky little shit. Jensen had the balls to refuse
his offer.

"Bradford Bottling and Imperial Cola have had a
profitable relationship. I don't think it would do your
career any good if we started having problems now."

He paused expecting some comment, but Jensen
merely kept silent, that half-assed smile still on his face.
Tony scowled, expecting to cow Jensen the way he did
everyone else.

"Let me spell it out for you, Jensen. Imperial likes its
executives to blend into the local society. They see themselves as our partners, not foreigners. If I start squawk-
ing about you being an ugly American causing trouble,
your career is finished. Mark Nolan won't be able to
leapfrog you over more experienced men into a position
at corporate headquarters."

Jensen continued to smile. The Texan obviously had shit for brains.

"Be sensible. Accept my offer or—"

"You're not in any position to threaten me." Jensen lounged in the chair, his long legs stretched out in front of him and crossed at the ankles. "Not when I can prove your son is concealing his involvement in Travis Prescott's murder."

"Curt? What the fuck are you talking about?"

"Curt and Rhonda. They know more than they're telling about his death, and I can prove it."

Rhonda? That no-account bitch. She'd been after Curt for years, trying to get her marriage to some old man annulled. Tony's gut feeling told him Jensen was bluffing, but he wouldn't be certain. His son, he admitted, not for the first time, was a sneak and a liar.

Nick rose and walked to the door. "Don't screw with my career. If I don't get promoted, I'm going to stay right here and help manage those hotels."

The door closed behind Jensen and Tony stared at it. He punched the monitor and yelled at his secretary to send for Curt. His son appeared moments later.

"Did you have anything to do with Travis Prescott's death?"

"Of course, not. Why?"

Either Curt was telling the truth, or he'd become a more accomplished liar. Tony couldn't decide which. "Jensen claims he can prove you're involved."

"I dare him to try."

Tony measured his son for a moment. He usually intimidated Curt, but now his son seemed uncharacteristically confident. They weren't close; they never had been. Tony didn't care. He'd slaved his entire life building an empire. It was Curt's duty—he'd shirked it long enough —to marry and produce a son. Tony wanted to know his name would live on long after he'd died.

NEVER KISS A STRANGER   253

Founder of a dynasty.

"Jensen insists"—Tony carefully gauged Curt's reaction—"Rhonda Sibbet was involved too."

Curt shrugged. "I wouldn't know. I haven't seen her since the *festa* party."

Nick tossed aside the earphones. The tape of John Sanford's *Shadow Prey* wasn't holding his interest. He roamed around the guest house asking himself if lying to Tony Bradford had been a wise move. Nick couldn't *prove* anything. Worse, the incriminating picture seemed to be on the slow boat to Malta. Austin had sent it, but it had yet to appear. Still, Nick's usually reliable instincts told him Curt and Rhonda were responsible for his friend's death.

He walked over to the French doors facing Falcon's Lair and looked up at Janna's window even though he'd promised himself that he wouldn't keep thinking about her. The light was on; she'd come home. She would work in her room until well after midnight.

He knew she was struggling to finish the last-minute details before the Blue Grotto opened. She was personally training the staff so this hotel, although larger than Pithany's other hotels, would have the same level of personal service.

In the week since Janna had returned from London, he'd seen her twice. Both times she'd waved to him as she drove down the drive. He'd upset her by not asking her to come with him to Lyme Regis. But he couldn't have taken Janna, he thought, recalling that day.

He'd walked out on the massive curving breakwater, known in Lyme Regis as the Cobb. It was deserted except for the gulls circling, spiraling on motionless wings held aloft by the breeze, cawing to their mates. He silently called along with them: *Amanda Jane. Amanda*

Jane. No answer. Only the rhythmic rush of the waves on the shore and the chirping of birds.

He'd sat down on the end of the stone Cobb and looked across the bay that had once been a haven for smugglers. The sea lolled, gently rocking the small fishing boats like contented ducks in the bright sunlight. It wasn't anything like what he'd expected, remembering watching *The French Lieutenant's Woman* with Amanda Jane. The scene with Meryl Streep struggling toward the end of the Cobb through a lashing gale that threatened to rip the cloak off the near-suicidal woman had always brought tears to Amanda Jane's eyes.

He'd bought her a videotape of the movie, and she'd watched it countless times. He'd promised to take her to Lyme Regis one day when he had the money. Even when Amanda Jane had been stricken with cancer, she'd never given up hope of coming to the village.

"You'd like it," he said, looking over his shoulder at the quaint seaport stair-stepping down a steep hillside flanked by limestone cliffs that had earned them the name Lyme Regis—Royal Lime. "John Fowles still lives here—so they tell me."

But Amanda Jane didn't answer. With heightened self-awareness, he realized she had been slipping, slowly slipping away. He couldn't pinpoint when he'd lost touch with her. It might have been the finality of seeing her grave tucked in between those of her mother and brother. It might have been returning to the home where they'd been so happy. It might have been a dozen things, but most of all his life had changed when he'd come to Malta. He'd reentered the land of the living and been swept up in other people's lives. And problems.

But traces of guilt remained. When he found himself having a good time, Amanda Jane's image intruded. He would think of all she'd done for him. Of all the things she'd missed—like Lyme Regis. He might be adjusting to life again, taking part when he wouldn't have just a few months earlier. But he couldn't help feeling guilty when he enjoyed himself.

Nick wasn't certain how long he'd sat on the Cobb, gazing unseeing at the water, but when he stood up, the tide had gone out. The boats were resting on their hulls, the sailboats cocked to one side like drunken sailors. The beautiful bay had become a lonely mud flat waiting silently for the sea to return.

Nick forced his thoughts back to the present. He walked into his bedroom and searched for his swimming trunks. Whenever he needed to escape, Nick swam, finding the physical exertion took his mind off his troubles and relaxed him. In Japan he'd gone to the gym to swim twice a day, but here in Malta Nick found a few laps after work were all he needed.

He stepped out into the pool area, the sultry night air warm against his skin, promising summer's arrival that would soon bring sweltering heat. The welcome scent of freshly mowed grass brought back memories of his childhood when he'd spent Saturday mornings mowing their front yard—a small patch of weeds that passed for grass. No one would call this mother a yard; it was over two acres, maybe three including the side yard. He glanced at the expanse of grass that stretched from the guest house to the bluff overlooking St. Julian's Bay where the swing was. He slung his towel over a lounge chair and plunged into the deep end of the pool with a dive that took him to the bottom.

He swam half a lap, then climbed out of the pool, noticing the movement at Janna's window. Whenever he swam, she watched him, but never came down to talk. "Hey, Shorty," he yelled. "C'mon down."

Janna stepped out onto the balcony. "I'm busy—"

"Take a break. Come for a swim."

She hesitated, then said, "All right."

Nick went over to the double swing facing the ocean. It creaked as he sat and he told himself to oil it before Pithany returned next week.

He gazed out at the sea. Miles and miles of water. It reminded him of Texas and the limitless expanse of prairie visible from his porch. Usually that comforted him. Not tonight. The endless stretch of ocean made him feel even more lonely.

He turned, seeking the comforting lights of shore. Even at this distance Valletta stood out, a black silhouette, a medieval fortress standing proud and tall against the moonlit sky. In the harbor below the ramparts, *luzzijiet* bobbed in the gentle swells of the protected bay. Lanterns swung from their bows sending pinpoints of light across the water, reminding Nick of the fireflies back home.

"Hi." Janna came up wearing a white bikini.

The towel she clutched to her chest concealed the top half of her body but not her shapely legs. He moved over, making room for her on the swing. She lowered herself, being careful to sit so their thighs didn't touch. The swing rocked slightly, threatening to tip and dump them on the ground, but Nick braced his leg and steadied it. He stole a downward peek at Janna's bikini top. Her half-bare breasts were sexy as hell, not full enough for a *Playboy* centerfold, but damn sexy. She had a natural, unaffected sensuality about her that he found extremely provocative.

"What happened with that psychic artist? Did you get a portrait for your aunt?"

"No . . . She couldn't help me."

Precisely what Nick figured, but he didn't say so because Janna sounded too disappointed. He began rocking the swing by pushing with his foot just enough to move it.

"Gerry found out Ralph Evans died last year," Janna

added. "I'll never know if he'd forgotten something Ian said before he went to meet that RAF pilot and disappeared."

"I've been in touch with the authorities in Bardia," Nick said. "They're checking the records—such as they are—for unidentified bodies that were buried the week MacShane disappeared."

Janna smiled at him, the first genuine smile he could remember her giving him. "I really appreciate it."

"Don't get your hopes up. Getting any information out of Libyan sources is tough. Since neither Americans nor the British have diplomatic relations with Khadafy's government, I went through the Maltese embassy."

"That's smart. Ever since the Maltese warned Kadafi that American bombers were heading for Libya, they've been very friendly to the Maltese."

"Yeah. Too bad we didn't get Khadafy. A friendly government might be in power now, and we would be able to go there to investigate."

"I don't care if the British government doesn't permit travel to Libya. If they find out anything helpful, I'm going there."

He put his arm across the back of the swing, rocking rhythmically now. Janna could be damn stubborn. "Don't even think about going to Libya without me."

She didn't reply. Instead she faced forward, concentrating on the view. The Big Dipper had joined a crescent moon, coating the wind-ruffled water with a silvery patina. They sat, silently rocking the swing and watching the starry reflections of the moonlight on the waves, listening to the murmur of the breeze rustling the palms lining the garden and the rush of the surf against the rocky shore below them.

For a moment Nick studied her profile. "Why didn't you tell me you were getting a divorce?"

"Who told you?"

"Clara, but don't be angry with her. She thought I knew." He'd wormed it out of her was closer to the truth.

"I didn't want to upset my mother, so I've kept it a secret. My father's death was hard enough on her. I want to give her time to adjust before I tell her."

Audrey Atherton seemed happy to Nick. But who was he to judge? He'd only met her once. Still, he would bet the death or the divorce—probably both—had hit Janna harder.

"I know how you feel," he said, looking into her questioning eyes. "My wife died of cancer. It hasn't been easy . . ." He shrugged, having trouble putting his thoughts into words. "What I mean is: A divorce is like a death. It takes time to adjust." He attempted a smile. "That's what the experts say."

She nodded slowly. He wasn't prepared for the raw emotion he saw in her eyes. Not knowing what to say, Nick lowered his hand and touched her shoulder. He only meant to give her a reassuring squeeze, but he found himself pulling her against his side, her thigh resting against his. Her skin felt unusually soft and warm. She stared at him, her eyes a metallic silver in the moonlight.

Unable to resist temptation, Nick lowered his lips to hers. She parted her lips even before his mouth touched hers. He gently kissed her, savoring her eagerness. Her tongue edged forward, brushing his lightly. The gentle massage sent hot currents of desire through his body. He tighted his grip, bringing her flush against him.

Janna commanded herself to stand up—get away from Nick. Some greater power kept her pressed against him. Returning his kiss full measure, she slid her fingers through the thick, wet hair at the base of his neck, twisting in his arms so she could feel the coarse texture of his chest against hers.

Don't that beat all, Nick thought. The night in Mdina, he'd attributed her behavior to being tipsy. Her response to the kiss in the car might have been his own eagerness. This time he was positive. Her fingers plowed furrows in his damp hair, sending a surge of heat through his body.

Janna gave herself up to the kiss, a deep probing kiss. How was it Nick could make her ache with longing, just by touching her? There were a thousand reasons she should pull away. But she wanted him, oh how she wanted him.

Nick kept kissing her, losing track of time, letting the hot ache in his groin build. Through the thin fabric of her bikini, he felt her nipples against his chest. He edged his hand downward, sliding across smooth skin until he felt the bikini. She tensed, then arched forward, filling his hand. He eased the fabric aside and rubbed his thumb across the nipple.

Janna's stomach tumbled in one long free-fall. She felt his other hand sliding up her back. With a flick of his wrist, he had the hook undone. Oh my, he's just too good at this. She considered protesting but her tongue refused to desert his. He whipped the strapless top off and flung it over his shoulder. She barely heard the splash.

Nick eased his lips from hers and kissed his way across her cheek and down her neck. He kissed her breast, gently sculpting her nipple with the tip of his tongue. She inhaled sharply, digging her nails into his shoulder and leaving tiny half-moon imprints.

Janna's heart beat lawlessly when he began sucking and pulling ever so slightly. She couldn't keep herself from touching him. She put her hand on his knee and slipped it up his firm thigh. Anticipating her next move, she shifted her body. The swing shot out from under her. She grabbed Nick, trying to keep her balance.

Too late. She hit the grass, bringing him down on top of her.

Nick rolled off Janna. "You okay?"

She nodded, blessing the moon for ducking behind a cloud. She knew her cheeks were scarlet. How clumsy could one person be?

Nick leaned over her, partially covering her body with his, bracing himself on one arm. "Y'know, Shorty, I keep getting this feeling you and I are destined to be on the ground together."

The teasing note in his voice made her smile despite feeling like a clumsy fool. "I guess so."

"I'll bet your friend Shadoe with her damn Tarot cards would have something to say about this." He ran his warm palm up her midriff to her breast. "I know. The crystal ball says"—he settled himself between her thighs, his arousal pressing against her—"I'm destined to be on top of you." He nuzzled the sensitive spot just below her ear. "Nothin' you can do about it. Must be fate."

He kissed her, much more insistently than before, pressing her into the soft grass. "What isn't in the cards is getting it on here on the ground."

Nick stood and extended his hand to Janna. She awkwardly covered her breasts, looking around for her bikini top. It was floating at the far end of the pool. Nick lifted her into his strong arms.

As he carried her into the guest house, Janna reminded herself that she shouldn't be letting this happen. She and Nick were involved in a business. Sex would only complicate their lives. But before she found the right words—was there a polite way of getting your nearly naked body out of a man's arms?—she was in his bed.

Nick took off his trunks and slung them into the corner. A ribbon of moonlight twined its way through the shutters, glazing the room with enough light for her to see his silhouette. For a second the fullness of his arousal surprised her, filling her with a sense of feminine power. He wanted her—unbridled lust, no doubt—but he wanted her.

She ignored the silver-framed photograph on his dresser, its outline a mere glimmer in the dark room. His wife. Watching them.

Nick reached into the nightstand. "I'm going to need some help here, Short-stuff." He handed her a foil wrapper. "Know how to put on a life jacket?"

She held the foil-wrapped condom in the palm of her hand, wondering if Nick slept with women on a regular basis. Of course he did. He was prepared, wasn't he?

Nick saw her hesitating. Sleeping with a man other than her husband wouldn't be easy for her. He didn't need a crystal ball to know that. Making her smile was the only way he knew to ease her tension. "Stealth bomber," he said as she unwrapped the condom.

She fumbled with it, gingerly touching him. He buried his face at the nape of her neck, whispering against her floral-scented skin, "Hurry up. The damn thing's cold."

Her soft fingers made him even harder. He reminded himself to take his time to make this good for her. Safe sex and no regrets. He couldn't let himself think about love, so he kept talking. "Don't you have any interesting trivia to throw in right now?"

She finally got the condom on Nick but couldn't resist stroking his erect penis a few times—just to make certain the condom was in place. "The life jacket was invented by a British army doctor named Colonel Condom. Then in 1840—"

He snuffed out her words with a kiss and pushed her back on the bed. He hovered over her, kissing her and nudging her thighs apart with his knee. "You're about to see why they call this one 'The Stealth.'"

He thrust inside her in an instant, a powerful act of

possession that left her breathless. She levered her hips upward, expecting him to immediately satisfy himself. But he didn't. He propped himself up on his forearms, his hands at either side of her head. Brushing the ringlets off her cheeks, he gazed into her eyes, studying her.

"Notice one thing, Janna. I'm not smiling."

15

✳

"There's Stirling Moss," Warren told Shadoe, indicating the Formula One champion mounting the souped-up lawn mower.

"Won't he find this race a little slow?" Shadoe's eyes were on Chloe who was crawling through the grass near the judges' platform.

"Undoubtedly." The din of the racers, which sounded more like chain saws than lawn mowers, gave Warren an excuse to lean very close to Shadoe so she could hear him. "The top speed isn't much more than fifty miles per hour. But you can see the teams are serious. Look at the pits."

The farmer's field was lined with bales of hay to mark the track. At regular intervals were turnouts where the crews refueled and made repairs. With all the zeal of Le Mans teams, men were changing tires on lawn mowers whose blades had been removed for safety.

When Warren had been asked to present the trophy to the winner of the 12 Hour Endurance Classic of the British Lawn Mower Racing Association, he'd accepted. He'd received scores of invitations for every conceivable social gathering, from turkey shoots to christenings, since being featured on television several times. He accepted this invitation because he believed it would be a great opportunity to take Shadoe and Chloe out of the city for a day.

The twenty-plus acre pasture in the glen outside Wisborough Green resembled a country fair. Booths selling food and souvenirs lined the course along with families spread out on blankets or lounging in beach chairs. Children romped in the grass with family dogs chasing them and barking deliriously.

Beyond the glen, tall grass, the verdant green of early summer, rippled like a silk scarf fluttering in a light breeze. The dew had long since evaporated from the fragrant grass and drifts of wildflowers. In a stand of beech trees, Warren noticed the distinctive bright yellow flash of a warbler.

"Do you think someone will let you take Chloe for a ride when the race is over?" Shadoe asked. "She'd love a ride on a lawn mower."

"Sure." Warren smiled to himself. Shadoe often used that universal mother's voice, positive she knew exactly what her daughter would say if she could talk. Chloe was still crawling through the grass fascinated by a butterfly, showing no interest in riding a lawn mower. But Shadoe's concern for her daughter charmed Warren. She was a great mother. She would make a fantastic wife too.

In the weeks since his father's death Warren had come to terms with himself and his future. His seat in the House of Lords gave him a unique forum. For years he'd been troubled by England's economic woes. Now he was in a position to help. If his efforts led to a cabinet position, he planned to be ready.

Part of the process of grooming himself for politics was educating himself about the issues. Nick Jensen's insights on Hensho inspired Warren to spend hours researching the situation. He was determined not to shoot from the hip the way he had when he'd made his first speech. He had his beliefs, but they must be backed by facts.

Shadoe rose from her seat and grabbed Chloe before

she stuffed a fistful of grass into her mouth. She tossed the grass aside and attempted to distract the baby by offering Chloe her bracelet. Warren smiled to himself. Bringing them had been one of his best ideas. British politics demanded more than just a media presence. Warren needed to get out among the people. His life promised to be a succession of ribbon cuttings and lawn mower races. This aspect of his career would be sheer boredom without Shadoe.

Warren saw Shadoe wasn't having any success. Chloe had a taste for grass. "Let's show Chloe the booths. I'll bet she'd like to see cotton candy being made."

"You're right," Shadoe said with a grateful smile. "She'd love to see that."

He picked up the baby, who immediately dusted his shoulder with blades of grass. Shadoe brushed them off, taking longer than necessary. He looked at her, wondering if he was imagining the heartrending tenderness of her gaze.

"Thanks for inviting us," Shadoe said, then gave him a kiss on the cheek, a sensual, fleeting kiss. "Chloe's been dying to see a lawn mower race."

"What about you?" he asked, aware of how rapidly his pulse was beating. "Are you glad you came?"

"I always enjoy being with you," she said, sending a giddy rush of pleasure through him.

Carrying Chloe in one arm with the other arm around Shadoe, Warren led them toward the cotton candy booth. As they walked, dozens of people greeted him. It still surprised Warren that he'd become a celebrity overnight, increasing the awesome weight of social responsibility.

Chloe had the cotton candy in her hair twenty seconds after they arrived at the booth. Naturally, Shadoe was prepared. She whipped out a washcloth from a Gladstone bag that weighed more than the baby.

"Look, Chloe, a clown." Warren pointed to a clown coming their way, juggling balls.

Shadoe rewarded him with a heartfelt smile. As they walked toward the clown, Warren saw Everett Braxton-Ames who'd been at Christ College with him. Everett motioned for Warren to join him at the Guinness booth.

Warren maneuvered Chloe and Shadoe up to the front of the group around the clown. "I'll be right back."

Warren exchanged greetings with Everett, but declined his offer of a Guinness. They'd never been particularly close, but they moved in the same circles.

"You've become the Tories' golden boy."

Warren changed the subject, unwilling to discuss his aspirations. "I'm surprised to see you here."

"Don't forget I'm with Bellview Advertising. The Royal Automobile Club sanctions this event, and they're one of our accounts."

His eye on Shadoe who was still watching the clown, Warren mumbled something to end the conversation and said good-bye.

Everett's hand came down on his arm. "A word of advice. Shadoe Hunnicutt will kill your career before it even gets off the ground. Your image calls for a proper wife." He waved his beer mug. "Believe me, I know. Advertising is selling an image."

"My personal life is—"

"Don't be naive. Hunnicutt's baby doesn't have a father. For Christ's sake, that woman is a political albatross."

"Anything interesting happening yet?" Rhonda asked.

"Are you kidding? They're still snorkeling. That damn dog's hanging over the side barking." Curt tossed the high-powered binoculars aside. He'd thought it might be fun to relieve the surveillance team assigned to watch Nick Jensen. Janna and the Texan had sailed out of the harbor early that morning for a *gala* on Comino. The inlet on the nearby island was a great spot for diving and snorkeling. Curt and Rhonda had followed them in a friend's speedboat. They'd anchored far away and stuck out a dive flag to avoid suspicion.

Curt watched Rhonda rubbing Piz Bruin on her bare breasts. He knew she was still pissed that he'd insisted she wear a blond wig, but after yesterday's confrontation with his father, he had to be careful. He didn't want Big Tony to find out he'd lied about not seeing Rhonda.

"I've been thinking about Jensen. You haven't gotten anywhere with him," Curt said.

"He never returns my calls. When I went to his office, they said he was too busy to see me." Rhonda's lower lip jutted out making her sexy pout even more pronounced.

"That's because he thinks you're involved in Prescott's murder."

"I'm still worried about the picture. What if Travis's father made a copy?"

Curt had explained over and over that he'd paid a postal employee to intercept the package from Austin Prescott. When he had the incriminating picture, he burned it and the entire collection of photographs they'd taken over the years. Big Tony had turned up the heat in the last few months, demanding Curt marry. He couldn't risk his father finding out about his secret life.

"If old man Prescott made a copy—which I doubt—I'll take care of it. The real problem here isn't the picture, it's Jensen." He turned around and picked up the binoculars again to check on the Texan. Nick and Janna were aboard the boat again talking and laughing. Curt turned to Rhonda. "Unfuckingbelievable! The solution to our problems just hit me."

Rhonda leaned over, her hand on his thigh, her bare breasts against his arm. "What's your idea?"

"Jensen doesn't seem to have a will. If he dies, his

mother gets everything. We shouldn't have any trouble persuading her to sell. That'll get Big Tony off my back for a year, maybe two. He'll be nose to nose with Pithany Crandall—in pigshit heaven. What he sees in that old bat, I'll never know, but he's always talking about her. Having so much stock will give him an excuse to poke his nose into her business. That'll keep him busy while we wait for your annulment to come through."

"Divine inspiration."

"You haven't heard the good part—" He adjusted the binoculars. "Holy shit! Look at this."

Rhonda grabbed the other pair of high-power binoculars and they watched Nick lift Janna's hair off the nape of her neck and slowly kiss it.

"What's the 'good part' you were talking about?"

"Get rid of Jensen, but throw the blame on Janna," Curt said, watching Janna kissing the Texan and running her hand up his thigh. She was a hotter number than he'd thought.

Rhonda didn't answer, so Curt peered at her. She faced forward. Watching. Curt smiled to himself. The little scene they were viewing might be boring compared to their shipboard activities, but Rhonda was fascinated. When they finished watching, she would screw his brains out.

"Cut the crap," Curt instructed Nick who was now letting his hands rove across Janna's breasts. "Get that damn top off." He nudged Rhonda. "Can you believe she doesn't go topless? Every beach from the Costa del Sol to Monte Carlo is topless. Only tightass Brits and Americans wear bikini tops," Curt insisted, still watching Nick caressing Janna's breasts. "Sonofabitch! He doesn't have the balls to—"

In one deft motion, Jensen unhooked the top and tossed it over his shoulder. It sailed through the air, hit the rail, dangled there for a moment, fell into the water, and disappeared. Curt slapped his knee and howled. "Do you see the look on her face? She's pissed."

"Don't be ridiculous," Rhonda said. "She loves it."

Jensen was peeling off trunks that didn't come close to concealing his erection. Curt trained his binoculars on Janna's breasts. Fuller than he'd expected, but nothing *Knave* would feature. He heard Rhonda's gasp and swung his binoculars back to Jensen, who had shed the trunks.

"He's well-hung," Curt admitted, mentally comparing himself. He came out ahead by a centimeter. Okay, maybe half a centimeter. Curt looked at Rhonda. She was running the tip of her tongue over her bottom lip.

Janna watched Nick step out of his wet trunks with Taxi, her puppy, at his feet, wagging his tail. Would she ever have the strength to tell Nick no? She doubted it. They'd made love twice last night and again at dawn. It should have been enough, but it wasn't. When he'd invited her to spend the day with him on his boat, she hadn't hesitated even though she'd seen him toss the stealth bombers in the picnic basket.

"Off with that bottom, Shorty."

"Me?" she said, unable to take her eyes off him. She'd had a few lovers before Collis, but no man compared to the athletic grace Nick had, the hint of power in every line of his body.

"No. Taxi." He turned to her puppy. "Get out of your coat. Can't you see no one has clothes on?"

Taxi barked and wagged his tail, totally in love with Nick. Janna felt the heat rising to her cheeks, but she slipped out of the bikini bottom.

Nick sat down beside her, easing Janna into a horizontal position. In one fluid motion that seemed casual yet unbelievably erotic, Nick ran his hand from her bare breasts to the curve of her hip. "Know what I like about your body?"

She shook her head, unable to imagine Nick actually liking her oh-so-average body.

He stretched out beside her, his erection nuzzling her thigh, his lips kissing the inner swells of her breasts. "We're a perfect fit."

She eased her hand down the rasp of hair on his chest until her fingertips finally reached his groin. "You're so much bigger—"

He pressed himself into her palm, encouraging her to stroke him. "It's not the size of the wand, Shorty. It's the magician."

"I meant you're taller. You're always teasing me about—"

His lips covered hers, his tongue dancing with hers before she could finish her sentence. It occurred to her, not for the first time, that Nick was so very different from Collis. Her husband had believed in sex by the numbers: a tickle here, a pinch there, a flick of the tongue. It was over before it had really started. The truth was, he'd never cared enough to find out what she liked.

Nick's hand edged between her thighs, expert fingers stroking her. He kissed her breast, then nipped playfully as he slipped downward. She tried to hug him, but he'd repositioned himself, now trailing moist kisses across her taut stomach, his fingers exploring her inner thighs.

"You know there's a nasty rumor going around Malta." Nick smiled up at her.

She craned her neck and peered down at him. "What rumor?" She heard the waver in her voice. No wonder. She'd never carried on a conversation with a man parked between her thighs. Only his naughty blue eyes and damp head were visible. He stroked her twice with his tongue. She lost all interest in the local gossip.

"There's a rumor that I'm a culinary Neanderthal.

They say all I like is fast food that's fatal to laboratory rats." He winked at her. "This should prove I have very sophisticated tastes."

Janna gripped the cushions, her eyes on the cerulean blue sky, white-hot heat unfurling inside her. Seconds later involuntary tremors began, dismaying her with the magnitude of her own desire. The sound of foil ripping filtered through the sound of the waves lapping the side of the boat and the blood pounding in her ears.

"Know what I like about these stealths?" he asked, unmistakable laughter in his voice.

She cocked her head forward and saw Nick poised above her, very erect, very sure of himself. Not trusting her voice, she shook her head.

"They hit the target every time."

With one explosive thrust, he was inside her. She wrapped her arms around him, arching her hips to meet his. She slid her hands into his hair and wound the damp waves through her fingers. Her breath came in pleasure-filled gasps as his body moved in a languid rhythm against hers, building slowly into a rapid, more powerful cadence. She lost track of time, letting raw emotions guide until her body surrendered completely. Moments later, Nick tensed, pressing into her for one final time.

"Know what, Janna? You're smiling."

Who wouldn't be? She brushed a damp curl off his forehead. She had no idea what to say at moments like this. Part of her screamed to say: I love you. Fortunately, she knew better.

Nick rolled onto his side, taking his weight off her. He studied her face, his eyes filled with an unreadable emotion. Kissing her gently, he hugged her body to his, splaying his hand against her hips as if he didn't want his body to separate from hers.

"I never made love to you before," Nick said.

"What about last night?" she asked, not understanding what he meant.

Nick winked at her. "In another life. I never made love to you in France. Even if I had to take off ten thousand petticoats, I would have made love to you. And remembered it."

"You're never going to let me live that down, are you?"

"Nope." He kissed the tip of her nose. "Of all the come-ons I've heard, that takes the cake."

"It wasn't a come-on, honest. Some people really believe they've lived before."

"Well, it worked. It made me really think about making love to you."

"Nick, I—" She flinched at a cold nudge on her upper thigh. "Taxi, get your nose off me."

"He's feeling left out."

Taxi responded to Nick's voice by yipping excitedly. Nick eased away from Janna. She reluctantly let him go, watching him sit up. He walked over to the galley area with Taxi at his heels and tossed the condom in the waste paper basket.

Nick motioned for Janna to follow him as he opened the transom door and went out onto the swim step. "Time for a dip."

"What about that boat over there?"

"They're too far away to see us without high-power binoculars with gyrostabilizers. Besides, they've got a dive flag up." He squinted thoughtfully at the boat. "The flag's been up for hours. They couldn't still be diving." He chuckled and put his arm around Janna. "Look at that boat rock. They're having too much fun to watch us."

Nick pulled her into the water and they swam with Taxi perched on the swim step worriedly barking. Afterward, they decided they'd had enough sun and went into the salon. Nick turned on the stereo and they lounged on the settee, wrapped in towels, sipping drinks.

"Are you sorry you're getting a divorce?" Nick asked, surprising Janna. So far, they'd steered away from personal questions.

"Yes. I am," she admitted with complete honestly. Part of her still loved Collis and fantasized about him begging her forgiveness. Another part of her wanted to kill him.

"Do you mind me asking what happened?"

"I don't mind," she said even though she didn't want Nick to know she was a failure. Obviously, his marriage had been a tremendous success. "But I'm not sure what went wrong exactly. I—I think he loved me . . . or at least was very fond of me. Even so, he married me for my money—what he thought was my money."

Taxi hopped up onto Janna's lap. She stroked the puppy's soft ears, her thoughts drifting to the moment she'd discovered Collis in the tub. The sharp knife of betrayal hurt just as much now as it had then.

"Collis was—is—an extremely handsome man. Not only that, he's very intelligent. Women can't resist throwing themselves at him. It wasn't his fault really. It was bound to happen sooner or—"

"That's bullshit. Looks or intelligence doesn't have anything to do with love and commitment."

"You're right," Janna conceded. The sympathetic look in his eyes unlocked her heart. "He didn't love me."

"I'm sorry, Shorty. That's a raw deal." Nick squeezed her hand, then held it in both his. "It'll take a while to get over it. The important thing is not to rebound into another relationship the way Mark Nolan did. The second time, you should choose even more carefully than you did the first."

Janna nodded, understanding what Nick was trying to say: Our relationship isn't serious. She knew that, Janna reminded herself. Nick was just marking time, waiting for his transfer. The only thing binding them was the stock. And sex.

"I was married for almost seven years," Nick said, quietly.

Janna listened intently. Ever since Mark Nolan had told her about Nick's marriage, she'd wanted Nick to open up and discuss his wife with her.

"Amanda Jane died of cancer. When someone's been everything to you, it's hard to adjust to living the rest of your life without her. I'm just beginning to come out of it."

"How awful for you. I—I'm so sorry. After all that, losing her brother must have been a terrible blow." She couldn't imagine a world without Warren. From the moment she'd been born, he'd been there. She loved him as much as she did Aunt Pith.

"Travis took the place of the brother I lost. I won't leave Malta until I find his killer." A somber expression came over Nick's face, shocking Janna with the depth of his emotion. "I have a hunch Curt Bradford is involved. I saw a picture of his girlfriend with Travis."

"What does that prove? Maybe she dated him."

"She denies knowing him yet a picture shows them buck-naked screwing—" Nick vaulted to his feet and looked out.

"What's the matter?"

He turned back to her, raking his fingers through his damp hair. "Nothing. He flopped onto the settee beside her. "The picture had been taken with a telephoto lens. It suddenly hit me that the boat you were worried about was there a long time. I thought maybe they were watching us, but they're gone now. Must be getting paranoid."

"You suspect Rhonda is covering up for Curt?"

"Yup. Soon as I get that picture, I'm forcing her to tell what she knows."

"Remember in Mdina when I—"

"This had better not be an apology."

"It's not. I'm trying to tell you that Curt put something in my drink—some kind of a drug to lower my inhibitions or make me pass out. I don't know what would have happened if you hadn't been there."

"You're sure? Why didn't you tell me?"

"I'm positive. I had less than one full glass of wine. I felt woozy even before you knocked on the library door." She shrugged, feeling incredibly immature for not telling him that night. "I hardly knew you then. I—I thought you wouldn't believe me. You'd think I was making an excuse for behaving like a slut."

"I would have believed you."

"I know that now, but then . . ."

Nick frowned, shaking his head. "What do you think Curt would have done?"

"I've asked myself a thousand times. I know a little about aphrodisiacs. They can't make you do anything you normally wouldn't. I can tell you with absolute certainty I would never have gone to bed with Curt Bradford."

"I don't think that's what he had in mind. His ego's too big to drug a woman to get her in the sack. The question is: What was he going to do with you when you were unconscious?"

Despite the warm strength of Nick's arm, goose bumps broke out across the back of her neck. "The thought terrifies me, but if he's killed once, he might again." She scooted closer, closing the small gap. "Now *I'm* being paranoid. Maybe there's a reasonable explanation for all this, but I've been wondering about the Bradfords. Remember, Ian MacShane was last seen just before he went to meet a RAF pilot? Tony Bradford was a pilot *and* he flew into Bardia a day or so after the *Nelson* sank."

"Didn't a lot of pilots fly between Malta and the mainland?"

"Yes, but none of them had a reason to kill Ian. Aunt Pith believed Ian had information that linked Tony to the disappearance of religious artifacts like Cleopatra's Chalice."

Nick considered her words for a moment. "Steer clear of the Bradfords."

"I want you to stay away from them too." She could tell Nick had no intention of heeding her warning.

They sat for a time, neither one saying anything but both thinking about the Bradfords.

"C'mon," Nick said. "We're missing the sunset. We're not going to solve this tonight."

They went out onto the deck and drank a glass of wine while watching the last rays of a perfect day disappear on the horizon, the sun slowly blending with the sea, glazing the deep blue water with coral.

"Clara's in Gozo for the weekend, isn't she?" Nick asked.

Janna nodded, grateful the housekeeper hadn't seen her this morning fishing her bikini top out of the bottom of the pool with a pool brush.

"That's what I thought, so I put some of my homemade chili in along with the sandwiches. Let's have it here, then sail back."

"Great," Janna agreed although she wasn't fond of chili. She didn't want to disappoint him. After all, he looked incredibly pleased with himself. Janna followed Nick into the galley. "Tomorrow Aunt Pith comes home. Audrey and Dr. Osgood will be with her."

"Too bad," Nick said, pouring thick, meaty-looking chili into a pot. "I liked having the place to ourselves."

"That's over. Warren is bringing Shadoe and her baby tomorrow about noon. They're all staying two weeks until the Blue Grotto's preview party for the travel agents.

While he's here, Warren is going to shoot that video you suggested."

"Really?"

"Yes. I sat down with the advertising people and developed an entirely new marketing concept. It's a little late to be changing, but I'm gambling it'll pay off with increased tourism from America." She didn't add that she should really be out at the Blue Grotto right now, going over other last minute details that she'd neglected while revamping the advertising campaign.

"You've really been working hard," Nick said. "I'm surprised that Pithany withdrew from the project when so many details were unfinished, aren't you?"

She noticed the chili was bubbling and motioned for Nick to stir. "Yes, but I think she wanted to give me a chance to really make the Blue Grotto my hotel. I rather enjoy the hard work and trying out new ideas. I've asked Shadoe to open a boutique in the Blue Grotto called Risqué Business. It'll feature expensive lingerie and skimpy swimsuits."

"Is she planning on selling Tarot cards too?"

"Very funny. She is going to carry the latest in—a-ah bath accessories."

"Okay. I'll bite. What?"

"It was my idea," Janna said. "I read in the *Economist* that bath shops are the latest craze. I want Risqué Business to feature a line of exotic bubble baths, fragrant shower gels, and unusual soaps, pleasure balms, and— that sort of thing. After all, every room has a sunken tub. I think the guests should be encouraged to use them—"

"Creatively."

"Exactly," she said with a laugh. "I arranged for a manufacturer to provide small samples of the products along with the usual soaps and shower caps most hotels carry. That way, if the guests like it, they can buy more in the hotel."

"Clever idea." Nick turned off the range and ladled the chili into bowls. She put them on the table while he got two beers out of the refrigerator. "It's not much, but it should hold us until we get back to the yacht club. If you're still hungry, I'll take you to dinner."

Janna sat opposite Nick who already had taken a bite. "Are there a lot of beans in this?"

"Nope," he said between spoonfuls, obviously savoring every morsel. "Texas chili. Mostly beef."

She took a bite and chewed thoughtfully. No beans. With a smile she swallowed and parted her lips to tell him what a great cook he was. The cool night air hit the roof of her mouth, igniting the aftertaste of the chili. Searing heat flared down her throat, burning her nostrils and making her eyes tear. She grabbed her bottle of beer, gasping for breath.

Nick took another bite of chili, chewing happily as she gulped beer. "An old family recipe—Kick Ass Chili."

part three

THE KISS
OF DEATH

16

✳

The late afternoon sun disappeared behind a cluster of clouds that reminded Nick of West Texas tumbleweeds trapped by a barbed wire fence. The welcome shadow temporarily brought relief to Falcon Lair's pool where Nick was sunning himself on a chaise near Shadoe and Warren. Nearby, Pithany sat under an umbrella with Chloe who was napping. Across the pool on the grass near the swing, Audrey and Ellis Osgood were drilling Von Rommel, preparing him for the next dog show.

"Would you like me to read your Tarot cards?" Shadoe asked.

"No, thanks." Nick glanced at Shadoe, stretched out, her body coated with tanning lotion that smelled like a coconut grove. Unlike most redheads, Shadoe had golden skin that tanned easily, but Warren kept checking to make certain she didn't burn. Any jerk could see Warren was in love with her. But Nick would give points that the two of them weren't sleeping together.

Nick joined Pithany under the umbrella before Shadoe said anything else. "Think Von Rommel will do as well as Millicent on the show circuit?" he asked. Millicent had come home with a first place trophy, and Audrey was determined to enter Von Rommel at the Athens show next month.

"It's hard to say," Pithany answered with a half-smile

that indicated she had her doubts. "The first show is always the hardest."

Nick put his hand down at his side and clicked his fingers. Taxi, his shadow, came immediately and Nick lifted him into his lap. "Taxi may only be pet quality, but he's a smart sucker. He's trained already."

"I don't put much faith in kennel club papers," Pithany said. "Von Rommel has a host of champions behind him, but we don't seem to be able to housebreak him, and he's unbelievably destructive, considering he's no longer a puppy." She adjusted the sunshade on Chloe's pram beside her. "He chewed to shreds an antique prayer rug that had been in the Atherton family for generations."

"Didn't Audrey stop him?"

"Discipline isn't her strong suit. It's a miracle that Janna and Warren turned out as well as they did."

At the mention of Janna's name, Nick stole a quick glance at his watch. Almost five. She was late. Janna had promised to come home early to be with her family, so Nick had left work early, too, hoping to see her. Janna insisted they play it straight while her family was around. Not only didn't she want Audrey to know she had filed for a divorce, but she didn't want her aunt to find out she was having an affair under her roof.

Nick had agreed, regretting it then, regretting it even more now. Over the last five years, he'd visited pros whenever he'd needed a woman. No comparison. Janna made him feel alive—happy—for the first time in years. That realization caused a too familiar pang of guilt, but he banked it. If he planned to join the living, he would have to learn to deal with the guilt.

"I was sorry to hear the police hadn't found out more about Travis's death," Pithany interrupted his thoughts.

"Do you think the authorities here would conceal evidence or destroy it?"

"No. This island isn't like any other place in the world. You won't find the Maltese language spoken anywhere else. Oh, we speak English, but first we're Maltese, and we're isolated on an island. We haven't printed a new telephone directory in years. Why should Telemalta bother? People don't move and they think twice before committing a crime that will disgrace their families."

"Falcon's Lair was robbed—the night Travis died."

"True, but you asked if the authorities were corrupt. I doubt it. I know you're thinking the police—"

"I was wondering about the postal workers. I've been expecting a package from Texas. It hasn't turned up. I thought maybe a worker . . ."

"Anything is possible, I suppose. What was in the package?"

"Pictures of Travis on his boat." Nick left it at that. He and Janna had agreed not to worry her family.

"While I was away, I spent a lot of time thinking about Travis. I wonder if we may have jumped to conclusions in assuming the Bradfords were involved. In the last few years, some pretty unsavory types who aren't natives have come through Malta. Interpol has proven that the bomb that brought down the Pan Am jet over Lockerbie, Scotland, had been in a suitcase filled with clothing bought in Malta."

"By Libyan terrorists."

"Yes, but the clothing was definitely purchased here. The shopkeeper is a reputable businessman. He remembers the Libyan who bought the clothing."

"How could he?" Nick couldn't imagine any of the Maltese shopkeepers, busy with tourists, recalling a certain customer.

"He purchased a sports coat the shopkeeper had in stock for years. It was far too heavy for this climate and had never sold. He'd been thrilled to get rid of it."

"Stupid mistake, but a break for the police."

"With Malta being so close to North Africa but with strong ties to Europe, it's become one way of shuttling between the continents without attracting suspicion."

"Terrorists? Here?"

"There's no evidence of a terrorist base here, none at all. But they trek through as do the British and American oil field workers whose national airlines won't fly into Libya. They're too greedy to heed their government's warnings and stay out, so they come through Malta." She paused and leaned closer. "I suspect items banned for sale to Libya come through Malta too."

Nick nodded, recalling a top secret memo in the file at his office warning him to beware of inconsistencies in shipments to Libya. "Like weapons or chemicals?"

"Yes. Is it possible Travis stumbled across some contraband being shipped with the soft drinks to Libya?"

"Maybe," Nick admitted, "but while you were gone Tony Bradford pressured me. He may not be responsible for Travis's death, but he's determined to corner your stock."

Pithany smiled at him, a secret smile, but she didn't ask him if he'd accepted Bradford's offer. Somehow—in this every-man-for-himself world—she knew him well enough to know he'd honor his promise to her.

"There's a private investigator who might—" Pithany jumped up. "Oh! My heavens! What does that dratted dog have now?"

Nick turned and saw Rommie circling the pool—hell-bent for leather—dragging something from his mouth.

"Nick, that must be yours. You left the door to the guest house ajar," Shadoe called.

Warren was already in pursuit when Nick joined him. They backed the growling dog into the wall that formed the bottom of the fountain. Nick pried Rommie's teeth open and extracted his jock strap.

Audrey dashed up. "Poor baby. He didn't mean any harm."

Warren winked at him as Nick wadded the jock strap up in his hand. Rommie in her arms, Audrey trotted off toward the swing where Ellis Osgood was waiting and Nick headed toward the guest house.

"Oh, Nick," Shadoe called, and he veered to the right, stopping in front of her, Warren and Taxi at his heels. "I was wondering if you'd be willing to model one of my new swimsuits that I'll be selling at Risqué Business."

"Maybe," he hedged, reminding himself to keep the door to his place shut. And toss his dirty clothes in the hamper. "What's it like?"

"It's a leopard print men's thong."

Nick had seen women's thongs—dental floss between the buns and a scrap of fabric across the crotch—and hated them. Nothing left to the imagination. Nothing.

"No way," he said over his shoulder, going to the guest house. "Get a friggin' frog." From what Nick had seen on Malta's beaches Frenchmen could make five pairs of swim trunks out of one pair of Speedos.

Janna peered at her reflection in the mirror and wondered if the one-piece swimsuit flattered her figure. She'd spent most of the afternoon at Marks and Spenser, the only department store in Valeetta. The soft peach color accentuated the tan she'd acquired, she reassured herself, but still worried that her bosom wasn't full enough for the strapless top. She grabbed her towel and raced downstairs, troubled that the dress she'd also purchased might not be right for the travel agents party that would officially open the Blue Grotto. Audrey certainly would never have selected anything for Janna in mauve pink, nor would she have ventured into "Marks and Sparks" and purchased anything for Janna off the rack.

"Stop it," she told herself when she reached the terrace overlooking the pool. Since when had she cared that much about clothes? Since Nick Jensen. She took three deep breaths, reminding herself that her family would be here for two weeks. She promised herself not to make love to Nick once while they were here. Surely, by the time they left, she would come to her senses.

Janna rounded the corner by the pool house and caught sight of Nick talking to Shadoe, who looked like every man's fantasy in an iridescent green bikini. For an instant, a deep ache welled up inside Janna, but she snuffed her jealous reaction. Shadoe was her dearest friend, and she'd been in love with Warren for years. Shadoe believed the Tarot cards had predicted their split when Reginald had insisted Warren stop seeing her. Now Shadoe relied on the cards, insisting they'd been correct before and she'd been foolish not to listen.

Right now, though, Shadoe was listening to Nick talking to Warren. Janna's throat tightened, but she reminded herself that she had no claim on Nick. One weekend didn't mean anything—not when Collis had tossed aside five years of marriage for some big-boobed blond bimbo.

Nick went into the guest house and Warren sat on the end of Shadoe's chaise, smiling at her. Without question, they loved each other, but Shadoe refused to give Warren another chance. Janna cursed her friend for relying too much on Tarot cards, rune stones—whatever. Janna decided to play matchmaker and get Shadoe and Warren together as much as possible. One day, she'd have to listen to her heart, not the cards.

Janna skirted the pool area and went over to Aunt Pith. "Hi. I was hoping you would come by the Blue Grotto today."

Aunt Pith smiled, that same loving smile she always

gave Janna. "I know you're doing a terrific job. I'm not going to hover over you."

"I wanted you to see the new computer system I had installed," Janna said. She half-anticipated Pithany remarking about an unnecessary expense, but her aunt merely looked at Janna, expecting her to continue. "I have small terminals mounted in housekeeping, the room service desk, the valet parking service—throughout the hotel. The minute a guest picks up his telephone, the staff will see the guest's name flash on the screen. Then the staff will address the guest by name. I want everyone to be on a name basis with the guests."

"What a clever idea," Pithany said. "I never thought of using computers to get around the impersonality of a large hotel."

"I personally trained the staff, too, not just to call the guests by name but to smile and ask if they can do anything to help."

"I understand you . . . ah . . . persuaded Georges Dumont to move from the Plaza Athénée in Paris to be the Blue Grotto's concierge. Now mind you, I'm not criticizing, but I am wondering why you didn't think one of the concierges from our hotels was better suited to the job."

"Our concierges are top-notch, but Dumont is young and innovative. He uses computers to track the guests' preferences and keep abreast of events in the area that might interest them. He'll be combining the data we have on guests who've stayed at our other hotels with the information he's gathered at the Plaza Athénée."

"So, the Blue Grotto will start off with all the polish and experience of an established hotel."

Janna nodded. "We'll be a large hotel, but we'll be friendly and personal just—"

"Janna"—Pithany craned her neck looking past her— "Nick wants you."

She turned and heard Nick yell, "Telephone." She hurried across the pool area, puzzled about who would know to call her at Nick's number. Something must be wrong at work. She should never have left early. Perhaps the electrical contractor she'd just hired had run into a lighting problem. Undoubtedly this was her punishment for spending time she didn't have shopping. She dashed inside the guest house saying, "Who—"

Nick's intimate look, surveying her from head to toe—as close to a caress as you could get without touching—told her there wasn't any phone call. He smiled his adorable smile, backed up by the one dimple. "Terrific suit."

His words wiped away all her anxiety, making every moment she'd spent choosing the suit worth it. "Thanks." She hoped her voice sounded casual.

He put both hands on her bare shoulders. She felt his touch from her collarbone to the soles of her feet. He motioned for her to turn around, and she did a quick pirouette.

"Strapless, huh," he said, stating the obvious and taking her into his arms. He kissed her, one long, lingering kiss. "Know what I like best about these suits?"

He had the same smirk on his face that he'd had when he'd served her the Kick Ass Chili. She backed up. Too late. He hooked his thumbs under the edge of the top and yanked it—in one swift movement—to her waist. He covered her exposed nipples with the warm palms of his hands, squeezing ever so slightly. "Easy access."

He pressed his lips to hers, his hands playing across her breasts. Heaven help her, she honestly didn't know if she could make it two long weeks with her family keeping her from Nick. "You are sooo bad. What am I going to do with you?"

"I have a great idea."

She hiked up the top, shimmying to get it back in

place. "Come on before everyone figures out what we're doing."

Nick reluctantly followed her. "Warren would love to get Shadoe out of her bikini. Trouble is, he doesn't know how to get her to cooperate. I told him to stay in the extra bedroom in the guest house, and I'd give him a few pointers."

"You didn't?" Somehow she imagined being able to dash down to Nick's—if she weakened—but not with her brother in the guest house's second bedroom.

"Just kidding. He's staying out here in the guest house with me, so we can go over the script for the video."

Outside, Xavier, Clara's cousin hired to help with the extra guests, was serving drinks. Nick noticed that Pithany served La Valette and Lachryma Vitis; neither Maltese wine came from the Bradford vineyards. The group settled around the table, sipping drinks. Nick sat beside Janna, but as much as he loved teasing her in private, he respected her too much to embarrass her, so he kept his hands to himself. But he did let his knee brush hers. She jerked back. Nick could have sworn Pithany caught her niece's reaction, but she quickly looked away.

"Rommie's upstairs having his 'tucky time,'" Audrey told Nick and he smiled inwardly. Audrey baby-talked to her dog and Shadoe talked to Chloe as if she were a rocket scientist. "I'm so sorry about your—your—"

"Supporter," Ellis Osgood supplied the polite term for jock strap.

Nick noted Janna's puzzled look, but she didn't question her mother.

"Now tell me, Nicholas—" Audrey began.

"Just Nick. It's not short for anything."

"Unique like Janna's name," Audrey said with a smile at Ellis. "Pithany suggested I name Janna after a Roman god, Janus. He had two heads. One looked back, the other forward."

"Looking back in time as well as living in the present," Shadoe added.

Nick smiled to himself. Maybe his mother wasn't so nutty, after all.

"Tell me about your people," Audrey asked Nick.

He felt the group's eyes on him, friendly eyes, really, but he couldn't envision them understanding life in West Texas. "I'm from Muleshoe, Texas. It's a small town."

"Like Pildowne Crossing," Audrey said. "It's very small. Isn't it about five hundred people, Ellis?"

"About that," Ellis Osgood answered with a very fond smile at Audrey, who blushed.

Nick doubted any of them, even Janna, could comprehend the difference between Muleshoe and Pildowne Crossing. Nick had been in England only once, but on the trip to Lyme Regis he'd seen plenty of manor houses. They didn't have signs but the message was clear in their golf-course-size lawns and storybook homes: No riffraff need enter.

"Did you find the seminars at the dog show interesting?" Janna asked before Nick could change the subject himself.

"Quite helpful, actually," Audrey said and Ellis nodded his agreement, but Nick noted Pithany merely sipped her wine. "I'm now able to asperate Rommie's anal glands myself."

Puleeze, we're drinking. Nick struggled to imagine the beautiful Audrey lifting her dog's tail and squeezing the pea-sized glands.

"It's very important," Audrey informed the group. "Those nasty little glands are a throwback to the days when dogs marked their territory by spraying on it. Of course, Rommie would never . . ."

Nick had his doubts about what Rommie would do

with his anal glands, but kept them to himself. In his book, any dog who would chew a hole in a jockstrap was perverted. "I don't believe I'd ever seen a Maltese before coming here," Nick dropped his hand and clicked his fingers. Taxi came and Nick lifted him into his lap. "Great dogs, but they remind me of Chihuahuas."

"Chihuahuas?" Warren and Shadoe said in unison.

"Not Taxi or Millicent so much," Nick admitted, "but Rommie looks a bit like the two Chihuahuas that lived up the street from us in Muleshoe. My brother, Cody, and I called them Cha-wee-wees. No one could housebreak them. They went all over until their owners had a polka-dot carpet."

"Rommie only widdles inside to punish me," Audrey said, "for leaving him."

Again, Nick had his doubts. Rommie reminded him of a sneaky Chihuahua wearing a fluffy white toilet rug.

"I also learned," Audrey announced with a flourish of her hand that held a wineglass like a scepter, "that chocolate can be fatal to dogs. Too much and they die. I have to watch Rommie. He has a terrible sweet tooth."

"I'll hide my box of Cadburys," Pithany said with a wry smile, her eyes on Nick.

"Beside the seminar on the dangers of chocolates, I attended a seminar that made me aware of those dreadful fleas," Audrey continued. "Of course, Rommie's *never* had a flea. But since I'm planning to breed him, I'll have to be careful."

"You're breeding him?" Shadoe gasped.

"Well, not right away. It may take some time to find a female with suitable credentials."

"What does breeding Rommie have to do with fleas?" Janna asked.

"Janna, surely you're aware"—Audrey blushed, a rosy pink that crept up her face to her cheeks. She stole a quick look at Ellis—"of diseases spread by sexual activity."

Nick nudged Janna with his knee. "Can't be too safe these days."

"You're right," Audrey agreed, looking at Warren. "I hope we're all taking precautions. I wouldn't want any of us to catch anything . . . unpleasant."

"I'm certain we're all aware of the problems," Warren said, "but you were talking about Rommie."

"The biggest danger when breeding a male is sexually transmitted fleas."

Warren stood, his still full glass in his hand. "I think it's time to dress for dinner."

"Mercy," Audrey said, "I'll have to hurry. Come along, Ellis."

Pithany rose, smiling at them. "I'm going to rest a bit before dinner. My legs are tired. Too much walking, I guess."

The older group went indoors and Warren said to Nick, "Don't mind my mother. She gets a bit . . ."

"You should meet my mother," Nick said.

Shadoe pointed to the terrace "Isn't that Rommie? What's he got in his mouth this time?"

"It looks like a rolled up map or something," Warren said.

Nick and Warren chased Rommie around a Pygmie palm before it dawned on Janna what the dog had in his mouth. She must have left her closet door open, and the sneaky little beast had found the sketch hidden at the back. She charged over to the tree crying, "Cookie, cookie." Rommie stopped; she pounced on him and snatched the rolled up sketch from his mouth. Rommie scampered into the house, yipping as if he'd been kicked.

Warren hurried up to her, Nick at his side, asking, "What's that?"

"It's nothing."

"It must be something important. You were in enough of a hurry to get it. Is it damaged?" Warren asked.

The paper was soggy but would dry. "It's fine." She looked into her brother's eyes; she'd never been able to hide anything from him. His blue eyes telegraphed astonishment that she was evading his question. "It's the sketch Laurel Hogel did for me," she said weakly.

Shadoe joined the trio. "You didn't give it to Aunt Pith?"

"She wouldn't want it. It isn't Ian MacShane."

"You left London before you could tell us what happened with the psychic artist," Warren said. "I gather she's a fraud."

Janna avoided Nick's curious stare. "No. She's a very nice lady, but she couldn't sketch Ian."

"Then why keep it?" Warren asked.

"I couldn't throw it away. She tried so hard. And she was helpful."

"She told you more about Ian," Shadoe said with complete certainty.

"Yes." Janna looked over her shoulder; she couldn't risk Aunt Pith finding out about this until she had more facts. "Let's talk in the gazebo."

In silence, the foursome walked to the side yard where a Victorian style gazebo overlooked the topiary garden. Wisteria draped the latticework, its purple blossoms swaying in the breeze, shielding the group from the brutal sun, and creating patches of shadow and light inside. Nick positioned himself beside Janna. She regretted not telling him what Laurel said earlier. After all, he'd taken the trouble to help her by contacting the authorities in Libya.

"I don't pretend to understand how Laurel does it, but she does see . . . or sense things she couldn't possibly know about. I told her what I knew, and I read her the transcripts of Ian's broadcasts."

"What did she tell you about him?" Shadoe asked.

"She says he was killed by a bullet to his brain during the war, but she doesn't know who killed him or why."

"Jee-zus. Don't tell your aunt that." Nick shook his head. "Sounds to me like this Hogel woman was b.s.ing you."

"I don't think so. Laurel knew the pet name Ian had for Aunt Pith. I'm the only one alive but Aunt Pith who knows."

"A lucky guess," Nick insisted.

"She also said Pithany and Ian's love was 'a love for all time.' That's the last line in a letter he wrote Aunt Pithany—exactly," Janna said. "But I never told her those words."

"That has to be more than luck," Warren said.

"Without locating his body we'll never know," Janna said, "if she's right about how he died."

"I believe her," Shadoe said.

"I don't know what to think," Warren admitted, "but if the picture isn't of MacShane— Hold everything. How do you know it isn't him? You never saw him."

Janna could see there was no way of avoiding showing them Laurel's sketch. And Nick would know the truth. She'd deliberately not discussed her visit to Laurel with him. She hadn't wanted him to know how often she thought about him. How much she cared.

She slowly unrolled the sketch, taking care not to tear it in the spots where Rommie's saliva had soaked the paper. She held it up for the group, but she didn't need to look at it again. She'd looked at it, puzzled, too many times.

A silence filled the gazebo. The only sound was the hum of the bees darting in and out of the wisteria and the distant crash of the waves hitting the shore. Warren looked at Nick, then at the picture, then at Shadoe, who was staring at the sketch, smiling.

Nick's laughter ricocheted through the small space. He put his arm around her saying, "We might as well tell them, Shorty."

Warren looked directly at Janna, but Shadoe's eyes were still on the sketch.

"Nick and I"—Janna didn't know how to put it—"have been seeing a lot of each other. I was thinking about Nick right up to the moment I knocked on Laurel's door. You see, we'd been discussing ways to promote the Blue Grotto, and Nick was on my mind. Evidently, Laurel picked up on my thoughts."

"That explains why she drew Nick instead of Ian," Warren said.

Nick hugged her, his blue eyes caught and held hers. "She read your mind."

Shadoe shook her head. "Why would she have sketched him in an RAF jacket?"

17

✳

Janna followed Shadoe upstairs to dress for dinner, holding the rolled sketch, still amazed that Laurel had read her mind and had drawn Nick rather than Ian Mac-Shane. Accompanying her astonishment at Laurel's unique ability was a sense of disappointment at not being able to present Aunt Pith with a picture of Ian. All Aunt Pith had were memories.

Janna's mind replayed Ian and Pithany's story, recalling how they'd met in the dark and Aunt Pith had believed Ian to be much older than he was. Aunt Pith had also thought she was too plain, too bookish to interest the handsome reporter. Not for the first time, Janna wondered what Ian had looked like. A tall, handsome Scot, had been all Aunt Pith had said. Somehow Janna had pictured him as blond even though she'd never been told this. What had he looked like? Even though he'd been a reporter, had he worn an RAF bomber jacket like the one in the sketch?

Halfway up the stairs, Janna realized that Shadoe had been uncharacteristically quiet since asking about the jacket. She and Shadoe hadn't had one of their intimate talks since Janna had confided in Shadoe that she'd discovered Collis with his girlfriend. "I'm sorry I haven't rung you lately. I've been so busy with the hotels and the upcoming opening of the Blue Grotto."

Shadoe paused on the landing, her hand on the freshly

polished newel post. "I understand. You're developing a relationship with Nick."

"Maybe," she said, reluctant to confess their relationship was based primarily on sex. "I can't explain what's happened to me since I moved here. I was devastated by my father's will and Collis's affair. When I was in London, I wondered how I could go on. But after arriving here, all that seemed"—she didn't know how to explain it—"as if it had happened to someone else. It hurts if I think about my father or Collis, but they aren't on my mind very often."

"Yet you think about Nick all the time."

"Yes," Janna admitted. "I'm very attracted to him physically."

"Are you sure that's all it is?" Shadoe opened the door to her suite.

"I hope so," Janna mumbled, her voice barely audible above the sounds of Chloe's nanny giving the baby a bath in the adjacent room. "I thought I loved Collis and look what happened. All I know for certain is that now isn't the right time for me to fall in love."

"Why not?"

"I'm still legally married, remember? My divorce won't come through for another six months. Anyway, Nick's not right for me. With his looks, women will always be after him—Collis all over again. He's still in love with his wife even if she's been dead for years."

"Do you think it's fair to hold his looks and the fact that he's capable of committing himself, against Nick?" Shadoe flung over her shoulder as she left the suite's sitting room for the bedroom and bath. Without waiting for Janna's answer, she called to the nanny to be careful not to get soap in Chloe's eyes.

Janna honestly didn't know what to think. She'd been grappling with her feelings about Nick Jensen since the night he'd tackled her in the dark. As usual, Shadoe asked insightful questions, but hadn't offered her opinion. The only way she would tell Janna what she was thinking was if Janna asked.

Shadoe returned with a burgundy shopping bag emblazoned with silver foil script that read: RISQUÉ BUSINESS. Janna was glad she had suggested Shadoe open a lingerie boutique in the Blue Grotto's shopping arcade and convinced Warren to make a promotional video for the Blue Grotto. If he and Shadoe were forced to spend time together, she would realize he really loved her and that he wouldn't leave her the way he had years ago.

"I brought these for you." Shadoe handed Janna the bag. "They're samples of some new items Risqué Business will feature."

"Thanks." Janna decided her comments about having an affair with Nick had prompted Shadoe to give her the sexy lingerie—the confection of black silk and lace—she saw in the bag. For years, Shadoe had hounded her about her cave-woman undergarments. She wondered what her friend thought about Nick, betting she liked him. "Shadoe, what do you think about Nick?"

"I like him. He isn't conceited."

Janna took that as a backhanded swipe at Collis. Shadoe had never criticized him, but Janna knew she hadn't liked him.

"I've studied Nick's astrological chart," Shadoe continued. "Saturn is in Leo. That means during all Nick's lives he's been a leader. A natural leader."

Janna studied the black lace peeking out of the bag. She'd never criticized Shadoe's obsession with astrology and Tarot cards. Janna had even listened enough to absorb many of Shadoe's theories. She knew Saturn was believed to be the key to past lives. Her own chart had Saturn in Sagittarius, making her a wanderer who'd lived in many different cultures. Now, Janna regretted nurturing Shadoe's ideas because her astrological chart was keeping her from Warren.

"What about my brother?" Janna asked, giving herself an opening to discuss their relationship.

"Saturn is in Capricorn for him. Throughout time, Warren's been a very correct person, someone who can be relied upon to do the right thing, but he has to learn to develop his own individuality."

Janna silently conceded Shadoe had accurately described her brother. "He's changed a lot since you dated him years ago."

"Yes. He's come into his own. He's just the sort of man England needs."

"What about you? Isn't he the man for you?"

"Our signs aren't compatible. Tarot cards confirm it. The last time I went against the cards . . ." Shadoe's voice trailed off.

"The cards had nothing to do with it. My fath—Reginald forced Warren to stop seeing you. Things have changed. Give him another chance."

"If the time is right, there'll be a sign."

Janna didn't argue. She valued Shadoe's friendship too much, deciding that throwing Warren and Shadoe together as often as possible would intensify the chemistry Shadoe could attribute to cosmic forces or karma.

Nick and Warren finished dressing for dinner early and sat in the sitting room of the guest house, talking about filming the video, which would begin the next morning.

"Just be natural," Nick advised. "Pretend you're talking to a close friend, telling him about an exciting resort you've recently visited."

"I'll do my best," Warren said. "I'm not really comfortable in front of a camera."

"I'd never know it. You come across as very relaxed

and, more important, sincere. That's what the public wants, someone they can believe in."

"Sincere? Believable?" Warren said with a slight shake of his head that shifted his blond hair. "Too bad everyone doesn't see me that way."

"You mean Shadoe?" Nick guessed. "Aren't your signs compatible?"

"It goes deeper than that," Warren said quietly.

Nick regretted prying, getting too personal. He liked Warren, but he hardly knew him. Warren's love life was really none of his business. Nick certainly didn't want Janna's brother asking him about his love life.

"Years ago, I'd wanted to marry Shadoe, but my father insisted it would be a mistake. I was young, impressionable. I listened to him and have never stopped regretting it."

"Shadoe hasn't forgiven you."

"Actually," Warren said. "Shadoe was very understanding. From the start, she claimed the Tarot cards had been against our relationship. She didn't blame me."

"Great," Nick couldn't help saying, "an instant excuse for your actions."

"I never used that as an excuse, nor did I blame my father. I could have stood up to him. I never blamed anyone but myself."

The forlorn expression on Warren's face and the bitter tone of his voice made Nick feel sorry for him. He genuinely liked Janna's brother. When he'd first learned Warren was an earl, Nick had assumed he'd be content to spend his time trotting around the English countryside yelling, "Tallyho!" But Warren had proved to be an interesting man with a sense of responsibility, not only toward his family but toward his country.

"Shadoe's convinced we aren't destined to be together. She believes we've been together in several past lives and I always let politics separate us."

"What a crock!" Nick was sorry the second the words were out of his mouth; he could see Warren was earnest. "Oooo-kay, I know Shadoe's a very successful business-woman, and a highly creative person, but this past lives bit is farfetched, don't you think?"

"I used to," Warren conceded, "but now I'm not so sure. Shadoe was regressed and under hypnosis she discovered we'd been together in ancient Greece. She was my slave."

"Your slave?" Interesting possibilities: Shadoe in a toga as Warren's slave. Sounded like an X-rated video.

"It took a long time for us to discover this because, when she was under, Shadoe spoke an obscure dialect of ancient Greek. It took a professor from Oxford to translate what she was saying."

"Really?" Nick admitted he had no explanation for this. It gave him an eerie feeling, the same feeling he'd had when he'd seen the sketch earlier.

"Shadoe, sobbed, brokenhearted—but still under hypnosis—when I gave her to another man in exchange for a political post."

"You were there when she was regressed?"

"No. Professor Olgesby from Oxford told me. Apparently in that life I was a very callow man."

"In that life?" Jcc-zus, was there no end to this?

"We were together in the Middle Ages." Warren hesitated.

The Middle Ages, Nick thought, wishing he'd studied the period more, but he did remember a professor calling it "a thousand years without a bath."

"Go on," Nick prodded. "What happened?"

"I loved Shadoe, but I married another woman in order to win the king's favor and obtain a court appointment."

Nick was sorry he'd mentioned Shadoe. She was an

intelligent, but very complicated woman. If she believed all this, Warren was in trouble.

"Then during the French Revolution—" Warren continued.

"You were there too?" Nick had teased Janna about this but he hadn't taken it seriously.

"Yes. Shadoe believes I was Robespierre."

"The leader of the Reign of Terror?" Nick knew little about the French Revolution except what he'd learned in one brief course in college, but he did remember the vicious Robespierre. Hard to believe that man was anything like Warren. If what Warren believed was true, Warren as Robespierre had been responsible not only for Shadoe's death but for Nick's and Janna's too. That probably meant good ole Marie Antoinette was hanging around somewhere. He almost laughed. If Marie had returned, she was now Audrey.

"If I were Shadoe," Nick joked, "I'd stay away from you."

"She thinks people change from life to life," Warren said, obviously taking Nick seriously. "She isn't afraid I'll kill her, but she does think I'll leave her."

"Isn't there some way to change Shadoe's mind?" Nick asked.

Warren shrugged. "I keep hoping she'll draw the ten of cups when she reads the Tarot cards. She believe the cards reflect change, that the world doesn't stay the same. The ten of cups indicates a happy family life."

Janna excused herself to get dressed and went down the hall, the bag in one hand the rolled sketch in the other.

Rommie was chasing Millie and Taxi up and down the wide hall, his muzzle full of crumbs. She bet Rommie had been into the stash of Harrods' ginger cookies Audrey always kept on her nightstand. At the turn in the hall, Janna paused and looked to the adjacent wing where Aunt Pith had her suite.

The niggling at the back of her mind since seeing Laurel's sketch returned. Janna had put off discussing Ian with Aunt Pith because she wasn't a good liar. Aunt Pith might sense something was wrong, and Janna would be forced to tell her Ian hadn't gone down with the *Nelson*. But her curiosity got the better of her. She walked down to the double oak door, and Aunt Pith immediately answered her knock.

"I like your new swimsuit," her aunt said with a smile, "but don't you think you'd better dress for dinner?"

"I just wanted to ask you a quick question. What did Ian MacShane look like?"

Aunt Pith motioned for Janna to come in, saying, "He had dark hair and blue eyes. He was a big man, over six feet tall. Why?"

"Just curious," she evaded, thinking the similarity between the description of Ian and Nick had to be coincidence. "Did he resemble Nick?"

Aunt Pith's gaze swung to the window overlooking the area of the garden with the swing. "Yes."

"A little?"

Pithany nodded.

Janna's sense of disbelief grew. "More than a little?"

Aunt Pith turned back to Janna. "When I last saw him he was twenty-six, so Nick's eleven years older."

"Right," Janna said, her mind scrambling for a plausible explanation. "Nick's older than Ian was when he died, but other than the age difference do they look alike?"

"They're dead ringers."

Janna stared at her aunt in utter disbelief, the truth hitting her full force. Dead ringers? Laurel Hogel hadn't made a mistake. She looked into the clear green-gray eyes, an echo of her own, filled with the certainty that

Laurel had also been correct on another count. Ian Mac-Shane *had* been murdered.

Aunt Pith put a comforting arm around Janna. "I didn't tell you because I thought you'd think me a foolish old lady for comparing Nick to Ian."

"You're anything but foolish," Janna said. "Since I took over for you, I've discovered how difficult it must have been to build the business. I don't know how you did it."

"It's been my life." She gestured toward the window. "But I do have my sentimental side. I named Falcon's Lair for Ian. And I built that swing so I could sit facing the sea. From there I can see the spot where the *Nelson* went down. I feel I've never really lost Ian because I know he's out there. Sometimes—now this is really silly —I've even talked to him."

Janna squeezed her eyes shut, forcing herself to be quiet, filled with love and a renewed determination to uncover the truth about what had happened to Ian. She slowly unrolled the sketch.

"My stars." Tears welled up in Pithany's eyes. "That's Ian in the RAF bomber jacket he always wore. See"— she pointed to a patch on the shoulder—"that was caused by a burning ember from a bombed out building. I patched it for him. Where did you get this?"

"A psychic artist did it for me." Janna's words came out in a rush; she didn't want to reveal what else Laurel had told her. "I was shocked when it looked exactly like Nick. I thought she'd made a mistake. How do you explain their resemblance?"

"I can't explain it. After I met Nick, I had a private investigator do a thorough check on him. He hasn't any relatives from Scotland." Her eyes never left the sketch.

"But surely there must be some reason—"

Looking at the picture, her emotions clearly expressed

in the tenderness of her expression, Aunt Pith said, "Some things can never be explained."

She looked up and met Janna's gaze. "During the war about a month after Tobruk fell, I had two whole days off. I cadged a ride to Mosta where I had friends, thinking it was out of the Nazis' regular bomb runs. That Sunday I went to St. Mary's church with them. In the middle of the service the air raid siren rang. We stayed where we were, assuming the Nazis were merely using a different route to Valletta to dodge the antiaircraft guns. Too late we realized they were bombing Mosta. A bomb struck the church, crashed through the centuries-old canopy and landed on the altar."

"You must have hidden under the pew."

"No. I looked in death's face and waited for the bomb to explode." She shrugged. "It didn't even though the bomb was perfectly good. Most thought it a miracle. I took it as a sign from God that he was on our side—the Nazis wouldn't win. They'd never take Malta."

"And they didn't."

"No. There were lots of dark days ahead, but I had faith. The same faith I feel about Nick Jensen. Some things can never be explained, like why he so closely resembles Ian. I like to think God's sending Ian back to me as a son."

A son? Janna was momentarily stunned, then decided her aunt's reaction was only natural. She'd wanted children, lots of them, but had had to content herself with mothering her sister's children. Knowing Nick resembled Ian certainly accounted for her fondness for him. And her trusting attitude about his owning Blue Grotto stock.

"I also think Nick's been sent here for you."

"For me?" Janna gasped, wondering if her aunt knew about their affair. She was sharp, observant; undoubtedly she did.

"In many ways your life has been parallel to mine. You remind me so very much of myself."

By the time she arrived at the dinner table the aspic had been served—Nick hadn't touched it—and the group was discussing the Beauchamp Place location Warren had rented for Audrey's boutique, Haute Dog. Nick was full of ideas: diet chow for dogs, bone-shaped breath mints, K-9 Wellies for rainy days, and a soft drink to be called "The Paws that Refreshes."

Aunt Pith smiled encouragingly at Janna and she managed a half smile. Since she'd left her aunt's room Janna had experienced a gamut of perplexing emotions. She realized Aunt Pith was more sentimental than she'd suspected. One great love had won her heart and left her determined to never let Ian's memory die.

Janna didn't want to bring the aunt she'd loved and looked up to her entire life any more grief, but Janna knew what she and Nick shared didn't approach the love Pithany and Ian had known. Nick's transfer would come through and he would leave. The very thought of Nick's leaving caused an ache like a too tight girth around her ribs, making it difficult to concentrate. She'd better learn to face the truth: Soon he'd be gone.

Even if he stayed, even if they elevated their relationship to more than a physical level, he still loved his dead wife. He hadn't said it—not in so many words. Still, Janna knew it. The picture of Amanda Jane with her brother and Nick stood on his dresser. Every time Janna and Nick made love, his wife watched. A silent reminder of true love.

She let Clara remove her half-eaten tomato aspic, her mind still on Nick. *Don't fall in love with him. Don't let Aunt Pith's romantic fantasies become yours.*

She concentrated on her own problems. Collis. She'd put off confronting him in person for too long. Some part of her expected him to come to her and beg her forgiveness, but all he'd done was send gifts. Trying to buy his way out of trouble—as always. She cursed herself for not having seen the truth earlier. How could she have mistaken her relationship with Collis for true love?

"I'll bet Janna has a great name for that handcast statue of a dog you're planning to put at Haute Dog's door," Nick said to Audrey, interrupting Janna's thoughts.

"Fido," she said automatically, "from the Latin *fidus* meaning faithful."

"Perfect," Audrey said. "Man's faithful friend like Rommie."

Janna didn't think there was anything particularly faithful about Rommie. When she'd been dressing she'd heard him yipping in the garden below. He was trying to get in Nick's door, but Taxi and Millie had come barreling out of the main house through the pet door and distracted him. Like Taxi, Von Rommel was crazy about Nick.

The group chatted amiably and ate *lampuka* with wheatberry sauce. Janna silently bet Nick wouldn't like the dolphin-fish native to Malta, but she was wrong. He winked at her and ate every bite.

Janna watched Aunt Pith, who was listening attentively as Nick explained to Audrey that Haute Dog was a perfect name—memorable and it targeted the upscale market. No one should ever underestimate the power of a name. Apparently, Imperial Cola had used the phonetic equivalent of its famous name when they brought their drink to China. No one bothered to check and find out *Em per al* meant "eat the waxy minnow," and they were forced to change it.

Aunt Pith laughed at Nick's story, and Janna reminded herself to find out the truth about Ian's death. If she couldn't please Aunt Pith by keeping Nick in Malta, she owed it to her aunt to find out about Ian. She intended to ask Nick who he'd contacted about Bardia and follow up herself.

After dinner Janna sat at her desk with Taxi chewing a bone at her feet and tried to concentrate on the computer printouts of staff scheduling that she'd brought home to analyze. She kept wondering how Nick and Warren were doing out in the guest house, rehearsing the script for the video. She talked herself into thinking they might need her help, only half admitting it was an excuse to see Nick. Opening the door into the hall, she caught a glimpse of Nick at the top of the stairs. Surely, he wasn't coming to her room, not with Audrey and Ellis in suites just down the hall from Janna.

She ducked back into her room, trying to decide what to do, thrilled that he wanted to see her as much as she wanted to see him. A few seconds passed—plenty of time to reach her room—and nothing happened. Janna opened the door a crack and peeked out. At the far end of the hall, she saw Nick going into Shadoe's room.

"Just a minute," Shadoe said, motioning for Nick to follow her into the bedroom, "I'm reading Chloe a bedtime story."

Nick leaned against the doorjamb, one hand in his pocket, and listened to the end of the story. Then Shadoe kissed the baby good night and returned to the sitting room. Nick took a seat across from her, asking himself why he was doing something he vowed never to do: mind someone else's business.

"You came to have me read your Tarot cards?"

"No," Nick responded. "I came to talk to you about Warren.

Shadoe reached for the pack of Tarot cards on the coffee table and shuffled the deck. "There's nothing to discuss. We're friends. That's all."

Something about Shadoe reminded him of his mother. Maybe it was the faraway look she sometimes had—as if she didn't quite know where she was. At other times she was the complete opposite of his mother, hardworking, full of creative ideas. On another, deeper level, she reminded Nick of himself. He'd asked Warren, who'd confirmed that Shadoe's childhood had been unhappy. Desperately lonely. No one like the Prescotts had come along to rescue her. To show her love.

"We tried being more than friends once about fifteen years ago," Shadoe said. "It didn't work."

Nick sensed rather than heard the hurt she still felt.

"I've never had a sign that things have changed."

From his discussion with Warren, Nick had concluded that a rational argument wouldn't carry any weight with Shadoe. In the bedroom just off the small sitting room, Chloe cried.

Shadoe dropped the Tarot cards. "Excuse me. Her nanny has the evening off."

Nick picked up the deck, shuffling them absentmindedly and listening to Shadoe comforting her daughter. His idea would take some finesse to pull it off, particularly since he knew diddly-squat about Tarot cards. When Shadoe returned, he said, "My great, great, great" —he hoped he'd counted the greats properly "great-grandmother was a witch."

"Really?" Shadoe's voice held more than a trace of skepticism. She wasn't Willy-off-the-pickle-boat; she was a very intelligent woman. He had to play this just right— and get lucky.

"Yes," he answered with total honesty. "She was hanged at Salem." He knew little about his father's side of the family, but his mother had used their famous ancestor to frighten Nick and Cody into behaving by threatening the witch would get them.

"That must have been terrible for your family." Shadoe's voice was now sympathetic.

Nick nodded sadly, shooting for an Academy Award winning performance. He'd never known his father's family. He'd been too young to even remember much about his father except for a vague impression of a tall man with brown hair and brown eyes. But Nick doubted his grandparents were proud of having a witch in the family. They certainly hadn't welcomed a dirt farmer's daughter. Or her two sons.

"Let me do a Tarot reading for you," he said, fanning the deck in his hand. "Pick a card."

"Just one?"

Aw, shit! A reading must take more than one; he should have gotten more details from Warren. Nick smiled, his good-guy grin that could have landed him the part of a born-again preacher in any movie. "This method has been in our family since Salem."

She looked doubtful but selected one card, pulling it partway out. Nick snapped the deck shut—not as fast as he had playing gin in the warehouse, but what the hell? He was out of practice—and flipped the card she thought she'd selected onto the table. The ten of cups landed face up.

"Well, I'll be. Looks like you're in for a happy relationship."

Shadoe stared at the card, incredulous. "I *never* draw the ten of cups."

"Maybe your life is changing."

"It's possible," Shadoe admitted. "Tarot cards don't rely on fate or a fixed fortune. Things can change." Her eyes narrowed, staring at the card with disbelief. "We should really do an entire reading, a gypsy reading, to be sure."

"What's the point?" He leaned forward, his eyes locking with hers. "Do you want this chance, or not?"

"Of course."

"Warren's out in the guest house. Why don't you go talk to him?"

"I can't leave Chloe. If she wakes up and I'm gone—"

"I'll stay with her. I'll come get you if she wakes up."

"Promise not to leave her? She'll be terrified if she wakes up in a strange place all alone."

"I'll stay right here."

Shadoe picked up the deck. "My turn. Before I leave, I want you to draw one card."

Janna studied herself in the full-length mirror and examined the black silk negligee that Shadoe had given her in the bag of samples from Risqué Business.

"I look good in it, don't I?" she asked Taxi. "But not good enough to keep Nick Jensen interested."

Hearing Nick's name, Taxi wagged his tail in double-time. She slipped out of the gown and tossed it on the bed. "Who was I kidding? Nick isn't any different from Collis."

Undoubtedly, Shadoe had sent him away. Determined to forget Nick, Janna flipped through the rest of the contents of the bag, marveling at Shadoe's creativity. Split panties? Panties trimmed in fur? Then she found the wrapped packages. She giggled out loud, momentarily forgetting being hurt by Nick.

Janna set the packages aside and slipped on a silk camisole the color of raspberry puree. This was more conservative than the other items in the bag, more her style. The expensive silk felt cool against her bare skin. She selected one of the packages, telling herself the bikini panties matched the camisole. Once on, they felt like tissue paper—never to be mistaken for fine silk like the camisole—but they passed for ordinary bikinis.

She twirled in front of the mirror, thinking the high-cut legs on the bikinis made her own legs look longer.

"Go to hell, Nick Jensen," she told her reflection. "I don't need you."

She walked over to the bed, set to take off the sexy lingerie and get back to work, when there was a soft knock on the door. Clara. Janna slipped her old terry robe over the underwear and answered the door.

Nick was leaning against the doorjamb, the same cocky grin on his face that she'd seen the night he'd tricked her into eating Kick Ass Chili.

Instead of returning his smile, she bristled. Obviously, Shadoe had tossed him out. She was damned if she would be second choice. Taxi hopped around, wagging his tail.

"Know how to change a diaper?" he asked.

"Of course, I've helped Sha—"

Nick grabbed her arm. "Then come with me. Chloe's wet."

"Where's Shadoe?"

"Shadoe's out with your brother. I'm babysitting."

"You're kidding?" she asked, a surge of relief arcing through her. He hadn't been after Shadoe. "How'd you manage that?"

"It was in the cards."

Janna hurried to Shadoe's suite followed by Taxi and Nick and tiptoed into the bedroom. Chloe was asleep in her crib. Her nappy was bone-dry.

"She doesn't need changing," Janna whispered to Nick as she tiptoed back into the sitting room.

One look at his face told her that she'd been had. Again.

"Now, Nick, we agreed—"

"Who's to know?" He came closer. Bedroom eyes. Most definitely.

"Audrey's just up the hall. Dr. Osgood gives her medication, but sometimes she can't sleep."

"The only medication Ellis is giving her is a beef injection."

It took a full five seconds before it dawned on Janna what Nick meant. "You're unbelievably crude!"

"But right." He leaned down to pet Taxi who immediately rolled over and offered Nick his tummy.

"Wrong. He's been my mother's personal physician for years. That's all." Privately, she admitted Ellis Osgood loved Audrey. But her mother believed Reginald's word had been gospel. He'd frowned on associating with "social inferiors" like a small-town doctor. Like Shadoe Hunnicutt. Warren dismissed his father's beliefs but Audrey had come to live with the Athertons during the war, fallen in love with the heir, and married him. Janna couldn't imagine Audrey defying Reginald even if he was dead. But she couldn't tell Nick any of this. She didn't want him to view her family as snobbish.

"They're sleeping together," Nick insisted, giving Taxi the tummy rub he adored.

"What makes you think so?"

"They get in each other's space." His eyes—bedroom blue—fastened on her lips and she found herself wishing he would stop talking and kiss her. "Don't you know our "space" is about a foot and a half radius around us? Ever notice that lovers naturally stand closer to each other than they do to other people? They trust each other enough to come into each other's space." He stood within inches of her, one hand draped across her shoulder, well within her "space." "If I'd been a stranger, you would have taken one step back. You wouldn't have been comfortable with me so close."

I love having you close. "I never noticed how close Ellis Osgood stands to my mother."

"I did. And I saw your brother watching Shadoe like a hawk but not ever getting into her space."

With a single yank, he opened her robe. She'd forgotten the camisole and skimpy bikinis.

"Wow! I'm thinking of smaller spaces," he said as he touched the filmy camisole.

So was she.

He ran the tip of his index finger up the scalloped edge of the bikinis. "Nice"—she felt her knees weakening—"my style. What kind of material is this?"

"It's man-made material."

"Feels like tissue paper to me." He stroked the material, his hand warm. Hot.

"I'll give you a hint. It comes in four flavors."

Nick's hand cradled the warm mound between her thighs. "We're talkin' food, here?"

"I guess"—the word stalled between her lips—"so. They're edible undies."

"Remember what happened last time you tricked me?"

"Honest. These bikinis come in Chocolate Truffle, Key Lime, Raspberry Mousse, and Tutti-Frutti."

Nick nuzzled her neck, nibbling his way south. Janna moaned, "Stop," but he didn't pay any attention.

"A new culinary experience," he said, "panties." He made munching sounds and smacked his lips. "Want a bite, Taxi?"

The dog enthusiastically stood on his hind legs and pawed the air.

"Nick," she murmured, her voice a shade shy of a whisper, "you're not planning on eating—"

"Of course, not. You know I'm a common-sewer, not a connoisseur. I never eat anything exotic."

"I want your word"—his hand moved provocatively between her thighs—"you won't eat these undies. They're Shadoe's samples."

"Eat? Be serious. Do you think I lured you into this

room to eat raspberry undies? The baby's in the next room, for God's sake."

"Well, I . . ."

"I invited you here, Shorty, not because I'm planning on having panties for dessert, but because"—he lowered his voice yet another notch—"I plan on transmitting a few fleas."

18

*

Warren answered the door and expected to find Nick, but found Shadoe instead with Rommie at her heels. He heard his own quick intake of breath, but recovered when he realized she hadn't come to see him. The serious look in her eyes told him something was wrong. He shuddered, astonished at his acute disappointment. What did he expect? He always called her, came to her. Only an emergency could bring her to him.

Then she smiled, the compelling smile that never failed to touch his heart. "Nick thought you might need help with the video script."

Stunned, Warren stepped aside to let her enter, silently blessing Nick and asking, "Who's with Chloe?" He knew the nanny had the night off; Shadoe would never leave her daughter alone. How often had she awakened as a child with a nightmare and no one had been there to comfort her?

"Nick's with her." Shadoe seated herself on the wicker sofa.

Rommie followed her, sniffing incessantly. Warren was tempted to toss the little devil out, but reminded himself that Shadoe had given the dog to his mother. He took a seat beside her, wondering how Nick had managed this.

"There isn't a television in my suite. Maybe we ought to take Nick a book."

Warren quickly looked around the small sitting room and saw the only bookshelf was stacked with books on tape. Thank God. Now that Shadoe had finally come to him, he had no intention of sharing her with anyone. "I'm sure he'll find something to do."

"I guess you're right. He said Janna would help him watch Chloe."

He recalled Janna showing them the sketch that should have been of Ian MacShane but had turned out to be Nick. Warren had instantly realized they were lovers. "I don't like Janna jumping into an affair so soon after filing for divorce, even with a guy as nice as Nick. I don't want her hurt again. She hardly knows Nick. They're barely more than strangers."

"No, they're not strangers. They're just getting to know each other again."

Warren refused to discuss the French Revolution and the possibility Nick had met Janna in a previous life. "I guess Janna's pretty taken with him. That sketch proves it."

"The sketch merely proves Nick looks like Ian."

"What makes you think that?"

She shrugged, her free-flowing red hair shifting across her shoulders. "I think Ian's spirit was drawn back to Malta, the place where he was the happiest. The place he found love."

In London, Janna had told them the tale of Ian and Pithany. Very romantic. Just the sort of love story to capture Shadoe's imagination. Once he and Shadoe had lived their own love story, but that had been years and several husbands ago. He wasn't sure what she felt now. But he had to know. Surely, her appearing at his door indicated she still had some feeling for him.

He gazed into her brown eyes, willing her to love him. "What about you? Have you found love?"

"Yes. I love Chloe." She looked down, the fringe of her lashes concealing her eyes. "What about you?"

He gently put his hand under her chin and tilted her head until she was looking directly at him, her eyes wide and questioning. Beneath his fingers her flawless skin felt smooth and invitingly warm. "You're the only woman I've ever loved."

His mouth slowly descended to meet her parted lips as he ran his hand over her cheek and burrowed his fingers into her thick wavy hair. Her lips trembled against his and he wondered if being together so much—without any physical contact—had been as difficult for her as it had been for him. Her arms stole around his neck, bringing him closer while her tongue welcomed his. He allowed himself one kiss, really more of a caress. They had things to settle before he would go any further. He eased away, reluctantly breaking the kiss. "I love you. I want to marry you and be Chloe's father."

For a moment he thought she might cry; tears were bordering her eyes. "You do?"

Her voice reminded him of a little girl. A little girl lost. No wonder she placed so much faith in rune stones and Tarot cards. "Yes. Forgive me for letting my father convince me to stop seeing you. It was the biggest mistake of my life. Give me another chance."

She hesitated for a moment, looking directly into his eyes as if she expected to find an answer there. Then she gazed down and inspected the folds of her skirt.

Each breath he drew brought an anguished sense of loss. He felt she wanted to love him, but had risked so much years ago—only to have him hurt her—that she would never trust him. "Listen to your heart, Shadoe. We belong together."

"Chloe does want a father."

Good Lord, no. Of all the times, over all the lonely years that this scene had played in his mind, he'd imagined her saying yes or saying no, but never agreeing to marry him for Chloe's sake. "Don't marry me to just to give her a father. Marry me because you love me."

Her expression became even more somber. "Of course, I love you. I've never loved anyone else. After you left me, I went into a tailspin, looking for someone to replace you. Finally, I realized no one could ever take your place. That's when I decided to have Chloe. I love her with all my heart." Shadoe hesitated, running the tip of her tongue across her lips. "I love you too. I always have."

Suddenly, it became impossible to steady his erratic pulse. She touched his hand, a gesture that was almost unbearable in its tenderness, and he pulled her into his arms. She buried her face against the curve of his neck. "I love you," he whispered into her hair. "Nothing will ever keep us apart." He put his arm around her, drawing her closer and she rested her head on his shoulder.

They held each other tightly as if each was afraid to let the other go. Finally Warren gently kissed her cheek, then her lips. The heady sensation of her willing lips parting for him, the tip of her tongue caressing his brought back poignant memories of the love he'd thought he'd lost forever.

"I drew the ten of cups," Shadoe whispered, her breath warm against his neck. "Nick has a way of doing a Tarot reading with just one card. The ten of cups says love will be firmly established and includes children and family."

What she's always sought, Warren realized, but he didn't point it out. He didn't know how Nick managed to get Shadoe to draw the ten of cups, but he definitely owed him a favor.

"One of Nick's ancestors was a witch who was killed at Salem, so he must be a warlock."

Warren had his doubts, but he didn't say anything because he wanted to kiss her again.

"I'm worried about Nick. I made him draw one card. Do you know which one he picked?" Warren shook his head. "The five of wands. Trouble. Danger."

"I'm sure Nick can handle—"

An insistent scratching interrupted Warren. He'd forgotten that Rommie had come in with Shadoe. What the hell had he been up to now? Reluctantly, Warren stood up. "Rommie wants out," he said to Shadoe, but told himself the feisty mutt probably hadn't found anything interesting to chew.

He opened the door and Rommie shot out, heading straight for the pet door into the main house.

Janna snuggled closer to Nick, her head resting on his chest, listening to the thudding of his heart as his pulse returned to normal. In the dark room she whispered, "Do you think we woke Chloe?"

"If your screaming 'More! More!' didn't wake the kid, nothing will."

She slapped his bare thigh. "I did *not* scream."

"No, but you moaned real loud. Real loud."

I couldn't help myself.

"It's all right." Nick explored her midriff with the tips of his fingers, gliding them across her skin and circling lower and lower. "I like knowing you enjoy making love to me."

She didn't want to tell him how much; she hadn't lasted one night even though she'd promised herself to put their affair on hold until after her family left. What had happened to her self-discipline? "Maybe I should find my clothes and get back to my room before Shadoe returns."

"Forget it. Shadoe isn't coming back so soon. Anyway,

your robe's a goner. I tossed it aside and it flew out onto the balcony. I think it went over the edge."

She jumped up and dashed out onto the balcony. The night was still warm, a harbinger of summer, and filled with clusters of crystal-white stars hovering around a full lover's moon. The bittersweet scent of the blossoming almond trees and the heady smell of near-ripe figs hung in the air. Above the throaty hum of crickets she heard the owl that lived in the carob tree. She peered over the wrought-iron rail, then went back inside. "It's decorating the mulberry bush!"

Nick pulled her down on top of him. "Could be worse," he whispered, nuzzling her ear. "Could have been those panties."

"Where *are* my panties?"

"Is that what Taxi's chewing?"

"Taxi, come here," Janna called softly.

No response.

"Yo Taxi," Nick whispered, and the puppy bounded out of the dark corner, the panties hanging from his mouth.

Janna slipped off Nick and snatched the edible undies away from Taxi, who was more interested in getting Nick to pet him than finishing off the raspberry panties. She held the panties up to the moonlight filtering into the room from the French door. "He's eaten the crotch."

"Better than Milk Bones?" Nick asked Taxi as the puppy settled down on his bare chest and licked his chin. "Now tell me what makes a great pup like this pet quality and a cur like Rommie show quality?"

"Rommie's ancestors are all champion show dogs."

"Which means they were only allowed to mate with other champions. Big deal."

"Taxi's nose is faded, not as black as India ink like Rommie's."

"So use a Magic Marker before putting him in the ring."

"Some owners tattoo their dogs' noses to bring them up to standards."

Nick gave Rommie a reassuring pat. "Don't worry, boy. No one's putting a needle in your nose."

"Aunt Pith would never allow it. She's never done anything like that to her dogs. But even if Taxi's nose was black-black, he still fails to meet kennel club standards. He has an overbite."

Nick started to laugh but a scream—a scream of stark terror—cut through the quiet villa.

"Jeezus!" Nick jackknifed to his feet, pushing Taxi aside.

He was across the room and getting into his trousers when another scream rent the night air.

"It's Audrey," Janna cried to Nick's back as he opened the door to the hall, Taxi at his heels. She grabbed the cashmere afghan off the sitting room chair and wrapped it around herself. She sprinted down the hall, nearly colliding with Aunt Pith, and halted in front of the door to Audrey's suite.

Nick was down on his knees beside Audrey and Ellis who were kneeling on the Persian carpet over Von Rommel. The dog was writhing on the floor, gasping for breath. A foul odor assailed Janna's nostrils, gagging her and bringing up bile in her throat. A viscous liquid— Rommie's diarrhea—covered the fringe of the Persian rug Aunt Pith had purchased at a Sotheby auction.

"He's dying. He's dying," Audrey moaned.

"I believe he's merely ill," Aunt Pith said.

"Probably something he ate." Nick winked at Janna.

Behind her noises came from the stairs and Warren appeared, his hair hopelessly mussed, with Shadoe following him, her blouse half-buttoned. Janna awkwardly wound the afghan around her body, ignoring the knowing look in her aunt's eyes.

"What's the matter?" Warren asked, rushing up to them.

"Rommie's ill," Janna said, mentally cursing the dog for exposing her affair with Nick. When she'd dashed into the hall, half-naked, she'd assumed something terrible had happened, not just a dog with an upset stomach.

"How could that be?" Warren asked. "He just left us. He was fine."

"Call the veterinarian," Ellis said, his arm around Audrey, who was sobbing softly.

"No," Aunt Pith said. "Let's take Rommie to him. Warren, you drive. Ellis, you bring Audrey." She turned to Nick. "Find out what he ate, so we'll know what to tell Dr. Zahra." She walked passed Janna, saying, "Call the veterinarian's emergency number and tell him to meet us at the hospital."

"Take Taxi too," Shadoe said, pointing to the puppy.

Taxi danced at Nick's feet, begging to be picked up, his muzzle bright pink.

Janna scooped him up, clutching the slipping afghan with her other hand. "He'll be fine, honest. He was with me. Whatever Rommie ate, Taxi didn't."

"That's right," Nick chimed in. "Taxi just sucked on a piece of raspberry candy."

Rommie moaned, a low piteous sound, then began panting, gasping for air.

"Let's go," Aunt Pith commanded.

Janna dashed into her room and dialed 990 for inquiries and asked for Dr. Zahra's telephone number. "Have Dr. Zahra meet Pithany Crandall at his office," she told his service. "Her Maltese is very ill." She hung up and turned to Nick. "Give me a minute to get dressed."

He flopped down on the sitting room sofa. "Check to

see if that mutt ate those chocolate undies. Maybe he's ODed on panties."

She went into her room, wondering for the first time if Rommie could be seriously ill. Many things were poisonous to dogs. She rifled through the shopping bag and counted the packages of undies. "They're all here," she called to Nick.

"Must have eaten something in my place," he called back. "Warren said he was just there."

She tossed the afghan on her bed, went to the closet, and took out a velour jumpsuit. Quickly putting it on, she hoped Rommie recovered quickly. Audrey was terribly attached to him. "Where's Shadoe?"

"With Chloe. All the commotion woke her."

Taxi at their heels, they went down to the guest house and found Shadoe's black lace bra slung across the back of the sofa. A wispy pair of matching underpanties lay on the floor. Taxi beelined for the panties.

"Yo Taxi."

The puppy froze, hovering over the underpants, drooling. Nick clicked his fingers, and Taxi charged over to him.

Nick said, "You're picking up all of Rommie's bad habits, aren't you?"

"I don't think Rommie ate anything in here," Janna said, looking around the sitting room. "He usually leaves a trail of crumbs or shredded paper."

They went into Nick's bedroom. While he checked the closet floor where Rommie had found the jock strap, Janna stared at the picture of Amanda Jane on his dresser. How could she ever compete with someone so beautiful? Someone whose memory still called to Nick from the grave.

"Nothing," Nick said. "Let's check the kitchen."

They flicked on the light in the small kitchenette. A blue box of cookies from Attard's Bakery had a gaping hole in its side. Crumbs and nuts were scattered across the table. A half-eaten cookie lay on the floor.

"What's in those cookies?" Nick asked, a strange look on his face.

"They're *tan-nar* cookies. All the local bakers make them. They're just flour, chopped almonds, cinnamon, and honey."

Nick yanked the receiver off the wall telephone. "What's the vet's number?"

Janna gave it to him, wondering why Nick suddenly seemed so alarmed. Earlier he'd been joking about Rommie's illness.

"Warren Atherton, please." He waited, watching her, an intense expression on his face. "Warren? . . . Aw, shit!" He covered the mouthpiece and said to Janna, "Dead on arrival." Removing his hand, he said, "Get back here right away. We've got a problem. Don't frighten the others. Meet Janna and me in the guest house."

He hung up and Janna asked, "What's wrong?"

"Honey. There's oleander poison in the honey. Travis brought a jar of honey with him the night he died. The same honey must be in those *tan-nar* cookies."

"But Clara said she used it later and it was fine."

"The pantry's bigger than most supermarkets. I counted eleven different types of honey in there. I bet she *thinks* she used that honey, but never did. Ants got to it and she threw it out before it could be tested."

"But those cookies are from Attard's. They wouldn't sell you poisoned cookies."

His brow furrowed into a deep frown. "I didn't buy them. They were sent to me at my office."

Shock siphoned the blood from her face; she could literally feel herself going white, her knees weakening. If his theory was correct, someone had tried to kill him. Intellectually, she realized there might be a logical explanation, but on a visceral level she felt he was right. Someone wanted him dead.

Until now, she hadn't totally admitted how much she cared for him. If he'd eaten a cookie, she might never have had the chance to . . . She suddenly became aware of the intensity in his expression, in his eyes. He picked up an envelope off the counter and withdrew a letter. She instantly recognized the stylized arch, the logo of the Blue Grotto Hotel. She reached for it.

"Don't touch it!" He held it up for her to read.

Darling,
    I had a wonderful time yesterday. You owe me a new bikini. While you're deciding which color to buy, here is a box of my favorite cookies.

Enjoy,
Janna

"I never sent that," she said, breathless with fury and stunned that someone had tried to kill Nick and blame her. "Look at it. It's been typed. Anyone could have gotten some of the hotel's stationery and sent you this note."

She stared at him, praying he believed her. His lively blue eyes were positively forbidding. His ready smile had vanished, replaced by a grim expression. *He didn't believe her.* In her heart she'd always known she would lose him. But not like this.

"I love you, Nick. I'd never do anything to hurt you."

Her words were spoken in a low, wretched voice, but they hit Nick with the impact of a shout. Love? The past few days had been fun; more fun than he wanted to admit. He'd taken care not to think about how much he was enjoying Janna, because it made him feel guilty that his life was continuing when Amanda Jane's had so cruelly been cut short. He'd deliberately not considered where their relationship was going. Now certainly wasn't the time.

"Shorty," he said, kissing the tip of her nose. "You aren't capable of murder." He pulled her into his arms and kissed the top of her head. She clung to him with a desperation that touched his heart. "What concerns me is someone's trying to frame you."

She drew back, no longer holding her breath and hoping against hope to hear that he loved her too. The startling realization that she loved him had consumed all her thoughts. Her normally rational, levelheaded thought process had gone haywire. Until he'd spoken she hadn't realized she was in terrible trouble. "Why?"

Nick studied her, thinking intently. "To get you arrested. To ruin the preview of the Blue Grotto. What could be worse with the hordes of travel agents and travel column writers set to arrive next week than to have you arrested for murder?"

The relief she felt at Nick believing her was extinguished, the full impact of the situation hitting her. How easily she could have been charged with murder. Even now she might be charged with attempted murder.

"It has to be the Bradfords. Who else would want to see you dead and me in jail?"

"What good would my death do the Bradfords?" Nick asked. "My mother would inherit my stock—"

"My point," Janna cut in. "They're counting on buying the stock from your heirs."

"You're right," Nick admitted. Pithany knew all she had to do was ask for the stock, and he'd return it. She'd have no reason to kill him. "That's why they killed Travis."

"This hotel is Aunt Pith's dream. If it's ruined and she finds out that no one knows what happened to Ian MacShane, she'll be devastated," Janna said, anger firing every syllable.

Nick admired Janna for not thinking of herself first; she could really be in trouble with the law. It reminded him of Amanda Jane. How lucky could one guy get? Twice blessed.

"And I don't want anything to happen to you," she said, her anger increasing with each second.

"We're not going to let the Bradfords sabotage the Blue Grotto, or kill me." Nick put his arm around her and brought her snug against his side. "Travis used to have a saying: Ride with the tide; go with the flow. For years, I believed in living my life that way. Now I see that's bullshit. I'm not waiting around like a sitting duck. We're going to make the Bradfords sorry they took us on."

"How? We don't have any proof that they're responsible."

"Don't tell the police anything about the note—"

"We can't do that. We would be withholding evidence."

"I plan to send the note to Scotland Yard along with one of these cookies. I believe that they'll prove the honey in the cookies and the honey the original autopsy found in Travis came from the same source."

She looked confused. "But how does that implicate the Bradfords?"

"Honey contaminated with oleander isn't an everyday occurrence. It should be easy to trace, and there should be latent prints on that paper. The Yard has sophisticated enough equipment to detect them."

"The prints would prove who sent the note."

"Damn right. Meanwhile we turn the heat up on the Bradfords. Let's see what happens."

Janna nodded thoughtfully. "I'm going to tell the police how Curt tampered with my drink."

"Great idea"—Nick admired her spunk—"but they'll

ask why he would want to and why you didn't report this before now."

"My aunt's feud with the Bradfords is public knowledge. Now that I've taken over for her, the Bradfords are desperate to get me out of the hotel business. I was afraid to go to the police before, but now I know they'll stop at nothing."

"Be careful how you say it. Imply they're responsible. You don't want to be sued for slander."

"I'm not afraid. If we don't do something, the next time it won't be a dog who dies."

Nick silently applauded Janna's courage. Undoubtedly the police would ask a lot of tough questions. She'd stand up to the pressure. With a fleeting thought, he wondered how Amanda Jane would have handled this problem. She had a maternal quality about her, but she wouldn't have gone on the offensive.

A knock on the door interrupted Nick's thoughts. Warren walked in, frowning.

"Rommie's death was no accident," Janna said. "Someone tried to kill Nick."

Warren slumped onto the sofa. They spent the next few minutes filling him in on the problems with the Bradfords.

"There's only one way anyone could have known what we were doing aboard the *Amanda Jane*," Janna said. "They were spying on us, the same way they spied on Travis."

"The point of casting suspicion on the Bradfords is to put them on the defensive and force the police to thoroughly investigate them," Nick said. "Anyone who would do this is probably hiding a lot."

"How can I help?" Warren asked.

"Take your plane with a sample of the cookie and the letter to Scotland Yard—"

"Better yet, to Fort Halstead in England. There isn't a

lab on earth equal to it. When the Pan American flight was bombed and went down over Lockerbie, Scotland, the boys at Fort Halstead analyzed fragments—some of them microscopic—and determined the garments in the suitcase with the bomb had been manufactured here in Malta.

"If there are latent prints on the paper, the team at Fort Halstead will lift them. They'll reevaluate the honey samples from Travis's autopsy report and cross-check it against the cookies."

"Meanwhile," Nick said, "I want a family conference. I want us to form a united front and blast those bastards. Let them know they've taken on the best."

"Aunt Pith's always game for a good fight," Warren said.

"Audrey will be outraged when she finds out the Bradfords were responsible for Rommie's death," Janna added.

Nick smiled, not the slow, one-dimpled smile Janna loved, but a vengeful grin. "Know what I want to play up the most?"

"What?" Warren asked.

"Tony Bradford is a coward. I spent an hour in his waiting room. The walls are plastered with his medals and pictures of him in his RAF uniform. He thinks of himself as a war hero."

"So do most people around here," Janna said. "No one mentions he led the black market. Everyone knows it, of course, but it's in their best interests to forget how one of Malta's leading citizens made his fortune."

"Let's remind them," Warren said.

"Great." Nick said. "Hit the coward part hard. A real man would shoot me or something. A coward sends cookies. Hell, if my secretary hadn't been on a diet— again—I would have offered her one." He turned to Warren. "You could have eaten one."

"You're right," Warren said. "A coward kills innocent people."

"You were lucky you didn't eat one of those cookies," Janna told Nick.

He put his arm around her and gave her a quick hug. "Luck had nothing to do with it, Short-stuff. You saved my life. I took one look at that note and remembered the black pudding and the *fenek*. I suspected there was something in the cookies I wouldn't like. Add to that the Kick Ass Chili I'd tricked you into eating and I knew better than to eat those cookies until I asked you what was in them."

Warren stood, saying, "I'm going into the house and tell everyone what's happening before I call the police. Put the letter and a cookie in plastic bags. As soon as the police leave, I'll take them to London. We want the results as soon as possible."

Warren left and Janna followed Nick into the kitchenette. "I'm wondering if Ian MacShane—"

"We'll work on that later. Right now, we've got our hands full." He used tongs to lift a cookie out of the box.

"I know but . . . I think perhaps he's part of this."

Nick turned to her and saw she was serious. Dead serious.

"I showed Aunt Pith the sketch Laurel made and . . . and . . ."

"Come on, Janna. Spit it out."

"You look exactly like Ian MacShane."

Silence.

"Aunt Pith says you're a dead ringer for Ian."

"Aw, shit!" Nick slumped back against the counter, unnerved by her revelation. Warning spasms of alarm ricocheted through him. His thoughts filtered back to the day he'd first met Pithany Crandall. She *had* looked like she'd seen a ghost. "That might account for the weird way Tony Bradford acted when I was in his office."

"What do you mean?"

"He threatened me, trying to force me to sell him my shares. But I had the gut feeling he was afraid of me."

"It must be an eerie feeling to see someone you think is dead, especially if you've killed him."

"Hold it! You really believe what that psychic artist told you about MacShane being shot in the head?"

"At first, I wasn't sure . . . but now, I think she may be right."

"Ooooo-kay. Suppose Bradford did kill him. What's it got to do with me? It's just coincidence that I resemble Ian. I'm no threat to Tony."

Janna shrugged. "I guess he just wants the stock."

Nick didn't answer; his thoughts were on the sketch. He looked like a man who'd been dead for over fifty years. He thought of Pithany and how much she'd loved Ian. It certainly accounted for her attitude toward Nick. He wasn't certain how he felt about the situation. Part of him accepted it as one of those mysterious coincidences that could never be explained. Another part of him sought a logical, reasonable explanation.

"I'm convinced Tony killed Ian," Janna said, more determination firing her words than Nick had heard before now. "I intend to prove it."

Nick doubted that she could locate MacShane's body let alone solve a murder that had taken place so long ago, but he didn't offer his opinion. He remained silent for a moment, an idea forming in the back of his mind. "When I speak, do I sound like Ian?"

"I've never met a Scot with a Texas accent."

"Forget the accent. Did your aunt mention if my voice sounds like his?"

"No, but we could ask her."

"If I do sound like Ian, could you teach me how to say a few sentences with a Scottish brogue?"

19

✵

Tony Bradford awoke, groggily wondering where the hell he was. He rolled over, and the crisp linen sheets reassured him. He'd been dreaming, the nightmare he'd had for as long as he could remember. In the dream, he was a little boy again, locked in a dank garret while his mother walked the streets.

The insistent rapping on the plank door to his bedroom caused him to sit up. He realized an earlier knock had awakened him. "Iva?" He said "yes" in Maltese, knowing something was wrong. The servants wouldn't dare wake him for anything short of an emergency.

"Telephone."

"Who is it?"

"A woman. She says it's an emergency."

His thoughts muddled, still half-asleep, Tony shrugged into his silk dressing gown and slipped into his Porthault slippers before shuffling down the long hall to his study.

"Hello," he mumbled, sleepy-eyed.

"This is Ian MacShane. Start looking over your shoulder, Bradford. I'm going to get you."

The line went dead before Tony could say one word. He clutched the receiver, looking up, still not focusing properly. Across the room he saw his reflection in the mirror. He blinked once. Twice. Again.

The damn mirror—once a door to some pharaoh's tomb—was playing tricks on him. He peered at the im-

age, suddenly short of breath. Tony saw himself with Ian
MacShane holding a gun to Tony's head.

Just above his left temple.

Tony blinked, and the haunting image vanished as
quickly as it had appeared. He sank into the chair, assur-
ing himself his sluggish brain—he never woke easily—
had tricked him. He took another look at the mirror.
Nothing. The voice on the line bore an eerie resemblance to Ian MacShane's, but it didn't fool him. It had
to be Nick Jensen. The prickle of alarm that had seized
him when he'd spoken with Jensen in the office returned. Tony silently told himself not to be concerned.
He could make more trouble for Pithany and her Texan
than they could for him. Still, he wondered why they'd
called—he checked his watch—at four o'clock in the
morning.

The metallic clang of the brass knocker on the front
door interrupted his thoughts. Who could that be? No
one lived in Mdina, and it was a long drive over winding
roads to get to the nearest city. He crossed the marble
foyer and swung open the door. In the courtyard a squad
car with two horizontal blue stripes was parked near the
fountain. Three policemen wearing silver Maltese
crosses with the word *Pulizija* in the center stood beside
Raymond Muscat, Inspector General of the Police. Tony
had known the pompous ass for years.

"Curt?" Instantly, Tony knew something had happened to his son. He wasn't particularly fond of Curt—
sometimes he outright hated him—but Tony counted on
his son to continue the Bradford dynasty into the next
century.

"I'm not here about Curt." Muscat looked uncomfortable. "There's been trouble at Falcon's Lair."

Tony motioned for Muscat to come in, remembering
the premonition of trouble he'd had from the moment
he'd seen Nick Jensen at the *festa* party and the phone

call he'd just received. He led the group into the study without saying anything, realizing the situation must be serious. No doubt, they'd gotten Muscat out of bed. The officers could have come alone, or the Inspector of Police District 3, in charge of Mdina, could have come instead. But no, this was important enough to merit sending Raymond Muscat, the highest ranking police official in Malta.

The Maltese police used the old watchtowers around Malta that had been built during the war to house anti-aircraft artillery as small police stations. They'd been colder than a witch's tit in the winter and hotter than Hades in the summer until Tony had paid to have heating and cooling systems installed. He had an ulterior motive for his generosity: He loved to drive his Lamborghini Contach like he was on the Le Mans circuit, and he didn't want to see any flashing red lights in his rearview mirror.

The Maltese police weren't really corrupt. To the contrary, they were notorious sticklers for thorough investigations. Most of them had trained in England at New Scotland Yard, but they did bend the rules for friends. All Big Tony could expect to get out of them was advance notice of whatever shit Pithany and pretty boy Jensen had cooked up.

"Tonight someone poisoned a dog staying at Pithany Crandall's home."

"For crissakes, you came all the way out here about a dog?"

"No." Muscat shifted from one foot to the other as if standing on the devil's own hearth. "He ate poisoned cookies. They thought you sent them to Nick Jensen. Your card was attached to the box."

"Cookies? Cookies?" Tony started to laugh, but stopped when he saw how serious Muscat was. "If I wanted to get rid of Jensen, I'd slit his throat."

"The Earl of Lyforth confirmed that you'd gone to great lengths to acquire stock in the Blue Grotto, and Jensen refused to sell you his stock. The earl believes you want Jensen dead so you can purchase the stock from his heirs."

Muscat was obviously swayed by Warren Atherton's title. That infuriated Tony; he liked to think of himself as the Duke of Malta. He didn't possess a title and he never would, but some little jerk like Lyforth could come along and impress everyone.

Muscat continued, "Lady Janna Atherton-Pembroke says your son tried to drug her with your help, right here in this villa."

"That's ridiculous." Tony had never figured out exactly what Curt had been trying to do with Janna. From behind the two-way mirror, Tony had seen his son put something in her drink and assumed it was an aphrodisiac. Heavy-handed, Tony admitted, but then, Curt's brains were in his dick.

"Nick Jensen confirms her story. He says he got her out of here and she lost consciousness."

"She was soused."

"Possibly, but she was pretty convincing." Muscat hesitated; Tony knew he hadn't heard the last of their accusations. "Jensen wants us to reopen Travis Prescott's murder investigation and focus on you."

"Me! Next they'll claim I'm plotting to kill the Pope." He poked the silver Maltese cross on Muscat's chest. The cluster of braid dangling from it, indicating Muscat had achieved the pinnacle of success, flopped up and down. "I'm not involved in any of this, and they can't prove I am."

"No," Muscat conceded, "but I thought you might want to know that they're trying very hard to hang this on you."

Muscat walked to the door, his men dutifully following. "If the tests on those cookies show poison, you'll have some explaining to do. Jensen is insisting you be charged with attempted murder."

Sonofabitch! Tony slammed the door behind them. That Texan with his half-assed smile. He hated him as much as he'd hated Ian MacShane. Ladies' men—always crooning to the women and flashing their baby-blues. Pithany had put Jensen up to this. Obviously, she was nervous because Tony had acquired so much of her stock.

They can't prove a thing, he assured himself. Even if the cookies had been poisoned, he hadn't sent them. Anyone could have stuck his business card in the box; Jensen probably did it himself. Undoubtedly he'd picked up one of Tony's cards when he'd come to his office. If the cookies contained poison, Tony knew he would have to do a lot of explaining and make his attorney even richer. It would be as embarrassing as hell. As much as he liked a good fight in the boardroom, Tony prized his image as a gentleman. A war hero. Owner of a palace. The Duke of Malta.

Sonofabitch! The papers would crucify him even if he hadn't done a damn thing. He'd blocked Pithany Crandall's efforts to build a hotel on her land by throwing around a lot of environmental crap. And he had grossly overpaid that wop fag for the stock. The situation could easily blow up and make him look guilty.

He calmed himself by pouring Le Paradis cognac in a brandy snifter and sipping it. An old adage popped into his mind: Where there's smoke there's fire. He remembered Curt slipping something into Janna's drink. Had that little prick done something really stupid like sending Jensen poison cookies? Why?

Tony hurried back to his room determined to change clothes and find Curt in his condominium in Sliema. No doubt he would be in bed with that new blonde he'd been seeing. The investigator that Tony had hired reported Curt spent every night with her. Tony didn't care if he caught them in the sack. He would be damned if he'd let his son ruin the reputation it had taken a lifetime to build.

Frantic banging on the penthouse door brought Curt out of a deep sleep.

"What's wrong?" Rhonda clutched the satin sheet to her bare breasts.

"I don't—" Curt recognized Big Tony's voice shouting for Curt to open the door. "It's my father." He jumped out of bed and grabbed his robe. "I'll stall him. You get out of here."

"I'm coming," Curt yelled, dashing from the bedroom across the living area overlooking St. Julian's Bay. Dawn's hazy light coated the water, casting a pearly sheen over the fishing boats as they put out to sea. What in hell could Big Tony want at this hour? The hair across the back of Curt's neck stood at full attention. A fine dappling of perspiration coated his brow. He swiped it with the back of his hand.

Certain Rhonda had sneaked out the back way by now, Curt opened the door and found Big Tony, his face purple with rage.

"It's raining shit!" His father barged past Curt, waving a newspaper.

"What are you talking about?" Relief swept through Curt. Tony hadn't found out about Rhonda.

Big Tony pointed to the morning edition of the *Times of Malta* that must have just been delivered. "Pithany Crandall and her brood are claiming I tried to kill Nick Jensen. They're even suggesting we poisoned Travis Prescott."

"That's ridiculous," Curt insisted. Once again he regretted using the poison a second time. Risky. Stupid. Not one of his better ideas.

"The paper insists some Greek sailor swears Rhonda tricked him into going out to *Siren's Song* where you beat him up."

Curt kept his face poker-straight, but something in his eyes must have given him away.

"You did it, didn't you?" Tony backhanded Curt with a crushing blow to the jaw that sent him reeling against the sofa. "Why?"

His ears ringing from the force of the punch, Curt managed to mumble, "It was just a little party that got out of hand."

"The paper says the Greek almost died. He was in the hospital for weeks. His ship sailed without him, so he went to the police. As soon as Jensen accused us of trying to kill him, the police dug up the Greek's report."

Tony eased into a leather chair and stared at Curt for a full minute, his silence more chilling than a beating.

"Is there anything you aren't telling me?" Tony asked at last, his voice a churchlike whisper.

Curt was positive nothing could link him or Rhonda to the poison. All right, it had been a stupid idea, but they had taken extraordinary precautions. He remembered the postal worker he'd paid off to give him the picture Austin Prescott had sent to Jensen.

"If you don't tell me the whole truth now, don't come to me later and expect help."

"Well"—Curt wavered—"there is a postal worker who might make trouble. I paid him to give me a package sent to Jensen."

"What the hell was in the package?"

"A picture," Curt hedged, not wanting to bring up Rhonda's name, but not seeing any way to avoid it. "Of Rhonda and Travis Prescott." He braced himself, finishing, "I didn't want her implicated in his death."

"Unfuckingbelievable! That stupid whore sucked you into this mess." Tony vaulted to his feet. "You two killed Prescott and tried to get Jensen, didn't you?"

Curt knew that tone of voice only too well. Even if he had been innocent, Tony's mind was made up. "Yes," Curt muttered.

Tony flopped into the chair opposite Curt. "Why the hell did you kill Prescott?"

Curt had to give his father some explanation. "Prescott had the hots for Rhonda. One night he came out to *Siren's Song* uninvited and discovered us having a party. There were drugs and stuff . . . Prescott was such a tightass that he threatened to go to the police. Rhonda was worried a scandal might hold up her annulment."

Curt managed an apologetic shrug while Tony stared at him, his jaw suddenly slack—disbelieving. The explanation was plausible. Malta was ardently Roman Catholic; the clicking of Rosary beads as constant as the trade winds. Although divorce was out of the question, annulments were regularly granted. But not to women thought to be immoral. Of course, the annulment had nothing to do with Prescott's death. He had stumbled into one of their private parties just in time to help an injured drifter Rhonda had hustled for the night. Prescott wanted to go to the police immediately, but Rhonda had persuaded him to wait until the extent of the man's injuries were known.

Curt and Rhonda had met with Travis the next day and convinced him that the man hadn't been hurt. The truth was the drifter had lost an eye, but they'd managed to get him onto a ship bound for Ceylon. They'd given Travis the honey as a peace offering, saying the whole incident had been a regrettable accident. Killing Travis had been Rhonda's idea, but Curt had gone along. Getting the shares while ridding themselves of a witness had seemed like a good idea. At the time.

Tony had been quiet for so long it unnerved Curt. "Don't worry. All they can prove is I bribed a postal worker."

Silence filled the room, but outside church bells pealed, announcing the first Mass of the day. Finally, Tony spoke, his voice barely discernable above the sound of the bells. "A lifetime on this island, building a name —an empire. For what? For you. And you throw it all away for some pussy who's married and can't even give you a son."

The desolate note in his father's voice made Curt want to comfort him. "I'm certain Rhonda will be granted an annulment, then we'll give you lots of grandsons."

"Brats with shit for brains." Tony snorted. "Any broad dumb enough to come up with this poison cookie bit will pass on worthless genes to her kids."

Curt braved his father's anger, compelled to defend Rhonda. After all, he'd been every bit as responsible for the poison as she had. "Her heart's in the right place. She loves me. All she'd let me do was bribe that worker. She handled everything else. Give her credit. She's loyal."

Big Tony's eyes narrowed, and Curt prepared for a tirade. Instead Tony lowered his head and shot him a shrewd smile, the same crafty grin he'd seen when Tony crushed a competitor. "You're smarter than I thought, boy."

Curt winced at "boy" but managed a cautious smile. With Big Tony you never knew. He could grin and backhand you in the same breath.

"You're stupid, but at least you let the broad do all the work. If anyone fries, it's Rhonda Sibbet."

Curt stifled a groan. He had never insisted Rhonda do anything. Helping him had been her idea. He'd gone along with it, not because he gave a damn whether or not his father got those shares, but because he wanted his father off his back so he could spend more time with Rhonda. He'd consoled himself, telling himself that the authorities couldn't *prove* Rhonda had done anything. She was smart enough to get out of town until this blew over.

Big Tony walked to the door and opened it. "Come in, boys."

The beefy Mifsud brothers ambled into the room. Their sloping foreheads reminded Curt of throwbacks to Cro-Magnon man. No more than thugs, they were kept on Big Tony's payroll to do the dirty work.

"Why are they here?"

"They're going to be your escorts. Let's call them bodyguards. It sounds classier." Big Tony smiled, a full, unnatural smile that revealed his gums above a glistening set of false teeth. "You're going to Marbella. I want you to check in at the Puente Romano. I've reserved their priciest villa."

The brothers lumbered across the room. The older one—Curt never could remember their names—lolled a toothpick from one side of his mouth to the other. The younger Mifsud stared sleepy-eyed at Curt. Their combined IQs didn't hit double digits. But they were masters of brute force. Curt knew getting away from them would be impossible.

"I want you at one of the Puente Romano's pools every day. All those topless women should keep you happy. At night, I want you to eat in the main dining room where everyone can see you, then dance all night at the hotel's nightclub. What's it called?"

"Regine's," Curt said glumly. Once he would have welcomed the opportunity to spend time in Marbella's jet-set hotel. But without Rhonda and with the Mifsud brothers dogging his every move, who cared?

"When can I come back?"

"I'll send for you." Big Tony motioned to the Mifsud brothers.

They grabbed Curt by his arms, hauling him backward without even giving him the chance to walk.

"Don't try to get away from them," Big Tony warned. "If you even *think* about it, they've got orders to kill you."

Janna glanced up from her desk in the executive offices of the Blue Grotto the following evening and saw Nick coming through the door.

"The tests for oleander poison came back positive." Nick dropped into the chair opposite her desk. He looked as tired as she felt; they'd been up all night. "Of course, there's not enough evidence to charge Tony Bradford with anything. We need to find his prints on the box or envelope, especially since only my prints were on the card that I gave the police."

"I still don't like lying to the police and tampering with evidence by taping Anthony Bradford's card to the cookie box."

"I intend to explain everything just as soon as Warren gets the report back from Fort Halstead. Meanwhile, turning up the heat is working. They've assigned two more men to investigate Travis's death."

"The picture still hasn't come?"

"No, but I insisted the police question everyone at the post office. I think someone intercepted the package."

He leaned back and closed his eyes for a moment, and she wondered why he'd come all the way across the island. It would have been easier to use the telephone. Watching him, she tried to swallow the lump that lingered in her throat. Until last night, she hadn't realized she loved him. She'd blurted it out like a lovesick adolescent only to have him ignore what she'd said. She couldn't blame him. He hadn't made her any promises, or told her any smiling lies. Still, looking at him, know-ing she'd never have his love almost made her cry.

Nick opened his eyes, but his lids remained at half-mast. "How much longer are you planning on working?"

"Midnight or so, I guess. There's so much to do with less than a week to go before the preview. When those travel agents get off the plane, I want everything to—"

"You're not staying out here all alone."

She struggled to conceal the surge of happiness racing through her. He was worried about her. He had to care —a little. "I'm not alone. We have security guards."

"I walked right in. No one stopped me."

"Do you think I'm in danger?"

Nick leaned forward and placed his elbows on her desk. "We all need to be very careful. These people are dangerous. I should have had the sense to think I might be their next target, but no. I waltzed around Malta hav-ing fun, never thinking I was in danger."

"We have been acting pretty silly, playing with Kick Ass Chili and edible undies. Exchanging fleas."

"We have a right to have fun," Nick said, suddenly realizing he'd enjoyed himself more in the past week than he had in the last five years. "I don't intend to let the Bradfords stop me. I'm just going to be more cau-tious." He rose, adding, "Come on. Bring what you need and work at home."

Outside, iridescent shafts of red-gold light flicked across the sea, gilding the water while the sky was streaked with the deepening mauves and plums of twi-light. In another few minutes the dark canopy of night would fall over the secluded lagoon.

Nick took her briefcase from her. "Let's watch." He pulled two deck chairs to the edge of the pool area where they were standing.

The Blue Grotto hotel was built on a bluff overlook-ing a series of grottos and stone arches so wide that *luzzijiet* sailed through them, the colorful boats a sharp contrast to the weathered limestone. Evening shadows deepened the irregular crevices time and the wind had eroded in the rocks. A wide ellipse of powdered-sugar sand wrapped around the tranquil cove of water that literally glowed a unique shade of peacock-blue. Scattered across the tranquil lagoon were *faraglioni,* tall upright rocks like pillars.

As a child, Janna remembered standing on this very spot, clutching Aunt Pith's hand, and listening to her explain that the phosphorus in the rock made the water glow and made the surf look like spun glass.

"One day people from all over the world will come to our hotel," Aunt Pith would say. "They'll swim on this beach and take *luzzu* rides into the grottos. We'll show everyone the isle of Capri can't compare to what we have."

Aunt Pith's dream was about to become reality. Next week the travel agents would preview the Blue Grotto and a few days later the first guests would arrive. Having shared her aunt's dream for as long as she could remember, Janna welcomed the chance to do something for the woman who'd spent her entire life giving to everyone else.

A jack-o'-lantern moon nudged its way up from behind the crest. The only sound Nick heard was the waves tumbling onto the beach below. He thoroughly enjoyed being with Janna. She was attractive, not glamorous with that hard edge of chic many women coveted. Last night, he'd lain awake; his plots of revenge frequently interrupted thoughts of her.

She loved him. Did she know what she was saying? Definitely. She wasn't the type to lie. Besides, she'd said it when her guard had been down. He wanted to take his time, get to know her, and see what happened. See if he could live with the guilt over Amanda Jane's death. But

Janna had forced his hand by telling him that she loved him. His silence was only hurting her. Yet he didn't know what to say. He cared about her. But did he love her the way she deserved to be loved? The way he'd loved Amanda Jane?

Sex bred a false sense of intimacy, he realized. She didn't know him, not the way Amanda Jane had. But then, he'd never given Janna that chance. He hadn't played fair. She'd shared her aspirations with him, but he hadn't even told her that he expected to be transferred to Atlanta soon. Now would be the worst time to tell her that he was leaving. She would feel rejected.

"When I was in school, I couldn't find Malta on the map," Nick said, breaking into her thoughts.

"Most Americans can't. That's why I had the ad agency put maps on all our brochures. When tourists realize how close we are to Italy, I think more Americans will come here."

There was a long pause before he added, "I wasn't your average kid. I had problems. A lot of problems."

Somehow she'd imagined him to be the all-American hero. Good looking, possessing the devil's own charm. A football star.

"I hated school. I pretended I was sick whenever I could get away with it. Played hookey a lot."

Janna had loved school. She'd dawdled her way through college, taking plenty of time to travel, just so she could prolong her school days. "What didn't you like about it?"

"I could barely read."

Involuntarily, she gasped, then prayed he hadn't heard. "How did you graduate?"

"I relied on my memory—and my smile—to slog through school until I graduated."

"Didn't your mother or the teachers or someone help

you?" The minute the words were out, she knew who'd helped him. Amanda Jane.

"My mother had too many of her own problems to be concerned with mine. Some teachers tried to help me, but dyslexia takes special training. One teacher didn't let me charm her. Old lady Mooth, my third grade teacher. She had me stand up in front of the class and try to read —every day. Thought embarrassing me would make me go home and study harder."

She winced, unable to imagine a teacher who could be so cruel. The strain in Nick's voice indicated some pain still lingered.

"I met the Prescotts and they persuaded me to go to a clinic where they discovered I have dyslexia. It took about a year of counseling and I learned to read well enough to get into college. But I still reverse words sometimes and I'm slow, so I avoid reading except at work."

Every time he said "the Prescotts," she knew he meant his wife. Janna realized Amanda Jane had given Nick something she could never give him: his self-esteem. No wonder losing her had created a void time hadn't buffered. With hopeless clarity, she knew no one was taking Amanda Jane's place.

"Throughout college Travis spent time tutoring me. I wouldn't have made it without him."

"Did you see Travis very often after he came here?"

"The day after Amanda Jane's funeral I left for Japan. I never spoke with Travis again."

"Why not?" she asked, stunned as much at his words as the bitter edge in his voice.

"I'd been in Denver, working in Imperial's "From the Bottom Up" program. Once a month, I'd go back to Houston. I sensed something was wrong, but Amanda Jane denied it. Travis and Austin didn't tell me a thing either. Finally, I noticed how thin Amanda Jane had become. Claimed it was a diet. She never told me about her liver cancer until I threatened to drag her to the doctor because she'd become so thin, so tired."

"Liver cancer moves very quickly, doesn't it?"

"Hers did. A little over four months from the initial diagnosis until we buried her."

"Oh, Nick. I'm so sorry. It must have been terrible."

"I wish she'd told me." His voice rose, tinged with anger. "Travis or Austin could have told me. But they didn't want to ruin my career." He stood, jammed his hands into his trouser pockets, and stared out at the Blue Grotto. "Hell, I didn't give a damn about the program. I would have gladly quit and spent time with her— taken her to Lyme Regis—before it was too late."

Janna's chest threatened to burst, the ache inside hurt so much. The pain and suffering rife in his words touched her heart. No wonder he'd insisted on going to Lyme Regis alone. It had special meaning for him that would never include her.

"I understand now that being angry with Travis for not telling me was a childish response," Nick said, his voice now level. "I discovered that when it was too late. He'd been murdered."

"Don't be so hard on yourself."

He didn't respond, instead he gazed up at the stars haloed by a warm mist that floated in from North Africa in the early summer. The gauzy vapor never descended on the island, but it rose touching the stars and screening their light like a honeycomb veil.

"I know it's hard to forgive. I was very angry with Aunt Pith right after my father died, but I forgave her. She thought she was protecting me"—Janna hesitated for a fraction of a second—"by not telling me I'd been adopted."

"Really?" Nick sat down again and studied her intently. "I'm surprised. Your green eyes fooled me."

"Mine are grayish, closer to Aunt Pith's than Audrey's. When I was young, I would look in the mirror and tell myself one day my eyes would be emerald-green like Audrey's. It wasn't until Reginald Atherton died that I found out why they weren't."

Nick listened as she told him the circumstances surrounding the earl's death and the will. Janna said she wasn't hurt, that she understood. He knew better.

"I think you were lucky the Athertons adopted you— even if Reginald didn't like you. Warren loves you, and Pithany might as well be your mother. Audrey's a little . . . different but I think she loves you too."

"I'm not complaining. I love my family."

"Sometimes the best parents aren't your natural parents. I've been closer to the Prescotts than I ever was to my own family. Hell, I'd be with Austin right now, but I owe it to him to find out who murdered his son."

After dinner at the Kosher Nostra Deli in St. Julian's Bay, Janna drove past the newly hired security guards into the garage at Falcon's Lair. Nick pulled in beside her. All through dinner, she'd told herself how lucky she was. Her childhood, like Nick's, could have been a desperately lonely nightmare. She'd been blessed, and until she'd heard Nick's story she'd never been fully aware of just how lucky she was. She jumped out of the car, set to dash upstairs and give everyone a kiss.

Nick stopped her, saying, "Don't run off. Spend the night with me. I could use a little protection."

Janna opened her mouth to say she couldn't compete with a ghost. But his joking tone of voice—protection, indeed—triggered something deep within her. Nick had exposed his innermost feelings—for the first time since his wife's death. Janna knew she wasn't just a one-night stand to Nick Jensen. She had her foot in the door of his heart. She would be damned if she would give up now.

"I'll be there in a minute," she said, handing him her briefcase. "I need to run upstairs and let everyone know I'm home safe."

Janna charged into the house and up the stairs, going straight to Aunt Pith's door. She knocked and heard her aunt call for her to come in. She found her in the bedroom, lying on her bed, her feet elevated on a tower of pillows.

"Are your legs bothering you again? Have you called the doctor?" Janna asked, but doubted that she had. Aunt Pith despised doctors—a holdover from all the hours she'd been kept waiting in their offices trying to help Audrey.

"I'm just a little tired, that's all. Too much gardening."

"You rest then." Janna bent over and kissed her aunt's cheek. "I just came in to tell you how much I love you."

The pleased look on Aunt Pith's face reminded Janna that she should tell her more often. Everyone needs to know they're loved. Aunt Pith had known love so briefly it didn't seem fair.

"I love you too." She squeezed Janna's hand and smiled the tender smile that colored even Janna's earliest memories. "I guess last night has made us all think about those we love."

"You're right. All day I kept telling myself how lucky I was that Rommie—not one of you or Nick—ate those cookies. And tonight, Nick and I watched the sunset on the Blue Grotto lagoon. I remembered all the times you and I stood on that spot, and you told me of your dreams about building a hotel. Now the hotel's ready to open, and I'm going to make you happy by seeing to it the Blue Grotto is the best hotel in the Mediterranean."

Aunt Pith's smile had faded. "Do you know what would really make me happy?"

Janna shook her head, wondering if she'd done something wrong.

"I would love it if you married Nick and had lots of children. I want to see them running all around Falcon's Lair, sliding down the bannisters, playing in the pool, and swinging in the swing." She smiled again, this time a forlorn smile. "I always wanted lots of children, you know."

Her aunt's words hung in the air, weighing heavily upon Janna. "I do love him but . . ."

"You feel he still loves his wife?"

"Most definitely. Tonight he talked about her. You can't imagine how much he loved her . . . still loves her. I'm convinced I'm fighting a losing battle. But I'm not giving up."

"That's my girl." Aunt Pith squeezed Janna's hand, her expression concerned. "Do you mind a little advice?"

"No. I can use all the help I can get."

"I have a theory about Nick Jensen. His mother never loved him. Everyone needs a mother's love—"

"Even if it comes from your aunt, not your mother?"

"Yes. I always pretended you were my daughter. You know I love you."

She nodded, unable to find the words to express herself. Across every memory, some pleasant, others not, she'd been fortified by the knowledge Aunt Pith loved her.

"Well, Nick never knew a mother's love until he met his wife. She filled both roles."

Janna considered Aunt Pith's observation for a moment, and decided she was correct. Nick clearly felt the Prescotts were family, not merely in-laws.

"He's different now," Aunt Pith continued. "Don't try to mother him. Treat him like a partner, or better yet, a lover."

Janna nodded, absorbing the wisdom of her aunt's words.

"But don't be afraid to tell him you love him. He needs to hear it. He hasn't had enough love in his life."

"I'm intimidated by his looks," Janna confessed.

"He's not Collis. Nick Jensen reminds me very much of Ian MacShane. They don't rely on their looks. They'll value love a lot more than a pretty face."

Janna stood up. "Thanks for the advice. I'm going down to Nick's in a bit and—"

"Everyone knows you're sleeping with him, Janna. Don't bother to hide it."

"You're right," Janna said, feeling foolish.

"Last night, it became completely clear that my family has very creative sleeping arrangements. Audrey was the only one in the right room and Ellis was in her bed."

"I noticed his door was shut and Audrey's was open. I wouldn't have thought much of it, if Nick hadn't mentioned he thought they were lovers."

"Nick Jensen is a very observant man."

"Do you think his fight to overcome dyslexia made him rely more on his memory and powers of observation?" Janna asked. She bet her aunt knew all about Nick's problems. Either Nick had told her or she'd discovered it when she'd had him investigated, but she'd waited for him to tell Janna.

"Yes," Aunt Pith said with complete conviction. "He's very much like Ian."

20

✳

Janna said good night to Aunt Pith. Halfway down the hall, she saw Taxi chasing Millie around a potted palm. "Come here, you little devil." With the puppy in her arms, she knocked on Audrey's door. The older woman answered immediately. "I brought you a present." Janna handed Taxi to Audrey.

"But he's yours." Audrey cuddled the wiggling puppy.

"I'm gone all day. It isn't fair to him. He isn't really show quality right now, but I made a few calls today. There's a canine dentist in Rome who can fit Taxi with braces. He'd only have to wear them a short while because his overbite isn't too pronounced. Then you could show him. All you would have to do is dab a little India ink on his nose before he went into the ring."

Tears welled up in Audrey's eyes and seeped down her cheeks. "This is so sweet of you. I know how much you love Taxi."

"I love you more," she said. "I know he won't replace Rommie, but he'll try his best."

Audrey motioned for her to come in and sit down. "Rommie was special. This morning I had him cremated. His ashes are in that urn." She gestured to a Sèvres vase on the mantle. "There'll never be another dog like him, but I'm thankful he ate those cookies before one of you did." Audrey toyed with Taxi's ear for a moment, then looked Janna directly in the eyes. "Ellis and I are getting married. We're planning a small wedding here in Falcon's Lair."

"That's wonderful!" Love was certainly in the air; hopefully, some of it would blow Nick's way.

She said good night to Audrey, who vowed never to let Taxi out of her sight, then went to say hello to Shadoe. By the time Janna got down to Nick's the lights in the guest house were off. Guided by filmy moonlight, she tiptoed into his bedroom. He was asleep on his bed, his earphones on with a tape playing. She gently removed the earphones and turned off the cassette.

Too weary to work on the schedule for the opening after going without sleep the previous night, she was folding her clothes and placing them over the back of the chair when she realized something was different. A chill finger of fear waltzed down her spine. She put her hand on Nick's bare chest. He was still breathing. Thank you, God.

She took a close look at the shadows. No one was lurking in the dark corners of the room. Then she peeped into the closet. Nothing. Still, something niggled at her. She padded barefoot to the kitchenette. Shafts of silvery moonlight slanted through the closed shutters, revealing an immaculate kitchen, a far cry from the mess the police had left.

It took her a moment to summon her courage to look into the second bedroom. The door creaked open. No one was in Warren's room. The closet door stood open, a reminder of his hasty departure last night.

Your imagination has the best of you. She should never have allowed Nick to call Tony. His bogus accent couldn't have fooled Chloe. All he'd done was aggravate an already explosive situation. Why had she let Nick make that call? It was tantamount to waving a red flag in front of a bull. Who could predict what Tony might do?

She went to the front door and slid the dead bolt into

place, then punched in the alarm code. Peeking out the
window, she saw one of the security guards Aunt Pith
had hired today patrolling the grounds. Nothing was
wrong.

She eased into bed beside Nick, careful not to wake
him. Once again, her eyes scanned the dark room and
found no one hiding in the shadows. She closed her eyes
and wished she'd thought to ask Aunt Pith for the derringer that Ian had given her so long ago. Janna knew it
was still in the bottom drawer of Aunt Pith's nightstand.

Sleep refused to come; her brain was on full alert. *It's
this room,* she assured herself. *You always feel as if
Amanda Jane is watching you.* Her eyes flew open. The
picture of Amanda Jane was gone.

Collis lounged on a padded chaise beside the Seacrest
Hotel's pool. His timer went off and he reluctantly
rolled over onto his stomach. Getting an even tan was
more important than watching the big German girl
swimming nearby. He didn't know what it was about her
that appealed to him anyway. She was broad-shouldered
and hefty verging on masculine—except for her full
breasts.

He reminded himself to keep his mind on business.
He wanted to look his best—a mellow tan always enhanced his blond hair and deepened the blue of his eyes
—when he appeared at the preview party Janna was
throwing for the travel agents at the Blue Grotto tomorrow.

The Athertons had thought they were rid of him, but
they were wrong. It had been incredibly, shamefully,
easy to get a clerk to photocopy Reginald Atherton's
will. From there it had been ridiculously simple. He'd
found the fag in Sheriff's Lench and tricked him into
revealing that "Reggie" had died in his Hammersmith
flat, not at Lyforth Hall.

Collis smiled to himself, almost laughing out loud. The Tories' golden boy would be a tarnished man. Moving a body. Filing false reports. Not much would happen to him, but he would be finished politically. Ruined. No more speeches on television.

Of course, the Athertons could avoid this little scandal if they pay me enough. Collis didn't know if he should take them for a huge settlement now or bleed them a little at a time for years to come. Both, he decided. This information might be worth much more later when, say, Warren was being considered for a cabinet post.

"Say old chop, have you seen the paper?" asked the elderly man sunning himself near Collis. The words whistled through the gaps in the old man's teeth, turning "chap" into "chop." He'd been pestering Collis all afternoon.

"Not today," Collis replied, trying to cut off the conversation. Naturally, the London papers had been following the events in Malta. *Anything* that happened to Lyforth concerned them. And Warren was certainly in the middle of this. Just yesterday, he'd returned from Fort Halstead with proof that the honey that had killed that worthless cur, Rommie, came from the same batch of honey that had killed some man named Travis Prescott.

"Says here"—the old man rattled the paper—"that poison honey comes from India's"—he squinted myopically at the paper—"Gir forest. Imagine, bees that make honey from oleander."

Collis's intellectual curiosity was mildly stimulated. "Who would sell honey knowing it's poison?"

"Says here natives packaged it, labeled it as poison, and sold it as a novelty item. They traced the honey to a doss house in the *Gut,* wherever that is."

"It's Malta's red-light district," Collis said, knowing

from experience there were shops there that specialized in whips and chains.

"Bloody hell." The old man, obviously British, shook his head. "Imagine, they almost killed the Earl of Lyforth with that poison."

"Mmmm," Collis mumbled, wishing Warren had eaten a dozen cookies. The resentment of all the attention Warren had garnered using his title to capture the media had hardened into hatred.

The old man said something, but his words were drowned out by the German girl backstroking in front of them. Collis had almost forgotten about her. He took a quick peek over his shoulder and caught a blur of churning legs and arms. He settled down on his stomach again, reminding himself not to think about sex.

"Well, what do you think, old chop?"

"Sorry, I couldn't hear you."

"I said our boys at Fort Halstead did it again. According to the paper, they'd lifted a partial fingerprint from the note sent with the poison cookies. It belongs to some woman called Rhonda Sibbet. She lives right here in Malta."

"No one can beat an Englishman when it comes to solving a crime," Collis said, and the man grunted his agreement.

The old man asked Collis if he wanted a drink, but Collis declined. He wiggled on his stomach, determined to catch a nap while "old chop" hobbled off toward the poolside bar in search of a gin and tonic.

Collis suddenly noticed the rhythmic splashing had stopped. He turned, pretending to be reaching for his tanning lotion. From behind his dark glasses, he watched the German girl get out of the pool. She was walking toward the crescent-shaped swim steps where some children were playing. Her breasts cleared the water first. Rivulets rushed off tightly spiraled nipples, then steadily dripped as she made her way to the steps. A slow heat built in his groin. She stepped out of the pool, wringing water from her long hair with strong arms. Her thighs looked powerful too.

Collis brought himself up short, remembering his appetite for sex had him in a jam and rolled onto his stomach. Annabelle. Before he'd left London she'd tearfully informed him that she was "in the family way." He'd told her to get rid of it. The thought of Annabelle's figure after a baby made the overdressed Cobb salad— what did he expect at a Bradford hotel?—turn over in his stomach. He was tired of her, anyway. He would get rid of her as soon as he returned to London. A rich man.

"Vurn."

Collis looked over his shoulder and found the German amazon standing over him. It took him a second to realize she'd said "Burn," meaning his back needed more tanning lotion. He handed her the lotion, his eyes quickly surveying her muscular thighs. He lay prone on his stomach—the heat in his groin had returned—offering her his back.

She dribbled a generous amount of lotion in a T pattern across his back. Instead of smoothing it on, she kneaded it in with amazingly strong fingers.

"You're good at this," he said.

"Ja."

Not much English, he decided as she trickled the lotion down the length of his leg. She worked his leg, starting at his ankle and moving upward, in the same way she had his back, and he wondered if she might be a professional masseuse. Taking special care with his thighs, she rubbed more slowly in tantalizing circles right up to the hem of his trunks. She smoothed the lotion across his inner thighs. One finger grazed his balls. Again. And again.

His willpower evaporated. He was about to ask her to

come up to his room when her hand swooped between his thighs, locking around his penis.

"Gut? Ja?"

"Good. Good. Yes. My room," he muttered.

She hoisted him to his feet. He held his towel in front of himself as she shoved him toward the bathers' elevator. Inside, he punched nine and the elevator creaked upward. He studied the amazon. She was much younger than he'd originally thought. Hausfrau material in another few years. But now—

She reached past him and jabbed the "Stop" button. The elevator lurched to a halt between floors. She slammed him against the side of the elevator and had his trunks down to his knees before he could open his mouth.

Alone, Pithany sat on the Blue Grotto veranda facing out over the picturesque lagoon. A light breeze ruffled the scarlet bougainvillea that festooned the veranda's wall of golden limestone, bringing with it the bittersweet scent of the almond trees' white blossoms. "Why didn't I think of lighting the grotto?" she said to no one in particular. Dozens of travel agents and writers were milling around at the preview party, sipping drinks, and enjoying the same view.

Janna had lined the bluff circling the lagoon with torches that flickered in the cat's-paw of wind that usually blew across the ridge, revealing drifts of wildflowers swaying gently on the top of the hill. Like a strand of diamonds, the lights sparkled in the darkness, highlighting the majestic rocks, sheer corniches that towered above the lagoon. Below, floodlights concealed in the grottos illuminated the deep caverns with an ethereal light. In the lagoon itself, Janna had cleverly hidden underwater lights among the coral so the water glowed with the same incandescent peacock-blue as it did during the day. Multihued fishes by the schools darted through the coral to the delight of those watching. The effect was quite breathtaking, Pithany reflected, proud of Janna.

For the party, Janna had arranged for local fishermen in their brightly colored *luzzijiet* to sail guests through the grottos and between the limestone arches that separated the peaceful cove from the rougher waters of the Mediterranean. The guests seemed to be enjoying themselves. They'd been arriving for the past two days until this evening when every room in the hotel had been filled.

Too bad they weren't paying guests, but then Pithany had never expected them to be. Every great hotel debuted—to the industry first—with complimentary rooms. Janna had taken the custom one step further by targeting events for special travel interests designed to acquaint the visitors, not just with the hotel, but with Malta as well.

The response had been tremendous. Trekkers International, headquartered in London, had sent representatives to hike across the island's prehistoric trails to the Hagar Qim temples. The site resembled Stonehenge, but predated it by several centuries.

Dive groups, especially those from America, had arrived two days ago and had already proclaimed the area the greatest "find" since the Barrier Reef. Pithany could have told them the Phoenicians had discovered the reefs around Malta first, free diving to amazing depths.

Pithany smiled to herself, thankful she'd handed the operation over to Janna. The Blue Grotto had been Pithany's dream since the day the Nazis surrendered. While the islanders toasted Hitler's fall, she'd hiked across the island to the lagoon her family owned. She'd marveled at the four hours of solitude—uninterrupted by an air raid, appreciating the natural beauty of the island she loved. The silvery leaves of the olive trees fluttered in the breeze and *api,* the sound of bees at work on the ripening fruit, filled the air along with the fresh scent of wild mint and fennel. She'd sat on the high bluff overlooking the lagoon, comforted by nature's timeless order, but enveloped by an overwhelming sense of loss. Ian would never return.

What was she to do with the rest of her life? The war, at least, had given her direction. She had no choice really except to rebuild the family's three hotels. Her father had committed suicide months before, leaving her alone.

Long before the surrender, the islanders had planned for the victory. Few buildings had been left undamaged by Nazi bombs, certainly none in Valletta. Reconstruct, the city fathers urged—not ugly modern bunkers—but buildings the knights would recognize. Rebuild with modern conveniences lacking before the war, but reconstruct a city proud of its medieval heritage, its place in history, its ability to withstand not only the greatest siege in ancient history, but in modern history as well.

Sitting on the bluff that day wishing Ian were with her to celebrate, Pithany had gazed down at the lagoon through tear-blurred eyes. "If only you could see this, darling," she'd said out loud, regretting that the war had kept them on the other side of the island and they'd never come here. "It's the most beautiful spot on Malta."

That day over fifty years ago, desperately longing for a love that was never to be, Pithany decided the hotels would be her life. She would build a tribute to Ian's memory, a hotel built on the site he surely would have loved.

Pithany looked up, telling herself to stop being a sentimental old fool, and saw Nick. He was talking with Clybourne Hooey VI, publisher of *Travel Logue,* the bible of the industry. She liked to think of Nick as the son she'd never had. Not only did Nick look like Ian, he had his moral integrity. Some men, like Collis, were for sale. If she could have bought Nick for Janna, Pithany would have.

Nick caught Pithany's eye and came over to her, a Bushwacker in his hand. "I assure you that I'm honored, deeply honored, to have spoken to a man with a Roman numeral that big after his name." He leaned closer. "Personally, I think his parents should have named him Phooey Hooey."

"He is a trife taken with himself."

"The ego has landed," Nick said, leaning against the railing, "but the good news is he loves the hotel. He's already booked the honeymoon suite for his son. He's positive Phooey Hooey the eighth will be conceived here."

Nick swirled the ice in his glass and scanned the crowd for Janna. She was talking to one of her staff, double-checking or giving last minute instructions, no doubt. They'd spent every night together. He made it a point to talk to her more, not just about casual things, but about themselves.

For the first time in over five years, Nick found himself enjoying a woman's company, looking forward to being with her, but as much as he liked Janna, a part of him held back. He knew Amanda Jane wouldn't have cared. Hell, her dying wish had been for him to have a happy life. Even so, he hadn't quite come to terms with a world without Amanda Jane. He told himself to take his time. Janna's divorce wasn't final yet anyway. Wait and see what happened.

A life is meant to be shared, not lived alone, he thought looking at Pithany Crandall. As much as he admired her, Nick didn't want to have the same fate, living his life loving someone who'd died. He'd wrestled with his conscience a dozen times or more, but somehow he wasn't quite ready to let go of the past.

He watched Janna, still speaking intently with one of her employees, thinking of how she awoke first each morning. When he opened his eyes, she would be sharing his pillow, watching him with undisguised love. She would kiss him, a tender early morning kiss and say, "I love you, Nick." Before he could answer, she would slip out of bed and into the bathroom. Obviously, she wanted to spare him from answering.

Warren had his arm around Shadoe, guiding her through the crowd, when someone tapped on his shoulder.

The waiter said, "Inspector General Muscat is waiting in the lobby to see you."

Warren took the shortcut from the veranda to the main lobby, cutting through the garden. The tamarisk trees' white blossoms gleamed from between green leaves while hundreds of tiny lights sparkled from the branches. Janna had a knack for adding drama, and knowing his sister, she had the paperwork necessary for running a hotel under control as well. He hoped Muscat didn't have bad news that would affect his sister's business. So far, the offensive the family had directed against the Bradfords had gone well.

Rhonda Sibbet had been implicated in Travis Prescott's murder. The police had filed extradition papers with the authorities in Monaco where she was staying. Put enough pressure on her, Warren thought, and she would implicate Curt Bradford. Linking Tony to the crimes might be more difficult, but he felt obligated to pursue the man. Tony had made Aunt Pith's life difficult enough for years. Warren didn't want him harassing Janna.

Warren entered the lobby, passing under the limestone portico. "Inspector General." Warren extended his hand.

"Sir . . . Your lordship—"

"Warren," he said, accustomed to the way many people stumbled over the title he preferred not to use.

"I'm afraid I have some bad news, sir."

Warren braced himself. "What's that?"

"Rhonda Sibbet has committed suicide."

Janna winnowed her way through the crowd on the veranda, almost giddy with success. Things were going so well, she couldn't believe her luck. She'd seen the pride in Aunt Pith's eyes as she'd arrived that evening. The hotel her aunt had dreamed about for years had joined the ranks of five-star hotels.

It was the least I could do for her, Janna thought. *All these years, she's given me love when she herself needed love.*

"You look great," Nick said, his eyes beaming his approval as Janna came up to them. "Isn't her dress a smash?"

"Yes. It's very becoming." Aunt Pith's sincere smile confirmed her words.

Janna had purchased the mauve sheath on the same day she'd bought the new swimsuit. At the time, she'd worried that it might not be the best selection for this evening. She'd wondered what designer gown Audrey might have chosen. Since that day, things had happened with such breakneck speed that Janna didn't have time to concern herself with the dress. Other things were much more important.

"Aunt Pith, do you mind if I borrow Nick for a bit? I want him to meet the editor of *Diver's World*. I was going to have Warren talk to him since it's his video on diving in Malta that the editor will be viewing, but Warren seems to have disappeared."

"Run along," Aunt Pith said. "I'll stay here and enjoy the view."

Nick slipped his arm around Janna and she smiled up at him. She couldn't honestly remember when she'd been this happy. They walked toward the bar where the editor waited. As they rounded the corner, Janna saw Collis coming toward her.

21

✳

Collis sized up the situation, observing from a distance as Janna walked toward him with the tall, rather good-looking man. Janna obviously liked him. Collis recalled receiving the same adoring look when he'd first met Janna. A spurt of jealousy hit him but he steadied himself, remembering hammerlock thighs. Gerte Wethstrude. He'd spent last night and the entire day, letting the German amazon make love to him.

He couldn't imagine Janna getting rough—really rough—with him. *Definitely not.* Candlelight dinners and long walks at dusk were more her style. Even if she'd appreciated the kinkier side of sex, Collis admitted Janna still didn't suit him. Let the stranger have her. The only thing Collis needed from Janna was money. It wasn't as if the Athertons didn't have plenty of it to go around. He deserved his share. With enough capital, he could travel from country to country lecturing—finding women like Gerte.

His most charming smile on his lips, Collis walked up to Janna, ignoring her angry grimace. "Darling." He kissed her lightly on the cheek. "You've done a wonderful job with this place. It's—"

"What are you doing here?" He'd only heard that tone once before—at Reginald's funeral.

"I knew you would want me to be here with you." Out of the corner of his eye, Collis studied the man with

Janna. He was even handsomer at close range. No doubt he was responsible for Janna's bitchy attitude.

"I'll see you later." The stranger left them alone.

"Why would I want you here?" Janna asked. "You did everything you could to discourage me from working with Aunt Pithany."

"I can see I made a mistake. You're a born business-woman."

"Don't patronize me. Why are you here?"

He had no intention of telling her. He planned to harry the Athertons a bit. "Let's be civilized about this. You don't have to be ugly just because you caught me with another woman. Where's the harm? Remember Karl Marx? His wife had an enlightened attitude toward extramarital affairs. She's buried with Karl and his mistress right in London's Highgate Cemetery. And remember Nelson and Lady Hamilton. They lived together with her husband. Why can't you be—"

"I don't give a damn about Karl Marx's love life, or Nelson's. Surely, you aren't suggesting some ménage? You know I would never be happy sharing the man I loved." She cast a sidelong glance in the direction of the man who'd been with her earlier.

Collis thought baiting her with all that trivia would fluster her, but it hadn't. When they'd argued, she'd always recited a litany of facts, which often confused him. He'd hoped to give her a dose of her own medicine. Tonight, though, she seemed to have an inner strength. He wondered if her attitude had anything to do with the stranger. He made a mental note to find out more about him.

"You didn't come here to wish me well, or to suggest a reconciliation. Why did you come?"

Collis smiled mysteriously. "After the evening's over I want to have a private chat with you . . . and Warren."

"Warren? What does he have to do with us? Our

problems are between you and me. You won't get any more money out of the family by approaching my brother."

For a moment Collis was startled that she'd so quickly guessed that he planned to ask for money. He shouldn't have been. Janna was sharp. It would be a relief to get rid of her.

"I know you married me for what you thought was my money," Janna said, her green eyes surveying him—the way Pithany always did—from his tanned face to the tips of his white loafers with an unmistakable look of dislike. "I can't imagine why I ever married you."

The disgust in her voice would have undermined a lesser man's self-confidence, but Collis knew Janna too well. The Marx comment might not have worked, but his next parry would. Collis directed his gaze at the tall man who stood not far away. "Is he any good in bed?"

Janna's gaze remained steady. "Your problem, Collis, is not knowing the difference between sex and love." She jabbed her finger against one of the mallards swimming across his tie. "I'm willing to give you everything—the house, the car, every pound in the Barclays' account— just to get rid of you as soon as possible. But don't you *dare* ask my brother for a single pence."

She spun around and merged with the crowd before Collis could respond. He wouldn't have admitted it to a soul, but he was shaken, not by Janna's anger—after all, she was a woman scorned—but by the fact she'd found someone so quickly. Janna was a careful woman who planned everything, usually researching the subject and spewing facts until she bored him to death. It wasn't like her to take up with a man so soon.

Her new lover was handsome, but no competition for Collis. Collis shouldn't have felt threatened, he didn't give a damn about Janna, but his self-confidence had been eroded by her imperious attitude. He rallied immediately, reminding himself that he could make plenty of trouble for her.

Pithany had observed the exchange between Janna and Collis with amusement. She couldn't hear a word they were saying, but Janna's assertive gestures and tight expression confirmed this wasn't a reconciliation. Not that Pithany had expected one, but the moment she'd seen Collis, she'd assumed that was why he'd come to Malta.

Pithany rose slowly, her legs tired despite her nap earlier, and walked to Nick who was talking to a man Pithany didn't know. She recognized his lapel pin, crossed gold keys, indicating he was a concierge at a major hotel. Nick quickly introduced her to Etienne Terrail, concierge of the Ritz Hotel in Paris.

She was welcoming him to the Blue Grotto when Collis ambled up to the group. Pithany was forced to introduce Etienne and Nick. Upon saying Nick's name, Pithany detected the slightest narrowing of Collis's eyes.

"You're with Imperial Cola, I understand," Collis said. "The plant manager."

Pithany cringed when he made "manager" sound like a dirty word, but the barb didn't trouble Nick who merely nodded.

"I know a lot about the company," Collis said with a superior tone and none of his usual charm. "I often use it when I give lectures at the London School of Economics."

Since Reginald's death, Collis had abandoned the smooth-talking method he'd used to try to charm everyone. Showing his true colors at last, Pithany decided, although she'd never been fooled by him. But Janna had. At least she'd changed enough since Reginald's death so that she was no longer susceptible to Collis's manipulations.

Pithany maneuvered the concierge away from Collis,

who appeared set on delivering one of his speeches. Nick could handle him. "You'll not believe our automated wine vault," she told Etienne. "My niece, Janna, designed it. A robot retrieves each selection and sends it down an airtight chute, so the vault door is only opened to receive new stock. The temperature never varies even half a degree."

Nick felt uncomfortable being left alone with Janna's husband. Until this evening Collis Pembroke had merely been a name, a faceless man who'd spurned Janna. Now here Collis was, eager to support his wife. Undoubtedly he wanted another chance. Nick believed in marriage— it had been his salvation—not divorce. But realistically he knew half the marriages in America failed and the divorce rate in Great Britain was similar. Still, he had no intention of being "the other man." He'd gotten the distinct impression that her marriage was over, the divorce merely a formality. But now, he wondered.

Nick swallowed the remainder of his Bushwacker, seeing it as his escape. "I need a refill."

"I could use a drink too."

Nick shouldered his way through the crowd with Collis dogging him.

"I read that Imperial lost the Balfour Hotels account," Collis said. "Dynasty-Cola came up with the seventy-five million dollar loan Balfour wanted. Do you think suppliers should give their customers low interest loans like that?"

Nick shrugged, the gut feeling he'd had upon meeting Collis intensifing. Even if he hadn't been Janna's husband, Nick wouldn't have liked him.

"I guess it doesn't matter." Collis didn't bother to hide a shit-eating grin. "With that deal, Dynasty captured a sizable portion of Imperial's market share."

Nick didn't respond. Personally, he considered it

against the company's best interests to loan money, but he didn't offer his opinion.

"Imperial Cola should have agreed to that deal with the Soviets," Collis pressed. "If they'd joint-ventured an Imperial operation with the Russians, Dynasty wouldn't have captured that market. I can just see the commercials: Hundreds of Rooskies dancing in Red Square singing 'Drink Dynasty-Cola.' "

"Dynasty accepted a pack of Soviet ships and vodka instead of cash as the Russians' contribution. Do you think that was a smart move? How'd you like to try to unload those tubs in this economy?"

"Perhaps, but unforseen economic eventualities . . ."

What an ass. Nick stopped listening. Like most "analysts" Collis Pembroke's insight was twenty-twenty hindsight. The man in front of Nick stepped forward, and Nick moved closer to the bar. Collis followed, delivering some bullshit theory about market shares. Janna's choice for a husband puzzled Nick. True, he'd expected some studious type complete with bifocals. Nick hadn't been prepared for a man who'd stepped from the pages of *GQ*, an overbearing jerk with a deep-fried tan.

The bartender asked for Nick's order, and he decided on another Bushwacker.

"Make one for me too," Collis said.

"You won't like it. It's—"

"I'll give it a go."

Nick spotted Warren coming toward them with Shadoe at his side. The bartender handed Nick and Collis their drinks just as Warren walked up.

Warren asked Collis, "What are you doing here?"

Collis smiled at Warren but Nick detected a trace of arrogance in his expression. He doubted if the two men really liked each other the way Nick and Travis had been friends as well as brothers-in-law. Warren's question demanded some answer, but Collis didn't give one. The tension in the group kicked up a notch. Collis took a swig of the Bushwacker, still grinning at Warren like a cat with its paw on a mouse. Collis swallowed hard and then gulped for air, sticking out his tongue and fanning it for all he was worth. Shadoe started to giggle and Nick had trouble not smiling.

"Nick," Warren said, ignoring Collis. "I need to have a word with you—in private."

Puzzled, Nick followed Shadoe and Warren to the far end of the terrace.

"Rhonda Sibbet is dead," Warren said.

"She shot herself," Shadoe added.

"Aw, shit!" Nick had been counting on the police locating her. He was positive she would implicate the Bradfords.

"The gendarmes in Monaco found her body early this morning. She'd died sometime last night."

"The Bradfords killed her," Nick said emphatically.

"I think you're right," Shadoe agreed.

"It seems suspicious," Warren said, "but the police did find powder burns on her hands, and her prints were on the gun. The servants insist she didn't have any visitors, and the villa is protected by guard dogs. She left a note saying she'd given Travis the poison honey."

"So the Bradfords put her up to it," Nick said, thinking that must be the reason they'd tried to kill him—to acquire his stock from his heirs. "Now the police—"

"Her note clears the Bradfords. She did it because she hoped to make Anthony Bradford like her by purchasing Travis's stock in the Blue Grotto. Apparently, she was waiting for an annulment of her marriage so she could marry Curt Bradford."

"We're supposed to believe neither Bradford knew about it? No way!"

"She also claimed to have acted alone when she sent you the cookies."

"The Bradfords forced her to write that note and then killed her."

"Tony hasn't left Malta. He's been at a golf tournament," Warren said. "Curt is at the Puente Romano in Marbella. He's been seen—"

"How convenient. They both have alibis." Nick told himself to lower his voice. Yelling at Warren didn't solve anything. "They hired someone to do it."

"That's what I think. I've put pressure on the authorities to thoroughly investigate this. I'm going to have the team at Fort Halstead go over the evidence."

Nick nodded, telling himself to be grateful for Warren's help, but the anger simmering inside him almost overwhelmed him. Thankfully, neither Bradford was around or Nick would have beat the crap out of them to get the truth.

Collis nursed his Macallan, letting the single malt scotch soothe his raw throat as he watched Nick and Warren. It was obvious the Texan had ingratiated himself with Warren Atherton, something Collis had never been able to do. For some reason—he couldn't imagine what —Warren had remained aloof, never respecting Collis's opinion the way Reginald had, but Warren had never been this cold, this rude. Evidently, his status as a media star had gone to his head. If Warren thought he could shunt him aside—Collis Coddington Pembroke of the Northumberland Pembrokes—he was very sadly mistaken.

As for the dumb Texan, let him have Janna. Even if she inherited all of Pithany Crandall's money, Janna wouldn't get it for years. That old bat would live to be one hundred. It would serve Nick Jensen right to get stuck with boring Janna. Yet despite not wanting Janna himself, Collis deeply resented being replaced. So soon.

* * *

The guests were moving into the main dining room for a five course meal. Janna scanned the crowd for Nick, but didn't see him. "Where's Nick?" she asked Warren.

"He had a telephone call."

Janna needed to talk to him. Shadoe had told her about Rhonda's death. They'd agreed it was too convenient. What did Nick think? She bet he was angry and she couldn't blame him. If the Bradfords had been involved in the attempt on Nick's life, it appeared that they'd gotten away with it. The last of the guests had taken their seats when Nick appeared, his face grave.

"I have to leave for Houston right away. Austin Prescott's in the hospital. He's not expected to live."

The anguish in Nick's voice wrenched at Janna's heart. "I'm so sorry, Nick." She put her hand on his arm, although she would rather have taken him into her arms to comfort him. "Is there anything I can do?"

"There's nothing anyone can do." He hesitated, measuring her for a moment, concern in his eyes. "You know about Rhonda?"

She nodded.

"They killed her."

"Maybe the police will be able to prove who forced her to write that note, or—"

"Don't count on it. Those bastards are smart."

She walked with him to the door, aware that all the guests had now been seated. They expected her at the head table, but Nick was more important.

"While I'm gone, I want you to be very careful."

"I will." She stood on tiptoe and kissed his cheek. "Whatever happens, remember I love you."

Nick nodded, moved by the sincerity he saw in her eyes. He wanted to pull her aside and discuss her relationship with Collis, but now wasn't the time. He squeezed her hand and mumbled good-bye.

Nick hurried through the nearly empty lobby, his

thoughts on Travis's father. Why hadn't Austin let Nick know sooner? When he'd last seen him, he'd told Nick he wanted to die quietly and without all the fuss that had accompanied Amanda Jane's death. His request had been a quiet reprimand. During the final weeks before Amanda Jane's death, Nick had lashed out at Travis and Austin, furious that they hadn't told him about her condition sooner.

Nick knew he could never repay Austin. He'd been the father that Nick had never had, encouraging him to go back to school. He'd even been happy Nick had married Amanda Jane. Hell, most fathers wouldn't have been thrilled to have a knockout of a daughter, who could have married anyone, marry a loser. But Austin Prescott, like Travis, had seen Nick's potential. Even when he himself hadn't.

After Travis's funeral, Austin had said his own battle with cancer wasn't going well. Nick had wanted to stay with him, but Austin insisted he "get on with his life." Coming to Malta seemed like the perfect solution. Nick could finally repay Austin by discovering what really happened to his son. But Nick was almost as far from the truth now as he'd been when he'd arrived here.

The frustrating sense of helplessness Nick had known his whole life threatened to overwhelm him. In school he'd been at the mercy of the teachers. The struggle to overcome his disability—learning to accept himself and not be embarrassed—had given him strength and courage. Those gains had suffered when Amanda Jane became ill. Once again, control had been snatched from him, leaving him feeling as powerless as he'd been as a boy quaking under Mrs. Mooth's stare. Now here he was —again—unable to help those he loved. He'd counted on telling Austin that his son's killer had been caught. He owed Austin that much, and damn it, he kept his promises.

Halfway across the parking lot, Nick heard someone yell, "Jensen. Leaving so soon?"

Nick turned and saw Collis. "Yeah." He had no intention of sharing his personal problems with this man.

"There are a few facts about Janna that I thought you might like to know."

Nick bristled, but managed to keep his voice even. "If she hasn't told me, then I don't want to know."

"Janna doesn't have any money of her own; Reginald Atherton cut her out of his will. Pithany Crandall could live another twenty years before she dies and Janna inherits. Who knows? Pithany mortgaged everything to build this hotel. She could very well lose it all, if this hotel fails."

Nick attempted to control his anger. Obviously, Collis knew about his wife's affair and thought Nick was after Janna's money. "I'm not interested in anyone's money. I have more of my own than I need."

"Really? As a bottling plant manager? That's a joke."

Nick unlocked the car and climbed in. What the hell could Janna have ever seen in this jerk?

"All you're going to get out of sleeping with Janna is bored."

Nick jumped out of the car and grabbed Collis by his prissy tie.

"Now don't get huffy," Collis said, trying to be cool, but Nick saw the fear in his eyes.

He let go of the tie and Collis smiled. Nick rammed his fist into Collis's stomach. He doubled over so unexpectedly that Nick's second punch, aimed for his gut as well, hit Collis just below his right eye. His head snapped back and he tottered backward, then collapsed butt first into the African daisies lining the parking area.

Nick glared down at him. "Fuck you and the horse you rode in on."

*   *   *

By midnight the party was winding down. A few people were still dancing but most had retired knowing they had a full day of activities scheduled for tomorrow.

"I told Collis to meet us at Falcon's Lair," Warren said. Shadoe stood silently at his side. "We might as well face him tonight."

"No matter what he says, you're not going to give him any money." Janna was still fuming. Despite her warning, Collis had arranged a meeting with Warren.

"All right," he agreed, then glanced toward the dance floor where Audrey and Ellis were the only couple still dancing. "You'd better tell Mother about your divorce."

"I've been planning to for days, but . . . Look how happy she is. I don't want to upset her."

"I think she'll be less upset about your divorce now than if it had happened when Reginald was alive," Shadoe said.

"You're right. I'd better tell her now."

The dance ended. "I'll go with you," Warren volunteered.

"No. This is my problem. I'll tell her." Janna crossed the terrace, thinking Audrey had been a good mother. She'd never really understood Janna, but she'd tried her best.

Janna managed to part the lovebirds and drew Audrey aside. "I've been meaning to talk to you."

"What's so important, dear? Are you concerned about Taxi? He's safely locked in my room."

"No. I'm not worried about Taxi."

"Well, what is it?"

"Collis and I aren't getting along."

"It'll all work out for the best. I'm certain."

"It's not a passing problem." She hesitated, then decided not to soften the blow and tell Audrey the truth. "Divorce seems to be the only alternative."

"I wondered when you were going to tell me."

"You knew?"

"Yes. Ellis overheard Warren talking with the solicitors."

"I would have told you sooner, but I didn't want to upset you."

Audrey shook her head. "I'm not upset. On the contrary, I never cared for Collis."

"But I thought—"

"I admit I was a bit of a mouse, always deferring to Reginald, but that didn't mean he controlled my every thought."

Janna glanced over to where Ellis Osgood and Aunt Pith stood talking with Warren and Shadoe. Reginald certainly hadn't controlled Audrey. She'd managed to carry on an affair right under his nose.

"As a matter of fact, I did everything I could to make certain you and Collis didn't get back together," Audrey said proudly. "I told him I would speak with you on his behalf, but I never did."

"Why not?"

Audrey looked directly into Janna's eyes. "I love you too much to let you make the mistake I made: staying married to a man who doesn't love you. All these years I could have been happy with Ellis but I stayed with Reginald. I tried to leave him several times but he talked me into staying. I didn't want that to happen to you."

With a pang, Janna realized she'd never given Audrey the credit she deserved. She'd been locked in a loveless marriage for years. As demanding as Reginald had been on his children, he'd held Audrey up to an almost impossible standard. Janna wondered if Audrey had known Reginald was a homosexual. If she had, she'd never alluded to it, not even once. "I think you understand, better than anyone, why I have to get a divorce."

Audrey hugged Janna. "Life's too short not to be happy. I only wish I'd realized that sooner."

* * *

Collis drove up to Falcon's Lair, ten minutes late. He'd rushed back to his hotel from the Blue Grotto. The time he'd spent with an ice pack on his eye had reduced the swelling, but had done nothing to hide the purple and blue bruise around his eye. That damn Texan. He'd nearly ruined a perfect face.

The anger simmering inside him had hardened into full-blown hatred, not of Jensen, but of the Athertons. He wanted what was rightfully his—now. Warren answered his knock. Collis was momentarily taken aback. True, it was very late, but Collis would have insisted a servant answer the door.

"What happened to your eye?"

"Jensen hit me. The man's crazy. I'm thinking of filing charges."

Warren smiled. Fuming, Collis followed him through the marble foyer into the grand salon. He came to an abrupt halt when he saw not only Janna but Shadoe and Ellis Osgood as well as Audrey waiting for him. Off to one side, her legs propped up on an ottoman sat Aunt Pith.

"I don't think you'll want everyone to hear what I have to say," Collis said, masking his surprise with a level voice, "especially your mother."

"I'm part of this family," Audrey said, having heard his comment from across the large room. "I'm entitled to hear what you have to say."

Collis assessed his options swiftly. He'd counted on playing Audrey as a trump card, knowing they wouldn't want her to discover Reginald had been a homosexual. He whispered, "Do you think she'll want to hear about Gian Paolo?"

Warren literally went white; his so-called Atherton blue eyes didn't look quite as clear. Before he could respond Audrey rose and walked over.

"Come in, Collis," she said. "Sit down." She gestured to the straight-backed chair nearby.

He took his seat, leaving Warren to get rid of his mother. There was a whispered exchange between mother and son while Collis poured himself a snifter of Le Paradis cognac from the decanter on the table in front of him although no one had offered him a drink.

Audrey returned to her place on the loveseat next to Ellis Osgood. "Don't *anyone* even *think* of asking me to leave. Anything that concerns this family is my problem as well."

Collis sipped the cognac, rapidly making a mid-course adjustment. He'd intended to use Audrey's emotional instability as a lever to extract money from Warren. But clever as he was, Collis instantly saw how to turn the situation to his advantage.

"I'm willing to agree to a divorce on Janna's terms."

"Generous of you," Janna said, "considering I'm giving you everything."

Collis shrugged off her comment. He knew he deserved more—much more—and he knew how to get it. "I think I should be compensated for my silence regarding a number of highly sensitive matters."

"Like what?" Janna asked, quickly looking at Warren whose face was grave as he held Shadoe's hand.

"Gian Paolo."

Only the ticking of the Cartier mystery clock on the mantel could be heard. Janna wondered how Audrey would weather this revelation. Her heart went out to the woman who'd sacrificed her own happiness for so long. She and Warren should have told her, found some way to soften the blow.

"We're all aware of my husband's preference for men."

Audrey's words, cool and to the point, startled

Pithany. She'd wondered if Audrey had suspected, but she had never mentioned anything to her sister.

The answer, coming as it did from Audrey, not one of the others, caught Collis off guard. He tried to gauge the reaction of the others to see if they were surprised, but was unable to read anything in their expressions except dislike of him. He recouped quickly, asking, "Do you want the whole world to know?"

Blackmail! So Collis was desperate enough to stoop this low. There was a time when Pithany would have told him to go to hell and tossed him out, but she commanded herself to remain silent. It was time for Warren and Janna to handle matters.

Warren didn't hesitate. "Go ahead. Make it public."

"You still won't get any money," Janna added.

Collis took another sip of cognac, certain they were bluffing. He'd been a fool to tip Janna by telling her in advance that he wanted to talk with Warren. She'd immediately known what Collis wanted and moved to stop him by alerting her brother. But it didn't matter, Collis held all the cards.

"Would you want everyone to know Janna isn't really your sister?"

"Janna is my sister. A piece of paper doesn't mean a damn thing."

Collis couldn't resist smiling. "Reginald didn't share your feelings. He cut her out of his will in favor of Gian Paolo." Collis saw he'd hit his mark with Janna. She wasn't a good enough actress to disguise the hurt in her eyes.

"I don't care what my father felt about Janna. I'm in charge of this family now. I love her. I'll do anything I can to help her."

"We're not giving you one pound to buy your silence." Janna's voice was choked with emotion, aware that Warren's words echoed her family's feelings. No matter who her parents were, no matter how Reginald had shunted her aside. She had a family; she had love.

Bravo, Pithany silently applauded.

"No?" Collis said with all the confidence he could muster. He had to admit, he expected the Athertons to fold at the first hint of scandal. He directed his gaze at Janna. "What value do you place on"—he cast a withering glance at Warren—"the golden boy's career?"

"The British people are too intelligent to judge a son by his father's actions," Janna said.

"True." Collis took another swig of cognac, purposely letting them dangle. Letting them wonder. He could tell by the look on Audrey's and Shadoe's faces that he'd hit the mark. They knew Warren had potential in politics. Audrey probably had her sights set on number 10 Downing Street. "But how would Warren's adoring public feel if they discovered he was a common criminal?"

"You bastard—"

"Let's hear what he has to say." Warren cut Janna off.

"Reginald died in Paolo's Hammersmith flat, not at Lyforth Hall." He gave a broad smile, thrilled at the stunned looks leveled at him.

"Warren committed at least one crime. Hardly adds to the credentials of a man bound for the cabinet, does it? The Tories are incredibly stuffy about those things."

"Please," Audrey said, her voice quavering. She reached for Osgood's arm. "Warren did it to protect me."

Collis had known she would be the first to crack, so he decided to go for the jugular. "I have the documents to prove your son is a common criminal. Don't force me to expose him."

"Now see here," Osgood boomed, surprising Collis. In all the years he'd known the doctor, he'd hardly heard the man talk. A silent shadow, he rarely spoke except to give medical advice. He *never* raised his voice.

Collis knew his battle plan was on track despite the rocky start. Warren gloried in his newfound fame. Collis would wager every pound he had—or hoped to extract from the Athertons—that Warren had set his sights on the glory trail of politics. The very worried expression on Shadoe's face told him that she knew this as well.

"It doesn't matter if you expose me or not. There are those in the Tory party who might consider Shadoe"— Warren put his arm around her"—a political liability. Before I asked her to marry me, I decided nothing was more important to me than the woman I love. I won't be seeking a political career."

"The worst that can happen to Warren is a fine," Janna added.

"I know what I did was wrong—"

"But you did it for all the right reasons," Shadoe said.

"I'm prepared to accept the consequences."

His mind reeling, Collis struggled to maintain his composure. Hope of blackmailing the Athertons out of millions evaporated. "I can sell the story to the tabloids."

"No gentleman ever would," Janna said, recalling the pride Collis had in his family name—the Pembrokes of Northumberland. "But then, everyone in this room knows you're not a gentleman."

Collis ignored the satisfied smile on Pithany's face. "I'm giving you all one last chance. . . ." His eyes swung around the room, searching for a vulnerable face.

"Get out." Janna stood and pointed to the door.

Collis sauntered across the large room, deliberately taking his time. He was in the dark foyer before he decided that he might have a better alternative than selling the story to the tabloids. Much better.

22

After Collis left, Janna decided to spend the night in the guest house even though Nick had returned to Texas. During the past weeks she'd grown accustomed to staying with him. But tonight the exhilaration she usually experienced at being here had vanished, and not even the memory of the triumphant opening of the Blue Grotto could bolster her self-esteem. How had she ever fallen in love with Collis? Even Audrey had seen through the veneer of charm Collis no longer bothered to maintain.

A gentle knock at the door interrupted her thoughts. She opened it and found Shadoe, smiling radiantly.

"I know it's late," she said, her words coming out in a breathless rush, "but I have to talk to you."

"Come in," Janna said, although Shadoe was already through the doorway and hugging her.

"I'm so happy," Shadoe said, still hugging her.

"Now we're really going to be sisters," Janna said.

"Yes. Warren asked me to marry him the night Rommie was killed. With all the trouble, we didn't have time to make plans so we hadn't told anyone, but tonight when Collis— Well, it just came out."

Janna motioned for Shadoe to sit. "I want to hear all about the wedding."

"It won't be a big wedding," Shadoe said as she sat beside Janna, "just family—your family."

"Yours now."

Shadoe smiled eagerly. "Chloe will have grandparents. She's always wanted a grandma and grandpa."

Janna knew Shadoe was the one who'd always yearned for a family. The Tarot card trick had given Shadoe an excuse to follow her heart.

"You're upset," Shadoe said, her face suddenly serious as she studied Janna. "Forget Collis."

"I was an idiot. A total idiot. He never loved—"

"You weren't the first woman to marry the wrong man. And you won't be the last." Shadoe pointed to herself. "You're looking at a three time loser."

"Warren is different. You two should have been together all these years."

"You're right. None of my previous husbands loved me the way Warren does. But I needed love so much that I married men that I should have realized didn't love me."

"None of your husbands were as bad as Collis. My entire family has to suffer for my mistake, especially Warren."

"I know you're worried about him. But remember, you had nothing to do with his decision to move his father's body. He takes complete responsibility for his actions."

"Still, our entire family—who's never had a breath of scandal—will be dragged through tabloid muck."

"We're strong enough to weather it."

"I hope so," Janna answered, unable to conceal how heartsick she felt. But as her eyes scanned the room, with its reminders of Nick, her thoughts returned to him. "We should be worrying about whoever murdered Travis and tried to kill Nick. I'm convinced the murderer is still out there."

* * *

"Shit for brains," Tony said to himself as he waited for one of the Mifsud brothers to haul Curt out of bed in Marbella and bring him to the telephone. His son didn't have the intelligence of an ant. Of all the half-assed ideas Tony had ever heard, the oleander poisoning was the stupidest.

"It's all Pithany's fault. That bitch." If Pithany had been Curt's mother, he would have been smart. And dedicated like Janna. Look at her. Janna didn't know a thing about hotels, but she jumped right in, working harder in the short time she'd been here than all the years Curt had worked for him. She would stick with it too. Anyone who spent years ferreting through musty reports on the French Revolution had a rare sense of dedication.

"H-hullo," Curt said.

"Did you read the papers?" Tony asked, his voice cautious, wondering how Curt would take the news.

"Wh-what?"

"Rhonda Sibbet killed herself."

"I—I know . . . I know." Curt's consonants slurred. How could he be drunk before lunch? "I love . . . I loved her sho much."

"Snap out of it! I want you to come home, but I don't want you bawling all over Malta about Rhonda."

"I'm not comin' back. You killed Rhonda. You—"

Tony slammed the receiver into the cradle. Shit for brains was a compliment. Zero brains. How could he accuse his own father over the telephone? The line could be tapped. Unlikely. Maltese laws were strict. But with Pithany's family in on the act—calling in the experts from Fort Halstead—Tony couldn't afford to take chances.

He flopped back in his chair and studied the ceiling. He was safe. No one could prove he'd ordered Rhonda killed. He'd taken a quick ferry ride from Malta to Sicily where he'd linked up with an old friend in the Mafia. Guiseppe Aldo had sent his most experienced hit man to take care of Rhonda.

If Tony had planned on killing anyone to get the hotel shares, which he hadn't, he would have hired Guiseppe to take care of it instead of pulling an amateurish poison stunt. How dumb could they have been? It didn't seem possible that anyone so asinine could really be his son.

For the first time in his life depression tugged at him. He'd spent a lifetime building an empire. How could he leave it to a son who would do something so stupid that it defied all logic? There was only one solution to this mess—a grandson. Curt should marry immediately— someone with brains, not tits—and produce an heir.

Meanwhile, damage control was the order of the day. Shoring up the image he'd cultivated over more than half a century was essential. He was mentally reviewing what he planned to say at the press conference he'd called for that afternoon when the monitor on his desk buzzed. His secretary announced Collis Coddington Pembroke.

"Make him wait fifteen minutes, then send him in."

Wary of anyone from the Crandall camp, Tony pondered the situation. He'd kept tabs on Janna from the moment she'd been born. Why Pithany allowed Janna to marry a lightweight like Collis mystified Tony. Then he thought of Curt's long-term relationship with Rhonda. Controlling his own son hadn't been easy. It gave him a measure of satisfaction to think Pithany had experienced the same troubles.

Collis Pembroke's affair and Reginald cutting Janna out of his will had played right into Pithany's hands. Now she had Janna living here where she would no doubt remarry and produce a brood of sons who would attend Oxford and then run around Malta flaunting their diplomas, claiming to be British aristocracy.

"Mr. Bradford, I've heard so much about you." Collis Pembroke extended his hand when Tony's secretary sent him in. "I often use Bradford Enterprises as an example when I give lectures on building corporate empires. Impressive. Most impressive."

"Really?" Tony said, forcing a pleased smile, but he didn't have to step in bullshit to recognize it.

"Absolutely. Top-drawer company. Absolutely first-rate."

Tony studied the man—handsome despite the bruise around his eye—seated opposite him. A blond Curt. No question about it. Janna could have done better. The unwelcome image of Nick Jensen intruded. Tony choked back a curse. "What can I do for you?"

"I know you've been having some difficulty with Pithany Crandall. The police are accusing your family of trying to murder people to get stock in her company."

"Not a word of truth to it," Tony said when Pembroke paused expectantly. "My son was involved with a mentally unstable woman who . . . Well, what can I say? She took matters into her own hands. Her suicide note cleared our family's name."

"The Athertons—and Pithany Crandall—have caused you a lot of trouble."

Tony shrugged, keeping his expression noncommittal, determined to stick to the story he intended to feed to the press. "Rhonda Sibbet was the problem. A disturbed woman. What a tragedy."

The smuggest smile Tony had ever seen crossed Collis Pembroke's face. A surge of relief, like a fine cognac, flowed through Tony, warm and sweet. Pithany had been cursed with her own problem—Collis Coddington Pembroke.

"Even so, Tony," Collis said, leaning forward, his expression suggesting he and Tony were intimate friends,

"I thought you might be interested in a few details about the family that aren't public knowledge."

Fat chance. Tony knew everything worth knowing about Pithany Crandall and her relatives. "Like what?"

"The details of Reginald Atherton's will. The *unreported* circumstances of his death."

Tony managed an "I'm interested" smile although he had complete reports on both subjects in the file behind Collis.

"The earl could be charged with criminal misconduct."

Tony didn't give a damn what charges Warren Atherton faced. Malta was less than three hours by plane from London, but it was light-years away. Barely a ripple, if that, would be felt on Malta should the Earl of Lyforth be arrested.

"There are other details but . . ."

"How much?" Tony asked, suddenly seeing a way to salvage his life's dream, his social position.

"A million pounds."

"For a little gossip? You're full of shit."

"I have embarrassing information about Janna's birth. Pithany Crandall wouldn't want it made public."

Tony forced himself to look surprised and interested. He knew the exact minute Janna had been born. Nothing this man could tell him would be news. It might cause Pithany some distress, but she was stronger, much tougher than Collis suspected.

"Half a million pounds," Collis said.

Tony put his hands together and steepled his fingers, pretending to weigh the situation. He let Collis squirm for a minute. "You have proof? Documents or something?"

"Photocopies of Atherton's will, his death certificate, Janna's birth certificate, and adoption papers."

"Mmmm," Tony muttered, striving to sound interested. Janna's birth certificate contained nothing but phony information. The adoption papers repeated the same bullshit. Only two people alive knew the truth—Pithany and Tony. Unless Pithany had told Janna. Tony discounted it. He knew Pithany too well.

"A quarter of a million?" Collis asked hopefully.

"All right," Tony agreed after a moment's hesitation. "I'll need copies that I can leak to the press." At Pembroke's enthusiastic nod, Tony added, "And something in writing from you."

A startled expression crossed Collis's face.

"It's nothing," Tony assured him. "I want you to sign a note that will say I'll pay you the money when you deliver the photocopies of personal records of the Athertons and Pithany Crandall. Keep it vague. But I want to protect myself should the documents you're offering turn out to be fraudulent."

Collis reluctantly agreed and Tony had his secretary draw up the papers. After Collis signed the document, he left to return to England for the photocopies.

Tony watched him go out the door, barely able to conceal his smile as he looked at the signature on the paper. Collis Coddington Pembroke. Sonofabitch. There were other men in the world as stupid as Curt.

Curt lay draped across the bed in his Puente Romano suite, his head hung over the side. In the distance he heard the Mifsud brothers laughing as they watched to the television in the sitting room. Curt studied the marble floor, its pattern, like clusters of clouds, reminding him of Rhonda and the hours they'd spent together lying naked on secluded beaches and watching the clouds float by. An ache of regret, of love lost forever, engulfed him. Even the bottle of vodka he'd consumed had failed to ease his pain.

"I hate 'im," Curt told the floor. "Big Tony sinks he

can order the world around. He didn't hafta kill Rhonda. No one could"—he lost his train of thought for a moment—"could prove nothin'."

He tried to envision a world without Rhonda, but couldn't. Ahead of him all he could see was a ball and chain connecting him to his father. Curt was positive that Big Tony had arranged for him to marry. Someone Big Tony had chosen.

"I can't do it. I can't," Curt muttered to the marble just inches below his nose. He sat up, intending to pick up the telephone and tell his father to go to hell. The room swam nauseatingly around him. He rolled onto his back, trying to steady the four walls that were whirling and collapsing inward on top of him.

In his mind, Curt heard his father's voice. For a moment, he froze, wishing he had a knife to plunge through Big Tony's heart. How had Rhonda felt in her final seconds of life as she was forced to put the gun to her head and pull the trigger? He shuddered to think of her terror. Had she regretted loving him? He prayed she hadn't, but he couldn't be certain.

The ceiling swirled, enveloping Curt in a miasma of emotions too intense to deny—or block out. No woman could replace Rhonda. To return to Malta would be to reject her, to deny the sacrifice she'd made because she'd loved him. He listened to the Mifsud brothers laughing at a Spanish translation of *The Three Stooges*. They thought he'd passed out and wouldn't check on him for hours. He slipped out the terrace door, over the railing, and onto the sand. Then he broke into a run, a mindless charge down the beach past the Club Marbella's exclusive bungalows.

It was almost eleven o'clock by the time Janna returned to Falcon's Lair on the day following the opening of the Blue Grotto. As she parked in the garage, her thoughts turned to Nick. She hadn't heard from him, but knew he must be in Houston by now. She tried to imagine Aunt Pith in a hospital bed like Austin Prescott, but couldn't. Janna's heart went out to Nick as she let herself into the guest house.

"Janna," called Shadoe as she came out of the main house. "Have you seen the television? Big Tony has given an interview."

"No," she replied, her voice echoing her weariness. The only news she'd heard had been when Warren had called to say the experts from Fort Halstead had flown to Monaco. Their findings confirmed the initial reports. They found no evidence to indicate Rhonda Sibbet's death had not been a suicide.

"If you hurry," Shadoe said, "we can catch Tony on the eleven o'clock news."

By the time they were inside the guest house and had the television on, Tony's interview was already being repeated. "I feel sorry for Pithany Crandall. This whole incident has been regrettable, most regrettable. But how was I to know my son had once dated a deranged woman who would resort to murder because she *thought* she would be able to marry him if she delivered shares in the Blue Grotto?"

"Can you believe his nerve?" Shadoe asked.

"How can he sound so sincere? He's obviously a good liar."

"To show Ms. Crandall my goodwill," Tony continued, "I'm willing to sell her my shares in her corporation for exactly what I paid for them." He held up papers.

"Amazing," Janna said.

"Malta is too small an island and tourism is too big an industry for us not to put aside our differences for the good of the country."

"Brilliant," Janna said, although she didn't believe his motive for selling the shares was altruistic. Aunt Pith had told her too many stories about Tony Bradford, but she had to admit it was a clever ploy. The police had failed to prove that Rhonda's death was anything but a suicide. Her suicide note explained Travis Prescott's death as well as what the papers had chosen to call "the cookie caper."

"It seems," Tony went on, "Pithany Crandall has numerous enemies, including her niece's husband."

With an overwhelming sense of humiliation, Janna sank into the nearest chair.

Again Tony waved a piece of paper, which a reporter took and examined carefully. "Collis Coddington Pembroke, husband of Janna Atherton-Pembroke, Pithany Crandall's niece and heir to her hotel chain, has offered to sell me documents that reveal family secrets. Apparently, there's a horrible scandal involving the Earl of Lyforth and another concerning his sister, Lady Janna."

In one moment of blind fury, Janna wished she could strangle Collis.

"Naturally," Tony added with a condescending smile, "I've refused this malicious offer. I don't know what these secrets are. No matter how dirty their family secrets, how offensive their behavior, I refuse to stoop to their level by purchasing the documents Pembroke is trying to sell. He'll never get any money out of me. What I want," he said, his voice oozing sincerity as if he'd invented it, "is for Malta to take its rightful place in the world as a center for travel and industry. Pithany Crandall will just have to handle her own problems."

"Don't you see?" Janna asked Shadoe. "He killed Rhonda. Tony is just covering his tracks."

"Of course," Shadoe agreed.

"He killed Rhonda as well as Travis and Ian MacShane. Rest assured, this time he isn't getting away with it."

* * *

Collis walked down the jetway and followed the signs for members of the European Community. Really, he'd expected more for the information he had to offer from Anthony Bradford, but considering the debacle at Falcon's Lair, Collis considered himself to be lucky to salvage anything. He added the money offered to the sum he expected to receive from the divorce settlement and the sale of the town house, car, and stocks. Not bad, he reasoned. With luck he could parlay it into a fortune using his superior knowledge of the stock market.

Meanwhile, he could continue to do what he liked to do best—give speeches. After Bradford leaked the news to the press, Warren wouldn't be any competition. He would be lucky to be covered on the fifty-seventh page of some third-rate tabloid—if he even had the guts to return to the House of Lords and give a speech. Collis couldn't help smiling. Maybe *he'd* pursue a career in politics.

He was still grinning when he passed the green checkpoint at customs and walked into the reception area. Out of nowhere flashbulbs exploded. Someone shouted his name. More flashbulbs. A horde of reporters, clamoring for his attention, descended on him. Microphones were thrust in his face. For a moment Collis thought they'd confused him with some famous movie star, but couldn't think of anyone whose good looks equalled his.

"Is it true you're selling out your family?" one reporter shouted, jamming a microphone in Collis's face.

"What are you talking about?"

"The Earl of Lyforth," another reporter answered, his minicamera rolling. "You're trying to sell his family secrets."

"Just what are those secrets?" Several reporters badgered him at once, blocking his exit.

"I—I don't know what you're talking about."

"How do you explain Anthony Bradford's allegations?"

For once, Collis was speechless.

23

✳

The muezzin's wail, calling the faithful to midday prayers echoed up and down the dusty alleys that passed for streets in Bardia, Libya. A blind beggar huddled on the steps of the Ministry of Libyan Health building, chanting verses from the Koran. Inside, Janna sat with Morris Wentworth, an expert from Fort Halstead, and Abram Mafhji, the Maltese attaché in Libya, listening to the beggar's singsong chanting coming through the open window. She gazed at the portrait of Muammar Khadafy hanging slightly off kilter on the wall behind the row of desks in the office as she waited for the clerks to finish their prayers.

"What takes five minutes in London, seven in Rome, and ten in Malta will take all day here," Abram informed them, his voice low. "Libya has no rivals when it comes to plodding bureaucrats."

"I'm prepared for a lot of red tape," Morris said as he gave her an encouraging smile.

Janna wasn't; she wanted to scream at the white-robed clerks who'd seemed content to shuffle papers all morning. She had to know if Ian had been among those unidentified bodies buried in Bardia shortly after he'd disappeared during the war.

Two weeks ago authorities in Bardia had finally answered her persistent telephone calls and informed her that four unidentified bodies had been buried during the week following Ian's disappearance. A great deal of baksheesh had been passed around Bardia before officials had been persuaded to exhume the bodies. Warren had willingly given her the money, the use of his jet, and had sent Morris with her. Should any of the bodies appear to be Ian's, Morris could render an opinion on the spot. If there was any question they could fly the body back to England where the experts at Fort Halstead could conduct further tests.

As they had so often in the three weeks since he'd been gone, Janna's thoughts turned to Nick. He had no idea she was in Libya. She'd spoken to him only once since he'd left. When two weeks had passed after the Blue Grotto opening, and she hadn't heard from him, she'd called Nick. He'd sounded so weary from his around-the-clock vigil at Austin's bedside that she decided not to tell him that she planned to go to Libya. She hadn't heard from him since.

Janna had contacted Abram Mafhji, the Maltese attaché, and had him deal with the Libyan officials. Since the British had expelled the Libyan terrorists and closed Khadafy's embassy in London, British subjects weren't welcome in Libya. Like the United States, the British no longer maintained a consulate here, but the Maltese did and Abram had been helpful.

Even worse than being British on Libyan soil, being a woman worked against Janna, and she knew it. A woman traveling alone in a Moslem country was thought to be a prostitute. Hotels wouldn't allow females to register without a husband or an adult male relative. Morris, with his brown eyes and ready smile, didn't look old enough to be her uncle, but he willingly went along with the charade.

Despite Abram's helpfulness, remaining behind the scenes and letting him conduct her business frustrated Janna. Her guilt about lying to Aunt Pith compounded her uneasiness, but Janna hadn't wanted to tell her aunt what she was doing until she knew whether or not one of the bodies was Ian MacShane's.

"Your brother's made quite a name for himself," Morris interrupted her thoughts. "I like the way he called that press conference and told everyone he'd moved his father's body and why."

Janna nodded, again wondering if Morris was flirting with her. He had a way of being a little too friendly, a little too personal. She wished Nick were here with her instead.

"No one blamed him for protecting his mother," Morris added.

"I would have done the same thing," Abram said. "I wouldn't have wanted my mother to know if my father had died at his lover's home."

Janna nodded again, noting Morris had tactfully not mentioned Reginald's lover had been a man. Warren had cleverly gone on the offensive and called a press conference just after Collis returned to England. Few words ignited passion in the hearts of self-contained Englishmen. "Mum" was one of these. The Queen Mum consistently topped popularity polls. And Mothering Sunday meant retail sales that were exceeded only by Christmas. Overnight, Warren became the perfect son. His forthrightness defused the situation and made Collis look like nothing more than a shoddy con man.

"They're back," Morris whispered.

Five men wearing ankle length white tunics, their heads covered by white headpieces resembling long scarves that had been anchored in place by tribal headbands appeared, carrying rolled-up prayer rugs under their arms.

Abram rose and crossed the room. Janna lifted her chin to adjust the knot on the scarf she wore over her head in deference to the Moslem culture. She refused to give them any excuse not to let her see the bodies. Abram had told her the four pine coffins had been unearthed from a pit lined in concrete to protect sacred Moslem soil from the bodies of infidels, then brought here. Somewhere in this very building were those bodies.

Abram returned, a smile on his face. "Minister Akbar will take us to see the coffins now."

Janna jumped to her feet, a surge of anticipation rocketing through her. She muted her high hopes by reminding herself that Nick was probably right. This was a long shot. They might never discover what happened to Ian MacShane.

With Morris and Abram on either side of her, Janna followed Minister Akbar and a servant carrying a crowbar down a long corridor lit only by a bare bulb that couldn't have been more than fifteen watts. The servant opened a door leading to another even darker hallway that eventually turned into yet another passageway. Finally, he opened a door into a room whose only light came from the sunlight filtering through the missing tiles on the roof.

Four wooden coffins caked with sand stood in the center of the room, almost lost among copper buckets of olives pickling in brine. Evidently the ministry wasn't too interested in health and made money on the side in the lucrative olive market. The sense of elation that had heightened with each turn in the labyrinth of corridors evaporated: All four of the coffins were the same size.

"There's no use opening the coffins," she said. "Ian was too tall to be in any of those."

"Coffins are a uniform size here," Abram said as the servant went to work on the first coffin with the crowbar. "The same families have been in the business for generations, constructing them exactly the way they were built in the Middle Ages."

"Min fadlak," Minister Akbar exclaimed as the last nail on the coffin gave way.

"Are you positive you want to see this?" Morris asked.

"Yes." She remembered his earlier warning. The bodies, baking in the desert for fifty years, would be macabre skeletons. She peered into the coffin. The bleached bones of a small skeleton, perhaps those of a child or an adolescent lay in the unlined pine box.

Morris shook his head and the minister moved to the next coffin. Janna's eyes were drawn to the third box. Sand filled knots in the pine; a long crack ran down the length of the lid. Undoubtedly, sand had seeped into the interior.

The second coffin opened more easily than the first. Janna glanced into it and saw a frail skeleton, fragments of disintegrating cotton still clung to its arms.

"No," Morris said. "Look at the pelvic bones. That's a woman."

Janna's gaze returned to the third coffin. Minister Akbar signaled to the servant who pried up one side. The lid split, a dry brittle sound, fracturing along the crack. The servant tossed the broken wood aside. The dim light in the room and the remaining wood covering the top made it difficult to see inside, but she could tell this skeleton was larger than the others.

Akbar rammed the crowbar under the remaining piece of wood and it popped off. Janna stared into the coffin. Bile rose up in her throat and Morris put a hand on her arm.

"They broke his legs to fit him in," Morris said.

Janna dropped to her knees beside the coffin. The skeleton was bleached a pure white. Bones piled upon bones, filled the lower half of the coffin. Sand had leaked in through the crack and had partially filled the rib cage and skull. The head was turned to one side so that his profile faced her.

Janna looked into the coffin, her mind playing a cruel trick on her. For a moment, she didn't see a skeleton. She saw Nick Jensen.

"Male Caucasian," Morris said. "A large man, tall."

She gingerly touched one of the skeleton's sand-covered hands and gently lifted it. Granules of powdery sand slid away from the bones. A ring, jet-black with years of tarnish, gleamed unnaturally dark against the white bone. A Maltese Cross.

She turned his skull to the side and saw a gaping hole, ringed with splinters of bone. Again she imagined Nick, then his face vanished from her mind's eye. Laurel Hogel's replaced it, pointing to the left side of her temple.

"It's Ian," she said, fighting back the hot sting of tears. The blood pounded in Janna's temples, each pulsing beat reminding her of how cruelly—how unnecessarily— Ian had been taken from Aunt Pith. Tears blurred her vision; she barely heard Morris.

"Look closely. That's a bullet lodged in the bone."

"Can you run a ballistics test on it?" Janna could hardly believe the calm voice was hers.

"Certainly, but what good would it do?"

"I know where the gun that killed Ian MacShane is."

Warren lay stretched out on the tester bed that every earl had used, his eyes on Shadoe who was sitting cross-legged beside him twirling her rune stone like a bolo over his groin. He caught her hand, stopping the circular motion, but the stone with its primitive markings still dangled over his crotch. "I don't need any help rising to the occasion."

She turned toward him, her eyes pensive.

"Hey. What's the matter?" he asked, the joking tone vanishing from his voice.

"Maybe we should postpone the wedding."

"Why?" Apprehension deflated the happiness he'd felt just moments earlier. "You're having second thoughts."

She kissed him lightly on the forehead. "Of course not. I'm afraid Nick won't be able to come is all."

"You know I spoke with him yesterday and he said to go ahead without him. Austin's hanging on. It might be . . . who knows?" Warren recalled the despair in Nick's voice. "In any case, I think it will be quite a while after Austin dies before Nick will be in the mood for a wedding."

"Maybe you're right, darling," Shadoe conceded. "Was he terribly upset when you told him the investigators from Fort Halstead couldn't prove Rhonda Sibbet didn't kill herself?"

"He accepted it, but I don't think he believed it." Warren sighed. "I admit I'm suspicious too."

"It's just a little too pat, isn't it?"

"Yes," Warren agreed. "Let's hope the laboratory at Fort Halstead has better luck with that bullet. We should be hearing sometime today. Morris said he would tell the ballistics experts to rush the tests to see if the gun Aunt Pithany loaned Tony was the weapon that killed Ian MacShane. Even if they're positive, I believe it will be impossible to prove Anthony Bradford killed Ian."

"Why?"

"All they'll have is circumstantial evidence. If they prove the gun fired the fatal shot, that doesn't mean Tony fired the gun."

"He had it in his possession during the time Ian was murdered."

"True, but he could have given the gun to someone else, or he could deny ever having had it. It'll be his word against Pithany's."

"I suppose you're right," Shadoe admitted, "but Janna won't accept him getting away with murder."

Warren nodded; he'd never seen his sister as upset as she'd been when she'd flown from Bardia to London with Ian's body. She was determined to avenge Ian's death. En route she'd stopped and picked up Aunt Pithany's gun without telling her.

"It's strange but the oleander investigation has played right into Tony's hand," Shadoe said. "If your family starts accusing him of a fifty-year-old murder, it'll appear to be nothing more than a continuation of a long-standing feud."

"You're right," Warren said, again admiring Shadoe's intuitiveness. "An investigation would make the family look bad." The telephone rang. "Maybe that's Morris, now."

She handed him the receiver. His eyes on Shadoe, Warren listened to Morris Wentworth read the ballistics report, then hung up. "Just what we thought. The bullet came from Pithany's gun."

Shadoe clasped the stone and mumbled a magic rune under her breath, then said, "Poor Janna, now she will have to tell Aunt Pith."

Collis sat in his office at the London School of Economics. He finished the current issue of *Economist* and set it aside, then stared at the telephone. Like everything else in the old building, it was a relic dating back to the Second World War. It hadn't rung in days. Collis didn't expect it to ring again. It was as if he'd never been born. Since the disastrous interview at the airport when he'd been caught off guard and lost the offensive, he'd become a pariah.

Warren, on the other hand, could do no wrong. His dim-witted explanation of his father's death had been accepted by everyone. Even when Lyforth had announced his engagement to Shadoe Hunnicutt—a nut if there ever had been one—the press applauded. Engaging, creative, they'd called her. They'd lauded her newest venture, the Panty of the Month Club, an elixir for ailing marriages.

Two days ago, the Japanese stock scandal had hit the papers. Heads of several top securities companies in Tokyo had resigned in disgrace when it was revealed they'd loaned millions to Japanese gangsters. Suddenly, Lyforth's warnings about letting *yakuza*-backed businesses joint-venture projects in the UK seemed brilliant. "Sage advice" the press called it. Hell, how lucky could Lyforth get?

The telephone on his desk rang. Collis looked at the thing as if it had spit on him. It rang again, the excited double ring British Telecom used.

"Collis Coddington Pembroke here." He tried to keep the excitement out of his voice.

"Chancellor Hilton would like to see you immediately," a nasal voice, clipped with the officiousness peculiar to secretaries of important men, informed him.

Four minutes later, Collis was standing before the same secretary, her carrot-red hair tied back in a neat bun, her expression grim. With a sense of foreboding, he entered the Chancellor's office.

Collis extended his hand, which Chancellor Hilton shook without enthusiasm.

"Well," he said, not asking Collis to have a seat. "It seems you've gotten yourself into a bit of difficulty."

"Yes, sir," Collis admitted. If only he hadn't been so foolish as to sign the document Anthony Bradford had drawn up. Then he could have denied everything. "I hope I haven't caused any embarrassment to—"

"Of course you have. I've removed your name from the speakers roster. This institution can no longer recommend a man like you."

Chancellor Harris continued, ranting about honor and decency, but Collis hardly heard him. Removing his name from the speakers list would make it impossible to continue on the speakers circuit. More than anything, he lived for those moments of glory, those minutes when everyone listened to his financial sermon. This couldn't be happening to him, Collis Coddington Pembroke of the Northumberland Pembrokes.

"Actually, what concerns me even more—the reason I called a meeting of the Board of Governors—is a telephone call I received yesterday."

Collis dropped into the nearest chair, knowing the worst was yet to come.

"You've been named in a paternity suit filed by"—he shuffled some papers on his desk—"by Annabelle Swarthmore."

Collis opened his mouth to deny everything, but shut it quickly. What would be the use? A blood test would confirm the truth: He was the father of Annabelle's baby.

"We can't have our professors seducing students."

"She wasn't a student. She worked in the Brunch Bowl."

"It doesn't matter. We pride ourselves on being gentlemen and scholars. Obviously, you're neither. Your position at this institution has been terminated. Effective immediately."

24

✳

With the blinds drawn the living room was dark despite the bright summer sunshine outside. Nick sat on the Prescotts' sofa, Houston's version of Danish modern, and waited for the real estate agent to arrive. After Austin's funeral, Nick had decided to put the house on the market.

He leaned back and closed his eyes, wondering when he'd again be able to sleep through the night without waking up haunted by the past. *You're alone now,* he told himself. But it was strange; he didn't feel alone. This house contained so many happy memories. It was almost like a person to him—the last Prescott.

He opened his eyes and tried to imagine the home stripped of its middle-class furniture. A fresh coat of paint. Squads of kids chasing through the living room to a brand new swing set in the backyard. The house would have happy times again. He shouldn't have qualms about selling it.

He rose and walked into the bedroom wing. Three small bedrooms opened off the hallway. He and Amanda Jane had shared one when they'd first been married. But he didn't go into that room. It was empty now with nothing left to fill it but memories. Instead he walked into Travis's room. The computer paper banner still hung from the ceiling: *Ride with the tide; go with the flow.*

"I'm sorry I let you down, buddy."

The whir of the air conditioner answered him.

Nick leaned against the doorjamb. "I let everyone down."

Until the moment Austin had breathed his last agonizing breath, Nick had prayed for a break in the case that would deliver the killer who'd really murdered Travis. Nothing. The Bradfords had gotten away with it. The old sense of helplessness returned as powerful as the bone-deep emptiness that had been his companion since Amanda Jane's death five years ago.

There had to be something the experts had missed, Nick told himself, going back into the living room. If not, there had to be some way of getting the Bradfords to admit they'd forced Rhonda to kill herself. There had to be something he could do. Anything.

Nick's eye caught the enormous plant Janna had sent when Austin died. For a moment, he wished she were with him, but guilt washed over him as if the walls themselves had read his mind and sat in judgment on him. Since returning to Houston, living in this house while Austin battled cancer, Janna often slipped into his conscious thoughts. At night he would awaken to find he'd been dreaming about her.

The tug of war between past and present raged within him. As usual the overriding guilt won. He was alive. Amanda Jane gone. Why did he keep tormenting himself, punishing himself? A wonderful woman had fallen in love with him. And he had enjoyed her. Hell, he had more than enjoyed her. Was that a crime? No, the rational part of his brain answered, but somehow depth charges of guilt sabotaged him.

The doorbell rang and Nick answered it, letting a blowtorch of humid air into the house along with a real estate agent sporting Madonna blond hair and neon-orange earrings the size of tennis balls. He paused in the doorway, on the edge of the air-conditioned sanctuary, thinking that by now Malta would be as hot as Houston, though not as humid. He missed the sea breeze, the wind-ruffled water surrounding Falcon's Lair—and Janna.

"Thelma Lou Riley." She handed him a card, batting cheap-looking false eyelashes, turning his thoughts back to the sale. "I'm the best in these parts."

He assumed she meant sales agent although the tone of her voice implied she meant something else. "I'm considering putting the house on the market." He stopped short of asking her what she thought it would bring. It was like selling a pet.

Thelma Lou cranked open the blinds with a hand capped by long pink nails, her eyes sweeping around the room. "Nice plant."

Nick followed her into the small kitchen. She stopped dead center, folded her arms under her breasts and said, "I reckon you've had lots of deferred maintenance with the illness and all. 'Spect you'll want the cabinets painted before we put 'er on the market."

Nick gazed at the chipped cabinets remembering Amanda Jane had painted them herself the first summer he'd met her. He could still see her dressed in tattered sweats, a glob of daffodil-yellow paint in her hair, talking with him while she painted. Smiling. Happy. Alive.

Thelma Lou traipsed off in the direction of the bedrooms, her earrings swaying like pendulums. Nick remained behind in the kitchen. He didn't want to give up this house. He could honestly say it was the only home he'd ever had.

Thelma Lou returned. "Well, Nick, this house has possibilities. I'm not rightly sure how much—"

"I've made a mistake. I can't sell."

She placed a reassuring hand on his arm. "Nick, many

folks have doubts about sellin' 'specially after a loved one passes on to his great reward, but—"

"I've changed my mind. I'm not selling this house."

"Now honey, don't go bein' too upset to make a wise decision. I have a nice young couple—"

"I'm not selling."

"All righty," she said, her smile as false as her eyelashes. "You have my card. When you see fit, give me a jingle, you heah?"

Nick listened to her stiletto heels clicking on the sidewalk and the grinding of her car's gears. For a few minutes he waited, looking out the window at the children across the street running through the sprinklers.

He walked into the kitchen and examined the cabinets, then he went into the garage. It took him a few minutes to rummage through the drawers in the makeshift workshop Austin had set up and find the sandpaper.

Janna slowly climbed the stairs to Falcon Lair's bedroom wing. She'd waited four days since the experts at Fort Halstead had confirmed Aunt Pith's gun had been the one used to murder Ian. Warren had urged her not to delay telling Aunt Pith any longer, but Janna settled as many details as possible first, wanting to spare Aunt Pith. Warren and Shadoe had selected a handmade coffin for Ian. His body was being transported from England to Malta on Warren's jet, which was set to arrive late tomorrow afternoon. Janna had arranged an immediate burial in the Crandall plot.

Everything was set except Aunt Pith didn't realize she would be attending Ian's funeral tomorrow. Janna reached the landing, dreading the task ahead, but knowing no one else could tell Aunt Pith. Audrey and John had taken Taxi to a canine orthodontist in Rome. Janna had insisted Warren remain in London with Shadoe who

couldn't leave Chloe's bedside because she had chicken
pox. Besides, even if the entire family were present,
Janna loved Aunt Pith too much to let anyone else break
the news to her.

"Come in," Aunt Pith called when Janna knocked.

Janna attempted a bright smile and patted her skirt
pocket, reassured to find Ian's ring there. She'd polished
it until it gleamed the way Aunt Pith always kept hers. "I
thought I would join you for tea."

Aunt Pith studied her a moment, obviously startled to
see her home from the Blue Grotto this early. "Something is wrong. Is it Nick?"

"No. I haven't heard from him since the telegram saying Austin Prescott had died." Janna eased onto the sofa
beside Aunt Pith, only too conscious of the newly framed
picture of Ian hanging on the wall. "I want to talk to you
about Ian MacShane."

Aunt Pith turned to the tea service to pour Janna a
cup of tea. "What about him, dear?"

"You know the psychic artist, Laurel Hogel, who
sketched Ian? Well, Dr. Kaye sent me to her." She accepted the cup Aunt Pith handed to her, taking a second
to collect her thoughts. "Gerry had worked with her on
several of his books."

"So you told me." Aunt Pith smiled up at Ian's portrait. "I'm most grateful."

Janna sipped her tea. She was off to a bad start.
"Gerry taught me that there is always a paper trail. Not
much of any importance has happened since the Middle
Ages that hasn't been recorded somewhere even if it's
only in a diary or personal letters. That's how I researched my paper on the actual cost of the French
Revolution—by following the paper trail." Janna
paused, angry with herself for rambling. "I thought Ian
might have left a paper trail and perhaps a photograph
accompanied that trail."

"But you found nothing," Aunt Pith said patiently. They'd discussed this once before. Aunt Pith had been relieved that Janna had discovered nothing more than the transcripts of Ian's radio broadcasts. The investigator Pithany had used just after the war to check on Ian's family had discovered nothing except those same transcripts. Aunt Pith would have been upset if her investigator had missed something.

"I didn't find anything," Janna hedged. For a speech rehearsed so many times, the words failed to come easily. "But Gerry uncovered something while researching one of his books."

"Oh?" Aunt Pith arched one eyebrow. "What was that?"

"Ian . . ." Janna put her cup down and took Aunt Pith's hand in both hers. "Ian . . . Ian wasn't aboard the *Nelson*."

For a moment Aunt Pith gazed blankly at Janna as if she hadn't heard her and Janna would have to repeat herself. "But—but he sent the message."

"Something must have happened. He never made it to the ship."

"Your friend must be mistaken. I'm—" Aunt Pith's voice lost some of its forcefulness. "What makes Dr. Kaye say this?"

"He interviewed several soldiers who made it from Tobruk to Bardia. Ian was with them."

"But . . . he never sent word." Her voice cracked.

"Apparently, there wasn't time." The pain deep in Janna's chest made it difficult to say the next words. She squeezed Aunt Pith's hand. "He died in Bardia."

Aunt Pith stared at the portrait of Ian. Finally she asked, "If there were documents about his death why didn't my investigator find them? I asked him to bring me everything he could about Ian."

"There weren't any documents on his death. Gerry

uncovered his presence in Bardia while conducting interviews for a book on some of the unsung heroes of the war."

"Heroes? Heroes?" Aunt Pith gazed up at Ian, her expression sad, her voice sadder still. "He had so much promise, yet people forgot him. To many, like your Professor Kaye, he's become nothing more than a footnote in a history book. To me, he'll always be a hero. The only man I ever loved."

Aunt Pith rose, slowly levering herself to her feet. The news had tired her, weakened her, Janna thought, watching her walk to the window overlooking the garden —and the swing that looked out to the sea. "What happened to him, Janna? How did he die?"

She went over to where her aunt stood and put her arm around her waist, wishing she could make up some story. "He was shot." She clutched Aunt Pith tighter. "Murdered."

"Murdered? Who would do such a thing?"

A tense silence enveloped the room. Janna forced herself to whisper, "Tony Bradford."

Aunt Pith recoiled as if she had been shot.

"It's true. Tony was in Bardia shortly after Tobruk fell," she reminded Aunt Pith, hoping to cushion the coming blow. "He brought you flowers when he returned and gave you back your gun."

Aunt Pith nodded soberly, recovering slowly from the shock, her already pale face now totally drained of color. She hadn't reacted to the mention of her gun, so Janna let it slide for the moment.

Janna drew the ring out of her pocket and handed it to Aunt Pith. "I located Ian's body in Bardia. When we opened the coffin, this ring was on his finger."

"Ian's ring," she whispered, gazing down at it, her eyes wide and brimming with tears. Aunt Pith turned to face Ian's portrait. "Murdered?"

"I know Tony did it," Janna insisted. "The ballistics experts at Fort Halstead proved the bullet taken from Ian's skull came"—Aunt Pith looked at her and Janna's throat constricted—"from your gun."

Aunt Pith gasped. "My gun? The one Ian gave me?"

Janna ushered Aunt Pith back to the sofa. She sagged back into the cushions, staring at Ian's portrait. "Dear God, not that gun."

"My theory is Tony discovered Ian's investigation of the black market and the selling of religious relics like Cleopatra's Chalice. Tony killed Ian to keep him from telling what he knew."

"But Ian told me he planned to report Tony to the authorities in Alexandria," Aunt Pith said, her voice distracted, her eyes on Ian's portrait. "He was there with the high command for months. He would have had plenty of opportunity."

"For some reason, he didn't. Gerry says there isn't any mention of a black market ring in Malta in the official papers."

Aunt Pith closed her eyes. Janna looked at the person who'd comforted her for so many years. Tears rolled in a silent stream down Aunt Pith's cheeks. There was nothing Janna could say to make up for Aunt Pith's loss—a lifetime of happiness—but Janna planned to make Tony Bradford pay.

"I know we don't have enough evidence to bring a murder charge against Tony. Perhaps if we went to the authorities we could make enough of a case so that someone who knew about the black market operation would come forward. If we could prove Tony sold religious treasures like Cleopatra's Chalice—"

"No." Pithany sat up, her tears still flowing, her voice choked. "Don't do it." She wiped her tears with a lace handkerchief she'd taken out of her pocket. "Please. Leave it be."

"I can't let him get away with it."

"No!" Aunt Pith beseeched her, "Promise me you'll leave Tony alone."

"Don't you want justice for Ian?"

"Of course, I"—her voice faltered—"I knew Tony was ruthless. Over the years I've experienced my share of his vindictiveness, but I never thought him capable of murder. Now that I know he's a killer, I . . ."

Aunt Pith bowed her head and studied her clasped hands for a minute before raising her eyes to meet Janna's. "I'm asking you to do this one thing for me. Forget you know Tony killed Ian. It's behind us. Let it go."

"But he's killed again. Travis, and now this Sibbet woman."

"Not even the experts from Fort Halstead could prove that her death wasn't a suicide."

"I know," Janna conceded, "but—"

"Please. Do it for me. Close the door on the past."

"All right," Janna conceded. She understood Aunt Pith's feelings. She'd suffered an emotional shock. In time, she would recover and want to avenge Ian's murder. Meanwhile Janna would proceed on her own.

Soft purple shadows of late afternoon cloaked the east-facing cemetery in Valletta, but the sky was a brilliant blue and the air as hot as it had been at midday. Earlier, Pithany and Janna had met the jet at Luqa Field and stood beside the plane while the mahogany coffin was loaded into the hearse. The new casket was long and sleek and gleamed in the sunlight.

Pithany was still in shock that Tony had killed Ian. She'd always known Tony was unscrupulous, determined to be rich, but she'd never felt physically threatened by him. During the course of the half-century she'd known him, Tony had schemed repeatedly to take over her business. Even so, she'd never imagined him to be the type of man who would resort to murder.

When Travis had died, Pithany didn't suspect Tony. A cowardly method like poison that might kill an innocent person wasn't Tony's style. He was brash, outspoken. Brave. She hated to admit it, but he'd had the courage to fly mission after mission, defending Malta against superior Luftwaffe forces, even volunteering to fly to North Africa in those frantic days after Tobruk fell to Rommel.

Still, Janna must be right. The gun Ian had given Pithany had killed him. Tony must have killed Ian to keep him from exposing his black marketing of art treasures. She couldn't think of any other reason why he would have murdered Ian.

But Pithany knew what she had to do now. If Tony killed Ian, he must have killed Travis and tried to kill Nick. At all costs, Pithany would protect Janna and Nick.

"There's Canon Amestoy," Janna said as they entered the cemetery. "He'll conduct a brief grave-side service."

She shouldn't be surprised, Pithany told herself. Janna's middle name should have been efficiency. She'd thought of everything, including the flowers surrounding the freshly dug grave.

"Here's my father," Pithany said, pausing in front of her father's tomb. "He never liked Ian, you know," she said, her voice low. She had to keep talking or she would break down.

Janna responded with an even tighter grip around Pithany's waist as she guided her up to where Canon Amestoy waited. Pithany smiled weakly at him as he held his prayer book open. The Protestants in Malta were outnumbered hundreds to one, and the elderly clergyman was eager for every opportunity to serve, officiating with zeal and a certain repetitiousness Pithany found annoying.

"Dearly beloved, we are gathered here," he began, but Pithany stopped listening.

She didn't glance around. Other than herself, Pithany knew the "beloved" consisted of the two men from Farquar's Funeral Home who served as pallbearers and Janna. Once, over fifty years ago now, her dreams about Ian's funeral might have been very different. She would have seen the "beloved" as an extended clan of children and grandchildren. Instead, there were only Janna and herself to mourn him.

You would be proud of her, Pithany mentally talked to Ian as his casket was lowered into the ground. *Had we had a daughter, she would have been exactly like Janna. You're here with me, now, where you belong because she cared enough not to let your memory die.*

"Even though I walk through the valley of the shadow of death"—the priest's voice rose, threatening to wake the dead—"I shall fear no evil." Pithany sighed, her thoughts again wandering, thinking Ian had feared no evil, yet he'd been murdered.

"And I shall dwell in the house of the Lord forever." Canon Amestoy's concluding tremolo made Pithany's head throb. "Amen."

Janna stepped forward and tossed a nosegay of delicate pink roses and Queen Anne's lace onto the coffin. Pithany gazed down into the deep grave, the late afternoon shadows and the walls of earth threw a veil of darkness over the casket. Pithany crumbled the dried flowers she held in her hand and watched as the petals floated downward, slowly downward.

To the onlookers, a wealthy woman like Pithany sprinkling dried flowers over a coffin might have seemed odd. Pithany didn't care. She knew Janna understood. Once Ian had told Pithany there wasn't a prettier sight in all the world than Malta's wildflowers. When Pithany had learned the funeral was to be this afternoon, she'd climbed the hill behind Falcon's Lair and picked a few of the wildflowers that had dried on their stems, victims of the cool fall weather.

Earth from the attendants' shovels rained down on the coffin. In moments, the nosegay disappeared and with it the wildflower petals. Janna drew Pithany back from the edge of the grave. Canon Amestoy offered his condolences. Pithany remained silent, letting Janna speak for her, not quite hearing what either of them said. He walked away, his prayer book tucked under his arm, his purposeful stride reflecting duty done.

Janna kissed Pithany's cheek. "I thought it was a beautiful ceremony, didn't you?"

Pithany gazed into Janna's eyes and saw that she'd been crying. "Lovely. You know, of all the things anyone has ever done for me, you've done the most. First, the portrait and now, bringing dear Ian home to me." Pithany saw the grave had been filled, the flowers arranged alongside of it. "Do you mind if I spend a moment alone with Ian?"

Tears filled Janna's eyes. "I'll wait in the car."

Pithany returned to the grave. The Crandall plot, high on the hill, overlooked Valletta's medieval buildings where shadows were just now tiptoeing across the roofs. Below, Grand Harbor sparkled like a blue mirror, its surface dotted by multi-colored *luzzis,* their wakes leaving billowing trails on the glassy water as the fishermen brought in their daily catches.

"Welcome home, darling," she said to the mound of fresh earth, still striving to accept Ian's return. "It's so beautiful here. You always liked the view of Grand Harbor. There's a breeze up here; it's never too hot."

She glanced around, her next words coming with difficulty. "There's a place for me. Where I've always belonged, right by your side." Not since the war when the threat of Nazi invasion loomed over Malta had Pithany considered dying. Now, it didn't seem so frightening. Not at all.

"I'm sorry, darling, for all you've missed. Birthdays, Christmas celebrations, weddings—Janna was the most beautiful bride." She dabbed at her eyes with a sodden handkerchief, not realizing until that moment she'd started to cry. "Janna made this possible. I told her what you'd written in your note: 'If anything happens to me, Ace, look for me in the shadows, in the darkness. We met without a light to guide us. And out of the dark came the greatest gift of all—love. A love for all time.' Janna was determined to bring you out of those shadows and home to me where you belong.

"I live nearby in Falcon's Lair. I took that name from our special code word. The falcon's lore; the falcon knows. You knew what so many have had to learn— nothing is more precious than those we love."

She bent down and touched the soft moist earth. "I hope you'll understand why I'm not avenging your death and seeking to destroy Tony Bradford. Call me a silly old fool, tell me I just don't want to risk Janna's life, say anything you will, but I believe Nick Jensen will take care of Tony. Don't ask me how or when, but in my heart I'm convinced he'll do it.

"He's so much like you it frightens me sometimes. He has your sense of justice, not to mention the face I've always loved." She turned to look at the car waiting beyond the cemetery gates. "Janna's too much like I was at her age. If I don't hold her back, she'll barge in and Tony will kill her. I can't risk that. I honestly, can't. I love her too much. You understand, don't you?"

She walked to the head of the grave where a careless attendant had placed a wreath in front of the tombstone. She moved it aside, admiring the Carrara marble and blessing Janna for somehow managing to have it inscribed on short notice. For the first time, Pithany read the inscription.

IAN MACSHANE
FOREVER IN MY HEART
A LOVE FOR ALL TIME

part four

✳

TWICE
BLESSED

25

✳

Tony stared out his window down at South Street where groups of men walked carrying small bird cages, taking their pets as usual for an early morning stroll. The stupid idiots pretended the birds needed exercise, but it was just an excuse to parade through Valletta to a sidewalk cafe and have coffee with their buddies before going to their jobs. Excuses, hell. He knew he was about to hear another one. "Nothing to report?"

"No, sir. Curt seems to have disappeared. We haven't found a trace of him," the private investigator replied.

"That's crap. He has to be somewhere."

"We're still checking. Something will turn up."

"It had better be soon." Tony spun around to face Robert Tarkington, whose receding hairline showed more than a trace of sweat. "What about MacShane?"

"Well, er, that is, Pithany Crandall had him buried."

"I know that, goddammit. I can read the papers." It pissed off Tony to read the war hero had come home. Hero, hell. He'd been a reporter. A world-class snoop. A troublemaker. Nothing more. "How the hell did she find him?"

"She didn't, sir. Janna Atherton-Pembroke located his body by checking records in Bardia. Apparently, a friend of hers . . ."

Tony stopped listening. Sonofabitch. That kid, Janna was as smart as Pithany. But there was no way they could even suspect what had really happened to MacShane. Bardia had been full of Nazi spies, deserters, and retreating Brits shell-shocked from Tobruk. It had been total chaos.

Anyone could have killed MacShane.

Blind luck, Tony thought. Running into MacShane in Bardia had been nothing more than coincidence, but it had been an opportunity Tony couldn't pass up. He'd had Pithany's gun to use if the men he worked with in the black market became too greedy. No one could prove he'd used it on MacShane.

Unless some smart ass like Janna had thought to check Pithany's gun—did she still have it?—against the bullet in MacShane's brain. They couldn't prove a thing. He could have lent the gun to anyone, gotten it back, and returned it to Pithany. But an investigation could create one hell of a stink just when he'd spent a fortune on a public relations firm to reestablish his image.

Still, if they had anything they would have mentioned it in the two weeks since MacShane had been buried, Tony assured himself. "What about Jensen?"

"His transfer has come through. He's been assigned to the marketing division of Imperial Cola headquarters in Atlanta. He's set to begin there in two weeks."

"What's he been doing in Texas all this time?" The last report on Jensen had indicated Travis Prescott's father had died, but that had been almost a month ago.

"Not much. He painted the Prescott house inside and out."

"The guy's a real no talent."

"Yes, sir." Tarkington chuckled nervously. "He moved his mother from some town called Muleshoe. It's so small one horse would cause major gridlock. His mother is living in the Prescott house now."

Tony digested the information and reminded himself not to underrate Jensen. He'd had the balls to call up and pretend to be MacShane. Jensen must suspect Tony had been responsible for MacShane's death. Tony told himself not to worry. Only two people knew what had happened in that alley in Bardia. Tony said to himself, "Dead men tell no tales."

Jensen, though, was alive, a dead ringer for Mac-Shane. The whole time the Texan had lived in Malta, Tony had been uneasy. There wasn't any explanation for why Jensen was the image of the reporter. That's why Tony would breathe easier knowing an ocean separated him from Nick Jensen.

Janna looked over the responses from her query letters. Nothing. None of the major museums, public or private, had Cleopatra's Chalice. A paper trail, she reminded herself, gazing around her office in the Blue Grotto. Even during a war, art required proper export permits and licenses. Tony had smuggled missing treasures like Cleopatra's Chalice out of Malta, but when they entered another country, there would have to be some sort of documentation.

Any museum adding the chalice to their collection even years later would check the documentation. Certificates of origin and authenticity were mandatory. Many countries had reclaimed their national treasures after losing them to art thieves by proving the necessary documents had been forged. Malta had attempted to located its stolen treasures after the war, but nothing came of the effort except to recover a few minor pieces. The chalice remained on the list of stolen treasures circulated among museums.

Perhaps it had been in a private collector's hands all these years. If so, she hoped the recent acceleration in the art market had flushed out the chalice. It might have sold recently, creating a paper trail.

The telephone on her desk rang, interrupting her

thoughts, and she answered it, telling herself it wasn't Nick.

"How are things going?" Warren's voice had a smile to it.

"Fine," she said, refusing to put a damper on his happiness just because she felt incredibly frustrated at not being able to locate the chalice. She was even more upset at not hearing from Nick.

"Did you find a dress for the wedding?"

"Not yet," she replied, thankful his question hadn't been the usual one: Have you heard from Nick?

"Any word on Cleopatra's Chalice?"

"No. None of the major museums have it. I'm sending out a second round of queries to smaller museums."

"You know my theory. I believe Tony sold it to a private party. If that's the case, we may never locate it."

She muttered her agreement. The religious significance of the piece, being St. Paul's gift to the Maltese who'd rescued him, gave it a deep value that placed it a cut above other art. Someone might have kept it for religious reasons.

"I've sent letters to Christie's and Sotheby's as well as the other auction houses, asking them if they auctioned any piece fitting the chalice's description in the last fifty years," Janna added.

Warren asked a few more questions, but she could tell he wasn't as obsessed with finding the chalice as she was. Still, she was grateful for his help, and for agreeing to keep her search secret. Janna hated deceiving Aunt Pith, but she had no intention of letting Anthony Bradford get away with murdering Ian MacShane. Adding Travis Prescott and Rhonda Sibbet to the list only fueled her determination even more. He wasn't getting away with murder.

Warren had persuaded her not to pursue Tony on the murder charge. It would boil down to Pithany's word against Tony's. Pithany refused to be involved; she had been satisfied with bringing Ian's body home. But Janna wanted revenge. If he couldn't be convicted for murder, then she would send Tony to jail by proving he'd stolen Malta's most treasured possession.

She'd just said good-bye to Warren when the intercom on her desk buzzed. "Mr. Jensen is here to see you."

"Send him in." She scrambled to her feet, smoothing her mussed hair, trying to remember if she'd put on any makeup that morning. Why hadn't Nick given her a little notice?

He strode through the door; her heart did a quick stutter-step. He was more handsome than she'd remembered, but that wasn't what caused her heart to stall. She realized she loved him more than she had thought. Not the girlish infatuation that had characterized her feelings for Collis, but a deep abiding love.

The timeless love Pithany had felt for Ian.

"Darling, it's great to have you back." She threw her arms around him and was hugging him before she realized she had a stranger in her arms.

Nick had to steel himself to keep from kissing her. It had been years since any woman had been so genuinely glad to see him. He struggled to conceal his feelings. Stepping out of her arms, he asked, "How've you been?"

For a moment she appeared hurt by his cold response, but recovered. "I'm sorry you lost Austin. It must have been terrible for you."

He nodded, his eyes on her, wishing he could think of an easy way out of this. "How are things going around here?"

She nervously launched into a rapid-fire explanation of locating Ian's body. "The ballistics tests proved he'd been shot with the gun he'd given Aunt Pith."

"The left temple, the way Laurel Hogel said?"

"Exactly," she answered, rushing over to her desk. "It's eerie, isn't it?"

Eerie? Christ! It raised the hair across the back of his neck. He'd assumed the woman made up the gun bit to enhance her talent for sketching people she'd never met. Knowing he resembled Ian made Nick wary because he had no explanation for it.

"Here's the report from Fort Halstead." Janna pointed to a file folder just as the telephone rang. "Excuse me."

She answered the call and Nick read the single page report. MacShane had been six-three. Nick's height exactly. He'd weighed approximately one hundred and seventy pounds when he'd died. Nick was a few pounds heavier, but of course he wasn't surviving on army rations. That comparison had barely crossed his mind before his eyes locked on the next sentence.

Fractured kneecap during adolescent years. Nick stopped reading. Jesus! He'd almost wrecked his own knee playing football. He would be limping today if his mother hadn't swallowed her pride and called his father for money to have a special operation. But his father never called to see how Nick was doing.

There has to be an explanation, Nick reasoned, his mind scrambling to sort out the facts. How could he be so much like Ian? He'd gotten his black hair and blue eyes from his mother, no mistake. His body was courtesy of his absentee father. The dimple? He couldn't think of anyone in the family with dimples unless one of the witches on his father's side had a satanic dimple.

Nick couldn't think of a plausible explanation. None. The whole situation gave him the willies. No matter how much he'd wanted to come back to Malta, he felt the urge to leave now. *Get out while you can.*

"Is something the matter?" Janna asked, and Nick realized she'd hung up the telephone, and he was staring at her.

"No," he lied, hoping to ignore the similarities between himself and MacShane without having Janna discuss them.

"Tony killed Ian," Janna said.

"Tough to prove after all this time," he answered, taking on an indifferent tone he definitely didn't feel.

"He killed Travis too," Janna insisted. "And tried to kill you."

"Hold it. The police proved Rhonda killed herself, and she confessed to everything. There's no reason to think the Bradfords are responsible."

Janna regarded him with stunned surprise. "You believe that story?"

"The evidence supports it."

"Travis was your best friend. Don't you care about the truth?"

"Of course, I care," Nick assured her. "But I have no reason not to accept the police version of Travis's death. Experts from Fort Halstead discovered no evidence not to rule Rhonda's death a suicide. Do you think they could have missed something?"

"No, but I think someone may have been standing there with a gun on Rhonda forcing her to kill herself."

"Be reasonable," Nick said patiently. "The authorities interviewed the servants. No one else was seen at the villa that night."

"I've been told Tony has connections in Sicily. Perhaps the Mafia—"

"Come on, Janna. That's straight out of a B movie. Life's too short to spend it on a wild-goose chase," he said, then changed the subject. "What I care more about is how Pithany took the news that Ian had been murdered."

Janna's clenched hands hung at her sides. She appeared ready to continue arguing, but she finally said, "She was shocked at first. Now she's thrilled he's here. She visits his grave several times a week."

"Hmm," Nick muttered. "I dropped by Falcon's Lair. I see you're living in the guest house."

She turned the brightest shade of crimson he'd ever seen. "I hope you don't mind."

"Nope," he said, as casually as he could manage. "I just dropped by to pick up my things."

"You're leaving," she said, her enormous green eyes imploring him to stay.

"I've been promoted to the corporate office. Marketing."

She didn't even attempt to disguise her unhappiness. "I see. It's what you've always wanted."

"Yeah." He felt like a heel, but forced himself to smile that good-ole-boy grin that usually got him out of jams. "I've made arrangements to transfer my stock in the Blue Grotto to you."

Her lips crimped into a tight line. "How much money do you want?"

"Nothing. I promised Pithany that I would return the stock when I left Malta."

"For what Travis had paid for it. Wasn't that the arrangement?" she asked, employing a sarcastic tone to disguise her hurt.

"Forget the money." He studied the ceiling, wondering if he had a rat's chance of getting away without crushing her feelings. "I want you to have the stock."

"Why?" Her voice held a challenging note he'd not heard before now.

"I had a wonderful time here. You . . . your family helped me through a difficult time."

"Nick," she said, her voice a shade shy of a whisper, "I love you. Give me a chance. Let's discuss this."

He'd intended to let her down as easily as he knew

how and counted on her allowing him to make a gracious exit. But no. In the few short weeks they'd been separated, her self-confidence had improved. He wasn't getting out of here without hurting her. "There's nothing to discuss."

"Doesn't my love mean anything to you?"

The stricken expression on her face told him how much his leaving was hurting her. "You think you love me but—"

"I do love you. I really do."

"You think you do—"

"The same way you *think* you still love Amanda Jane?"

"Think"—he raised his voice for the first time—"think? I know I still love her. I'll always love her." As soon as the words were out of his mouth he wanted to retract them. It wasn't that they weren't true; they were. But the mortified look on Janna's face told him that he should have softened his words, as he'd intended, with a few white lies.

"I'm not trying to take her place, Nick." Her clear green eyes looked directly into his. "I know no one will ever take her place. But you've grieved for her for over five years. That's long enough." When he didn't respond, she added, "Do you plan to spend the rest of your life alone?"

He hadn't gotten any further in planning for the rest of his life than the task ahead. Things had snowballed. He didn't want to discuss this, not now. The only way out was to go on the offensive. "Did you tell Collis you loved him?"

She grabbed his arm. "Yes, but it wasn't the same, not at all."

He took a quick step back. She left him no alternative but to get the hell out. "Is your divorce final?"

"It will be in two weeks."

He yanked the door open. "We'll talk when it is."

The champagne cork sailed through the fall air, arcing high over the terrace and landing in Lyforth Hall's garden. Glasses extended, Janna and Pithany waited to toast the newlyweds. Audrey and Ellis, who'd been married several weeks earlier at Falcon's Lair, stood off to one side beaming at Warren and Shadoe.

"Chloe's always wanted a father," Shadoe said, her bright eyes on Warren's.

"She has one now," Warren said, then turned to the small group. "I'm adopting her."

"That's wonderful," Audrey said first, and everyone agreed.

Things had worked out perfectly for Warren, Janna thought, justifiably proud of her brother. He'd weathered the crisis with his image—and his personal happiness—intact. The media chased him more than ever; his opinion was sought by the most powerful men. None of this had gone to Warren's head. He remained concerned for England's future; he took his seat in the House of Lords seriously, rarely missing a vote.

"Here's to Shadoe and Warren," Aunt Pith said when the glasses had been filled. "Love everlasting."

The melodic tinkle of crystal rims being touched followed. Then Warren drew Shadoe into his arms and gave her a kiss that would have scorched the screen had one of the television crews that followed him around been present. Janna briefly closed her eyes, fighting the thought of herself in Nick's arms. Her divorce had been final for weeks, but she hadn't heard from Nick. She hadn't expected to; the scene in her office had replayed countless times in her mind.

He didn't love her. To give him credit, he'd never said that he did. She'd been the one to say—over and over—

how much she loved him. In the end, it hadn't mattered. Nothing mattered except his job. And Amanda Jane.

"You're next," Aunt Pith whispered, and Janna smiled indulgently. Nick had been courteous enough to visit Aunt Pith when he'd been in Malta. He'd given her no hope that he would return. "You and Nick belong together."

Janna longed to believe that was true, but reality told a very different tale. Her course had been charted, without Nick, placing her at the helm of Aunt Pith's hotel chain. The Blue Grotto had been so successful that Janna was being badgered to open similar hotels on Costa Esmerelda and Menorca.

The butler wheeled the wedding cake, Shadoe's favorite, Death by Chocolate Torte, out onto the terrace. Warren winked at Janna and came over to stand beside her.

"I tried to reach Nick in Atlanta," he said, "several times, but he never returned my calls."

Janna wanted to scream at everyone: Stop talking about Nick. But it wasn't their fault her wound was still too fresh for her to casually discuss him. "I guess his new job has him quite busy."

"Speaking of new jobs, I understand Collis is teaching at Durham University. Quite a comedown, isn't it?"

Janna didn't share her brother's elitist attitude. Oxford and Cambridge weren't the only institutions of higher education that counted. "He was married two days ago."

"Go on," Warren laughed, his eyes on Shadoe.

"I'm serious. Annabelle Swarthmore is now Mrs. Collis Coddington Pembroke."

"Of the Northumberland Pembrokes," Warren said. "How do you know all this? I haven't read anything."

"I bought his share of our place in Minera Mews. The

market has been bad and Collis needed the money to get married and relocate."

Warren studied her. "Did his remarriage upset you?"

"No." Not hearing from Nick hurt far more.

Shadoe motioned for Warren to come and help her cut the cake. Janna watched, thankful her brother had found happiness. Audrey brought Janna a fresh glass of champagne.

"Taxi's almost ready for the dog show in Athens."

Janna sipped the champagne, grateful to Audrey for taking her mind off her troubles. The canine orthodontist Janna had suggested had cured Taxi's overbite. Hours of professional training had readied the Maltie for the ring. Janna missed Taxi, perhaps because he reminded her so much of Nick, but she knew he was better off with Audrey. She doted on him, rarely letting him out of her sight—he was upstairs now for a little "tucky time"—for fear he'd get hurt.

"I want to thank you"—Audrey's voice became grave —"for bringing Ian home. All these years Pith has looked after me, after this whole family. We've never been able to do anything to help her. What you did was special . . . so special." Audrey gave Janna a kiss on the cheek.

Janna hugged Audrey, a long hard hug. Audrey had rarely shown anyone any affection even in private, but since Reginald had died she'd gradually lost those inhibitions.

"Let's go check on Chloe," Audrey said. "I'm certain Taxi is ready to get up now too."

They took the shortcut, the backstairs usually reserved for the servants, to the bedroom wing. They entered the newly redecorated nursery and found Nanny Forsythe changing the baby into a white dress edged in lace.

"I bought that for Chloe in Paris," Audrey said proudly. "I love having a granddaughter." She reached out and took the baby from the nanny. "I'm counting on you having lots of brothers and sisters."

Chloe gurgled and Audrey laughed. "Did you hear that, Janna? Chloe said, 'Gram.' Audrey cooed, then added, "Say Auntie Janna."

Auntie Janna? Audrey's words flashed through Janna's mind. How had Aunt Pith done it? she wondered, looking ahead to years of running the business but sitting on life's sidelines as far as her own happiness was concerned. Janna had thought she'd come to terms with her situation, but now watching Chloe in Audrey's arms, she experienced an ache of longing to hold her own baby. Nick's baby.

Janna backed out of the room, telling herself she had plenty of time to adjust to living a life of being "auntie" the way Aunt Pith had been. But right now it hurt too much to look at Chloe and realize she wasn't going to have Nick's children. "I'll go get Taxi."

In the hall she met Shadoe. "Don't worry about Chloe. Her grandmother has her and is putting in her order for brothers and sisters."

"Just what Chloe wants," Shadoe said. "Lots of brothers and sisters. No more sperm banks for me."

Janna didn't have the heart to spend any more time thinking about big, happy families. "I'm getting Taxi."

"I'll come with you. Chloe would rather be with her grandmother."

They went to Audrey's suite and found Taxi patiently waiting just inside the door. Janna scooped him up and kissed his silky topknot.

"Nick will be back," Shadoe said suddenly.

Janna vowed to strangle the next person who mentioned Nick Jensen, but it was impossible to be angry with Shadoe. Even now, with a solemn look on her face, she radiated happiness. Shadoe hadn't known a happy family; she'd been lonely until recently. Now, Janna knew how Shadoe had felt.

"I'm not counting on Nick returning," Janna said, hearing more bitterness in her voice than she'd intended.

"But he will be back—to stay. He may not remember Varenne, but deep inside, he knows he belongs with you."

"As I said: I'm not counting on it. What I am counting on," she continued, determined to change the subject, "is seeing Tony Bradford in jail. He may think he's gotten off scot-free, but he hasn't."

"Have you located Cleopatra's Chalice?"

"No," Janna admitted. "But I had an idea. The word 'chalice' implies that it's a cup, right?" Shadoe nodded, so Janna continued, "but it isn't. It's described as a crescent-shaped drinking bowl. It was called Cleopatra's Chalice because it's so beautiful and in that era Cleopatra set the standard for beauty."

"Isn't there a picture of it?" Shadoe asked.

"No. They were all destroyed in the war. But one of the parish priests was an altar boy who used to polish the chalice twice a week. He's done a pen and ink drawing of it for me. I've sent that drawing around to several museums. I'm hoping someone recognizes it."

"Why don't you and Nick work together?"

"Nick accepts the official version of his friend's death. He's too involved in his career to help me."

Shadoe shook her head, sending tumbles of red hair across her shoulders. "He's afraid to expose you to danger."

"No," Janna said, thinking Shadoe was impossibly romantic.

"I believe Nick's right," Shadoe continued, an edge to her words. "I want you to be careful. Never forget Tony Bradford is a cold-blooded killer."

26

✠

Tony tossed back his brandy in one gulp and eyed the private investigator opposite him. In the dim light of the study in Mdina, the tall well-dressed Frenchman didn't appear to be the best detective on the continent. He seemed more suited to the snobby confines of the Jockey Club where French aristocrats spent evenings sipping Le Paradis and comparing prices of stock traded on the *Bourse*. Yet, Gespard's reputation—and his outrageous fee—claimed he was the detective's detective.

"Your son should be easy enough to find."

"I've heard that before. No money. No passport. So how far could he go? He isn't on the Costa del Sol."

Gespard smiled, a smug smile that infuriated Tony. If finding Curt was so easy, the two previous detectives would have already pounced on the bonus Tony offered.

"Curt has been missing almost four months now," Tony restated the most worrisome fact. "All he knows is boats and cars. He's probably found a job—"

"That's the first place you'd look and your son knows it. He doesn't want you to find him, so he's gone to ground. I won't waste your time and money rechecking those leads." He rose and left saying, "I'll keep you posted."

Tony grunted, silently admitting this man was smarter than the others. He hadn't had much use for the frogs since the war when the French had danced with the Nazis in Algeria while the Allies suffered. But he was willing to update his opinion should Gespard find Curt.

Pouring yet another cognac from the bar in the sarcophagus, Tony cursed himself for not anticipating Curt's emotional tailspin over Rhonda's death. He'd been sleeping with the brainless broad for years; she hadn't been just a casual lay. Evidently, Curt had really loved her. Tony knew that feeling. Too well. The kid could come home—forgiven for his stupidity—and choose one of the two brainy women Tony had selected for him.

Then Tony could go to his grave knowing a competent heir to his empire bore his name. He took another swig of cognac and mulled over the situation. He needed more than one heir. The Princess of Wales had given Queen Elizabeth two grandsons. "The heir and the spare," the British tabloids called Diana's boys.

"That's what I want. That's what I need," Tony said to his glass as if it were a wishing well. "Two grandsons. I'll live long enough to train one of them to take over for me."

He felt mellow, the cognac at work, as he assured himself the game with Pithany wasn't over yet. He could still win. Her heir, Janna, had no heirs and certainly no spares. She wasn't even dating. Tony chuckled. He'd heard Nick Jensen had breezed into town and left the same day. For a while there, Tony had thought Nick and Janna might have fallen in love. A ghostly reminder of Ian and Pithany.

He remembered Jensen's call. The guy had the balls to imitate MacShane's voice. That one call had shaken Tony, not because Jensen had sounded enough like Ian to pass for a ghost, but because Tony let his imagination get the best of him. For a crazy moment he'd thought he'd seen the future: Jensen putting a bullet through Tony's brain, exacting revenge for Ian MacShane.

He'd even seen himself, standing in this very room in front of the mirror that had once been the door to some damn pharaoh's tomb, with a gun to his head. Just as he'd shot MacShane.

Of course, that had merely been a confused thought, a result of being awakened so suddenly. Jensen hadn't had the guts to call again. He'd returned to Atlanta to sell the world just what it needed—more Imperial Cola.

Swilling the last of his cognac, Tony returned to his desk, determined to clear away some paperwork. For weeks now he'd been too preoccupied with finding Curt to attend to his personal business. It had been all he could do to keep up with things at the office. He sorted through a stack of invitations and made a note for his secretary to check his schedule and accept as many as possible. His public relations firm had advised him to rebuild his image by attending many social functions. And donating his hard-earned money to worthy causes.

Curt had almost ruined him, but clever footwork had saved the Bradford name. Tony's reputation as a civic leader and successful businessman meant everything to him. He intended for his grandsons to tell their children how a brave RAF pilot had founded the family dynasty.

"I'm a hero," Tony assured himself, fondly recalling his daring missions. "MacShane was just another reporter. A nothing, like Jensen."

Tony shoved the invitations aside and found Westbury, Nimrod, and Houser's final report still sealed in a plain manila envelope. It probably contained a report on one of the business associates he no longer cared about. The postmark indicated it had arrived just after he'd fired the private investigators he'd used for years to keep an eye on Pithany and whoever else he found troublesome.

Once he would have immediately hired another detective to keep an eye on his business associates and

Pithany, but since Curt had disappeared nothing except finding his son seemed important.

He almost pitched the report into the wastepaper basket, but he changed his mind. Inside the envelope he found a single page report on Nick Jensen. Tony scanned it. Stopped. He reread every word. Then he wadded the paper into a tight ball and threw it at the mirror.

Sonofabitch. Jensen hadn't returned to Atlanta. He'd resigned his position. And disappeared.

Warren spotted Janna in the gallery while he was delivering a speech in the House of Lords. He strode out of the chamber afterward to a chorus of "Jolly good, Lyforth," "Congratulations, Lyforth," and "Keep the PM on his toes." In the loggia he found his sister.

"You've located the chalice," he guessed, noting her pleased smile. Earlier that month the Burrell Collection in Glasgow had responded positively to the sketch Janna had sent them. She'd been in Scotland since then, trying to prove they had Malta's prize possession.

"It's definitely Cleopatra's Chalice," she said, her voice low as if spies were keeping the chambers under surveillance. "Its papers claim the chalice is an ancient Etruscan piece from Turkey, but it came from an antiques dealer there who's known for selling stolen art."

"How can you prove it isn't Etruscan?"

Janna smiled, proudly. "The silver content."

"Clever." Most people didn't know that Maltese silver differed from other silvers and was purer. Simple tests could verify the silver content of the chalice. "Shall we have lunch?" He guided her down the corridor toward the members-only Bishops Bar.

"The museum officials have agreed to let experts from the International Foundation of Art Research arbitrate the case," Janna added, as the waiter immediately seated them at Warren's table. "I'm certain they'll decide this piece is the chalice. Meanwhile, I sent an art fraud investigator to Turkey. They have the original documents that supposedly authenticate the chalice as an Etruscan piece. What do you think he discovered?"

"Forged papers." He signaled to Chapman to bring two servings of his usual order: cold poached salmon, light on the dill sauce.

"Exactly, and what's more those papers show the chalice came into Turkey from Libya just after the war. Supposedly, the piece had been in the hands of a private collector. The investigator is bringing me copies of those Libyan exit papers. I'm betting the paper trail leads right back to Tony Bradford."

"If he was careful, his signature won't be on any papers."

"Maybe, but I suspect he hung on to the chalice until after the war, so he could keep all the proceeds himself."

"You should have Scotland Yard's art and antiques squad have a look at those documents. Detective Sergeant Anthony Russell is tops in his field," he said, mentally crediting Janna for her tenacity. She'd inspected thousands of documents and sent countless queries in her search for the chalice.

"As soon as I have proof, I'm going to expose Tony Bradford."

"Let's take care that he doesn't get wind of your investigation beforehand," Warren said as they were served.

"Don't worry, the museum board is anxious to keep this a secret. They don't wish to be accused of receiving stolen property—and not reporting it. Anyway, it wasn't really their fault. The sketch I had done was necessary to identify the chalice." She paused while they were served their salmon. "Just in case Tony does discover the investigation and tries to tamper with the evidence, I've placed a duplicate set of papers in a Lloyds vault."

"Still, be careful. I don't want anything to happen to you."

"Then why are you trying to poison me?" Janna asked with a mischievous smile, ignoring his seriousness.

"What are you talking about?"

She poked at the salmon with her fork. "Didn't I read that over a hundred peers contracted salmonella poisoning after eating here?"

"That was a year ago, smart aleck. The lords' kitchen is safe. I eat here every day." He watched Janna take a bite. He wanted to ask her about Nick, but she seemed so happy that he didn't. No one had heard from Nick. Warren's initial impressions of people weren't usually far from the mark—he'd disliked Collis the moment he'd shaken his hand—but he'd been mistaken about Nick. "Are you staying in London long?"

"I'll be here until the committee completes its report on the chalice and we have Russell go over the documents."

"Shadoe will be thrilled to see you. There's something she wants to show you."

"She's expecting a baby?"

"No, but we're still working on it. She's developed a new flavor for those edible panties—passion fruit. At dinner tonight she'll serve them for dessert for the fourth night in a row. No doubt, the servants have spread the tale all over Belgravia. She'll want your opinion on the new flavor."

Janna laughed, the first sincere laugh that he'd heard from her since Nick left. "Shadoe hasn't changed, has she?"

Warren shook his head, chewing thoughtfully. "She's just what I need, even though she drives me nuts with those Tarot cards and astrological forecasts." He didn't mention how fervently she believed Nick would return to

Janna. "Oh, I almost forgot to tell you. Mother called last night. Taxi won best in show."

"You're kidding. Nick would howl and say: so much for pet quality."

"Well, they did have to put India ink on his nose." Warren skirted over her reference to Nick Jensen. What good did it do to talk about him? Granted, Shadoe believed Nick and Janna were fated to be together, but Warren wondered. He worried that Janna would never fall in love again. Another Aunt Pith.

Nick stood on the balcony of his hotel room in Marbella, staring out at the Mediterranean several miles in the distance. The tattered canvas awning, once forest-green but now a brackish olive, fluttered in the breeze. On the horizon he saw the usual early evening procession of oil tankers, mammoth even at this distance, chugging their way past the Rock of Gibraltar, leaving a billowing wake behind them. Weeks ago, when he'd first arrived in Marbella, Nick used to take pleasure in the impressive sight. He would sit in the rickety tin chair, feet up on the balcony rail, and review the leads on Curt Bradford while watching the ships.

No more.

Armed with a photograph of Curt that he'd gotten from the *Times of Malta,* Nick had worked the Costa del Sol like a coon dog primed for the kill, searching for Curt. The days had merged, becoming endless weeks, lonely weeks without a trace of Curt. Nick no longer experienced any pleasure at the majestic scenery or the white sand beaches.

He turned and walked inside his small room. Institutional green paint and utilitarian furniture, a chair and a bed, greeted him. He flopped down on the bed; it sagged under his weight and he gazed up at the cracked ceiling.

"Give up," he said aloud.

"You can't," his inner voice answered.

Ride with the tide; go with the flow. Travis's favorite saying came to him. It would be simple to take the easy way out. Give up. Go along with the official version of Travis Prescott's death. But Nick couldn't do it. He owed it to the Prescotts to find out the truth.

Nick was convinced Tony or Curt—maybe both—had arranged Rhonda's death. They had been frightened she would talk and tell the truth about who had poisoned Travis. Curt was the key to the mystery. Why had he disappeared?

Leaving Marbella without Curt wasn't an option. Nick wasn't riding with the tide and going with the flow any longer. He wasn't spending the rest of his life with the nagging sense of helplessness that had dogged him until he'd met the Prescotts.

Not for the first time, he wished Janna were with him. She had a methodical approach to things, a rare intelligence. She might think of something he'd missed. Just as leaving wasn't an option, neither was calling her. He refused to expose her to danger.

"Where would be the last—the very last—place anyone would look?" he asked the ceiling.

The cracked plaster formed the Costa del Sol coastline in Nick's mind. Torremolinos to Puerto Banus covered a lot of territory, but Nick doubted Curt had ventured as far east as Torremolinos. On foot, without money or a passport, it would have been difficult to get that far. But Nick had covered his bases and checked the entire length of Costa del Sol. Not a trace.

"Where would be the last place—the absolute last place—anyone would look?" he again asked the ceiling.

"Out in the open. Where anyone could find him."

Nick silently thanked the ceiling. He'd been searching, and had run into one of Tony's detectives tracking Curt, assuming he'd hide and take a job like a night clerk or a car wash attendant.

"That's too crazy," Nick told himself. He must be going over the edge. Here he was talking to the ceiling and thinking Curt Bradford, who wasn't the brightest bulb in the chandelier, had the brains to hide right where everyone could see him.

He'd have to be in a disguise, Nick reasoned. Curt had enough jet-set friends plus Tony's dicks looking for him to know better than to brazen it out and take no precautions. Nick continued to study the ceiling, his hunch gnawing at him and giving him renewed hope of finding the bastard.

The last place anyone would look. Out in the open. Someplace you could work with no questions asked.

The answer hit Nick two seconds later. "No. No way."

It's worth a shot, he decided.

For the next two weeks, he searched methodically each night, starting at Torremolinos and working his way west. By the time he reached Puerto Banus, he'd decided his idea wasn't worth a damn.

Sleek yachts filled the small harbor, glistening under a crescent moon. Elegant bistros lined the pier, their waterfront terraces closed for the winter, but the interiors filled with diners eating late in the Mediterranean fashion. Nick glanced around, checking the nightclubs to see if he'd missed a new one. He'd been to Puerto Banus half a dozen times, checking various leads, thinking Curt might be drawn to the expensive resort. No one had recognized the picture Nick had shown them.

He trained his eyes on the huge yacht permanently moored at the far end of the harbor. Its transom faced Nick: *La Cage aux Faux.* He rode the shore boat out to the floating nightclub.

Once aboard, he cautiously examined every face. He'd given up showing the picture, knowing that the community of female impersonators was a tight group. If Curt were working at one of the many clubs featuring acts by female impersonators, word would spread along the coast overnight.

Satisfied the stewards and the maître d's weren't Curt, Nick walked into the bar and eased his way into a spot between a man who could have been a woman and a woman that he strongly suspected was a man.

"¿Cómo está?" asked the woman, looking pointedly at Nick's crotch.

"No speak Spanish." Nick turned to the bartender and ordered a Bushwacker. He was served a watery tomato concoction with two drops of tequila. Nick nursed his drink and examined every face at the bar.

By now, twenty-odd nightclubs later, he wasn't shocked at how much like women—beautiful women— many of the impersonators were. Still, being in a club like this gave him the willies. Aggressive men in drag always made passes at him. He could handle them, but it still made him uncomfortable.

Satisfied Curt wasn't among those gathered at the bar, Nick turned and idly sipped the piss-poor excuse for a Bushwacker and checked the tables surrounding the stage. By now, he knew the routine. Soon a show would begin and the performers would impersonate well-known female celebrities. Some of them were European actresses or singers that he didn't know, but several were Americans. Judy Garland, Marilyn Monroe, Barbra Streisand, and Bette Midler were sure crowd pleasers.

The house lights dimmed and the stage lights focused on a small stage. He doubted Curt would be among the talented performers who had to sing and dance as well as impersonate women. Nick had no reason to think Curt possessed theatrical skills. Even so, he checked each face carefully and studied with even more care the chorus girls who did little more than kick and strut.

By the fourth act, Nick was discouraged. No one even vaguely resembled Curt. Nick had two more clubs to check, but he was beginning to think this was a hare-brained idea.

"¡Cigarillos! ¡Cigarillos!" chanted an impersonator selling cigarettes between acts.

Nick turned and saw her holding a tray of cigarettes like a character from a forties movie. Tall, heavy ankles, hair the color of beet juice and makeup as thick as pâté.

Nick turned away, set to order a beer instead of a Bushwacker. Something clicked in the remotest part of his brain. Nick slowly turned back, gazing through the darkness to the nearby table where the woman was selling a customer a pack of cigarettes.

Curt? Absolutely. The eyes, though heavily caked with violet shadow and false lashes as long as feather dusters, gave him away. Nick pulled back into the shadows of the bar, suppressing a triumphant laugh while the urge to cry choked him. He didn't want to tip his hand. He needed to catch Curt alone.

Nick hurried from the bar and took the shore boat back to the pier. He waited, hunkered down in the shadows where he could see every person leaving the nightclub. Hours later, the customers left the boat, coming in small groups to the pier on the shore boat. Finally, the female impersonators began to come ashore.

The moon sulked, hidden off and on behind clouds that promised more rain before morning, but Nick still spotted Curt as he stepped from the shore boat. The beet-colored hair gave him away. Many of the other impersonators had come off in pairs or with customers, but Curt emerged alone. Nick hung back in the shadows of the building, then silently followed Curt down the street.

When he was well away from the busy harbor area, Nick pounced on Curt, knocking him to the ground with a flying tackle. They hit the cobbled pavement and rolled over twice. The wig flew off, sailed through the air, and landed in a puddle. Nick grabbed Curt's throat and choked, hard. Curt's eyes widened in fear and he struggled to breathe.

"You've got two choices." The words came out from between Nick's clenched teeth. It was all he could do to keep himself from squeezing the life out of the bastard. "You can talk. Or I'll kill you."

It was almost dusk when Janna's plane landed at Luqa Field the following day. The early winter sunset, muted hues of coral and plum, wasn't as brilliant as the summer sunsets that had astounded the guests at the Blue Grotto, but it still gave Malta the amber glow Janna loved. She took a taxi from the airport to Falcon's Lair, her sense of elation making it impossible not to smile. She could prove Tony Bradford had stolen Cleopatra's Chalice. Not only had Sergeant Detective Russell proven Tony Bradford's signature was identical to the handwriting on the documents purporting the chalice to be part of a private collection, but Interpol had located a dealer in Libya who would positively identify Tony Bradford as the man who'd sold the chalice to the dealer in Turkey.

Putting Tony behind bars would never compensate for Ian's death, but seeing Tony ruined would give Aunt Pith some satisfaction, Janna hoped. She could hardly wait to give her the news. It had been difficult, not calling Aunt Pith to give her a daily update these past weeks as they closed in on Tony, but Janna had wanted all her facts in order before telling Aunt Pith. Janna felt guilty about going back on her promise to leave Tony alone. She believed Aunt Pith would forgive her once she learned Janna could prove Tony had stolen a national treasure.

When she arrived at Falcon's Lair, Janna opened the unlocked door. The welcoming smell of Clara's dill bread baking in the oven greeted her. From the library came the sound of the telephone ringing. No one answered it, so Janna hurried into the room, wondering where Clara and Aunt Pith were.

"Janna? This is Gerry Kaye. I have that information you wanted."

"Great." She tried to sound upbeat, but she was upset with herself for not letting Gerry know that she was no longer interested in discovering if Ian MacShane had ever filed a report about the missing chalice. She had what she needed to put the noose around Tony's neck.

"MacShane did report to the high command in Alexandria that Anthony Bradford had stolen numerous religious relics. I don't know how MacShane did it, but he included a list of properties and the names of men who were in Tony's ring. This information wasn't in the official documents. It was buried in an attaché's notes that were never transcribed. That's why I didn't uncover it years ago when I was checking the reports for my book. It took me weeks to find it this time."

"A list? You found a list?" How lucky could she be? The final nail in Tony's coffin. She wrote down the names of those involved in Tony's black market ring. "Thanks so much. Your information will really help." She automatically lowered her voice even though no one seemed to be nearby. "Gerry, don't mention this to anyone. I found Cleopatra's Chalice. What did you always teach me? Follow the paper trail." She took a few minutes to explain how the authorities had proven Tony's involvement.

Gerry congratulated her, pride in his voice for having taught her well. "I find it odd," he remarked, and she imagined his quizzical expression, "that Bradford would kill Ian. The notes I read clearly stated MacShane kept his investigation a secret. And the attaché's notes were never transcribed. How could Bradford have discovered it?"

"I don't know," Janna admitted.

"Is it possible Bradford had another reason entirely for killing Ian?"

"I suppose," Janna said. "I intend to find out. My aunt deserves to know why Ian died."

"When do you think the authorities will arraign him?"

"Not for a few days. Interpol and Scotland Yard have contacted the Maltese officials. They want to make certain they have an airtight case." She paused to take a deep breath; she was so excited she was talking far too rapidly. "I can't thank you enough. I'm positive that list of men involved in Tony's ring will help. Some of them must still be alive. One of them will talk."

They chatted for a few minutes and then said good-bye. Janna sat a moment, the receiver in her hand. Once again the urge to call Nick tempted her. She didn't understand him, not at all. Travis Prescott had been like a brother to Nick. How could he accept that Rhonda had killed him? He'd been so positive the Bradfords had been responsible. Then Austin had died, and Nick had returned to Malta—a changed man.

She picked up the telephone and waited while the operator placed her call. It would give her a tremendous satisfaction to personally tell Nick that she'd avenged Travis's and Ian's deaths. *That's not why you're calling*, an inner voice said. *You love him. You want to give him another chance.*

"I'm not finding a Nick Jensen on our roster," the switchboard operator in Atlanta told Janna.

"He's in marketing or maybe advertising."

"Nothing. Sorry."

Janna swallowed her pride. "Connect me with Mark Nolan." It took a few minutes before he came on the line. "This is Janna Atherton. I'm a friend of Nick Jensen's. I met you in London."

"Sure. I remember. How are you?"

"I'm fine, thanks. How's Glennis?"

"Great. Redecorating the house again." He laughed, and Janna pictured Glennis as she'd been in London. "Dyin', simply dyin' " to cheat on him.

His friendly voice encouraged her. "I'm trying to reach Nick."

"Nick?" he asked, his tone guarded.

"Yes. I have some news for him."

"News?" Now his voice sounded positively forbidding.

"It's personal."

"I'll be glad to give Nick a message," he said, but he didn't sound the least bit happy about it.

She'd all but convinced herself Nick would want to hear from her. How wrong she'd been. "It's not important."

"You're sure?"

"Positive," she answered, then said good-bye, gazing at the rows of books on the library shelves, her high spirits deflated. Evidently Nick had been transferred to another location, probably New York where the major advertising agencies were. Obviously, Nick had told his friend enough about their relationship for Mark to know Nick didn't want to talk to her.

Taking a deep breath, she tried to put Nick out of her mind. Janna wrinkled her nose, then sniffed. The bread, the wonderful smelling dill bread, was burning. She hurried into the kitchen, yelling to Clara. Smoke filled the room. She managed to turn off the oven, but it took her a minute to find the mitt and take out the blackened hunk. Where on earth was Clara?

She checked the servants' quarters, calling, "Clara."

Unable to find the housekeeper, Janna rushed up the stairs. On the landing she discovered one of Aunt Pith's blue bedroom slippers. With a growing sense of alarm, she charged up the stairs, raced down the hall, and into Aunt Pith's suite.

It was dark inside except for the faint light coming from the lights in the yard. She switched on the lamp and saw the door to the bedroom stood open. At first she thought the bed hadn't been made after Aunt Pith's afternoon nap, but as she walked in, Janna saw the eiderdown comforter thrown on the floor, its pristine whiteness marred by a dirty smudge that looked suspiciously like a footprint. Suddenly, she wished the experts at Fort Halstead had returned the gun she'd secretly taken out of Aunt Pith's nightstand.

Had Tony Bradford somehow discovered Janna had exposed him? Would he have blamed Aunt Pith? Anything was possible, she decided. The whole story from Ian's death to Travis's poisoning and Rhonda's alleged suicide was bizarre. Tony was capable of anything. She prayed her lust for revenge hadn't gotten Pithany into trouble.

She reached for the telephone, set to call 991 for the police, but the sound of a car coming up the drive stopped her. *Please, let it be Aunt Pith.* She dashed down the hall, took the stairs two at a time, and skidded to a halt in the entry just as the front door opened.

"Clara," she cried, seeing the housekeeper, "where's Aunt Pith?"

"Upon my word, Miss Janna, upon my word, I had no idea she was ill until I took up her tea." Clara broke into sobs, her hefty shoulders heaving. "Miss Pithany was in pain something terrible. She couldn't breathe."

Primal fear overpowered Janna, almost panicking her. "Oleander poisoning."

27

✳

Janna rushed up the steps of St. Paul's Hospital. Aunt Pith had been alive when Clara had returned home, but the housekeeper had been too flustered to find out exactly what was wrong with her. All she knew was Aunt Pith's condition was "guarded." Had Tony somehow managed to poison her? Janna wondered, recalling Travis had experienced trouble breathing just before he'd died.

Inside, Janna didn't immediately see a reception desk. She stopped an orderly wheeling a cart laden with dirty plates and utensils, the remains of the evening meal. He sent her down a long hall past rooms marked in Maltese and English: *Qassis*/Priest, *Klinika*/Clinic.

"Which room is Pithany Crandall in?" she asked the receptionist.

The woman scanned a list, then said, "No visitors, sorry."

"I'm Janna Atherton, her niece. I want to speak with her doctor."

"Just a minute." The woman picked up the telephone and spoke in Maltese.

Janna listened, catching the Maltese word *tabib,* doctor. She tried to reassure herself that Pithany was receiving excellent care. This was a teaching hospital used by the university with doctors who'd graduated from the top medical schools in Europe and the United States.

The hospital had been built in the Middle Ages by the Knights of Malta to nurse crusaders wounded in the Holy War. The first modern facility of its kind, the hospital still retained the highest standards. Those facts ran through Janna's mind, but failed to comfort her.

A man walked toward her. The blue badge on his white jacket identified him as Dr. Vidal. "You're here about Pithany Crandall?"

"Yes. I'm her niece. What's wrong with her?"

"We'll know more in a few hours," he hedged, "when we have test results."

"Check for oleander poisoning," Janna said, hoping it wasn't too late to save Aunt Pith.

"She hasn't been poisoned," he said, and Janna let out a sigh of relief. "We know she's suffering from a pulmonary embolus. We're just waiting for tests that will tell us how extensive the damage is."

"What is a pulmonary embolus?"

"It's a blood clot that's migrated to her lungs. This one started in her calf. It lodged in her lung and was literally suffocating her."

"Omigod! Why didn't I make her go to the doctor? Her legs have been bothering her for months."

"Why didn't she consult a doctor herself? The pain must have been terrible these last few days."

"She doesn't like doctors. I should have insisted she see one, but I accepted what she told me. She thought her age was catching up with her and that she needed more rest."

He shook his head, his expression incredulous.

"May I see her now?"

"She's sedated. If you come back around midnight, I'll have test results and she'll be awake."

"I want to see her—just for a minute."

He reluctantly escorted her down a long hall into the intensive care unit. Aunt Pith lay on the bed, a drip IV attached to one arm, pale green oxygen tongs inserted in her nostrils. Her face was a pallid white except for the dark fringe of eyelashes.

The woman who'd seemed invincible now looked frail, her breathing labored as if the next breath might be her last. A choked sob escaped Janna's lips. "She's going to live, isn't she?"

Dr. Vidal's eyes evaded hers. "I'll have a better idea when I see the test results."

"Give me your opinion. What do you think?"

His eyes met hers. "Fifty-fifty. She may live, but it's more than possible your aunt is going to die."

Janna swayed for a moment, his words a punishing blow, but she steadied herself. "You said she'll be awake around midnight. Will I be able to talk to her?" To tell her how much I love her?

"I'll allow you to speak with her then," he responded, his voice stern, "if you keep it brief."

"And you'll have test results. You'll know more," she said, and he nodded. "If she needs anything we're . . . I can get the money." Her mind scrambled for possible ways to help. "I'll send for specialists or—or fly her to Zurich. Anything. Anything at all."

"We're doing all that can be done. Moving her would be fatal."

"I know you're doing everything possible. It's just that I don't want her to die. She's more than an aunt to me. She's been like a mother."

"I suggest you get the rest of your family here quickly."

Moving like a windup doll, her motions jerky, Janna called Warren and Shadoe. She left a message at the Vienna hotel where Audrey and John were staying while Taxi was entered in a show.

The Roman numerals on the clock in the hall read a few minutes after eight. Aunt Pith wouldn't be awake for hours. Suddenly, Janna knew what she had to do. There might not be a tomorrow for Aunt Pith. Tonight could very well be the last time she would ever speak to her again. The very thought of losing Aunt Pith made tears well up in Janna's eyes, but she fought the urge to cry.

She wanted to tell Aunt Pith exactly what had happened to Ian. Even though Janna had proven Tony had stolen Cleopatra's Chalice, Janna needed to know why Tony had killed Ian. The more she thought about what Gerry had said, the more disturbed she became. If Tony hadn't known Ian reported his black market activities, why had he killed the reporter? Aunt Pithany deserved to know the truth.

Janna sprinted out to her car, then drove as fast as she could toward Mdina. She prayed Tony Bradford would be home. The car clambered along the lonely road, hitting every bump and pothole, rattling her already tattered nerves while she mentally rehearsed what she would say to Tony. She'd never met him, but she'd seen him from afar on several occasions. A portly man now, he must have been built like a bull in his youth. Even at a distance he was intimidating.

Knowing he was a killer frightened Janna, but she fortified herself with the knowledge that she owed this to Aunt Pith. Tony had murdered the man she'd loved.

She drove into the silent city, surprised at how dark it was. The moonless night was even darker because Mdina had no streetlights. Naturally, the lights that had been strung along the walls for the *festa* celebration the previous spring had been taken down. She parked the car outside Tony's palace, the eerie quiet making her even more aware that she was all alone.

The servant that answered her knock opened the door a crack and peered at her suspiciously.

"Is Mr. Bradford home?" she asked, and he nodded. "Tell him Janna Atherton is here to see him."

He slammed the door and left Janna standing outside, her stomach roiling spasmodically. Minutes later he returned and motioned her inside with a jerk of his head. She followed him down the shadowy hall and into the study decorated like a mummy's tomb.

She walked in, bolstered by the knowledge this was her final chance to discover the truth about Ian's death. "I'm Janna Ath—"

"I know who you are." Tony stood behind his desk with a brandy snifter in his hand. At close range, he looked older, but he was still an imposing man. "Care for some cognac?"

"No thank you. This isn't a social call."

"I never imagined that it was. What do you want?"

"An answer. I want to know why you killed Ian Mac-Shane."

He stared at her as if she'd just announced visitors from outer space. "You've got your goddamned nerve. First, you accuse my family of murdering that Pierce kid—"

"Prescott. Travis Prescott."

"Who cares? Then you try to pin some poison cookies on me. Haven't you done enough?"

His injured tone astounded Janna. Of all the reactions she'd anticipated—even envisioning him trying to kill her—this had never entered her mind. She remembered the televised press conference. Tony was a consummate actor when he wanted to be.

"I haven't done anything to you," Janna insisted, forcing confidence she didn't feel into her voice. "You did it to yourself."

"You cost me my son."

"You cost Aunt Pithany a lifetime of happiness by killing Ian."

Tony laughed, a cruel chortle that raised goose bumps across the back of her neck. "She could have been happy, but she didn't want to be. *I* would have made her happy."

"You? Never."

"I would have given her everything." He swept his arm through the air, indicating the room. "This palace, a yacht, a villa on Cap Ferrat . . . anything."

Her mind reeled as if short-circuited as the truth hit her. "You're in love with Aunt Pith. You always have been."

He stared at her, transfixed.

"That's why you killed Ian."

"I never said I killed him." His voice sounded sincere, but his eyes told a different story.

"I know you lured him to his death. You used the gun he'd given Aunt Pith. We have Ian's body, you know. Ballistics prove that gun killed him. You fired the fatal shot."

"You can't prove a damn thing."

"I don't want to prove it. I just want to tell Aunt Pith the truth. She deserves—"

"She deserves nothing. You act like she's some saint. She's nothing more than a slut, like any whore on Strait Street." He flung open a drawer and withdrew a folder. He dropped it on the desk in front of her. "Here read this. She slept with three men. Three. Never married any of them."

Janna quickly glanced down and saw the date on the top page read 1945. He'd been keeping track of Aunt Pith's activities for half a century. Obsessive love. He had to be crazy. She mustered her courage, knowing any show of weakness would prevent her from learning the whole truth. "I wouldn't call three men in fifty years promiscuous. She probably was looking for someone to replace Ian, and never found him."

"I was the right man for her. Where was MacShane when she needed food? Where was he when she had to get her father out of Malta? Parading around Africa tooting his own horn. He didn't love her. Not the way I loved her."

The distress in his voice brought an unwelcome surge of compassion in Janna. She forced herself to remember he was a murderer. "She thought you asked her to marry her because you envied her family connections."

He belted back the last of his cognac. "I told her that. Who wants to beg a woman who loves another man?"

"But you did kill Ian."

"I'm not admitting anything."

"Look, you know I can't prove it, so I can't send you to prison for his death, but please tell me the truth. Aunt Pith is in the hospital."

"In the hospital? What's wrong with her?"

"A blood clot is lodged in her lungs. There's a good chance she won't live. I don't—"

"She can't die." Tony sank into his chair. "She can't do this to me. She can't die."

The anguish in his voice tore at Janna. She sat down opposite him, scooting her chair close to his desk and looking him in the eye. "You did kill Ian."

"I thought she'd love me if he were out of the picture," he said, his words hardly more than a whisper.

Janna held her breath, not wanting to interrupt his confession, but itching to scream: I knew it! I knew it!

"But would she marry me? No, she was too proud, too stubborn. Even when she was pregnant with you—" He stopped, halted by her gasp.

"M-m-me?" Janna stammered, gripping the top of the desk with both hands.

Tony laughed, a low diabolical laugh. "Sonofabitch. She never told you even after all this time."

Soul-wrenching shock left her speechless. Aunt Pith was her mother? Not Audrey? She sat immobile, a thousand childhood memories ricocheting through her mind.

Across every one was Aunt Pith's smiling face. Suddenly many things made sense. Their personalities were alike. They both had gray-green eyes. But why had Aunt Pith never told her? More important, why had she given her up?

"Your father," Tony scoffed, "was some American naval officer stationed here. He was killed in a freak accident."

At least, Janna thought, her mother had told her this much. Why hadn't she told her the whole truth?

"Even if he'd lived, Pithany wouldn't have married him."

Janna could tell by his self-satisfied smile that he relished telling her the details.

"Pithany didn't want his baby. She didn't want you." He grinned. "She went to Zurich to have an abortion, but didn't have the guts to go through with it."

Janna inhaled sharply, struggling to imagine Aunt Pith who doted on children, going to have an abortion. Janna realized with mind-numbing shock that she might never have been born. Her certainty about Aunt Pith's love ebbed. Her confusion, the ache in her heart almost reduced her to tears, but she stopped short when she saw the look in his eyes. He was taking perverse pleasure in destroying her image of Aunt Pith.

"She loves me. Aunt Pith has always been there when I needed her."

"Yeah, right. That's why she foisted you off on her sister, isn't it?"

"She spent months at a time living with us when I was growing up. She called me every other day when she was away."

"But she didn't keep you, did she?"

Janna refused to allow him to shake her faith in Aunt Pith's love. Granted it hurt to know she hadn't chosen to keep Janna, but Aunt Pith must have had her reasons.

She'd never given Janna any cause to doubt her love. She refused to let a madman change her mind.

"It didn't matter if I lived with her or with the Athertons. I love her, and if I'm her daughter that's even better."

Janna rose and looked at Tony. "You're nothing more than a pathetic, bitter old man with no one, not even your own son, to love you. If you die, who'll care? But if Aunt Pith dies our entire family will mourn her loss. She means so much to me that I can't risk her dying and not knowing I'm responsible for sending you to prison."

His eyes darkened dangerously.

"I've located Cleopatra's Chalice."

"So?" he said uncertainly. "What does that prove?"

"I traced it back to Libya. Experts will testify that your handwriting is on those exit papers. Saluu Zerafa will identify you as the person who sold the chalice to the Turkish dealer."

"You're bluffing," he said, but he didn't sound convinced.

"And I have the names of the men in your black market gang," she added, unmistakable triumph in her voice. She rattled off a few of the names she remembered from the list Gerry had given her.

He glared at her, his expression one of utter disbelief. A cryptlike silence filled the room, an eerie reminder of the long-dead pharaohs whose tombs had been looted to decorate Tony's study.

Finally, Tony spoke. "You think you're so goddamned smart. How do you plan on getting out of here alive?"

She couldn't resist smiling at him. "You won't kill me because the authorities already have all the information. Getting rid of me won't prevent your arrest." She headed for the door, hoping he wasn't too crazy to understand the logic of her argument. "You'd just face a murder charge." For insurance, she added a lie. "I told everyone at the hospital I was coming to visit you."

She opened the door, turned her head, and smiled over her shoulder at him.

Tony stared at the door, unnerved by her cleverness. Who the hell would have thought anyone could have linked him to the chalice? He would be finished in Malta, now. No question about it. Cleopatra's Chalice was a national treasure. No one would forgive him for stealing it.

Grandsons? Hell, their names would be worthless on this island. All the years he'd slaved to build a dynasty had been wasted. He would die in prison.

The thought of death reminded him that Pithany might die, and he sighed, the old sadness returning. He stood, his legs weak, and walked over to the mirror. Looking into it, he didn't see his reflection. Instead, he saw the proud RAF pilot he'd been when he'd arrived in Malta over half a century ago.

The islanders had greeted them with wild enthusiasm. The RAF was going to save them from the Nazis. The girls had been crazy about Tony, clamoring for his attention. He could have had any one of them. Except Pithany.

She'd leveled those matchless green eyes on him. "You don't expect to defend us by flying those rusty old Hurricanes, do you?"

She'd been right on target. Flying the Hurricanes had been a death wish. They weren't any challenge for the Luftwaffe planes. But Tony did his best, and his bravery impressed everyone. Except Pithany. He never had been able to impress her, not even years later when he'd amassed a fortune.

The insistent ringing of the telephone brought Tony back to the present. He debated whether or not to answer it. Then he remembered the decrepit Hurricanes and all the missions he'd flown always knowing death was his copilot. Hell, he'd survived. There was a way out of this.

What did they have on him, anyway? Handwriting experts could be challenged. He could discredit Zerafa, a slimy Libyan antiques dealer. Most of the men who'd worked with him in the black market were dead. Those that weren't could be bought off or buried.

"You're a survivor. A hero." He strode across the room and picked up the telephone. The static on the line indicated an international call. Tony's hopes soared. Perhaps that frog had located Curt. "Bradford here."

"Ian MacShane calling."

"Cut the crap, Jensen. Your accent sucks."

Jensen laughed, a triumphant laugh. The same laugh Janna had used earlier. Tony sank into his chair like a punch drunk fighter. What now?

"I'm calling for Ian MacShane, for Travis Prescott, and for Rhonda Sibbet."

"They're dead." Tony thought he sounded tough.

"And you're as good as dead."

Jensen's victorious tone left Tony immobile. The vision he'd had the last time Jensen called flashed through Tony's mind: Ian MacShane with a gun to Tony's head.

"I found your son."

"Where?" Tony croaked.

"In Puerto Banus. I'm at police headquarters with him now."

Just up the road from Marbella where he'd disappeared. Unfuckingbelievable! A dumb Texan could find Curt when the best in the business couldn't.

"He'd been working in a club as a female impersonator."

Tony gave the kid credit. No wonder he'd been hard to find. But he gave Jensen even more credit for locating him.

"Curt was actually damn glad to see me."

"I'll bet," Tony said, his mind reeling. What was coming next?

"He was ready to give himself up."

Tony opened his mouth to deny it—a Bradford didn't give up—then clamped it shut. Curt was a piss-poor excuse for a Bradford. Janna had gotten the genes that should have been Curt's. She didn't give up. Jensen didn't give up. Two of a kind.

"He's in the custody of the Spanish police. He's confessed to giving Travis the poison and sending me those cookies."

Tony's mind faltered. He couldn't imagine a way to salvage the situation.

"Curt's insisting you had Rhonda killed. He's come up with some interesting names of friends of yours in Sicily. He claims you hired a professional hit man."

Tony discounted the threat of anyone in Sicily fingering him. The Mafia had a code of silence that Tony envied. In his next life he was coming back as a Mafia don. "Why are you telling me all this?"

"I wanted to tell you all this in person," Jensen said, "but I'm still in Spain. I didn't want to risk anyone else telling you first that you're finished."

His reserve of strength sapped, Tony sat clutching the receiver. *No way out,* his mind kept saying. *No way out.* He dropped the receiver into the cradle. He rose slowly on unsteady legs and walked over to the mirror. He tried to convince himself that he would survive this. It was possible. But with Curt in jail, he would never have grandsons.

All this for nothing. A lifetime wasted.

He stood looking into the mirror.

28

✳

Janna floored the accelerator, anxious to get back to the hospital. *Please, God, let her live.* Nothing could convince Janna that Aunt Pith didn't love her. But as brave a front as she'd presented to Tony, lingering doubts troubled her. Why hadn't her mother kept her? She had so many questions she wanted to ask . . . her mother.

Ahead the serpentine road from Mdina to Valletta twisted through rolling farmland, winding through countless switchbacks. Janna tried to concentrate on the dangerous road while driving as fast as she could, but her thoughts filtered back to her childhood. She'd always loved Malta. Once she would have said the balmy climate and the sunny beaches lured her. Now she realized that the attraction was Aunt Pith. She and Warren had spent every summer at Falcon's Lair and most holidays. Those were the happiest memories of her youth.

Aunt Pith let her have a puppy, something Reginald would never allow. Over the years she'd had several puppies, Abbie, Lexi, and Dodger. She would sob uncontrollably when she had to leave them, but Aunt Pith would call with weekly reports and send pictures.

Pithany had flown to London to be with Janna on every important occasion. Janna laughed remembering Aunt Pith, sitting in the front row applauding loudly when Janna had played the part of the box of myrrh in the Christmas pageant. She never put the hotels first. If

Janna—or anyone in the family needed her—Aunt Pith came.

She loves me. She always has.

The luminous clock on the dashboard read a few minutes after midnight when Janna arrived at the hospital. She went directly to the intensive care unit and found Dr. Vidal standing outside the door conferring with a nurse.

"Is she awake?" Janna asked.

"Yes, but she's groggy." His grave expression frightened Janna.

"Do you have her test results?"

"Yes, and I've discussed them with her."

Aunt Pith must be better. It was just like her to demand to hear the facts.

"The news isn't good, I'm afraid."

The surge of hope vanished, replaced by all-consuming fear.

"The gas analysis of her blood shows her system is being starved of needed oxygen. The lung scan shows multiple emboli. Any of them can prove fatal."

"She has a chance, doesn't she?"

"One in a million."

Janna refused to accept the diagnosis. Aunt Pith was a fighter. "She's one in a million. She'll make it."

"Why don't you go in?" he said. "I told her you wanted to see her." He touched Janna's arm. "She's in a great deal of pain, so she's heavily medicated. Don't upset her."

She tiptoed into the room and saw Aunt Pith's eyes were closed. Janna moved the bedside chair closer and eased into it. She took Aunt Pith's hand in hers. Around the IV shunt a violet bruise stood out against the pale skin. Her fingers were cold, Janna thought, but soft and loving, the way they'd always been. Aunt Pith's eyelids fluttered and she slowly opened her eyes.

A thousand questions clamored for attention, but Janna reminded herself not to upset Aunt Pith. "I love you. You know that, don't you?" *Mother.*

"Of course." Her words came out slowly in the measured pace of someone heavily medicated.

"You're going to get better. You just—"

"No. I spoke with the doctor. I know the truth."

"He says you have a chance. You can't give up. You can't. I won't let you." Janna swallowed hard, her throat constricting.

"I'm ready, Janna. Really, darling, I am." She gazed fondly at Janna, her expression so wistful that she looked very young. "After we buried dear Ian, I made my own arrangements, selected my own coffin and tombstone. Bury me quickly. I don't want a lot of fuss. And whatever you do, don't let Dr. Amestoy conduct the service. You just say a few words. That's all I want."

"Please don't give up."

"I'm not giving up. I'm accepting the inevitable." She closed her eyes and for one heart-stopping moment, Janna thought she'd lost her. But Aunt Pith slowly, very wearily opened her eyes again. "I would have loved to see your children, though. I know you and Nick are going to have wonderful children. Beautiful, happy children."

Dear God, not Nick. Janna forced a nod, reminding herself not to upset her. If it made her happy to think Nick would come back, what was the harm?

"I counted on playing with them at Falcon's Lair. But I'll be with you always. Remember that."

Janna took a deep breath, marshaling her thoughts and choosing her next words more carefully than anything she'd ever said. "Part of you will live on in me." She squeezed Aunt Pith's hand. "I love you and I know you love me."

Aunt Pith studied Janna for a long minute. Tears

pooled in her eyes. Janna grabbed a tissue from the table and dabbed at the drops.

"Don't cry, please. I didn't mean to make you sad."

"You know I'm your mother."

"Yes, but I'm not upset you didn't tell me."

"I wanted to tell you a thousand times, but I didn't know how to explain the biggest mistake of my life."

"Hush," Janna said. "It's not important." But to herself Janna thought: A mistake! A mistake. Her mother had wanted her, had loved her.

"It's important to me. I thought I was doing the right thing by letting Audrey adopt you. I wanted the best for you. At that point I thought the Athertons were a family with two parents and a brother, not to mention prestigious social connections. I thou—" She gasped, clutching her side, then relaxed, sagging against the pillows.

Janna quickly looked at the heart monitor. It showed a steady blip. "Talking about this is upsetting you. I know you did what you thought best."

"Talking about it isn't bothering me," she said, her voice sounding weaker. "The pains keep coming and going. That's all."

"I'll call the doctor. You need more medication."

"I'm so medicated now that I feel as if I have angel's wings. Any more and I'll be unconscious. I want to know what's happening right up to the end. And I want to tell you why I allowed Audrey to take you.

"Thirty-five years ago this country's Roman Catholics would never have accepted a single woman with an illegitimate child. I was afraid they would make your life miserable. I thought you would be better off with Audrey. She had everything I wanted: a home and a family. I've regretted my decision since the moment you were out of my arms."

Janna leaned over and kissed her cheek. "My happiest

times were always with you. I guess deep down I always knew I belonged to you."

"You're so much like me that I'm frightened for you."

"Don't be," Janna said, doubting that she could ever live up to her mother, but feeling much stronger just knowing Pithany was her mother. Through a war and years of strife, she'd brought the family through everything. True, they had their problems—what family didn't?—but they'd made it for the most part due to Aunt Pith's guidance. Still, Janna had one remaining question that would haunt her until she knew more. "Would it"—she hesitated—"bother you to talk about my father?"

Aunt Pith looked at Janna, her expression forlorn. She waited a few seconds before responding, "No, it won't bother me. I wish—you don't know how I wish—I could honestly tell you that your father, Steve Sanford, was the love of my life, but he wasn't. In all fairness to him, I'll say that he loved me, but no one could ever take Ian's place. I didn't love Steve."

"Would you have married him, if he hadn't been killed?"

"No, Janna, I wouldn't have. His life was in America. He wanted to return to Kansas. If I'd loved him the way I had Ian, I wouldn't have cared, but I didn't."

Janna hesitated a moment, trying to come to terms with the facts. Her mother had never loved her father. She thought of Reginald, the cold imperious man who'd ruled her life for so many years. She had to admit that knowing he wasn't her father, that she didn't need to kowtow to his memory, lifted a burden from her shoulders.

Now that they were squaring the tables, Janna decided it was time to tell her about Tony. There might never be a better moment. "I found Cleopatra's Chalice. I have proof that Tony Bradford stole it. He'll be indicted any day now."

Aunt Pith grimaced, and Janna checked the heart monitor. The electric line's pace remained constant.

"I did it for you . . . Mother." Janna went on to give her the details: "I couldn't let him kill the man you loved and not pay for it. Granted, the punishment won't fit the crime, but at least he knows that I'm responsible for his downfall."

"Knows? Tony knows?"

"Yes. I went to see him earlier this evening. I wanted him to tell me why he'd killed Ian."

"What did he say?"

Suddenly, Janna was sorry she'd brought up Tony's motive. Now was no time to tell her Ian had been murdered because of her. With her gun. Janna loved her too much to hurt her further. Why should she die blaming herself because, in his own warped way, Tony loved her?

"Why, Janna? Why did he kill Ian?"

"The chalice. Tony sold it through a dealer in Libya," Janna said, hoping this half-truth would suffice.

Pithany closed her eyes and lay silent. Seconds passed and Janna thought perhaps she'd fallen asleep. She studied the heart monitor and saw the beat remained regular.

Strange, Janna thought, revenge didn't taste as sweet as she'd anticipated. But then, she hadn't expected the truth to hurt Aunt Pith. She knew Pithany would have married Tony if she'd suspected the marriage would have saved Ian.

"You know," Aunt Pith said, her eyes still closed. "I had the oddest feeling Nick was going to deal with Tony."

Janna held her tongue, blocking the urge to tell Aunt Pith that Nick hadn't cared enough for his friend, Travis, to even do any investigating on his own.

Aunt Pith opened her eyes. They appeared hazy, slightly out of focus. The concern that had ebbed slightly while they'd talked, bringing Janna hope that her mother would survive, returned full force.

"Janna, I don't want you to make the mistake I made. I should have sold the hotels, kept you, and moved to England." She squeezed Janna's hand, but her grip lacked its usual strength. "Never think the company is the most important thing in your life." Her voice trailed off and Janna had to bend closer to hear her next words. "Nick is more important.

"I purposely threw you together by convincing him to hold onto Travis's shares even though Nick wanted to sell them back to me. It worked. You two fell in love."

Janna wanted to remind her that Nick still loved Amanda Jane, but she saw how weak Aunt Pith had become. "You rest now. We've talked too long."

"I am tired, and my side hurts terribly. I want you to stay, though. Talk to me. Tell me all about Warren and Shadoe, about Audrey, about Taxi . . . about everything."

"All right." Janna kissed her cheek and smoothed the hair back from her face.

"Promise me." Aunt Pith clutched her hand, then paused to take a deep breath. "Promise me you won't leave me. Stay with me right to the end. I'm not afraid. I'm really not. Ian's waiting for me. But I love you, too, just as much. I want to be with you as long as I can."

Aunt Pith closed her eyes and Janna fought the tears. Willpower alone kept her from breaking down. "Well Shadoe . . . Shadoe has developed a new flavor for those edible undies. You won't believe it, but it's really delicious. Now, you know Shadoe"—Janna commanded herself to keep her voice upbeat—"she's always doing something interesting. She tested the new flavor by serving itty-bitty pieces of undies for dessert. The night I stayed with them, Warren had the MP from Ripon for dinner. Shadoe served the undies. Of course, he didn't recognize them as such. He loved them and asked her for the recipe."

Her eyes still closed, Aunt Pith smiled a faint but amused smile.

"Audrey, as you know, is giddy with Taxi's success. He's won several ribbons. Two days ago, I visited the shop she'll be opening. Haute Dog is straight across from Janet Reger's lingerie shop on Beauchamp Place. You know the spot. It's where Ravell Men's Furnishings used to be. The bronze statue of the dog is already at the front door. She didn't name it Fido, after all, but called it Rommel in Rommie's memory."

Janna checked her watch. Warren and Shadoe should arrive any minute. Hours ago, he'd said he was leaving immediately.

"Go on. I'm listening."

"Chloe has her first tooth, it's a little crooked—"

"Oh!" gasped Pithany. She sat bolt upright, clutching her side. The IV ripped from the back of her hand and dangled along the side of the bed leaving a trail of blood. "Oh, no! Please, no!"

Janna grabbed her. She hugged Janna, holding tight. "Are you all right?"

Pithany relaxed her grip and Janna started to ease her back onto the pillows, thankful the attack had passed. Her eye caught the monitor. The line went flat.

A bell clanged in the room and an even louder bell rang in the hall. "I love you . . . Mother. Bless you for loving me."

A nurse whipped into the room followed by an orderly with a red cart and Dr. Vidal. "Leave."

Janna jumped back, praying they could save her. She slowly walked into the hall and waited where she could see the heart monitor. The team scrambled around Aunt

Pith, frantically shouting orders at each other. The electric line remained flat.

Bright sunlight streamed into Falcon Lair's breakfast room as Warren watched Janna toy with her lunch. He and Shadoe had arrived last night shortly after Aunt Pith died. Janna had been inconsolable.

"She'd always been more than an aunt to me," Janna had said. "Much more."

Warren had been shocked to learn Aunt Pith was Janna's mother. He supposed he shouldn't have been. They resembled each other especially those gray-green eyes. And their personalities were similar. Warren hadn't noticed the similarity until recently. Since leaving Collis, Janna had come into her own. With each day, she became more like the Aunt Pithany he remembered from his youth.

"I should have insisted she consult a doctor," Janna said for the hundredth time.

"Don't blame yourself for Aunt Pith's death," Warren told Janna.

"None of us even suspected Pithany's life was in danger," Audrey said.

Warren silently thanked God that his mother hadn't gone into an emotional collapse. He'd met the plane she and Ellis had chartered when it arrived slightly after dawn. Audrey had taken the news stoically, clutching Taxi and leaning against Ellis.

"Would Aunt Pith want you to blame yourself?" Shadoe asked, her voice soothing.

"Of course not," Janna admitted.

"Then you must go on," Shadoe said. "Make her proud."

Janna nodded, her eyes bloodshot and red-rimmed. He'd thought a good night's sleep might help. Now Warren doubted she'd slept at all.

"Trust Pithany to be efficiency itself," Audrey said, tears welling up in her eyes. "Ellis tells me the funeral parlor says she'd taken care of everything. All we have to do is order the flowers."

"I'll take care of that," Shadoe volunteered.

Warren studied his sister. "Are you certain you want to deliver the eulogy yourself? Canon Amestoy volunteered—"

"She didn't want him."

Warren saw his mother was now on the verge of tears. Ellis put his arm around her.

Shadoe quickly said, "Then we must honor her wishes."

Janna rose. "I'm going to walk in the hills a bit. Don't worry about me. I'll be back in time for the funeral."

Warren watched his sister slowly leave. He glanced around the table, thankful that he had Shadoe and grateful that his mother had Ellis. He had a terrible feeling that Janna would go through life alone.

Aunt Pith all over again.

The doorbell rang and Audrey looked anxiously at Warren. "Who could that be?"

"Not a condolence call, I hope," Ellis said, a comforting arm still around Audrey.

"I doubt it," Shadoe said. "The article in this morning's paper said the funeral would be private, and we wouldn't be receiving callers."

Warren had been touched by the front page article recounting Pithany's work with the special services during the war and the rebuilding of her family's hotels. Commendations on her contributions to various charities and her success in saving the flocks of migrating birds from hunters had been cited as well.

Clara appeared at the breakfast room door. "Inspector General Muscat wants to speak to you," she told Warren.

He rose, casting a worried glance at Shadoe. He motioned for her to come with him. In the foyer he found Raymond Muscat.

"My sympathies on the loss of your aunt," Muscat said. "She was a fine woman. A credit to Malta."

"Thank you," Warren said as Shadoe slipped her hand into his.

"I came because I thought your family should be prepared." He shifted from one foot to the other, acutely uncomfortable. "That is, I thought you might want to know before you hear it elsewhere that Tony Bradford has killed himself."

"My God! He's dead?" Warren shook his head. "Why did he kill himself?"

"I was hoping your sister might help us. She visited him last night—"

"Janna went to see Tony?"

"Yes," Muscat said. "Do you know why she went? I mean, it is a bit surprising that after the trouble with the cookies and everything . . ."

"I didn't know she'd seen him. She didn't mention it."

"She's very upset about Pithany's death," Shadoe said.

"I understand," Muscat said, his tone sympathetic. "It's probably not important. His valet tells us that just after she left Tony received a telephone call. He remained in his study, standing in front of an Egyptian mirror until dawn."

"He stood all night in front of a mirror?" Shadoe asked.

"That's what the valet tells us. Apparently he didn't say a word. The man tried to get him to have a cup of coffee at sunrise, but couldn't."

"I find all this very peculiar," Warren said, "but what does this have to do with us?"

"I want you to be prepared when reporters question you."

"Question me?"

"I meant question the family. You see, Tony shot himself when his man came in with the morning paper and told him that Pithany Crandall had died."

Shadoe gasped and Warren drew her closer, putting his arm around her. "I never understood their feud," he told Muscat. "Evidently there's more to it than we realized. I don't think anyone knows the whole story."

"Well, I thought you'd want to know."

"I appreciate your thoughtfulness. I want to prepare my sister for any questions. She's taken this pretty hard, you know."

Muscat nodded sympathetically and turned to leave. Shadoe placed her hand on his arm, stopping him.

"How did Tony die?" she asked.

"Darling, the inspector just said Tony shot himself."

"I know, but where did he shoot himself?"

"He fired the gun at his head. Point-blank at his left temple."

As the limousine followed the hearse to the cemetery, Warren glanced at his mother seated beside Ellis. She seemed to be in control unlike at his father's funeral when she'd had to be sedated. To his right sat Janna, more composed than she'd been earlier, but silent. Shadoe squeezed his hand and he smiled weakly at her, thankful for her love, her strength.

The shock of Aunt Pith's death had just begun to hit him. His father might have shaped his life—almost ruining his chances with Shadoe—but he knew he would miss Aunt Pith more. Her warmth and support had been an antidote for his father's negativism and disapproval.

"Oh my," Audrey said.

Warren's spirits sank even lower. He hoped his mother wasn't going to succumb to a crying jag, not now when Janna seemed better.

"Who are these people?" Ellis asked.

Seated in the middle between Janna and Shadoe, Warren had to crane his neck to look around his sister. He saw people clad in dark clothing lining the street, clogging it so that the limousine had to slow down. Many of the women held bouquets of flowers.

"Oh my," Audrey said, "they're waiting to say goodbye to Pithany."

Shadoe looked questioningly at Warren.

He was so moved that he could hardly whisper. "There's a tradition here on Malta that when a loved one passes away the following Sunday friends place nosegays on the grave. I guess they couldn't wait."

"She would have been so moved," Janna said. "So pleased."

It took another ten minutes for the hearse to pass through the wrought-iron gates into the deserted cemetery. Warren helped Shadoe and Janna from the car, then brought Clara out of the front seat where she'd been riding with the chauffeur. He and Janna had decided that Clara, Aunt Pith's housekeeper for almost thirty years, was just like a member of the family. She'd sobbed uncontrollably when he'd told her the family wanted her to attend the private service with them.

"Heavens," Audrey said as they walked up to the grave site.

Roses, orchids, tulips, lilies of the valley—more flowers than Kew Gardens—surrounded the open grave. There couldn't be a flower left on the island, he thought, remembering the bouquets many of the mourners outside were carrying. He glanced at Janna who was staring at the flowers, a small nosegay of dried wildflowers in her hand. They'd be lost, but he didn't think it mattered. Pithany would have said it's the thought that counts.

Warren and Ellis, assisted by men from the funeral home, carried the coffin from the hearse to the grave. It was a polished mahogany coffin with gold-plated handles. Identical to the one they'd had made for Ian Mac-Shane, Warren thought, willing himself to concentrate on details. Anything to keep himself from thinking that this was his aunt that he was carrying.

They placed the coffin on the apparatus that would lower it into the grave as soon as the final blessing had been given. The honorary pallbearers withdrew and left the family around the coffin.

"Move in close," Janna said, sounding far more composed than Warren felt.

The group edged nearer the coffin. Without realizing it, Warren had his arm around Shadoe. He took his sister's gloved hand and gave her a reassuring squeeze.

"Aunt Pithany, we're all here," Janna began.

Clara openly sobbed; Audrey dabbed at her eyes with a lace-edged handkerchief. Warren stared at his toes, keeping his eyes open as wide as possible so tears wouldn't gather. Janna kept talking but Warren forced himself to concentrate on the tombstone to keep the tears at bay.

"I'm going to quote a man that I never met, Aunt Pith," Janna continued, the slightest waver in her voice. "His name is G. K. Chesterton. He said: 'The way to love anything is to realize that it might be lost.' That's the lesson you taught us. When you lost Ian, you learned that any one of us might be lost.

"You lived remembering that. Whenever any of us needed you"—Janna paused; Audrey was weeping now —"you were there. Remember, Ian said that the greatest gift of all is love. You gave us that gift, a love to treasure for all time."

Warren felt hot tears seep from his eyes. Shadoe pressed against him, her body trembling.

Janna placed the nosegay of wildflowers on top of the

coffin, which had already been covered by a blanket of lavender orchids ordered by the family.

Janna's voice faltered; she paused and looked around at her family. She gazed up at the sky, then out at the harbor. "God, we trust you with our Pithany. Bless her, and keep her with Ian until we join her."

"That was beautiful," Warren said when seconds passed and he realized Janna had finished. He motioned to the pallbearers to lower the casket.

Janna watched as the moist dirt was shoveled into the grave. The heavy weight perched on her shoulders since she'd left Pithany's bedside intensified; she wondered if she could move. Maybe she would just stay here.

"She's not gone," Shadoe whispered. "Not really. She lives on in you. You're exactly like her."

Janna didn't feel the least bit like her mother. She felt weak, incompetent. Warren put his arm around her. He stood, one arm around her, the other around Shadoe. Janna kept her eyes on the ground, telling herself Aunt Pith would want her to be strong. She looked up and saw a tall man hurrying toward them.

Nick? She blinked back her tears. *Dear Lord, it is Nick.* He stopped a short distance away in front of Ian's grave.

Warren released Janna, nudging her forward. Confused thoughts rushed through Janna's mind as she walked toward Nick. She stopped in front of him. He opened his arms, then drew her into them, hugging her fiercely, saying, "I'm so sorry about Pithany. She was a wonderful lady."

She'd forgotten how strong he was. She buried her face in the curve of his neck, thankful that at the moment she'd needed him the most he'd returned. Please, dear Lord, she silently prayed, don't take him from me. Ever.

"I came the minute I heard," Nick whispered into her

hair. "I was in Spain making sure Curt pays for killing Travis."

"That's why you didn't call?"

"Darling, I couldn't risk your life. I did my best to get rid of you, but you made it damn hard," he said with a smile. "I tracked Curt down and he's confessed to helping Rhonda give Travis that poison honey."

Guilt surged through her. How could she have doubted he would avenge his friend?

Janna glanced toward Aunt Pith's grave where the others waited. "You know, Aunt Pith never lost faith in you. She said you'd return."

"I told you I would be back." He pressed his lips to hers, then gently kissed her. "I'm back, Shorty. Back to stay."

"Does that mean . . . ?"

He smiled, the single-dimpled smile she loved. "I love you. I needed the time after Austin's death to think. As I painted the house, I realized what I had to do. My mother's spent her life living in the past, pretending my brother is still alive."

Janna nodded, remembering clearly Nick telling her about Cody's accident and how his mother mourned him to this day.

"She became a shell of a person. As I painted the Prescotts' house, I realized what I had to do. I forced my mother to move into the Prescotts' house. It was hard, but I even convinced her to join a local church and volunteer at a child care center."

"How's she doing?" Janna asked, admiring his tenacity. During one of their late-night discussions, he'd told her about his mother's problems.

"Better. I spoke with her last week and she sounded happier than she has in years.

"While I painted, I didn't just think about my mother. I took a close look at myself. I was in danger of becoming exactly like her—living in the past. I've been twice blessed. Amanda Jane and you. Part of me will always love her, but I love you more. I couldn't imagine going through my life without you."

Tears crept into Janna's eyes, brought on by the sincerity in his voice. The love. *Oh, Aunt Pith, are you listening?*

"Are those happy tears?"

She bobbed her head, unable to speak. He pulled her to him, his embrace almost unbearable in its tenderness.

"Marry me," he whispered.

"Of course," she answered, blinking back the tears.

Nearby Warren watched his sister. The passionate kiss she was now receiving from Nick indicated that he'd come back for her. Warren looked down at Shadoe to get her reaction. Her eyes were on Nick and Janna.

"Ian and Pithany," Shadoe said, "together at last. A love for all time."

Although my plots are entirely fictional, I'm often inspired by real people and actual events. Malta, at the crossroads of the Mediterranean, almost halfway between Gibraltar and Greece, has such a rich history beginning with the Phoenicians to the present day that I couldn't resist writing about it. Malta's ties to America are quite strong. Maltese fought in the Revolutionary War, aided in recasting the Liberty Bell, and sent mules when gold was discovered in California. Today there are sizable Maltese communities in San Francisco and New York. For this book I focused on the unique contribution the Maltese made to the Allied forces during the Second World War.

Pithany Crandall is a composite of many Maltese who spent the war below ground—as described in this book—monitoring Axis radio traffic. The suffering the islanders went through—and their amazing courage—is described as accurately as possible from interviews I conducted in Valletta and from written accounts of the ordeal.

Ian MacShane is a character roughly based on an actual reporter for London's *Daily Mirror*, Bernard Gray, who smuggled himself to the besieged island aboard an RAF bomber. He brought to the world's attention the tremendous bombing campaign the Luftwaffe was waging against the almost defenseless island. Until the nuclear attack on Hiroshima, more bomb tonnage fell on tiny Malta than any other place on earth. Gray died when the submarine he'd taken, hoping to reach the British forces in Egypt, was hit by a torpedo.

The character, Laurel Hogel, is based on a psychic artist who lives in Surrey, England. No one can explain her rare talent, but I've found it fascinating to use in this book.

St. Paul was shipwrecked on Malta while being sent to be tried before Caesar. He spent the winter there, converting the islanders to Christianity, but he did not give them any chalice. Cleopatra's Chalice was invented to forward the plot.

Another subject that has captivated me is past lives. Have we lived before? Could we live again? Many people have been hypnotized and regressed in time. With astonishing accuracy they've described places and events of which they had no prior knowledge. They've even spoken languages they didn't know and, in some cases, languages like Middle English, which are no longer spoken. It's a riddle to which there is no answer, but I found the following book, among many that I read on the subject, most helpful:

Life Between Life
by
Joel L. Whitton, M.D., Ph.D.
and
Joe Fisher

Many things in life simply cannot be explained. A live Nazi bomb did fall on a cathedral full of people in Mos tra. Why it didn't explode remains a mystery just as a psychic artist's talent is an enigma, and how some people can be regressed in time remains a mystery. To me, there is nothing more exciting or challenging than an interest ing mystery.